THE RETURN OF THE DANCING MASTER

Henning Mankell

THE RETURN OF THE DANCING MASTER

Translated from the Swedish by
Laurie Thompson

THE HARVILL PRESS

LONDON

First published with the title *Danslärarens återkomst*
by Ordfront Förlag, Stockholm, 2000

2 4 6 8 10 9 7 5 3 1

First published in Great Britain in 2003 by
The Harvill Press
Random House
20 Vauxhall Bridge Road
London SW1V 2SA

Random House Australia (Pty) Limited
20 Alfred Street, Milsons Point, Sydney,
New South Wales 2061, Australia

Random House New Zealand Limited
18 Poland Road, Glenfield,
Auckland 10, New Zealand

Random House South Africa (Pty) Limited
Endulini, 5A Jubilee Road, Parktown 2193, South Africa

The Random House Group Limited Reg. No. 954009
www.randomhouse.co.uk/harvill

A CIP catalogue record for this book is available from the British Library

ISBN 1 84343 0584 (hardback)
ISBN 1 84343 0614 (paperback)

Maps drawn by Reg Piggott

Papers used by Random House are natural, recyclable products made from wood
grown in sustainable forests; the manufacturing processes conform to the
environmental regulations of the country of origin

Typeset in Minion by Palimpsest Book Production Limited,
Polmont, Stirlingshire
Printed and bound in Great Britain by Clays Ltd, St Ives plc

Contents

Prologue Germany / December 1945   1

I   Härjedalen / October–November 1999   11

II   The man from Buenos Aires /
     October–November 1999   119

III The woodlice / November 1999   253

Epilogue Inverness / April 2000   389

Afterword   407

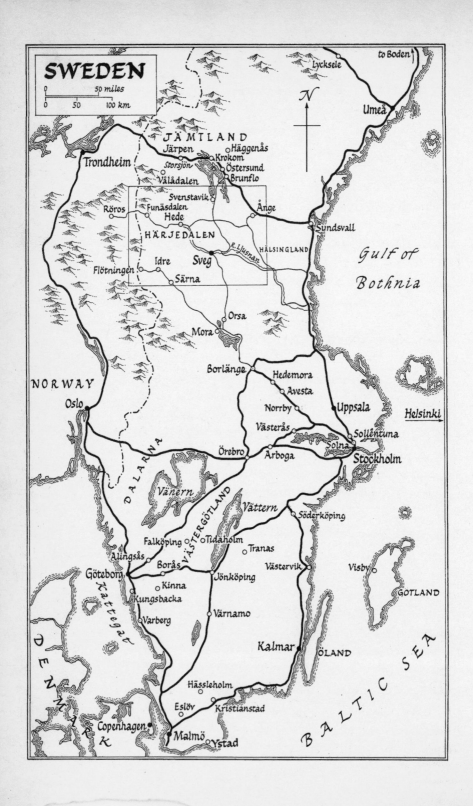

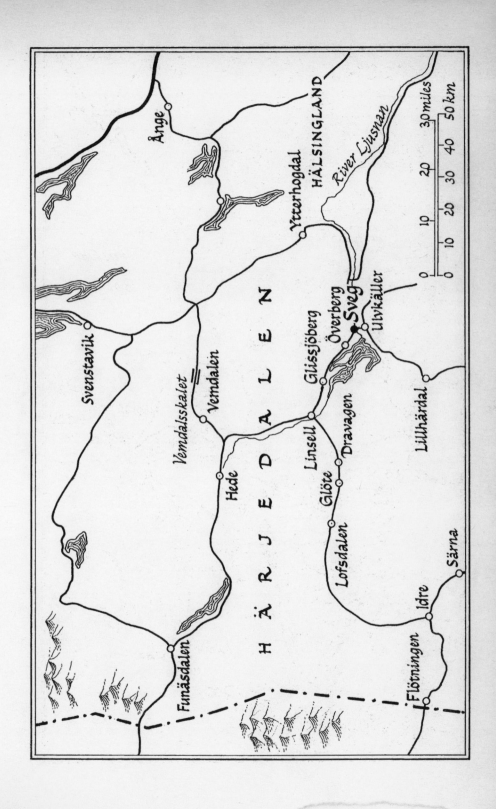

PROLOGUE

Germany / December 1945

The plane took off from the aerodrome near London shortly after 2 p.m. It was December 12, 1945. It was drizzling and chilly. Occasional gusts set the wind sock fluttering, then all was calm again. The aircraft was a four-engined Lancaster bomber that in the autumn of 1940 had taken part in the Battle of Britain. It had been hit several times by German fighters and forced to make emergency landings, but they had always managed to patch it up and send it back into the fray. Now it was used for transport jobs, taking essential supplies to British troops stationed in defeated and devastated Germany.

Mike Garbett, the captain, had been told that he would fly a passenger to somewhere called Bückeburg. The passenger would then be picked up and flown back to England the following evening. Who he was and why he was going to Germany, Major Perkins, his immediate superior, did not tell him, nor did he ask. Even though the war was over, he sometimes had the impression that it was still going on. Secret missions were not unusual.

After being issued with his flight instructions, he was sitting in one of the messes with his first officer, Peter Foster, and the navigator, Chris Wiffin. They spread out the maps on a table. The airfield was some miles outside the town of Hamelin. Garbett had never been there, but Foster was familiar with it. There were no hills in the vicinity, so the approach should not be a problem. The only potential difficulty was fog. Wiffin went off to consult the weather boffins, and came back with the news that clear skies were expected over northern and central Germany all afternoon and evening. They plotted their route, worked out how much fuel they would need, and rolled up the maps.

"We'll have just the one passenger," Garbett said. "I've no idea who he is."

Nobody asked any questions, nor did he expect any. He'd been flying with Foster and Wiffin for three months. What united them was that they were survivors. Many RAF crew had fallen in the war, and each of them had lost many friends. Having survived was not only a source of relief: they were also dogged by the sense of having been granted the life denied to their dead comrades.

Shortly before 2 p.m. a closed car drove in through the gate. Foster and Wiffin were already aboard the big Lancaster, going through the final checks before take-off. Garbett was waiting on the cracked concrete apron. He frowned when he saw that their passenger was in civvies. The man who emerged from the back seat was short. In his mouth was an unlit cigar. He took a black suitcase from the boot just as Major Perkins drove up in his jeep. The man who was to be flown to Germany had his hat pulled down and Garbett could not see his eyes. Something about him made Garbett feel uncomfortable. When Major Perkins introduced them, the passenger mumbled his name. Garbett didn't catch what he said.

"Right, you can take off now," Perkins said.

"No more luggage?" Garbett said.

The man shook his head.

"It's probably best not to smoke during the flight," Garbett said. "This is an old crate. There could be leaks. You don't usually notice aviation fuel fumes until it's too late."

The man made no reply. Garbett helped him aboard. There were three uncomfortable metal seats in the plane, which was otherwise empty. The man sat down and placed his suitcase between his legs. Garbett wondered what valuable he was about to fly into Germany.

Once they were in the air Garbett banked to the left until he was able to settle into the course Wiffin had set for him. When they had reached the designated height, Garbett handed over the controls to Foster. He turned to look at the passenger. The man had turned up his overcoat collar and pulled his hat even further down. Garbett wondered if he was asleep, but something told him that the man was wide awake.

The landing at Bückeburg went smoothly, despite the fact that it was dark and the lighting dim. A car guided the aircraft to the edge of the long operations building. Several military vehicles were already standing by. Garbett prepared to help the passenger off the plane, but when he reached for the suitcase the man insisted on taking it himself. He got into one of the cars and the convoy drove off immediately. Wiffin and Foster had clambered to the ground and watched the rear lights fade away. It was cold, and they were shivering.

"Makes you wonder what's going on," Wiffin said.

"Best not to ask," Garbett said.

He pointed to a jeep approaching the aircraft. "We're putting up at a base near here," he said. "I assume that's our car."

After they'd been allocated their quarters and had their evening meal, some of the mechanics suggested they go into town for a beer in one of the bars that had survived the bombing. Wiffin and Foster agreed at once, but Garbett felt tired and stayed in camp. He had trouble getting to sleep, and lay awake wondering who their passenger was. What was in that suitcase he hadn't let anybody else touch? The passenger must be on some secret mission. All Garbett had to do was to fly him back home the following day. The rest was not his concern. He looked at his watch. Midnight already. He adjusted his pillow and when Wiffin and Foster got back at around 1 a.m., he was fast asleep.

Donald Davenport left the British prison for German war criminals soon after 11 p.m. He had a room in a hotel that served as a base for British officers stationed in Hamelin. He needed some sleep if he were going to carry out his duties efficiently the following day. He was a little uneasy about Sergeant MacManaman, his nominated assistant. Davenport disliked working with people unused to the job. All manner of things could go wrong, especially when the assignment was as big as the one in store.

He declined the offer of a cup of tea and went straight to his room. He sat at the desk and sorted the notes he'd made during the meeting that had begun half an hour after his arrival. The first paper he addressed, however, was the typewritten document he'd received from a young major by the name of Stuckford, who was in charge of the operation.

He smoothed out the paper, adjusted the desk lamp and read the names. Kramer, Lehmann, Heider, Volkenrath, Grese . . . Twelve in all, three women, nine men. He studied the data on their weight and height, and made a few more notes. It was a slow process. His professional pride required him to be absolutely meticulous. It was 1.30 by the time he put down his pen. Now he had it all sorted. He'd made his calculations and double-checked them. He had overlooked nothing. He checked again, just to be certain. He got up from the desk, sat on his bed and opened his suitcase. Although he never forgot anything, he checked to make sure everything was in place. He took out a clean shirt, closed the case, then washed in the cold water that was all the hotel had to offer.

He never had any difficulty in dropping off to sleep.

When they knocked at his door just after 5 a.m., he was already up and dressed. They had a light breakfast and then drove through the dark, drab town to the prison. Sergeant MacManaman was waiting for them. He was deathly pale, and Davenport wondered again whether he would be up to the job. Major Stuckford seemed to sense Davenport's misgivings, took him on one side and told him that although MacManaman might look shattered, he wouldn't let anybody down.

By 11 a.m. everything was ready. Davenport had chosen to start with the women. Their cells were in the corridor closest to the gallows and they could not have avoided hearing the trapdoor open. He wanted to spare them that. Davenport paid no mind to the crimes of the individual prisoners. It was his own sense of decency that made him start with the women.

All those required to be present had taken up their positions. Davenport nodded to Stuckford, who signalled to one of the warders. Orders were barked, keys were rattled, a cell door opened. Davenport waited.

The first to appear was Irma Grese. A fleeting sensation of surprise disturbed Davenport's icy calm. How could this slight, blonde 22-year-old possibly have whipped prisoners to death at the Belsen concentration camp? She was hardly more than a child. But when her sentence had been passed, no-one had been in any doubt. She looked him in the eye, then glanced up at the gallows. The warders led her up the steps. Davenport adjusted her feet so that they were immediately above the trapdoor, and placed the noose round her neck while checking to make sure MacManaman made no mistake with the leather strap he was fastening around her legs. Just before Davenport pulled the hood over her head he heard her utter one scarcely audible word: "*Schnell!*"

MacManaman took a step back and Davenport reached for the

handle that operated the trapdoor. She fell down straight, and Davenport knew he'd calculated the length of the rope correctly. Long enough to break her neck, not so long that her head would be wrenched from her body. He and MacManaman went down under the scaffold on which the gallows were standing and, once the British Medical Officer had listened for her heartbeat and confirmed death, he released the body. The corpse was put onto a stretcher and carried away. Davenport knew that graves had been dug in the prison yard. He went back up onto the scaffold and checked in his papers the length of rope he should allow for the next woman. When he was ready he nodded to Stuckford again and before long Elisabeth Volkenrath was standing in the doorway, her hands tied behind her back. She was dressed exactly as Irma Grese, in a grey smock that reached down below her knees.

Three minutes later she too was dead.

The executions took two hours and seven minutes. Davenport had reckoned on two and a quarter hours. MacManaman had done everything expected of him. All had gone according to plan. Twelve German war criminals had been put to death. Davenport packed the rope and the leather straps into his suitcase, and said goodbye to Sergeant MacManaman.

"Come and have a glass of brandy. You did a good job."

"They deserved all they got," MacManaman said. "I don't need any brandy."

Davenport left the prison with Major Stuckford. He wondered whether it might be possible to go back to England earlier than planned – he was the one who recommended the return flight be in the evening, in case anything went wrong. Not even Davenport, England's most experienced hangman, was in the habit of executing twelve people in one day. But in the end he decided to stick with the arrangements.

Stuckford took him to the hotel dining room and ordered lunch. They had a side room to themselves. Stuckford had a wound that caused him still to limp with his left foot. Davenport approved of him, not least because he asked no unnecessary questions. There was nothing Davenport disliked more than people asking him what it had been like, hanging this or that criminal who'd become notorious after being written about in the newspapers. They exchanged pleasantries as they ate, about the weather, and if the English would be awarded extra rations of tea or tobacco for Christmas, not far away now.

Only over a cup of tea, afterwards, did Stuckford refer to what had happened that morning.

"There's one thing that worries me," he said. "People forget it could just as easily have been the other way round."

Davenport wasn't sure what Stuckford meant, but he had no need to ask. Stuckford provided an explanation himself. "A German hangman flying to England to execute English war criminals. Young English women beating people to death in a concentration camp. We could just as easily have been overwhelmed by evil as the Germans were, in the form of Hitler and Nazism."

Davenport didn't respond. He was waiting for what came next.

"No people is inherently evil. On this occasion the Nazis happened to be Germans, but nobody is going to convince me that it couldn't have happened just as easily in England. Or France. Or the USA, come to that."

"I understand your line of thought," Davenport said. "I don't know whether or not you're right, though."

Stuckford refilled their cups.

"We execute the worst of the criminals," Stuckford went on. "The really monstrous war criminals. But we also know that lots of them are getting away with it. Like Josef Lehmann's brother."

Lehmann was the last to be hanged that morning. A little man who'd met his death placidly, almost nonchalantly.

"He had an exceptionally brutal brother," Stuckford said. "But that brother succeeded in making himself invisible. Maybe he's slipped away through one of the Nazis' escape routes. He could be in Argentina or South Africa, and we'll never track him down there."

They sat in silence. Outside the window rain was now falling.

"Waldemar Lehmann was an incredibly sadistic man," Stuckford said. "It wasn't just that he was ruthless with the prisoners, he also took a devilish delight in teaching his subordinates the art of torturing people. We should have hanged him, as we did his brother. But we haven't caught him. Not yet, anyway."

*   *   *

8

Davenport returned to the aerodrome at 5 p.m. He was cold, even though he was wearing his thick winter overcoat. The pilot was standing by the plane, waiting for him. Davenport wondered what he was thinking. He took his seat in the chilly fuselage and turned up his coat collar to shield him from the roar of the engines.

Garbett settled in the cockpit, the Lancaster gathered speed and flew into the clouds.

Davenport had completed his assignment. He had justified his reputation as England's most accomplished hangman.

The aircraft tossed and shuddered its way through some air pockets. Davenport reflected on what Stuckford had said about the ones who had got away. And he thought about Lehmann deriving pleasure from teaching people the most horrific forms of torture. He pulled his overcoat more tightly around him. The air pockets were behind them now. The Lancaster was on its way back home to England. The day had gone without a hitch. None of the prisoners had struggled on being led to the scaffold. Nobody's neck had been severed. Davenport was content. He could look forward to three days' holiday. His next job would be hanging a murderer in Manchester.

He dozed off in the uncomfortable seat, despite the roar of the engines, and Mike Garbett was still wondering about the identity of his passenger.

PART I

Härjedalen / October–November 1999

CHAPTER 1

He woke in the night, besieged by shadows. It had started when he was 22. Fifty-four years of sleepless nights, constantly besieged by shadows. He'd only managed to sleep after taking heavy doses of sleeping pills. He knew the shadows had been there when he woke, even if he'd been unaware of them.

This night, now drawing to its close, was no exception. Nor did he have to wait for the shadows – or the visitors, as he sometimes called them – to put in an appearance. They generally turned up a few hours after darkness fell. Were there without warning, by his side, with silent white faces. He'd got used to their presence after all the years, but he knew he couldn't trust them. One of these days they'd be bound to break loose. He didn't know what would happen then. Would they attack him, or would they betray him? There had been times when he'd shouted at them, hit out in all directions to drive them off. He'd kept them at bay for a while. Then they'd be back and stay until dawn. He'd sleep in the end, but usually for only a few hours because he needed to get up and go to work.

He'd been tired all of his adult life. He had no idea how he'd got by. Looking back, he could recognise only an endless string of days that he'd somehow or other muddled through. He had hardly any memories unconnected with his tiredness. In photographs taken of him he always looked haggard. The shadows had also taken their revenge on him during his two marriages: his wives had been frustrated by his constant state of unease, and the fact that when he wasn't working, he was always half asleep. They'd lost patience with finding him up for most of the night, and he'd never been able to explain why he couldn't sleep like a normal person. In the end they'd left him, and he'd been alone again.

He looked at his watch. 4.15 a.m. He went to the kitchen and poured himself coffee from the thermos he'd made before going to bed. The thermometer outside the window showed minus two. If he didn't remember to change the screws holding it in place, before long it would fall. He moved the curtain, and the dog started barking out there in the darkness. Shaka was the only security he had. He'd found the name he'd given his Norwegian elkhound in a book – he couldn't remember the title. It had something to do with a powerful Zulu chieftain, and he'd thought it a suitable name for a guard dog. Short and easy to shout. He took his coffee into the living room. The thick curtains were securely drawn. He knew that already, but felt compelled to keep checking. He checked the windows.

Then he sat at the table again and contemplated the jigsaw pieces spread out before him. It was a good puzzle. It had lots of pieces and demanded imagination and perseverance to solve it. Whenever he finished a puzzle, he would burn it and immediately start on a new one. He made sure he always had a store of puzzles. It was a bit like a smoker and his cigarettes. For years he'd been a member of a world-wide club devoted to the culture of jigsaw puzzles. It was based in Rome, and every month he'd get a newsletter with information about puzzle-makers who had ceased trading and others who had entered the field. As early as the mid-'70s it had struck him how hard it was to find really good puzzles – that is, hand-sawn ones. He didn't think much of the mechanically produced ones. There was no logic in the way the pieces were cut, and they didn't fit in with the patterns. That might make them hard to solve, but the difficulties were mechanically contrived. Just now he was working on a puzzle based on Rembrandt's *The Conspiracy of the Bathavians under Claudius Civilis*. It had 3,000 pieces and had been made by a specialist in Rouen. He'd once driven down to visit the man. They'd talked about how the best puzzles were the ones with the most subtle nuances of light. And how Rembrandt's colour schemes made the greatest demands.

He sat holding a piece that obviously belonged in the background of the painting. It took him nearly ten minutes to find where. He checked his watch again: 4.30. Hours to go before dawn, before the shadows would withdraw and he could get some sleep.

It seemed to him that on the whole everything had become much simpler since he'd turned 65 and retired. He didn't need to be anxious about feeling tired all day. Didn't need to be frightened of nodding off at work. But the shadows ought to have left him in peace ages ago. He had served his time. They had no need now to keep their eye on him. His life had been ruined.

He went to the bookcase where he kept his CD player. He'd bought it a few months ago, on one of his rare visits to Östersund. He put the disc in the machine back on – he'd been surprised to find it among the pop music in the shop where he'd bought the player. It was a tango, a genuine Argentinian tango. He turned up the sound. The elkhound out there in the dark had good ears and responded to the music with a bark, then was quiet again. He went back to the table and walked round it, studying the puzzle as he listened to the music. There was plenty yet to do. It would keep him going for three more nights at least before he burnt it. He had several more, still in their boxes. Then he would drive to the post office in Sveg and collect another batch sent by the old master in Rouen.

He sat on the sofa to enjoy the music. It had been one of his life's ambitions to visit Argentina. To spend a few months in Buenos Aires, dancing the tango every night. But it had never happened; something always cropped up to make him draw back at the last minute. When he'd left Västergötland eleven years ago and moved north to the forests of Härjedalen, he'd meant to take a trip every year. He lived frugally, and although his pension wasn't a big one, he could afford it. In fact, all he'd done was once or twice to drive round Europe looking for new jigsaw puzzles.

He would never go to Argentina. He would never dance the tango in Buenos Aires. But there's nothing to stop me dancing here, he thought. I have the music and I have my partner.

He stood up. It was 5 a.m. Dawn was a long way off. It was time for a dance. He went to the bedroom and took his dark suit from the wardrobe. He examined it carefully before putting it on. A stain on the jacket lapel annoyed him. He wet a handkerchief and wiped it clean. Then he changed. This morning he chose a rust-brown tie to go with his white shirt. Most important of all were the shoes. He had several pairs of Italian dancing shoes, all expensive. For the serious dancer, the shoes had to be perfect.

When he was ready, he studied his appearance in the mirror on the wardrobe door. His hair was grey and cropped short. He was thin; he told himself he should eat more. But he looked considerably younger than his 76 years.

He knocked at the spare bedroom door. He imagined hearing somebody bidding him enter. He opened the door and switched on the light. His dancing partner was lying in the bed. He was always surprised by how real she looked, even though she was only a doll. He pulled back the duvet and lifted her up. She was wearing a white blouse and a black skirt. He'd given her the name of Esmeralda. There were some bottles of scent on the bedside table. He sat her down, and selected a discreet Dior which he sprayed gently onto her neck. When he closed his eyes it seemed to him that there was no difference between the doll and a living human being.

He escorted her to the living room. He'd often thought he should take away all the furniture, fix some dimmed lights in the ceiling and place a burning cigar in an ashtray. Then he'd have his own Argentinian dance hall. But he'd never got around to it. There was just the empty stretch of floor between the table and the bookcase with the CD player. He slid his shoes into the loops attached to the bottom of Esmeralda's feet.

Then he started dancing. As he twirled Esmeralda round the floor, he felt he had succeeded in sweeping all the shadows out of the room. He was very light on his feet. He had learnt a lot of dances over the years, but it was the tango that suited him best. And there was nobody he danced with as well as Esmeralda. Once there'd been a woman in Borås, Rosemarie, who had a milliner's shop. He used to dance the tango with her, and none of his previous partners had followed him as well as she did. One day, when he was getting ready to drive to Göteborg where he'd arranged to meet her at a dance club, he had a call to say she'd been killed in a road accident. He danced with lots of other women after that, but it wasn't until he created Esmeralda that he got the same feeling as he'd had with Rosemarie.

He had the idea many years ago. He had tuned in to a musical on the television: he'd been awake all night as usual. In the film a man – Gene Kelly, perhaps – had danced with a doll. He'd been fascinated, and decided there and then that he would make one himself.

The hardest part was the filling. He'd tried all sorts of things, but

16

it wasn't until he'd filled her with foam rubber that it felt as if he were holding a real person in his arms. He had chosen to give her large breasts and a big backside. Both his wives had been slim. Now he'd provided himself with a woman who had something he could get his hands round. When he danced with her and smelled her perfume, he was sometimes aroused; but that hadn't often happened over the last five or six years. His erotic desires had started to fade.

He danced for more than an hour. When finally he carried Esmeralda back to the spare room and put her to bed, he'd been sweating. He undressed, hung the suit in the wardrobe and took a shower. It would soon be light, and he'd be able to go to bed and sleep. He'd survived another night.

He put on his dressing gown and made himself some coffee. The thermometer outside the window was still showing minus two degrees. He touched the curtains, and Shaka barked briefly out there in the darkness. He thought about the forest surrounding him on all sides. This was what he'd dreamt of. A remote cottage, modern in every way, but no neighbours. And it was also a house at the very end of a road. It was a roomy house, well built and with a big living room that satisfied his need for a dance floor. The vendor was a forestry official who had retired and moved to Spain.

He sat at the kitchen table with his coffee. Dawn was approaching. Soon he'd be able to get some sleep. The shadows would leave him in peace.

A single bark from Shaka. He sat up straight. Another bark. Then all was quiet. It must have been an animal. Probably a hare. Shaka could move around freely in his large pen. The dog kept watch over him.

He washed up his cup and put it next to the cooker. He'd use it again seven hours from now. He didn't like changing cups unnecessarily. He could use the same one for weeks on end. Then he went into the bedroom, took off his dressing gown and snuggled into bed. It was still dark, but usually he lay in bed as he waited for dawn to break, listening to the radio. When he noticed the first faint signs of light outside the house he would turn off the radio, switch off the light and lie comfortably, ready for sleep.

Shaka started barking again. Then stopped. He frowned, listening intently, and counted up to 30. No sound from Shaka. Whatever animal it had been, it had gone now. He turned on the radio and listened absent-mindedly to the music.

Another bark from Shaka. But it was different now. He sat up in bed. Shaka was barking away frantically. That could only mean that there was an elk in the vicinity. Or a bear. Bears were shot every year in this area. He'd never seen one himself. Shaka was still barking just as frenziedly. He got out of bed and put on his dressing gown. Shaka fell silent. He waited, but nothing. He took off his dressing gown again and got back into bed. He always slept naked. The lamp by the radio was on.

Suddenly he sat up again. Something odd was going on, something to do with the dog. He held his breath and listened. Silence. He was uneasy. It was as if the shadows all around him had started to change. He got out of bed. There was something odd about Shaka's last barks. They hadn't stopped in a natural way, they seemed to have been cut off. He went into the living room and opened one of the curtains in the window looking directly out onto the dog pen. Shaka didn't bark, and he felt his heart beating faster. He went back into the bedroom and pulled on a pair of trousers and a jumper. He took out the gun he always kept under his bed, a shotgun with room for six cartridges in the magazine. He went into the hall and stuck his feet into a pair of boots, listening all the time. Not a sound from Shaka. He was imagining things, no doubt, everything was as it should be. It would be light soon. It was the shadows making him uneasy, that was it. He unlocked the three locks on the front door and slowly opened it. Still no reaction from Shaka. Now he knew for certain that something was wrong. He picked up a torch from a shelf and shone it into the darkness. There was no sign of Shaka in the pen. He shouted for Shaka and shone the torch along the edge of the woods. Still no reaction. He quickly shut the door. Sweat was pouring off him. He cocked the gun and opened the door again. Cautiously he stepped out onto the porch. No sound. He walked over to the dog pen, then stopped in his tracks. Shaka was lying on the ground. His eyes were staring and his greyish-white fur bloodstained. He turned on his heel and ran back to the house, slamming the door behind him. Something was going on, but he had no idea what. Somebody had killed Shaka, though. He switched on every light in the house and sat down on his bed. He was shaking.

The shadows had fooled him. He hadn't caught on to the danger in time. He'd always supposed the shadows would change, that they would be his attackers. But he'd been fooled: the threat came from outside. The shadows had persuaded him to look in the wrong place. He'd been misled for 54 years. He thought he'd got away with it, but he had been wrong. Images from that awful year of 1945 came welling up inside him. He hadn't got away with it after all.

He shook his head and resolved not to give himself up without a fight. He didn't know who was out there in the darkness, the person who had killed his dog. Shaka had succeeded in warning him even so. He wasn't going to surrender. He kicked off his boots, put on a pair of socks and took his trainers out from under the bed. His ears were alert all the time. What had happened to the dawn? If only daylight would set in, they'd have no chance. He dried his sweaty palms on the duvet. The shotgun gave him some sense of security. He was a good shot. He wouldn't allow himself to be taken by surprise.

And then the house collapsed. That's what it felt like, at least. At the explosion he flung himself to the floor. He'd had his finger on the trigger and his gun went off, shattering the mirror on the wardrobe. He crawled to the door and looked into the living room. Then he saw what had happened. Somebody had fired a shot or maybe thrown a grenade through the big window facing south. The room was a sea of splintered glass.

He had no time to think any further as the window facing north was demolished by another shot. He pressed himself against the floor. They're coming from all directions, he thought. The house is surrounded and they're shooting out the windows before coming in. He searched desperately for a way out.

Dawn, he thought. That's what can save me. If only this accursed night would come to an end.

Then the kitchen window was shot out. He lay on his stomach, pressing down against the floor with his hands over his head. Then the next crash, the bathroom window. He could feel the cold air gushing in.

There was a whistling noise, then a thud right next to him. He raised his head and saw it was a tear gas canister. He turned his head away, but it was too late. The gas was in his eyes and his lungs. Without being able to see anything, he could hear more canisters landing through the other windows. The pain in his eyes was so bad that he could stand it no longer. He still had his shotgun in his hands. He had no choice but to leave the house. Maybe the darkness would save him after all, not the dawn. He scrambled to the front door. The pain in his eyes was unbearable, and his coughing threatened to tear his lungs apart. He flung the door open and rushed out, shooting at the same time. He knew it was about 30 metres to the trees. Although he couldn't see a thing, he ran as fast as he could. All the time he was expecting a fatal bullet to hit him. It was only a short run to the forest, but far enough for him to think that he was going to be killed; but he didn't know by whom. He knew why, but not who. That thought was as painful as his eyes.

He barged into a tree trunk and almost fell. Still blinded by the tear gas, he staggered through the trees. Branches made deep wounds in his face, but he knew he must not stop. Whoever it was was somewhere behind him. Maybe several of them. They'd catch him if he didn't get far enough away into the forest.

He stumbled over a rock and fell. He was about to get up when he felt something on the back of his neck. A boot on his head. The game was up. The shadows had defeated him.

He wanted to see who it was that was going to kill him. He tried to turn his head, but the boot prevented him. Then somebody pulled him to his feet. He still could see nothing. He was blinded. For a moment he felt the breath of the person placing the blindfold over his eyes and tying the knot at the back of his head. He tried to say something. But when he opened his mouth, no words came out, just a new attack of coughing.

Then a pair of hands wrapped themselves round his throat. He tried to resist, but he didn't have the strength. He could feel his life ebbing away.

It would be nearly two hours before he finally died. As if in a border-land of horror between the nagging pain and the hopeless will to live, he was taken back in time, to the occasion when he gave rise to the fate that had now caught up with him. He was thrown to the ground. Somebody pulled off his trousers and jumper. He could feel the cold earth against his skin before the whiplashes hit him and transformed everything into an inferno. He didn't know how many were the lashes. Whenever he passed out, he was dragged back up to the surface by cold water thrown over him. Then the blows continued to rain down. He could hear himself screaming, but there was nobody there to help him. Least of all Shaka, lying dead in his pen.

The last thing he felt was being dragged over the ground, into the house, and then being beaten on the soles of his feet. Everything went black. He was dead.

He couldn't know that the last thing that happened to him was being dragged naked to the edge of the forest and left with his face pressed into the cold earth.

By then it was dawn.

That was October 19, 1999. A few hours later it started raining, rain that barely perceptibly turned to wet snow.

CHAPTER 2

Stefan Lindman was a police officer. Once every year at least he had found himself in a situation where he experienced considerable fear. On one occasion he'd been attacked by a psychopath weighing over 100 kilos. He'd been on the floor with the man astride him, and in rising desperation had fought to prevent his head being torn off by the madman's gigantic hands. If one of his colleagues hadn't succeeded in stunning the man with a blow to the head, he would certainly have succumbed. Another time he'd been shot at approaching a house to deal with domestic violence. The shot was from a Mauser and narrowly missed one of his legs. But he had never been as frightened as he felt now, on the morning of October 25, 1999, as he lay in bed staring up at the ceiling.

He had barely slept. He had dozed off now and again only to be woken with a start by nightmares the moment he lost consciousness. In desperation he'd finally got out of bed and sat in front of the television, zapping the channels until he found a pornographic film. But after a short while he'd switched off in disgust and gone back to bed.

It was 7 a.m. when he got up. He'd devised a plan during the night. A plan that was also an invocation. He wouldn't go directly up the hill to the hospital. He would make sure he had enough time not only to take a roundabout route, but also to circle the hospital twice. He would all the time search for signs that the news he was going to receive from the doctor would be positive. To give himself an extra dose of energy, he'd have a coffee in the hospital cafeteria, and force himself to calm down by reading the local paper.

Without having thought about it in advance, he put on his best suit. Generally, when he wasn't in uniform or other working clothes, he would be in jeans and a T-shirt. Today, though, he felt his best suit was called for. As he knotted his tie he contemplated his face in the bathroom mirror. It was obvious he hadn't been sleeping or eating properly for weeks. His cheeks were hollow. And he could do with getting his hair cut. He didn't like the way it was sticking out over his ears.

He didn't at all like what he saw in the mirror this morning. It was an unusual feeling. He was a vain man, and often checked his appearance in the mirror. Normally he liked what he saw. His reflection would generally raise his spirits, but this morning everything was different.

When he'd finished dressing he made coffee. He prepared some open sandwiches, but didn't feel like eating anything. His appointment with the doctor was for 8.45. It was 7.27. So he had exactly one hour and 18 minutes for his walk to the hospital.

When he came onto the street it had started drizzling.

Lindman lived in the centre of Borås, in Allégatan. Three years ago he lived in Sjömarken outside the town, but then he'd happened to hear about this three-roomed flat and hadn't hesitated to sign a contract for it. Directly across the street was the Vävaren Hotel. He was within walking distance of the police station, and could even walk to the Ryavallen stadium when Elfsborg were playing at home. Football was his biggest interest, apart from his work. Although he didn't tell anybody, he still collected pictures and press cuttings about his local team in a file. He had daydreams about being a professional footballer in Italy, instead of a police officer in Sweden. These dreams embarrassed him, but he couldn't put them behind him.

He walked up the steps taking him to Stengärdsgatan and kept on towards the City Theatre and the grammar school. A police car drove past. Whoever was in it didn't notice him. His fear stabbed into him. It was as if he'd gone already, was already dead. He pulled his jacket more tightly around him. There was no real reason why he should be expecting a negative verdict. He increased his pace. His mind was buzzing. The raindrops falling into his face were reminders of a life, his life, that was ebbing away.

He was 37. He'd worked in Borås ever since leaving Police College. It was where he wanted to be posted. He was born in Kinna and grew up in a family with three children; his father was a second-hand car salesman and his mother worked in a bakery. Stefan was the youngest. His two sisters were seven and nine years older than he was – you could almost say he was an afterthought.

When Lindman thought back to his childhood, it sometimes seemed strangely uneventful and boring. Life had been secure and routine. His parents disliked travelling. The furthest they could bring themselves to go was Borås or Varberg. Even Göteborg was too big, too far and too scary. His sisters had rebelled against this life and moved away early, one to Stockholm and the other to Helsinki. His parents had taken that as a failure on their part, and Lindman had realised he was almost bound to stay in Kinna, or at least to go back there when he'd decided what to do with his life. He'd been restless as a teenager, and had no idea what he wanted to do when he grew up.

Then, purely by chance, he'd got to know a young man devoted to motocross. He'd become this man's assistant and spent a few years travelling around race-tracks the length and breadth of central Sweden. But he tired of that eventually and returned to Kinna, where his parents welcomed him with open arms, the return of the prodigal son. He still didn't know what he wanted to do with his life, but then he happened to meet a policeman from Malmö who was visiting some mutual friends in Kinna. And the thought struck Lindman: maybe I ought to become a police officer? He thought it over for a few days, and made up his mind to give it a try at least.

His parents received his decision with a degree of unease, but Lindman pointed out that there were police officers in Kinna – he wouldn't need to move away.

He set out immediately to turn his decision into reality. The first thing he did was to go back to school and collect some A-levels. As he was so keen, it had been easier than he'd expected. He occasionally worked as a relief school caretaker in order to earn his keep.

To his surprise he'd been accepted by Police College at his first attempt. The training hadn't caused him any problems. He hadn't been outstanding in any way, but had been among the better ones in his year. One day he'd come back home to Kinna in uniform and announced that he would be working in Borås, just 40 kilometres down the road.

For the first few years he'd commuted from Kinna, but when he fell in love with one of the girls at the police station, he moved into Borås. They lived together for three years. Then one day, out of the blue, she announced that she'd met a man from Trondheim and she was moving there. Lindman had taken the development in his stride. He'd realised that their relationship was beginning to bore him. It was a bit like going back to his childhood. What intrigued him, though, was how she could have met another man and started an affair without Lindman noticing.

By now he'd reached the age of 30, almost without noticing it. Then his father had a heart attack and died, and a few months later his mother died as well. The day after her funeral he'd inserted a lonely hearts advert in the local paper. He had four replies, and met the women one after the other. One of them was a Pole who had lived in Borås for many years. She had two grown-up children, and worked as a dinner lady at the grammar school. She was nearly ten years older than him, but they'd never really noticed the difference. He couldn't understand at first what there was that had attracted him to her straightaway, made him fall in love with her. Then it dawned on him: she was completely ordinary. She took life seriously, but didn't fuss about anything unnecessarily. They'd started a relationship, and for the first time in his life Lindman had discovered that he could feel something for a woman that was more than lust. Her name was Elena and she lived in Norrby. He used to spend the night there several times a week. It was there, one day, that he was in the bathroom and discovered he had a strange lump on his tongue.

He interrupted his train of thought. He was in front of the hospital. It was still drizzling. It was 7.56 by his watch. He walked past the hospital and quickened his pace. He'd made up his mind to walk round it twice, and that was what he was going to do.

It was 8.30 by the time he sat down in the cafeteria with a cup of coffee and the local paper. But he didn't read a word in the paper, and never touched his coffee.

He was scared stiff by the time he got as far as the doctor's door. He knocked and went in. It was a woman doctor. He tried to work out from her face what he could expect: a death sentence, or a reprieve? She gave him a smile, but that only confused him. Did it

25

denote uncertainty, sympathy or relief at not needing to tell some-body they had cancer?

He sat down. She organised some papers on the desk.

"I'm afraid I have to tell you that the lump you have on your tongue is a malignant tumour."

He swallowed. He'd known all along, ever since that morning in Elena's flat in Norrby. He had cancer.

"We can't see any sign of it spreading. As we've found it in the early stages, we can start treating it straightaway."

"What does that mean? Will you cut my tongue out?"

"No, it will be radiotherapy to start with. And then an operation."

"Will I die of it?"

This wasn't a question he'd prepared in advance. It burst out without him being able to stop it.

"Cancer is always serious," the doctor said, "but nowadays we can take measures. It's been a long time since diagnosing cancer meant passing a death sentence."

He sat with the doctor for more than an hour. When he left her office he was soaked in sweat. In the pit of his stomach was a spot as cold as ice. A pain that didn't burn, but it felt like the hands of that psychopath on his throat. He forced himself to be calm. He would go for a coffee now and read the paper. Then he'd make up his mind whether or not he was dying.

But the paper was no longer there. He picked up one of the previous day's national papers instead. That ice-cold knot was still there. He drank his coffee and thumbed through the paper. He'd forgotten all about the words and the pictures the moment he turned over a page. Something caught his attention. A photograph. A headline about a brutal murder. He stared at the photograph and the caption. *Herbert Molin, age 76. Former police officer.*

He pushed the paper aside and went for another cup of coffee. He knew it cost two kronor, but he didn't bother paying. He had cancer and was entitled to take certain liberties. A man who had shuffled quickly up to the counter was pouring himself a cup of coffee. His hands shook so badly that hardly any of it arrived in the cup. Lindman helped him. The man gave him a grateful look.

He picked up the paper again, and read what it said without any of it really sinking in.

When he'd first arrived in Borås as a probationer, he'd been introduced to the oldest and most experienced detective on the staff, Herbert Molin. They had worked together in the serious crimes division for some years until Molin retired. Lindman had often thought about him afterwards. The way in which he was always looking for links and clues. A lot of people spoke ill of him behind his back, but he'd always been a rich source of learning as far as Lindman was concerned. One of Molin's main lines was that intuition was the most important and most underestimated resource for a true detective. The more experience Lindman accrued, the more he realised that Molin was right.

Molin had been a recluse. Nobody Lindman knew had ever been to Molin's house opposite the district court-house in Brämhultsvägen. Some years after he'd retired, Lindman heard quite by chance that Molin had left town, but nobody could say where he had moved to.

Lindman put the newspaper down.

So Herbert Molin had moved to Härjedalen. According to the paper, he had been living in a remote house in the middle of the forest. That is where he had been murdered. There was apparently no discernible motive, nor any clues as to who the killer might have been. The murder had been committed several days ago, but Lindman's nervousness about his hospital appointment had meant that he shied away from the outside world and the news had only got through to him via this much-thumbed evening paper.

He got to his feet. He'd had enough of his own mortality to be going on with. He left the hospital in a heavy drizzle. He started downhill to the town centre. Molin was dead, and he himself had been informed that he belonged to the category of people whose days might be numbered. He was 37 years old and had never really thought about his own age. Now it felt as if he'd suddenly been robbed of all perspective. A bit like being in a boat on the open sea, then being cast into a narrow fjord surrounded by high cliffs. He paused on the pavement to get his breath back. He wasn't just scared, he also had the feeling that somehow or other he was being swindled. By something invisible that had smuggled its way into his body and was now busy destroying him.

It also seemed to him rather ridiculous that he should have to explain to people that he had cancer of the tongue, of all places. People got cancer, you heard about that all the time. But in the tongue?

He started walking again. To give himself time he decided to make his mind a complete blank until he got as far as the grammar school. Then he'd decide what to do. The doctor had given him an appointment for further tests the next day. She'd also extended his sick leave by a month. He would start his course of treatment in three weeks' time.

Outside the theatre was a group of actors and actresses in costumes and wigs, being photographed. They were all young, and laughing very loudly. Lindman had never set foot inside the Borås theatre. When he heard the players laughing, he quickened his pace.

He went into the library and proceeded to the newspaper room. An old man was perusing a newspaper with Russian characters. Lindman collected a speedway magazine before sitting at one of the tables. He used it to hide behind. Stared at a picture of a motorbike while trying to make up his mind.

The doctor had said he wasn't going to die. Not yet, at least. There was a risk that the tumour would grow and the cancer might start to spread. It would be a head to head battle: he'd either win or lose. There was no possibility of a draw.

He stared at the motorbike and it struck him that for the first time in years he missed his mother. He'd have been able to discuss things with her, but now he had nobody he could talk to. The very idea of taking Elena into his confidence was unthinkable. Why? He didn't understand. If there was anybody he should be able to talk to and who could give him the support he needed, it was Elena. Even so he couldn't bring himself to phone her. It was as if he were ashamed of having to tell her that he did have cancer. He hadn't even told her about his hospital appointment.

He leafed through all the pages with pictures of bikes. Leafed his way to a conclusion.

Half an hour later he knew what he was going to do. He'd talk to his boss, Superintendent Olausson, who'd just got back from holiday – he'd been shooting elk. He'd tell him he'd been given a medical certificate without mentioning why. He'd just say he had to undergo a thorough examination because of the pains he'd been having in his throat. Nothing serious, no doubt. He could hand the doctor's certificate in to the staffing office himself: that would give him at least a week before Olausson knew the reason for his absence.

Then he'd go home, phone Elena and tell her he was going away for a few days. Maybe to Helsinki to see his sister. He'd done that before. That wouldn't arouse her suspicions. Next, he'd go to the wine shop and buy a few bottles. During the course of the evening and the night, he'd make all the other necessary decisions, the main one being whether or not he thought he could cope with fighting a cancer that might turn out to be life-threatening. Or whether he should simply give up.

He put the magazine back on its shelf, continued through the reading room and paused at a shelf with medical reference books. He took down one about cancer. Then he put it back again without opening it.

Superintendent Olausson of the Borås police was a man who laughed his way through life. His door was always open. It was midday when Lindman entered his office. He was just finishing a telephone call, and Lindman waited. Olausson slammed down the receiver, produced a handkerchief and blew his nose.

"They want me to give a lecture," he said, with a laugh. "Rotary. They wanted me to talk about the Russian Mafia, but there is no Russian Mafia in Borås. We don't have any Mafia at all. So I turned 'em down." He gestured to Lindman that he should sit down.

"I just wanted to let you know that my doctor's certificate has been extended."

Olausson stared at him in surprise. "But you're never ill."

"I am now. I have pains in my throat. I'll be off for another month. At least."

Olausson leaned back in his chair and folded his hands over his stomach. "A month sounds a long time for a sore throat, don't you think?"

"It was the doctor who signed the certificate, not me."

Olausson nodded. "Police officers do catch cold in the autumn," he said. "But I get the impression that the criminal classes never catch flu. Why's that, do you think?"

29

"Maybe they have better immune systems?"

"That could be. Perhaps that's something we should let the Commissioner know about."

Olausson didn't like the National Commissioner. Nor did he think much of the Justice Minister. He didn't like any superiors, come to that. It was a standing joke in the Borås police force that some years previously a Social Democratic Justice Minister had visited the town to open the new district court, and at the dinner afterwards had got so drunk that Olausson had to carry him up to his hotel room.

Lindman stood up to leave. "I read that Herbert Molin was murdered the other day."

Olausson stared at him in surprise. "Molin? Murdered?"

"In Härjedalen. He lived up there, it seems. I saw it in one of the evening papers."

"Which one?"

"I don't remember which one."

Olausson accompanied him out into the corridor. The evening papers were piled up in reception. Olausson found the article and read what they'd written.

"I wonder what happened," Lindman said.

"I'll find out. I'll ring our colleagues in Östersund."

Lindman left the police station. The drizzle seemed set to keep falling for ever. He queued up in the wine shop and eventually took home two bottles of an expensive Italian wine. Before he'd even taken off his jacket he opened one of the bottles and filled a glass that he proceeded to empty in one go. He kicked off his shoes and threw his jacket over a kitchen chair. The telephone answering machine in the hall was blinking. It was Elena, wondering if he would like to come round for dinner. He took his glass and the bottle of wine with him into the bedroom. The traffic outside was reduced to a faint buzz. He lay down on the bed with the bottle in his hand. There was a stain on the ceiling. He'd lain in bed the night before staring at it. It looked different by day. After another glass of wine he rolled over onto his side and fell asleep without further ado.

*   *   *

It was nearly midnight when he woke up. He'd slept for almost eleven hours. His shirt was soaked in sweat. He stared into the darkness. The curtains kept out any light there was in the street.

His first thought was that he was going to die.

Then he decided that he would fight it. After the next set of tests he would have three weeks in which to do whatever he liked. He'd spend that time finding out all there was to find out about cancer. And he'd prepare for the fight he was going to put up.

He got out of bed, took off his shirt and tossed it into the basket in the bathroom. Then he stood in the window overlooking Allégatan. Outside the Vävaren Hotel garage a few drunken men were arguing. The street was shiny with rain. He thought about Molin. A vague thought had been nagging at him since he'd read the report in the paper at the hospital. Now it came back to him.

They'd once been chasing an escaped murderer through the woods north of Borås. It was late autumn, like now. Lindman and Molin had somehow become separated among the trees, and when Lindman eventually found him he'd approached so quietly that he surprised Molin, who turned to stare at him with terror-stricken eyes.

"I didn't mean to scare you," Lindman said.

Molin just shrugged.

"I thought it was somebody else," he said.

That was all. I thought it was somebody else.

Lindman remained standing at the window. The drunks had dispersed. He ran his tongue over his top teeth. There was death in that tongue of his, but somewhere or other there was also Herbert Molin. I thought it was somebody else.

It dawned on Lindman that he'd known all the time. Molin had been scared stiff. All those years they'd worked together his fear had always been there. Molin had usually managed to hide it, but not always.

Lindman frowned.

Molin had been murdered in the depths of the northern forests, having always been frightened. The question was: of whom?

CHAPTER 3

Giuseppe Larsson was a man who had learnt from experience never to take anything for granted. He woke up on October 26 when his back-up alarm clock rang. He looked at his front-line clock on the bedside table and noted that it had stopped at 3.04. So, you couldn't even rely on alarm clocks. That's why he always used two. He got out of bed and opened the roller blind with a snap. The television weather forecast the night before had said there would be a light snowfall over the province of Jämtland, but Larsson could see no sign of snow. The sky was dark, but full of stars.

Larsson had a quick breakfast made for him by his wife. Their 19-year-old daughter, who still hadn't flown the nest, was fast asleep. She had a job at the hospital and was due to start on a week-long night shift that evening. Shortly after 7 a.m. Larsson forced his feet into a pair of Wellington boots, pulled his hat down over his eyes, stroked his wife's cheek and set off for work. He was faced with a drive of a couple of hundred kilometres. This last week he'd done it there and back several times, apart from one occasion when he was so tired, he'd felt obliged to book into a hotel in Sveg.

Now he had to drive there yet again. On the way he had to keep a lookout for elks, while also trying to summarise the murder investigation he was involved in. He left Östersund behind, headed for Svenstavik, and set his cruise control to 85 kilometres per hour. He couldn't be sure that he'd be able to stay under the speed limit of 90 kilometres per hour if he didn't. An average of 85 would get him there in good time for the meeting with the forensic unit arranged for 10 a.m.

He seemed to be driving through tightly-packed darkness. The northern winter was at hand. Larsson was born in Östersund 43 years ago, and couldn't understand people who complained about the darkness and the cold. As far as he was concerned, the half of the year usually described as winter was a time when everything settled down and became uneventful. Needless to say, there was always somebody now and then who couldn't stand the winter any longer and committed suicide or battered some other person to death – but that was the way it had always been. Not even the police could do anything about that. However, what had happened not far from Sveg was hardly an everyday occurrence. Larsson found himself having to rehearse all the details one more time.

The emergency call had reached the Östersund police station late in the afternoon of October 19. Seven days ago now. Larsson had been on the point of leaving for a haircut when somebody thrust a telephone into his hand. The woman at the other end was shouting. He'd been forced to hold the receiver away from his ear to grasp what she was saying. Two things were clear from the start: the woman was very upset, and she was sober. He'd sat at his desk and fumbled for a notepad. After a few minutes he'd made enough notes to give him a fair picture of what he thought she was trying to make him understand. The woman's name was Hanna Tunberg. Twice a month she used to char for a man called Herbert Molin, who lived some miles outside Sveg in a house called Rätmyren. When she arrived that day she'd found a dog lying dead in its pen, and seen that all the windows in the house were broken. She didn't dare stay as she thought the man who lived there must have gone mad. She'd driven back to Sveg and collected her husband, who had retired on health grounds. They'd gone back to the house together. It was about four in the afternoon by then. They'd considered phoning the police right away, but had decided to wait until they'd established what had actually happened – a decision they both bitterly regretted. Her husband had entered the house but emerged immediately and shouted to his wife, who'd stayed in the car, that the place was full of blood. Then he thought he saw something at the edge of the forest. He'd gone to investigate, taken a step back, then sprinted to the car and started vomiting into the grass. When he'd recovered sufficiently, they'd driven straight to Sveg. As her husband had a weak heart, he'd lain down on the sofa while she phoned the police in Sveg, and they'd passed the call on to Östersund. Larsson had noted down the woman's name and telephone number. When they'd finished talking he'd rung her back in order to check that the number was correct. He also made sure he'd got the name of the dead man right. Herbert Molin. When he put the receiver down for the second time, he'd abandoned any thought of having his hair cut.

He'd gone immediately to Rundström, who was in charge of emergencies, and explained the situation. Just 20 minutes later he was on his way to Sveg in a police car with blue lights flashing. The forensic boys were making preparations to follow as soon as possible.

They'd reached the house some time after 7.30. Hanna Tunberg was waiting for them at the turn-off, along with Inspector Erik Johansson, who was stationed in Sveg and had just got back from another call-out, a lorry laden with timber that had overturned outside Ytterhogdal. It was already dark by then. Larsson could see from the woman's eyes that the sight awaiting them would not be a pretty one. They went first to the spot on the edge of the forest that Hanna Tunberg had described to them. They found themselves gasping for breath when they shone their torches on the dead body. Larsson understood the woman's horror. He thought he'd seen everything. He had several times seen suicides who'd fired a shotgun straight into their faces, but the man on the ground in front of them was worse than anything he'd been obliged to look at before. It wasn't really a man at all, just a bloody bundle. The face had been scraped away, the feet were no more than blood-soaked lumps and his back had been so badly beaten that bones were exposed.

They'd then approached the house with guns drawn. They'd established that there was indeed a Norwegian elkhound dead in the pen. When they entered the house they found that Hanna's description of what her husband had told her was in no way exaggerated. The floor was covered in bloody footprints and broken glass. They'd closed the door to make sure that nothing was disturbed before the forensic team arrived.

Hanna had been in the car all the time, her hands clutching the steering wheel. Larsson felt sorry for her. He knew that what she'd been through today would stay with her for the rest of her life, a constant source of fear or a never-ending nightmare.

Larsson had sent Johansson in Hanna's car to the junction with the main road to wait for the forensic team. He'd also told him to write

34

down in detail everything the woman had to say. Precise times especially.

Then Larsson had been on his own. He suspected he was faced with something he wasn't really up to coping with, but he also knew that there was nobody else in the whole of the Jämtland police force who was better equipped than he was to lead the investigation. He decided to tell the chief of police straightaway that reinforcements would have to be called in from outside.

He was approaching Svenstavik. It was still dark. Several days had passed, but they were no nearer to solving the mystery of the murdered man in the forest.

There was another major problem. It had transpired that the dead man was a retired police officer who had moved up to Härjedalen after working for many years as a detective in Borås. Larsson had spent the previous evening at home, reading through documents faxed to him from Borås. He was now familiar with all the basic information that forms an individual's profile. Nevertheless, he had the impression he was staring into a vacuum. There was no motive, no clues, no witnesses. It was as if some mysterious evil force had been let loose, emerged from the forest to attack Molin with all its might, and then disappeared without trace.

He passed through Svenstavik and continued towards Sveg. It was getting light now, and the wooded ridges surrounding him on all sides were acquiring a shade of blue. His mind turned to the preliminary report he'd received from the coroner's office in Umeå where pathologists had been examining the body. It explained how the wounds had been inflicted, of course, but hadn't provided Larsson with any clues as to where this savage attack might have come from, nor why. The pathologist described in detail the violence inflicted on Molin. The wounds on his back appeared to have been caused by lashes with a whip. As there was no skin left on his back, it was only when they discovered a fragment of the lash that they realised what had happened. A microscopic examination revealed that the whip had been made from the hide of an animal. Just what animal they were unable to say, as it did not correspond with any animal in Sweden. It was highly probable that the injuries to the soles of Molin's feet had been caused by the same instrument. He had not been beaten in the face: the scrape marks indicated that he had been dragged face down over the ground. The wounds were full of soil. The doctor was able to state that on the basis of bruises on the victim's neck, it was clear that an attempt had been made to strangle him. *An attempt* was a wording that should be taken literally, the report stressed. Molin had not been choked to death. Nor did he die from the residue of tear gas found in his eyes, throat and lungs. Molin had died from exhaustion. He had, literally, had the life whipped out of him.

Larsson pulled into the side of the road and stopped. He switched off the engine, got out of the car and waited until a lorry had driven past on its way up north. Then he opened his flies and had a pee. Of all the joys that life had to offer, having a pee at the side of the road was the best. He got back into the car, but before starting the engine, he tried to think objectively about what he now knew concerning the death of Molin. Slowly and deliberately, he tried to let everything he'd seen and read in various reports filter through his mind and find its own way into appropriate pigeon holes. Something among that information might give a lead. They had found no trace of a motive. Nevertheless, it was obvious that Molin had been subjected to protracted and savage violence. Frenzy, fury, Larsson thought. That's what it's all about. Perhaps this furious frenzy is in fact the motive. Fury and a thirst for vengeance.

There was something else that suggested he might be on the right track. Everything gave the impression of having been carefully planned. The guard dog had had its throat cut. The murderer had been equipped with whips and tear gas cartridges. That can't have been coincidental. The fury must have been an outburst within the framework of a meticulous plan.

Fury, thought Larsson. Fury and vengeance. A plan. That means that whoever killed Molin had most probably been to the house before, possibly on several occasions. Somebody ought to have noticed strangers hanging around in the vicinity. Or maybe the opposite applied: nobody had noticed anything. Which would mean that the murderer, or murderers, would have been friends of Molin.

But Molin didn't have any friends. That was something fru Tunberg had been very clear about. Molin didn't have a social life. He had been a recluse.

Larsson went over what had happened one more time. He had the feeling that the attacker had been on his own. Somebody had turned up at the isolated dwelling, armed with a whip made from an unidentified animal hide, and a tear gas pistol. Molin had been killed with ruthless and planned sadism, and the body had been abandoned naked at the edge of the forest.

The question was: had Molin simply been murdered? Or was it an execution?

Expert reinforcements would have to be brought in. This wasn't just a run-of-the-mill murder case. Larsson was increasingly persuaded that they were faced with an execution.

It was 9.40 by the time Larsson drove up to Molin's house. The scene-of-crime tapes were still in place, but there was no sign of a police vehicle. Larsson got out of his car. There was quite a wind now. The swishing sound from the forest imposed itself upon the autumn morning. Larsson stood quite still and looked slowly round. The forensic unit had found traces of a car parked exactly where he was standing now: the tracks didn't correspond to Molin's ancient Volvo. Every time Larsson came to the scene of the murder, he tried to imagine exactly what had happened. Who had clambered out of this unknown car? And when? It must have been during the night. The pathologists still hadn't been able to establish the precise time of death. Even so, the writer of the preliminary report had hinted in carefully chosen words that the assault could well have been going on over an extended period of time. He couldn't say how many strokes of the whip Molin had received, but the beating – with pauses – might well have gone on for several hours.

Larsson rehearsed yet again in his head the thoughts that had occurred to him during the drive out from Östersund.

Fury, and the thirst for revenge. A solitary murderer. Everything meticulously planned. No killing on the spur of the moment.

The phone rang. He gave a start. He still hadn't got used to the fact that he could be reached by telephone, even in the middle of the forest. He retrieved his mobile from his jacket pocket and answered.

"Giuseppe Larsson."

He'd lost count of the number of times he'd cursed his mother for giving him his first name after, as a young girl, she'd heard an Italian crooner at a concert in Östersund's People's Park one summer night. He'd been teased ruthlessly throughout his school years, and now, every time anybody phoned him and he said his name, whoever was at the other end of the line always paused to consider.

"Giuseppe Larsson?"

"Speaking."

He listened. The man at the other end said his name was Stefan Lindman, and that he was a police officer. He was ringing from Borås. Lindman went on to say that he'd worked with Molin and was curious about what had happened. Larsson said he'd phone him back. He'd had cases when reporters had pretended to be police officers, and he didn't want to run that risk again. Lindman said he appreciated that. Larsson couldn't find a pencil, and instead marked the phone number in the gravel with the toe of his shoe. He rang back, and Lindman answered. He might be a reporter nevertheless, of course. What he ought to do was to phone the station in Borås and ask if they had an officer by the name of Stefan Lindman. Even so, the way the man at the other end of the line expressed himself suggested to Larsson that he was telling the truth, and he tried to answer Lindman's questions. But it wasn't easy to do so on the phone. In any case, reception was not good, and he could hear the forensic team approaching.

"I've got your number," Larsson said. "And you can get hold of me at this number or at the station in Östersund. Meanwhile, is there anything *you* can tell *me*? Did Molin feel under threat? Any information could be of value. We don't have much to go on. No witnesses, no apparent motive. Nothing at all, really. We're ready to grab at any straw."

He listened to the response without comment. The scene-of-crime van drove up to the house. Larsson concluded the call, and made the number he'd traced in the gravel more obvious with the toe of his shoe.

The policeman who'd phoned from Borås had said something important. Molin had been scared. He'd never explained why he was uneasy, but Lindman had no doubt. Molin had been scared all the time, wherever he'd been, whatever he'd done.

There were two forensic officers, both of them young. Larsson liked working with them. They were full of energy, meticulous and efficient. Larsson watched them enter the house they were destined to investigate, and try to take in the blood splattered over the walls and floor. As the young men donned their overalls, Larsson began once more to think about what had happened.

He was clear about the main outline. It started with the death of the dog. Then the windows had been smashed, and tear gas canisters shot in. It wasn't the tear gas canisters that had broken the windows. They'd found some cartridges from a hunting rifle outside the house. The man who'd carried out the attack had been methodical. Molin was asleep when it all started – at least, it looked as if he'd been in bed at the time. He was naked when his body was found at the edge of the forest, but his jumper and trousers were found soaked in blood at the bottom of the steps leading down from the front door. From the remnants they'd found of the tear gas canisters it would seem that the place must have been filled with the gas. Molin had run out of the house with his shotgun. He'd also managed to fire a few shots. Then he'd been stopped in his tracks. The gun was discarded on the ground. Larsson knew that Molin must have been more or less blind when he left the house. He'd also have had great difficulty in breathing. So Molin had been hounded out of his house, and had been incapable of defending himself as he staggered from the door.

Larsson picked his way carefully into the room leading off the living room. It contained the biggest riddle of all. In a bed a bloodstained doll, life size. He thought at first it was some kind of sex aid used by lonely Molin, but the doll had no orifices. The loops on its feet suggested that it was used as a dancing partner. The big question was: why was it covered in blood? Had Molin moved into this room before the tear gas made it impossible for him to stay in the house? Even so, that wouldn't have explained the blood. Larsson and the other detectives who had spent six days going through the house with a fine-tooth comb still hadn't come up with a plausible reason. Larsson was going to spend this day trying to work out once and for all why the doll was covered in blood. There was something about the doll that worried him. It concealed a secret and he wanted to know what it was.

He left the house to get some fresh air. His mobile rang. It was the chief of police in Östersund. Larsson told him the current state of affairs, that they were hard at work, but they'd not yet found anything new at the scene of the crime. Fru Tunberg was in Östersund, talking to Artur Nyman who was a detective sergeant and Larsson's closest colleague. The chief of police was able to inform Larsson that Molin's daughter, who was in Germany, would soon be on her way to Sweden. They'd also been in touch with Molin's son, who worked as a steward on a cruise ship in the Caribbean.

"Any news about his second wife?" Larsson wondered.

The first wife, the mother of his two children, had died some years ago. Larsson had spent several hours looking into her death, but she'd died of natural causes. Moreover Molin and his first wife had got divorced 19 years ago. His second wife, a woman Molin had been married to in Borås, had proved difficult to trace.

Larsson went back into the house. He stood just inside the door and scrutinised the stains of dried blood on the floor. Then he took a couple of paces sideways and looked hard at them again. He frowned. There was something about the marks that puzzled him. He took out his notebook, borrowed a pencil from one of the forensic officers, and made a sketch. There were 19 footprints in all, ten made by a right foot and nine by a left foot.

He went outside. A crow was disturbed and flew off. Larsson studied his sketch. Then he fetched a rake he knew was in the shed, and smoothed out the gravel in front of the house. He pressed his feet down into the gravel to reproduce the pattern he'd sketched in his notebook. Stepped to one side and studied the result. Walked all the way round, examining the marks from different angles. Then he carefully stepped into the footprints, one after the other, moving slowly. He did it again, faster now, with his knees slightly bent. The penny dropped.

One of the forensic officers came out onto the steps and lit a cigarette. He stared at the footprints in the gravel. "What are you doing?"

"Testing a theory. What can you see here?"

"Footprints in the gravel. A replica of the ones we have inside the house."

"Nothing else?"

"No."

The other officer came out. He had a thermos flask in his hand.

"Wasn't there a disc in the CD player?" Larsson asked.

"That's right," said the man with the flask.

"What kind of music was it?"

The technician handed the flask to his colleague and went inside. He was back in a flash.

"Argentinian stuff. An orchestra. I can't pronounce the name."

Larsson walked round the footprints in the gravel once again. The two forensic officers watched him as they smoked and drank their coffee.

"Does either of you dance the tango?" he said.

"Not normally. Why?"

It was the man with the thermos flask who answered.

"Because what we have here are tango steps. It's a bit like when you were little and went to dancing classes. The teacher used to tape footprints onto the floor, and you had to follow them. The steps are tango steps."

To prove his theory Larsson started to hum a tango tune that he didn't know the name of. At the same time he followed the footprints in the gravel. The steps fitted.

"What we have on the floor in there is a set of tango steps. Somebody dragged Molin round and placed his blood-soaked feet on the floor as if he'd been attending a dancing class."

The forensic officers stared at him incredulously, but knew he was right. They all went back into the house.

"Tango," said Larsson. "That's all it is. Whoever killed Molin invited him to dance a tango."

They contemplated the footprints in silence.

"The question," Larsson said, when he spoke again, "is who? Who invites a dead man to dance with him?"

CHAPTER 4

Lindman began to have the feeling that his body was being drained completely of blood. Even though the laboratory assistants were very gentle with him, he felt increasingly weary. He spent many hours at the hospital every day, having blood taken for testing. He also talked to the doctor on two more occasions. Each time he had lots of questions, but never got round to asking any of them. In fact, there was only one question he really wanted answering: was he going to survive? And if that question couldn't be answered with any degree of certainty, how much time did he, for sure, have left? He'd read somewhere that death was a tailor who measured people for their final suit, invisibly and in silence. Even if he did survive, he had the feeling that his span had already been measured out. It was much too early for that.

The second night he went to Elena's in Dalbogatan. He hadn't phoned in advance, as he usually did. The moment she saw him in the doorway, she knew something was wrong. Lindman had tried to make up his mind whether or not to tell her, but he was unsure right up to the moment he rang the doorbell. He'd barely had time to hang up his jacket before she asked him what was wrong.

"I'm ill," he'd said.

"Ill?"

"I've got cancer."

That left him with no more defences. He might as well tell the truth now. He needed somebody to confide in, and Elena was his only choice. They sat up far into the night, and she was sensible enough not to try to console him. What he needed was courage. She brought him a mirror and said look, the man on her sofa was very much alive, not a corpse, that was how he ought to approach the situation. He stayed the night, and lay awake long after she had gone to sleep.

He got up at dawn, quietly, so as not to wake her, and left the building as discreetly as possible. But he didn't go straight back to Allégatan:

42

instead he made a long detour round Lake Ramna and turned for home only after he'd got to Druvefors. The doctor had said that they'd finish all the necessary tests today. He'd asked if he could go away, possibly abroad, before the treatment started, and she said he could do whatever took his fancy. He had a cup of coffee when he got home, and played back his answering machine. Elena had been worried when she woke up and found that he'd gone.

Shortly after ten he went to the travel agent's in Västerlanggatan. He sat down and started going through the brochures. He'd more or less made up his mind that it would be Mallorca when the thought of Herbert Molin came to him. He knew there and then what he was going to do. He wasn't going to fly to Mallorca. If he did, all he'd do was to wander around a place where he knew no-one, worrying about what had happened and what was going to happen. If he went to Härjedalen, he would be no less alone, as he didn't know anybody up there either; but he'd be able to devote his attention to something other than himself and his problems. What he might be able to do, he wasn't sure. Nevertheless he left the travel agent's, went to the bookshop in the square and bought a map of the neighbouring provinces of Jämtland and Härjedalen. When he got home he spread it out over the kitchen table. He reckoned it would take him 12-15 hours to drive there. If he got too tired, he could always spend the night somewhere on the way.

In the afternoon he went to the hospital for the final tests. The doctor had already given him an appointment for when he should return for the start of the treatment. He'd noted it in his diary, in his usual sprawling handwriting, as if he'd been recording some holiday date, or somebody's birthday. On Friday, November 19, 8.15 a.m.

When he returned home he packed his suitcase. He looked up the weather on teletext and saw that the temperature in Östersund was forecast at between 5° and 10°C. He assumed there would be no significant difference between Östersund and Sveg. Before going to bed it occurred to him that he ought to tell Elena that he was leaving. She'd be worried if he simply disappeared. But he put it off. He had his mobile, and she had the number. Perhaps he wanted her to worry? Maybe he wanted to hurt an innocent party to make up for his being the one who was ill?

*   *   *

43

The following day, Friday, October 29, he left Borås before 8 a.m. Previously he'd driven to Brämhultsvägen and taken a good look at the house where Molin had lived. That had been his home as a married man, for a time on his own, and that was the place he'd left when he moved north on his retirement.

Lindman recalled the farewell party for Molin in the canteen on the top floor of the station. Molin hadn't drunk very much – he'd probably been the most sober of all present. Detective Chief Inspector Nylund, who retired the year after Molin, had given a speech: Lindman couldn't remember a word of it. It had been a pretty insipid affair, and had ended early. It was the practice for newly retired officers to invite their colleagues round, as a sort of thank you: Molin had not done so. He'd simply walked out of the police station, and a few weeks later left Borås altogether.

Now Lindman was about to make the same journey. He was following in Molin's tracks, without understanding why Molin had moved – or perhaps fled – to Norrland.

By nightfall Lindman had come as far as Orsa. He stopped for an evening meal, a greasy steak in a roadside café, then settled down on the back seat of his car. He was tired out, and fell asleep at once. The plasters on his arm were itching. In his dreams, he was running through an endless succession of dark rooms.

He woke up while it was still dark, feeling stiff and with a splitting headache. He wriggled his way out of the car, and as he was having a pee he noticed that his breath was coming out like steam. The gravel crunched under his feet. It was obvious that the temperature was around or even below zero. The previous evening he'd filled a thermos flask with hot coffee. He sat behind the wheel and drank a cup. A lorry parked beside him started up and drove off. He switched on the radio and listened to the early news. He felt uneasy. Being dead would mean he could no longer listen to the radio. Death meant many different things. Even the radio would fall silent.

He put the thermos on the back seat and started the engine. It was another 100 kilometres or so to Sveg. He drove out into the main road, and reminded himself that he must be on the look-out for elks. It grew gradually lighter. Lindman was thinking about Molin. He tried to sift through what he could remember about him, every conversation, all those meetings, all that time when nothing special had happened. What were Molin's habits? Had he had any habits at all? When had he laughed? When had he been angry? He had difficulty in remembering. The image was elusive. The only thing he was sure about was that Molin had that time been frightened.

The forest came to an end, and after crossing the River Ljusnan Lindman found himself driving into Sveg. The place was so small that he nearly drove out of it on the other side before realising that he'd reached his destination. He turned left at the church and saw a hotel sign. He'd assumed it wouldn't be necessary to book a room, but when he went to reception the girl behind the desk told him that he'd had a stroke of luck. They had one room, thanks to a cancellation.

"Who wants to stay in a hotel in Sveg?" he said, in surprise.

"Test drivers," the girl told him. "They book in up here and test new models. And then there are the computer people."

"Computer people?"

"There's lots of that sort of thing just now," the girl said. "New firms setting up. And there aren't enough houses. The council is talking about building hostels."

She asked him how long he intended staying.

"A week," he said. "Maybe longer. Is that possible?"

She checked in the ledger.

"Well, I think so, but I can't promise," she said. "We're full up more or less all the time."

Lindman left his case in his room and went downstairs to the dining room, where the breakfast buffet was open. Young people were sitting at all the tables, many of them dressed in what looked like flying suits. When he'd eaten he went back to his room, stripped down, removed the plasters from his arm and took a shower. Then he crept between the sheets. What am I doing here? he wondered. I could have gone to Mallorca. But I'm in Sveg. Instead of walking along a beach and looking at a blue sea, I'm surrounded by endless trees.

When he woke, he didn't know at first where he was. He lay in bed and tried to construct some sort of plan. But first he'd have to see the place where Molin had died. The simplest thing of course would be to talk to the detective in charge of the case in Östersund, Giuseppe Larsson; but something told him it would be better to take a look at the scene of the crime without anybody knowing about it. He could talk to Larsson later, maybe even drive to Östersund. On the way north he'd wondered if there were any police stationed in Sveg, or did the police have to drive nearly 200 kilometres from Östersund to investigate petty crimes? Eventually, he got up. He had no end of questions, but the crucial thing was to see the scene of the crime.

He dressed and went down to reception. The girl who'd checked him in was on the phone. Lindman spread out his map and waited. He could hear that she was talking to a child, no doubt her own, something about coming to the end of her shift shortly and being relieved, so that she could go home.

"Everything OK with the room?" she asked as she put the receiver down.

"All in order," Lindman said. "I have a question, though. I haven't come here to see if cars can cope with extreme conditions. Nor am I a tourist, or a fisherman. I'm here because a good friend of mine was murdered not far from here last week."

Her face turned serious.

"The bloke who lived out at Linsell? The retired policeman?"

"That's the one." He showed her his police ID, then pointed to his map. "Can you show me where he lived?"

She turned the map round and took a good look at it. Then she pointed to the spot.

"You have to head for Linsell," she said. "Then turn off towards Lofsdalen, cross the River Ljusnan, and you'll come to a signpost directing you to Linkvarnen. Carry on past there, for another ten kilometres or so. His house is off to the right, but the track isn't marked on this map."

She looked at him.

"I'm not really nosy," she said. "I know lots of people have come here just to gape. But we've had some police from Östersund staying here, and I heard them describing how to get there over the telephone. Somebody was supposed to be coming here by helicopter."

"I don't suppose you get much of that sort of thing here," Lindman said.

"I've never heard of anything of the kind, and I was born in Sveg. When there was still a maternity hospital here."

Lindman tried to fold his map together, but made a mess of it.

"Let me help you," she said, flattening it out before folding it neatly.

When Lindman left the hotel he could see that the weather had changed. There was a clear sky, the morning clouds had dispersed. He breathed in the fresh air.

Suddenly he had the feeling that he was dead, and he wondered who would come to his funeral.

He reached Linsell at around two in the afternoon. To his surprise, he saw a sign advertising an Internet café. The village also boasted a petrol station and a general store. He turned left across the bridge and kept going. Between Sveg and Linsell he'd seen a grand total of three cars going in the opposite direction. There was no hurry. About ten kilometres, she'd said. After seven kilometres he came to an almost invisible side turning into a dirt road that disappeared into the forest on his right. He followed the badly potholed track for about 500 metres, at which point it petered out. A few home-made signposts indicated that various tracks going off in all directions were snowmobile tracks for the winter months. He turned round and returned to the main road. After another kilometre he came to the next turning. It was practically impassable, and after two kilometres came to a stop at a log pile. He'd scratched the bottom of his car several times on stones projecting from the badly maintained track.

When he got to Dravagen, it was obvious that he'd gone too far. He turned round. A lorry and two cars passed him in the opposite direction. Then the road was empty again. He was driving very slowly now, with the windows wide open. He kept thinking about his illness. Wondering what would have happened if he'd gone to Mallorca. He wouldn't have needed to search for a road there. What would he have been doing instead? Sitting in the depths of some dimly lit bar, getting drunk?

Then he found the road. Just after a bend. He knew it was right the moment he saw it. It led him uphill and into three bends, one directly after the other. The surface was smooth and covered in gravel. After two kilometres he saw a house behind the trees. He drove into the parking area at the front and came to a halt. The police tapes closing it off were still there, but the place was deserted. He got out of the car.

There wasn't a breath of wind. He stood still and looked round. Molin had moved from his house in Brämhultsvägen in Borås to be in this remote spot in the depths of the forest. And somebody had found their way here in order to kill him. Lindman looked at the house. The smashed windows. He approached the front door and tried it. Locked. Then he walked round the building. Every window was broken. From the rear he could see water glittering through the trees. He tried the shed door. It was open. Inside it smelled of potatoes, and he took note of a wheelbarrow and various garden implements. He went out again.

Molin was isolated here, he thought. That must be what he'd been looking for. Even in his Borås days he'd longed to be alone, and that's what attracted him to here.

He wondered how Molin had discovered this house. Who had he bought it from? And why here, in the depths of the Härjedalen forests? He walked up to one of the windows on the short wall. There was a kick-sledge parked next to the house wall. He used it as a step-ladder to open the broken window from the inside. Carefully he removed the protruding bits of glass and clambered into the house. It struck him that there was always a special smell in places where the police had been. Every trade has its own smell. That applies to us as well.

He was in a small bedroom. The bed was made, but it was covered in patches of dried blood. The forensic examination had no doubt been completed, but he preferred not to touch anything. He wanted to see exactly the same things as the forensic officers had seen. He would start where they had left off. But what did he think he was doing? What did he think he might be able to uncover? He told himself he was in Molin's house as a private person. Not as a policeman or a private detective, just a man who had cancer and who wanted to find something other than his illness to think about.

He went into the living room. Furniture had been overturned. There were bloodstains on the walls and on the floor. Only now did he realise how horrific Molin's death must have been. He hadn't been stabbed or shot and fallen on the spot. He'd been subjected to a violent attack, and it looked as though he'd been chased and had resisted. He walked carefully round the room. Stopped at the CD player, which was standing open. No disc in it, but an empty case beside the player. Argentinian tango. He continued his exploration. Molin had lived a life devoid of ornament, it seemed. No pictures, no vases. No family photographs either.

A thought struck him. He went back to the bedroom and looked in the wardrobe. No police uniform. So, Molin seemed to have got rid of it. Most retired police officers kept their uniforms.

He went back to the living room, and from there into the kitchen. All the time he was trying hard to imagine Molin walking at his side. A lonely man of about 75. Getting up in the morning, making meals, getting through the day. A man is always doing something, it seemed to him. The same must have applied to Molin. Nobody just sits on a chair all day. Even the most passive of people *do* something. But what had Molin done? How had he spent his days? He went back to the living room and scrutinised the floor. Next to one of the bloodstained footprints was a piece of a jigsaw puzzle. There were other pieces strewn over the floor. He stood up, and felt a shooting pain in his back. The cancer, he thought. Or had he just slept awkwardly in his car last night? He waited until the pain had gone. Then he went over to the book-case with the CD player. Bent down and opened a cupboard. It was full of boxes that he thought at first contained various games. He took out the top one, and saw that it was a jigsaw puzzle. He looked at the picture on the front of the box. A painting by an artist called Matisse. Had he heard that name before, perhaps? He wasn't sure. The subject was a large garden, with two women dressed in white in the back-ground. He turned to the rest of the pile. Nearly all of them were based on paintings. Big puzzles with lots of pieces. He opened the next cupboard. That was full of jigsaw puzzles too, none of them opened. He stood up gingerly, afraid that the pain might return. So, Molin spent a lot of his time doing jigsaw puzzles, he thought. Odd. But there again, maybe no odder than his own hobby, collecting pointless press cuttings about Elfsborg football club.

He looked round the room again. It was so quiet he could hear his own pulse beating. He really ought to get in touch with the Östersund police officer with the unusual first name. Maybe he ought to drive there on Monday and have a chat with him? There again, the murder investigation was nothing to do with him. He ought to be quite clear about that. He hadn't come to Härjedalen to carry out some kind of private investigation into who had killed Herbert Molin. No doubt there was a straightforward explanation. There generally was. Murder was nearly always to do with money or revenge. Alcohol was generally involved. And the culprit usually came from a circle of close contacts – family and friends.

It could be that Larsson and his colleagues had pinpointed a motive already and been able to point the finger at a possible suspect. Why not?

Lindman took another look round. Asked himself what the room had to say about what had happened in it. But he heard no answers. He looked at the bloodstained footprints. They formed a pattern. What surprised him was that they were so clear, suggesting they'd been put there in that form intentionally, and were not the accidental traces of a struggle or the staggering steps of a dying man. He wondered what the forensic team and Giuseppe Larsson had made of that.

Then he walked over to the big broken window in the living room. Stopped in his tracks, and ducked down. There was a man standing outside. Holding a rifle. Motionless, staring straight at the window.

CHAPTER 5

Lindman had no time to be afraid. When he saw the man with the gun outside, he took a pace back and crouched by the side of the window. He at once heard a key in the front-door lock. If he had for a second thought that the man outside was the murderer, he shed it now. The man who killed Molin would hardly have had his front-door key.

The door opened. The man paused in the entrance to the living room. He was holding the gun pointing down at his side. Lindman saw that it was a shotgun.

"There's not supposed to be anybody here," the man said. "But there is."

He spoke slowly and distinctly, but not like the girl in the hotel reception. His dialect was different. Lindman couldn't tell what it was.

"I knew the dead man."

The stranger nodded. "I believe you," he said. "I just wonder who you are."

"Herbert Molin and I worked together for several years. He was a police officer, and I still am."

"That's about all I know about Herbert," said the man. "That he'd been a police officer."

"Who are you?"

The man gestured to Lindman, suggesting that they should go outside. He nodded towards the empty dog pen. "I think I knew Shaka better than I knew Herbert," he said. "Nobody knew Herbert."

Lindman looked at the dog pen, then at the man. He was bald, in his sixties, tall, thin and dressed in bib-and-brace overalls and jacket, and rubber boots. He turned his gaze from the dog pen and looked at Lindman.

"You wonder who I am," he said. "Why I have a key. And a shotgun."

Lindman nodded.

51

"In these parts distances are long. I don't suppose you met many cars on the way here. I bet you didn't see many people either. I live about ten kilometres away, but even so I was one of Herbert's nearest neighbours."

"What sort of work do you do?"

The man smiled. "Isn't it usual to ask a man first his name," he said, "and then what he does?"

"My name's Stefan Lindman, police officer in Borås. Where Herbert used to work."

"Abraham Andersson. But round here they call me Dunkärr, because I live at a farm called Dunkärret."

"Are you a farmer, then?"

The man laughed and spat into the gravel. "No," he said. "I don't go in for agriculture. Nor forestry. Well, I go to the forest, but not to cut down trees. I play the violin. I was in the symphony orchestra in Helsingborg for 20 years. Then one day I simply felt I'd had enough. And moved up here. I still play sometimes. Mostly to keep my fingers moving. Old violinists can have problems with their joints if they stop just like that. In fact, that was how I met Herbert."

"How so?"

"I take my violin into the forest. I settle down where the trees are densest. The violin sounds different there. At other times I go up a mountain, or to a lakeside. The sound is always different. After all those years in a concert hall it's as if I've got a new instrument in my hands." He pointed at the lake that was just visible through the trees. "I was standing down there, playing away. Mendelssohn's violin concerto, I think it was, the second movement. Then Herbert appeared with his dog. Wondered what the hell was going on. I can understand him. Who expects to find an old fellow in a forest playing a violin? Plus he was upset because I was trespassing on his land. But we became friends after that. Or whatever you'd call it."

"What do you mean by that?"

"I don't suppose anybody became a friend of Herbert's."

"Why?"

"He'd bought this house in order to be in peace. But you can't entirely cut yourself off from other people. After a year or so, he told me that there was a spare key on a hook in the shed. I don't know why."

"But you used to see a bit of each other socially?"

"No. He let me play down by the lake whenever I wanted. To tell you the truth, I never set foot in this house before today. He never came round to me either."

"Was there anybody else who visited him?"

The man's reaction was almost imperceptible, but Lindman noticed the slight hesitation before he answered. "Not as far as I know."

So, he did have visitors, Lindman thought. But he said: "So, in other words, you're a pensioner as well. And you've hidden yourself away in the forest, just like Herbert."

The man started laughing again. "Not at all," he said. "I'm not a pensioner, and I haven't hidden myself away in the forest. I write a bit for a few dance bands."

"Dance bands?"

"The occasional song. Light hearts, broken hearts. Mostly crap, but I've had some hits. Not as Abraham Andersson, of course. I use what's known as a pseudonym."

"What do you call yourself?"

"Siv Nilsson."

"A woman's name?"

"I once knew a girl at school I was in love with. It was her name. I thought it was a rather nice way of declaring my affection for her."

Lindman wondered if Andersson was pulling his leg, but decided that he was telling the truth. He looked at the man's hands. His fingers were long and slim. He could indeed be a violinist.

"You've got to ask yourself what on earth happened here," the man said. "Who can have come out here and finished Herbert off. The place has been crawling with police until yesterday. There's been folk coming in helicopters and roaming around with dogs; police knocking on doors for miles around. But nobody knows a thing."

"Nobody?"

"Nobody. Herbert came here from somewhere or other and wanted to be left in peace. But somebody didn't want to leave him in peace, and now he's dead."

"When did you last see him?"

"You're asking the same questions as the police."

"I am the police."

Andersson looked at him quizzically. "But you're not from the local police. That means you can't be on the case."

"I knew Herbert. I'm on holiday. I came here."

Andersson nodded, but Lindman was sure he hadn't been believed. "I leave here for one week every month. I go to Helsingborg to see my wife. It's odd that it should happen when I wasn't here."

"Why?"

"Because I never go away at the same time. It could be in the middle of a month from Sunday till the following Saturday, but it might just as easily be from Wednesday to Tuesday. Never the same. And yet it happens when I'm away."

Lindman thought that over. "So you think that somebody was keeping watch and made his move when you weren't around?"

"I don't think anything. I'm just saying that it's odd. I'm probably the only one who wanders about around here. Apart from Herbert."

"What do you think happened?"

"I don't know. I've got to go now."

Lindman walked him to his car which was parked at the bottom of the slope. He could see a violin case in the back seat.

"Where did you say you lived?" he said. "Dunkärret?"

"Just this side of Glöte. Keep going when you get there. About six kilometres. There's a sign pointing to the left. *Dunkärret. 2.*"

Andersson got into the car. "You've got to catch whoever did this," he said. "Herbert was a one-off, but harmless. Whoever killed him must have been mad."

Lindman watched the car drive off, standing there until the sound of the engine had died away. It struck him that sound travels a long way in a forest. Then he went back to the house and along the path that led to the lake. All the time he was chewing over what Andersson had said. Nobody knew Molin. But somebody had paid him visits. Andersson hadn't been prepared to say who, however. And the murder had taken place when Andersson wasn't in the vicinity, always assuming that Dunkärret could be counted as in the vicinity. Lindman paused to think. That could only mean one thing. Andersson must suspect that whoever killed Molin knew that Andersson was away, and that in turn could mean only two things: either the murderer was local, or he'd been keeping watch on Molin for some considerable time – at least a month, possibly longer.

He came to the lake. It was bigger than he'd expected. The water was brown, with only a very few gentle ripples. He squatted down and dipped his hand in. It was cold. He stood up and suddenly saw Borås hospital in his mind's eye. It was several hours since he'd last thought about what was in store for him. He sat on a rock and gazed over the lake. Wooded ridges stretched away into the distance on the other side, and he could hear a motor saw somewhere a long way off. I have no business being here, he thought. Molin might have had a reason for coming up north to the gigantic forests and the silence, but I haven't. On the contrary, I should be preparing myself for what's going to happen. My doctor has given me a good chance of surviving. I'm still young, and I'm strong, but the bottom line is that nobody can know for sure whether I'm going to make it or not.

He started along the shore. When he turned to look, he could no longer see the house. He was alone in the world now. He continued along the stony shore and eventually came to a rotting rowing boat that had been beached. In the decaying remains was an ant hill. He kept on walking, with no aim in mind, until he came to an opening in the trees, and sat down again, this time on a fallen tree trunk. The ground seemed to be well trodden. He noticed some cuts on the trunk that could only have been made by a knife. Perhaps Molin used to come here, he thought vaguely. Between jigsaw puzzles. Maybe he brought his dog with him? What was its name? Shaka? An odd name for a dog.

His mind was a complete blank. The only thing he could see was the road ahead, the long road he'd driven from Borås to get here. Then something intruded, spoiling the image. Something he ought to give thought to. He knew what it was. Something that had just occurred to him: that perhaps Molin came here with his dog.

It could have been somebody else, he thought. Somebody else sitting here. He started to look around, more attentively this time. The site had been cleared. Somebody had removed the undergrowth and levelled the ground. He got up from his tree trunk and squatted in the middle of the levelled area. It wasn't big, hardly more than 20 square metres, but pretty well shielded from view. Fallen trees and some large rocks made it more or less impossible to get there unless one came at it from the water's edge. He looked hard at the ground. If he screwed up his eyes, he could just make out a faint shape in the moss. A square. He felt with his fingers in the four corners. There were holes there. He stood up. A tent, he thought. Unless I'm much mistaken, there's been a tent pitched here. No knowing how long ago, but it must have been this year, otherwise the snow would have obliterated all the marks.

He looked round again, more slowly, as if every detail he saw might be crucial. At the back of his mind he kept thinking that what he was doing was pointless. But then again, he had nothing else to do at the moment. Nothing else to distract him.

He could find no trace of a fire, but that was irrelevant. People nowadays used camping gas stoves when they were in the forest. He examined the ground around the tree trunk one more time, but found nothing.

Then he went back down to the water's edge. There was a big stone on the waterline. He sat on it. Looked into the water, then felt at the back of the stone and the moss came loose. When he scraped it to one side he saw the remains of cigarette ends. The paper was brown, but they had certainly been cigarettes. They'd rotted away, but there were unmistakable flakes of tobacco there. He explored further with his hands. There were cigarette ends everywhere. Whoever had sat here had been a heavy smoker. He found a butt where the paper was discoloured but still retained a bit of whiteness. He picked it up carefully and searched in his pockets for something to put it in. The only thing he could find was a receipt. *The Hospital Cafeteria, Borås.* He placed the cigarette end carefully in the receipt, then folded it to form a parcel. He kept on searching and asked himself what would he have done if he'd pitched a tent here. You'd need a shit hole, he thought. It was possible to clamber into the forest past the side of one of the biggest rocks. It looked as if the moss had been scraped from one side of the stone. He examined the ground behind the stone. Nothing. He worked his way into the forest, a metre at a time. He thought about the police dogs Andersson had told him about. If they hadn't found any tracks, they could not have come this far.

He stopped short. Next to the trunk of a pine tree was a pile that had clearly been made by a human. Faeces and paper. His heart started beating faster. He was right. Somebody had camped by the side of the lake. A person who smoked cigarettes and didn't trouble to bury his excreta.

Even so, there was nothing to link the camper with Herbert Molin. He went back to where the tent must have been. There had to be some connection with the main road, or a track where the man in the tent might have left his car.

The shortcomings of his argument were immediately obvious to him. The camping site could well have been a meticulously arranged hiding place. The idea of a car parked near the main road didn't fit in with that. What were the alternatives? A motorbike or an ordinary bicycle would be easier to hide than a car. Or perhaps somebody else had driven the camper here.

He looked over the lake. There was another possibility, of course. The camper could have come that way. But where's the boat?

Larsson, he thought, is the man I have to talk to. There's no reason why I should be playing the private detective here. It's the police in Jämtland and Härjedalen that have to sort this out. He sat on the fallen tree again. It was colder. The sun was setting. There was a flapping noise in the trees. When he turned to look, the bird had already disappeared. He started retracing his steps. A brooding silence prevailed around Molin's house. The chill emanating from the events that had taken place here was getting to him.

He drove back to Sveg. He stopped at the Spar shop in Linsell and bought the local newspaper, *Härjedalen*, published every Thursday (except public holidays). The man behind the counter gave him a friendly smile. Lindman could see he was curious.

"We don't get very many visitors here in the autumn," the man said. His identity disk said that his name was Torbjörn Lundell. Lindman thought he might as well tell him the truth. "I knew Herbert Molin," he said. "We worked together before he retired."

Lundell looked doubtfully at him. "You're police," he said. "Can't our own force cope with this, then?"

"I've got nothing to do with the investigation."

"But even so, you've come here, from as far away as . . . Halland, was it?"

"Västergötland. I'm on holiday. But Herbert told you that, did he? That he came from Borås?"

Lundell shook his head. "It was the police said that. But he used to shop here. Every other week. Always on a Thursday. Never said a word unless he had to. Always bought the same things. He was a bit choosy when it came to coffee, though. I had to order it specially for him. French coffee."

"When did you last see him?"

"Thursday, the week before he died."

"Did you notice anything unusual about him?"

"Such as what?"

"Was he different at all?"

"He was same as ever. Didn't say a word more than he had to."

Lindman hesitated. He ought not to have lapsed so easily into his role as a police officer. Rumours would get out that there was a policeman from some distant place, asking awkward questions. Nevertheless there was one question he simply couldn't resist asking.

"Have you had any other customers lately? Ones you don't usually have?"

"That's what the fuzz from Östersund asked me. And the officer from Sveg. I told 'em the way it was – apart from a few Norwegians and some berry pickers from Belgium last week, I haven't seen a soul here that I didn't know."

Lindman thanked him, left the shop and continued towards Sveg. It was dark by now. He was feeling distinctly hungry.

He'd got an answer to one of his questions, though. There was a police presence in Sveg. Even if the investigation was based in Östersund.

Shortly before he came to Glissjöberg an elk ran over the road into his headlights. He managed to brake in time. The animal disappeared into the trees at the side of the road. He waited to see if others would follow it, but none did.

He parked outside his hotel. There was a group of men in overalls chatting away in reception. He went up to his room and sat on the bed. Before he knew where he was, he had visions of himself lying in bed with tubes attached to his body and face. Elena was in a chair at the side of his bed, crying.

He jumped up and slammed his fist hard into the wall. Suddenly there was a knock at the door. Another of the test drivers.

"Did you want something?" the man said.

"What on earth would I want?"

"You knocked on the wall."

"It must have been from somewhere else."

Lindman slammed the door in the driver's face. I've made my first enemy in Härjedalen, he thought. Just when I should be concentrating on making friends. That set him thinking. Why did he have so few friends? Why didn't he move in with Elena and start living the life he really yearned for? Why did he lead a life that left him all on his own, now that he was faced with a serious illness? He had no answer to that.

He thought about phoning Elena, but decided to eat first. He went down to the dining room and chose a window table. He was the only customer. He could hear the sound from a television set coming from the bar. To his surprise he found that the girl in reception had been reincarnated as a waitress. He ordered a steak and a beer. As he ate, he thumbed through the newspaper he'd bought in Linsell. He read all the deaths column, and tried to imagine his own obituary. He ordered a coffee after the meal, and stared out into the darkness.

He left the dining room and paused in reception, wondering whether to go for a walk or to return to his room. He chose the latter course. He rang Elena's number. She picked up immediately. Lindman had the impression she'd been sitting by the phone, waiting for him to ring.

"Where are you?"

"In Sveg."

"What's it like there?" she asked hesitantly.

"Cold, and I feel lonely."

"I don't understand why you've gone there."

"Nor do I."

"Come back home, then."

"If I could, I'd start back right away. But I'll be here for a few more days."

"Can't you tell me you miss me, at least?"

"You know I do."

He gave her the hotel telephone number, and hung up. Neither of them liked talking on the phone. Their conversations were often short. Even so, Lindman had the feeling she was close by his side.

He was tired. It had been a long day. He untied his laces and kicked his shoes away from the side of the bed. Then he lay down and stared at the ceiling. I must make up my mind what I'm doing here, he thought. I came here to try to understand what had happened, to understand what Molin had been so frightened of. Now I've seen the house where he was murdered, and I've found a camping site that might have been a hiding place.

He wondered what to do next. The obvious thing would be to drive up to Östersund and meet this Larsson.

But then what?

Maybe the journey here was pointless. He should have gone to Mallorca. The Jämtland police would do what they had to do. One day he'd find out what had happened. Somewhere out there was a murderer waiting to be arrested.

He lay on his side and looked at the blank television screen. He could hear some young people laughing in the street below. Had he laughed at all during the day that had just passed? He searched his memory, but couldn't even remember a smile. Just at the moment I'm not the person I usually am, he thought. A man who's always laughing. At the moment I'm a man with a malignant lump on his tongue who's scared to death about what's going to happen next.

Then he looked at his shoes. Something had stuck to one of the soles, he discovered, trapped in the pattern of the rubber sole. A stone from the gravel path, he thought. He reached to winkle it out.

But it wasn't a stone. It was part of a jigsaw puzzle piece. He sat up and adjusted the bedside lamp. The piece was soft and discoloured by soil. He was certain he hadn't stood on any pieces inside the house. It might have been outside the house. Nevertheless, his intuition told him that the jigsaw piece had stuck to the sole of his shoe at the place where the tent had been pitched. Whoever killed Herbert Molin had been camping at the lakeside.

CHAPTER 6

The discovery of the broken jigsaw puzzle piece livened him up somewhat. He sat at the table and started making notes about all that had
happened in the course of the day. It took the form of a letter. At first,
he couldn't think to whom it ought to be addressed. It occurred to
him that it should go to the doctor who was expecting to see him in
Borås in the morning of November 19. Was there nobody else to write
to? Perhaps it was that Elena wouldn't understand what he was talking
about? At the top of the page he wrote: *The fear of Herbert Molin,* and
underlined the words with forceful strokes of his pen. Then he noted
one by one the observations he'd made in and around the house, and
where the tent had been. He tried to draw some conclusions, but the
only thing that seemed to him definite was that Molin's murder had
long been planned.

It was 10 p.m. He hesitated, but decided to phone Larsson at home
and tell him he would come and see him in Östersund the following
day. He looked for the number in the phone book. There were a lot
of Larssons, but predictably only one Giuseppe, a police officer. His
wife answered. Lindman explained who he was. She sounded friendly.
While he was waiting, he wondered what Larsson's hobby might be.
Why didn't he have a hobby himself, apart from football? He hadn't
managed to find an answer before Larsson came to the phone.

"Stefan Lindman," he said. "From Borås. I hope this isn't too late."

"Not quite. Another half hour and I'd have been asleep. Where are
you?"

"In Sveg."

"Just down the road, then." Larsson roared with laughter. "A couple
of hundred kilometres is nothing to us up here. Where do you get to
if you drive two hundred kilometres from Borås?"

"Almost to Malmö."

"There you are, you see."

"I thought I might visit you in Östersund tomorrow."

"You're welcome. I'll be there from quite early in the morning. The police station is behind the National Rural Agency building. It's a small town. You'll have no trouble in finding it. When had you thought of coming?"

"I can fit in with you. Whenever you've got time."

"How about 11 a.m.? We have a meeting at 9.00 of our little murder squad."

"Have you got a suspect?"

"We've got nothing at all," said Larsson, cheerfully. "But we'll solve this one in the end, we hope. We'll be discussing tomorrow if we need any help from Stockholm. Somebody who can draw up a profile of the fellow we're looking for would be useful. Could be interesting. Up here, we've never been faced with anything like this before."

"They're good at that," Lindman said. "We've had some help from them in Borås now and then."

"See you tomorrow, then. 11 a.m."

Then he went out. The driver next door was snoring. Lindman went down the stairs as quietly as he could. His room key also fitted the front door. The lights were out in reception, the door to the restaurant closed. It was 10.30. When he emerged into the street he found that a wind had blown up. He pulled his jacket tightly round him and started walking through the empty streets. He came to the railway station, which was dark and locked. He read a notice and learned that trains no longer came here. The old "Inland Railway", he thought. That's what the line used to be called, if I remember rightly. Nothing left but rusting rails. He continued on his nocturnal ramble, passed a park with swings and tennis courts and came to the church. The main door was locked. In front of the school was a statue of a lumberjack. He tried to make out the features of the man. In the poor light of the street lamps they seemed to be expressionless.

He hadn't seen a single person. When he got back to the hotel, he lay down on the bed for a while and watched the television with the sound turned down. He could still hear the man next door snoring through the paper-thin wall.

It was 4.30 before he got to sleep. His head was a vacuum.

He was up again at 7 a.m. His head throbbed with tired thoughts. He sat at a table alone in the dining room, which was teeming with early-bird test drivers. The girl from reception was playing the part of waitress again.

"Did you sleep well?" she asked.

"Yes, thank you," he said.

It was raining by the time he came to Östersund. He drove around the town until he discovered the gloomy building with a red sign for the "National Rural Agency". He wondered what on earth an organisation like that actually did. Was its function just to facilitate the abandonment of Swedish rural communities?

He found a parking place in a side street and stayed in the car. Still 45 minutes to go before his meeting with Larsson. He reclined his seat and closed his eyes. I have death in my body, he thought. I have to take that seriously, but I can't get my head round it. You can't pin down death – not your own, at least. I can understand that Molin is dead. I've seen the traces of his death struggle. But my own death? I can't cope with imagining that. It's like the elk that ran across the road just before I came to Linsell. I'm still not sure that it really existed, or whether I just imagined it.

At 11 a.m. precisely, Lindman walked through the front door of the police station. To his surprise, the woman in reception looked very like one of the receptionists in Borås. He wondered if the National Police Board had passed a motion requiring all police receptionists to look alike.

He explained who he was.

"Larsson told us to expect you," she said, pointing to the nearest corridor. "His office is down there, the second room on the left."

Lindman knocked on the door with Detective Inspector Larsson on it. The man who opened it was tall and very powerfully built. His reading glasses were pushed up over his forehead.

"You're punctual," he said, almost hustling him into the room and closing the door behind them.

Lindman sat in the visitor's chair. He recognised the way the office was furnished from the police station in Borås. We don't only wear uniforms, he thought. Our offices are uniform as well.

Larsson sat in his desk chair and crossed his hands over his stomach. "Have you been up in this part of the world before?" he asked.

"Never. Uppsala once, when I was a child, but that's as far north as I've been before."

"Uppsala is southern Sweden. Here in Östersund you still have half of Sweden to go as you travel north. It used to be a very long way from here to Stockholm. Not any more. Flights can take you to wherever you like in Sweden in just a few hours. In the space of a few decades Sweden has turned from a big country into a little one."

Lindman pointed to the large wall map.

"How big is your police district?"

"Big enough and more besides."

"How many police officers are there in Härjedalen?"

Larsson thought for a moment. "Five, maybe six in Sveg, a couple in Hede. And the odd one more here and there, in Funäsdalen, for instance. Possibly 15 in all, depending on how many are on duty at a given time."

They were interrupted by a knock on the door. It opened before Larsson could react. The man in the doorway was the polar opposite of Larsson, short and very thin.

"I thought Nisse should sit in on this," Larsson said. "We are the ones in charge of the investigation."

Lindman stood up to shake hands. The man who'd joined them was reserved and serious. He spoke very softly and Lindman had difficulty gathering that his surname was Rundström. Larsson seemed to be affected by his presence. He sat up straighter in his chair, and his smile disappeared. The mood had changed.

"We thought we ought to have a little chat," Larsson said, cautiously. "About this and that."

Rundström had not sat down, although there was a spare chair. He leaned against the door frame and avoided looking Lindman in the eye.

"We had a call this morning," he said. "From a man who reported that a police officer from Borås was conducting an investigation in the region of Linsell. He was a bit upset, and wondered if the local police had handed the investigation over to outsiders." Before going on he paused to examine his hands. "He was a bit upset," Rundström repeated. "And it would be fair to say that we were upset as well."

Lindman had broken out in a sweat. "I can think of two possibilities," he said. "The man who phoned was either Abraham Andersson – he lives in a farmhouse called Dunkärret – or it was the owner of the Spar shop in Linsell."

"I expect it was Lundell," Rundström said. "But we don't like police officers from faraway places coming here and poking their noses into our investigations."

Lindman saw red. "I'm not conducting my own investigation," he said. "I've spoken to Larsson here. I told him I'd worked with Molin for quite a few years. I'm on holiday, and so I came here. It doesn't seem all that strange that I would have visited the scene of the murder."

"It creates confusion," Rundström said, in his soft, barely audible voice.

"I bought the local paper," Lindman said, no longer bothering to conceal his anger. "I told the man who I was and asked if Molin did his shopping there."

Rundström produced a sheet of paper he'd been holding behind his back. "You asked quite a few more questions as well. Lundell read them to me over the phone."

This is lunacy, Lindman thought. He looked at Larsson, but he was staring down at his stomach.

For the first time Rundström looked him in the eye. "What exactly do you want to know?" he asked.

"Who killed my colleague."

"That's what we want to know as well. Needless to say, we've given this investigation top priority. It's a long time since we've set up such a broadly based investigative team as this one. We've had some pretty violent crimes up here over the years. We're not exactly unused to it."

Rundström was making no attempt to disguise the fact that he resented his presence, but he could also see that Larsson was upset by the approach Rundström had adopted. That gave him an escape route.

"It goes without saying that I'm not questioning the way you are working."

"Have you any information you can give us that would be of use to the investigation?"

"No," Lindman said. He didn't want to tell Rundström about the tent site until he'd discussed it with Larsson. "I have no useful information to give you. I didn't know Molin well enough to be able to tell you anything about the life he led in Borås, never mind here. No doubt there are others who would be better at that than I am. And in any case, I'll be leaving soon."

Rundström nodded and opened the door. "Any news from Umeå yet?"

"Nothing so far," Larsson said.

Rundström smiled curtly at Lindman and was gone. Larsson stretched out an arm apologetically.

"Rundström can be a bit abrupt at times. But he means well."

"He's within his rights to complain about my poking my nose in."

Larsson leaned back in his chair and eyed him speculatively. "Is that what you're doing? Poking your nose in?"

"Only in the sense that sometimes you can't avoid stumbling over things."

Larsson looked at his watch. "How long are you thinking of staying in Östersund? Overnight?"

"I haven't decided anything."

"Stay overnight, then. I'll be working here tonight as well. Come here some time after seven. With a bit of luck everything will be quiet here then. I have to be on call tonight, because so many officers are off sick. You can make yourself at home in my office."

Larsson pointed to some files on a shelf behind him. "You can look through the material we have. Then we can talk."

"And Rundström?"

"He lives in Brunflo. You can bet your life he won't be here tonight. Nobody will ask any questions."

Larsson rose from his chair. Lindman understood that the conversation was over.

"The old theatre's been converted into an hotel. A good hotel. There's no question of their being full in October."

Lindman buttoned up his jacket.

"Umeå?" he wondered.

"That's where we send our dead bodies."

66

"I thought that was Uppsala or Stockholm."

Larsson smiled. "You're in Östersund now. Umeå's a lot nearer."

Larsson accompanied him as far as reception. Lindman noticed that he was limping. Larsson saw that he'd noticed.

"I slipped in the bathroom. Nothing serious."

Larsson opened the front door and went out into the street with him. "There's winter in the air," he said, looking up at the sky.

"Herbert Molin must have bought the house from somebody," said Lindman, "Privately, or through an estate agent."

"We've looked into that, of course," Larsson said. "Molin bought the house from an independent estate agent. Not one of the big companies. A rural estate agent. His name's Hans Marklund and he runs the business on his own."

"What did he have to say?"

"Nothing yet. He's been on holiday in Spain. He's evidently got a second home down there. He's on my list for tomorrow."

"He's home, then?"

"Yesterday." Larsson thought for a moment. "I can tell my colleagues that I'll take the responsibility for interviewing him. Which in turn means that there's nothing to prevent you from talking to him."

"Hans Marklund?"

"He works from his house in Krokom. Take the road north. In Krokom itself, you'll see a sign saying "Rural Properties". Ring the doorbell here at 7.15 p.m., and I'll come and let you in."

Larsson went back inside. Rundström's attitude had annoyed Lindman, but at the same time it had given him renewed energy. And Larsson wanted to help him by letting him go through the material they had so far accumulated. In doing so, Larsson was putting himself at risk, even if there were no real impropriety in allowing a colleague from another force to take part in the investigation. Lindman found the hotel Larsson had suggested. He got a room under the eaves. He left his case there and returned to his car. He phoned the hotel in Sveg and spoke to the girl in reception.

"Nobody will take your room," she assured him.

"I'll be back tomorrow."

"You come when it suits you."

Lindman found his way out of Östersund. It was only 20 kilometres to Krokom, where he found the estate agent's straightaway. It was a yellow-painted house with a large garden. A man was walking around the lawn vacuuming up dead leaves. He switched the machine off when he saw Lindman. The man was tanned and about Lindman's age. He looked fit and trim, and had a tattoo on one of his wrists.

"Are you looking for a house?" he said.

"Not exactly. Are you Hans Marklund?"

"That's me."

Then he turned serious. "Are you from the Tax Authority?"

"No. Giuseppe Larsson told me I'd find you here."

Marklund frowned. Then he remembered who that was. "The policeman. I've just got back from Spain. There are quite a lot of Larssons there. Or something of that kind. In Östersund there's only one. Are you a police officer as well?"

Lindman hesitated. "Yes," he said. "I'm a police officer. You once sold a house to a man called Herbert Molin. As you know, he's dead now."

"Come inside," Marklund said. "They phoned me in Spain and told me he'd been murdered. I didn't expect to hear from them until tomorrow."

"You will."

One of the rooms on the ground floor had been fitted out as an office. There were maps on the walls, and coloured photographs of houses up for sale. Lindman noticed that the prices were significantly lower than in Borås.

"I'm on my own at the moment," Marklund said. "My wife and children are staying on in Spain for another week. We've got a little house in Marbella. I inherited it from my parents. The kids have their autumn half-term holiday, or whatever it's called."

Marklund made some coffee and they sat down at a table strewn with files.

"I had some problems with the tax people last year," Marklund said apologetically. "That's why I asked. As the local authority is hard up, I supposed they have to squeeze out every krona they can."

"Eleven years ago, or so, you sold the house near Linsell to Herbert Molin. I used to work with him in Borås. He retired and moved up here. And now he's dead."

"What happened?"

"He was murdered."

"Why? By whom?"

"We don't know yet."

Marklund shook his head.

"It sounds nasty. We like to think that we live in a pretty peaceful area up here – but maybe there aren't any of those any more?"

"Maybe not. What can you tell me about that sale eleven years ago?"

Marklund disappeared into an adjoining room. He came back with a file in his hand. He soon found what he was looking for.

"March 18, 1988," he said. "The deal was signed and sealed here in this office. The seller was an old forester. The price was 198,000 kronor. No mortgage. The transaction was paid for by cheque."

"What do you remember about Molin?"

The reply surprised Lindman.

"Nothing."

"Nothing?"

"I never met him."

"I don't follow."

"It's very simple. Somebody else looked after the matter for him. Got in touch with me, took a look at a few houses and eventually made the decision. As far as I know, Molin was never here."

"Who was the middleman?"

"A woman by the name of Elsa Berggren. With an address in Sveg." Marklund passed the file over. "Here's the authorisation. She had the right to make decisions and sign the deal on Molin's behalf."

Lindman examined the signature. He remembered it from the Borås days. It was Molin's signature.

"So you never met Herbert Molin?"

"I never even spoke to him on the phone."

"How did you come into contact with this woman?"

"The usual way. She phoned me."

Marklund leafed through the file, then pointed.

"Here's her address and telephone number," he said. "She's no doubt the person you should talk to. Not me. That's what I'll tell Giuseppe Larsson. Incidentally I wonder if I'll be able to resist the temptation to ask him how he came by his name. Do you happen to know?"

"No."

69

Marklund closed the file.

"Isn't it a bit unusual? Not meeting the person with whom you were doing business?"

"I was doing business with Elsa Berggren, and I did meet her. But I never met Molin. It's not all that unusual. I sell quite a lot of holiday cottages in the mountains to Germans and Dutchmen. They have people who sort out the details for them."

"So there was nothing unusual about this transaction."

"Nothing at all."

Marklund accompanied him as far as the front gate.

"Maybe there was, though," he said, as Lindman was walking through the gate.

"Maybe there was what?"

"I remember Elsa Berggren saying on one occasion that her client didn't want to use any of the big firms of estate agents. I recall thinking that was a bit odd."

"Why?"

"If you're looking for a house you wouldn't as a rule start off with a small firm."

"How do you interpret that?"

Hans Marklund smiled. "I don't interpret it at all. I'm merely telling you what I remember."

Lindman drove back towards Östersund. After ten kilometres or so he turned off onto a forest track and switched off the engine.

The Berggren woman, whoever she might be, had been asked by Molin to avoid the big estate agents. Why? Lindman could only think of one reason. Molin had wanted to buy his house as discreetly as possible.

The impression he'd had from the very start had turned out to be correct. The house in which Molin had spent the last years of his life wasn't really a house at all. It was a hiding place.

CHAPTER 7

That evening Lindman wandered through the life of Herbert Molin. Reading between the lines of all the notes and reports, statements and forensic details that had already been collected in Larsson's files, despite the fact that the investigation hadn't been going for very long, Lindman was able to compile a picture of Molin that was new to him. He discovered circumstances that sometimes made him thoughtful and at others surprised. The man he thought he'd known turned out to be a quite different person, a complete stranger.

It had turned midnight when he closed the last of the files. Larsson had occasionally called in during the course of the evening. You could hardly say they indulged in conversation; they drank coffee and exchanged a few words about how the evening was going for the police emergency service in Östersund. Everything had been quiet for the first few hours, but soon after 9 p.m. Larsson had to sort out a burglary in Häggenås. When, eventually, he returned, Lindman had just reached the end of the last of the files.

What had he found? A map, it seemed to him, with large, blank patches. A man with a history with large gaps. A man who sometimes strayed from the marked path and disappeared, only to turn up again when least expected. Molin was a man whose past was elusive and in places very difficult to follow.

Lindman had made notes as the evening progressed. When he'd finished the last file and put it on one side, he looked through his notebook and summarised what he'd discovered.

The most surprising thing as far as Lindman was concerned was that according to the documents the Östersund police had requested from the tax authorities, Herbert Molin had been born with a different name. On March 10, 1923 he had come into this world at the hospital in Kalmar

71

and been baptised August Gustaf Herbert. His parents were the cavalry officer Axel Mattson-Herzén and his wife Marianne. That name had disappeared in June 1951 when he'd been allowed by the Swedish Patent and Registration Office to change his surname to Molin. At the same time he had changed his Christian name from August Gustaf Herbert to Herbert.

Lindman had sat staring at the name. Two questions occurred to him immediately. Why had Mattson-Herzén changed his surname and his Christian names? And why Molin, which must be about as common as Mattson? So many people in Sweden had the same surname that changing it was not unusual. But most people who changed their surname did so to escape from a common one so as to acquire one that nobody else had, or at least one that was not forever being mixed up with somebody else's.

August Mattson-Herzén was 28 years old in 1951. At the time he'd been serving in the regular army, a lieutenant of infantry in Boden. It seemed to Lindman that something must have happened then, that the early 1950s were important years in Molin's life. There was a series of significant changes. In 1951 he changed his name. The following year, in March 1952, he applied for a discharge from the army. He received a positive testimonial. He married when he left the army, and had children in 1953 and 1955, first a son christened Herman, and then a daughter Veronica. He and his wife Jeanette moved from Boden in 1952, to an address in Solna outside Stockholm, Råsundavägen 132. Nowhere could Lindman find any information about what Molin did to earn a living. Five years passed before he appeared again as an employee, in October 1957, in the local authority offices in Alingsås. He was posted from there to Borås, and after the police force was nationalised in the 1960s he became a police officer. In 1981 his wife filed for divorce. The following year he remarried, but wife number two, Kristina Cedergren, divorced him in 1986.

Lindman studied his notes. Between March 1952 and October 1957, Herbert Molin earned his living in some way unexplained in the files. That is a relatively long time, more than five years. And he had changed his name. Why?

When Larsson returned from the break-in in Häggenås, he found

Lindman standing by the window looking at the deserted street below. Larsson explained briefly about the burglary, no big deal in fact: somebody had stolen two power saws from a garage.

"We'll get them," he said. "We have a pair of brothers in Järpen who specialise in jobs of that kind. We'll nail them. What about you? What have you found out?"

"It's quite remarkable," Lindman said. "I find a man I thought I knew, but he turns out to be somebody else altogether."

"How so?"

"The change of name. And the strange gap between 1952 and 1957."

"Obviously. I've thought about that name change as well," Larsson said. "But we haven't really got that far in the investigation as yet, if you see what I mean."

Lindman understood. Murder investigations followed a certain pattern. In the beginning there was always the hope that they would catch the murderer at an early stage. If that didn't happen, they would set out on the long and often tedious gathering and then sorting of the material.

Larsson yawned. "It's been a long day," he said. "I need to get some sleep. Tomorrow is going to be just as long. When are you thinking of going back to Västergötland?"

"I haven't decided."

Larsson yawned again. "I gathered that you had something to tell me. It was obvious from what you said and how you reacted when Rundström was here. The question is: can it wait until tomorrow?"

"It can wait."

"You can't produce a murderer from out of a hat, then?"

"No."

Larsson got to his feet. "I'll come to your hotel tomorrow morning. Perhaps we can have breakfast together? 7.30?"

Lindman agreed. They put the files back on a shelf and switched off the desk lamp. They walked together through the dimly lit reception area. An officer was sitting in an inside room, taking a call.

"It always boils down to motive," Larsson said. "Somebody wanted to murder Molin. That's for sure. He was a specifically targeted victim. Somebody saw in him a motive to commit murder." He yawned again. "But we can talk about that tomorrow."

Larsson walked to his car, which was parked down the street. Lindman waved to him as he drove off and walked up the hill to the hotel. The town was deserted. He felt cold. He thought about his illness.

When Lindman came down to breakfast at precisely 7.30 a.m., Larsson was already waiting for him. He'd picked a corner table where they would be undisturbed. As they ate, Lindman told him about meeting Abraham Andersson and his walk along the shore of the lake that led him to the site where the tent had been. At that point Larsson pushed his half-eaten omelette to one side. Lindman produced the little parcel with the cigarette end and the piece of the jigsaw puzzle.

"I can only assume the dogs didn't get that far," he said. "I don't know whether it might still be worth sending a handler there now."

"There was nothing to go on," Larsson said. "We brought in three dogs by helicopter the day after we found him, but they didn't find a single scent."

He picked up his briefcase from the floor and produced a xerox of a map of the area around Molin's house. Lindman took a toothpick and indicated the spot where the tent had been pitched. Larsson put on his reading glasses and examined the map.

"There are some snowmobile tracks marked," he said, "but there's no road that could take a car to that part of the shore. Whoever set up camp there must have walked for at least two kilometres over quite difficult ground. Unless he used the track to Molin's house, and that seems unlikely."

"What about the lake?"

"That's a possibility. There are several forestry roads on the other side with turning places at the edge of the lake. It would obviously be possible to paddle over in a canoe or an inflatable."

He scrutinised the map for a few more minutes. Lindman waited.

"You might be right," Larsson said, pushing the map aside.

"I wasn't following a track. I just happened to land up there."

"It's not often that police officers just happen to stumble onto something. You could have been searching for something without realising it," Larsson said. He turned his attention to the bits of tobacco and the jigsaw puzzle piece.

"I'll take these and get forensic to give them the once-over," he said. "Your campsite must also be examined, of course."

"What's Rundström going to have to say about this?"

Larsson smiled. "There's nothing to stop me telling him that I was the one who found the place."

They both went for more coffee. Larsson was still limping.

"What did the estate agent have to say?"

Lindman told him. Again, Larsson was all attention.

"Elsa Berggren?"

"I've got her address and telephone number."

Larsson peered at him. "Have you spoken to her already?"

"No."

"You'd better leave that to me."

"Of course."

"You've weighed in with some very useful observations," Larsson said. "But Rundström's right of course, when he says that this is something we have to sort out ourselves. I wanted to give you the opportunity of seeing how far we've got, but I can't let you get further involved than that."

"I never expected you to."

Larsson slowly drained his coffee.

"Tell me, why did you really come to Sveg?"

"I'm on sick leave. I had nothing else to do. And, after all, I knew Molin quite well."

"Or you thought you did."

Lindman was aware that the man sitting opposite him was somebody he didn't know at all. Even so, he had an urge to tell him about his illness. It was as if he could no longer bear the burden alone.

"I came here from Borås because I'm ill," he said. "I've got cancer, and I'm waiting for the treatment to start. I had to choose between Mallorca and Sveg. I chose Sveg because I wanted to know what had happened to Molin. Now I'm wondering if I did the right thing."

They sat in silence for a minute or so.

"People always ask me where I got Giuseppe from," Larsson said. "You haven't asked. Because you've had something else on your mind, no doubt. I wondered what it was. Do you want to talk about it?"

"Not really. But I wanted you to know."

"Then I shan't ask any questions."

Larsson bent down and took a notepad out of his briefcase. He found the page he was looking for and passed the pad over to Lindman. On the page was a sketch of footsteps forming a pattern. Lindman saw that this was the pattern of the bloodstained footsteps in Molin's house. He'd been reminded of them by the photograph in Larsson's files. It also occurred to him that he hadn't mentioned to Larsson that he'd been inside Molin's house. It would be stupid to conceal it any longer. Andersson had seen him there, and he was bound to be questioned again by the police. So he told him exactly what had occurred. Larsson didn't seem to be surprised, and pointed once more to his notepad.

"This is a depiction of the basic steps for the fascinating dance known as the tango."

Lindman stared at him in surprise. "The tango?"

"There's no doubt about it. But this means that somebody carted Molin's corpse around and made those bloody footprints. No doubt you read the provisional report from the pathologist? His back cut to bits by lashes from the skin of some animal we have yet to identify. And the soles of his feet lacerated in similar fashion."

Lindman had read the pathologist's report with great distaste. The photographs had been horrific.

"This gives us food for thought," Larsson said. "Who would lead him round the floor like this? Why? And who is it that's supposed to see these bloody footsteps?"

"It could be a greeting to the police, of course."

"Correct. But the question remains: why?"

"No doubt you've thought of the possibility that they were photographed or filmed?"

Larsson returned the pad to his briefcase.

"It also leads us to draw the conclusion that this is no ordinary little bloody murder. There are other factors at work here."

"A madman?"

"A sadist. Look at what Molin was subjected to."

"Torture."

Larsson nodded. "There's no other word for it. But it worries me."

He closed his briefcase. "Did Molin use to dance the tango while he was in Borås?"

76

"Not as far as I know."

"We'll find out sooner or later, no doubt."

A child started screaming somewhere in the breakfast room.

"This used to be the theatre foyer," Larsson said. "Over there, behind the bar, was the auditorium."

"There was a beautiful old wooden theatre in Borås once upon a time," Lindman said. "But they didn't convert it into a hotel. They pulled it down, upsetting a lot of people at the time."

The child was crying still. Lindman went out with Larsson into reception.

"Maybe you ought to go to Mallorca after all," Larsson said. "I can keep you posted as the case develops."

Lindman didn't answer. Larsson was right, of course. There was no reason for him to stay in Härjedalen any longer.

They said their goodbyes in the street. Lindman went up to his room, collected his things, paid his bill, and left Östersund. He drove too fast along the straight road to Svenstavik. Then he slowed down. He tried to make a decision. If he returned to Borås now, today, he would still have time to go to the Mediterranean. To Mallorca or wherever. He could be away for two weeks. If he stayed in Sveg, he'd only get more and more restless. Besides, he'd told Larsson that he wouldn't interfere in the case more than he'd already done. Larsson had let him examine the investigation files. He couldn't go on intruding on scenes of crime. It was up to the Östersund police to find the motive for the murder. Up to them to track down the murderer.

The decision made itself. He'd go back to Borås the very next day. The excursion to Sveg was at an end.

He was driving slowly. Just under 60 kilometres per hour. Again and again he was passed by vehicles whose drivers eyed him with interest. He was churning over in his mind what he'd read in Larsson's files the night before. The investigation appeared to be being conducted meticulously and efficiently. When the call came, those on duty had reacted by the book. The first officers had been very quickly on the spot, the scene of the crime had been cordoned off exactly as it should have been, three dog patrols had arrived by helicopter from Östersund, and the forensic work seemed to have been performed with all thoroughness.

Lindman's discovery of the site where a tent had been pitched was pure coincidence. One of the local police would have made the same discovery sooner or later. The interview with Hanna Tunberg had confirmed the picture of Molin as a recluse. The house-to-house operation had produced one clear result: nobody had noticed any suspicious movements of vehicles or people in the area. Torbjörn Lundell in the Spar shop in Linsell had noticed no sign of Molin being nervous, or anything out of his normal routine.

Everything was as usual, thought Lindman.

Nevertheless, the placid scene is interrupted by the arrival of somebody, possibly paddling over the lake, who puts up his tent and then some time later attacks the retired police officer. He kills the dog and uses tear gas. He drags the dead or dying man around the floor and makes carefully mapped-out footprints. Steps describing the basic pattern of a tango. Then he paddles back over the lake again, and silence descends once more on the forest.

It seemed to Lindman that he could legitimately draw two conclusions. The first was that his original reaction had been correct: Molin had been afraid, and his fear had driven him to his hideaway in the forest.

The second conclusion was logical. Somebody had traced him to his refuge. But why?

Something must have happened in the early 1950s, he thought. August Mattson-Herzén abandons his military career and hides behind a new name. He marries and has two children, but there is a gap: how does he earn his living, until he turns up in the local council offices in Alingsås in 1957?

Could the events of nearly 50 years ago have caught up with him?

That was as far as he got. He ran out of ideas. He stopped in Ytterhogdal and filled up with petrol before driving on to Sveg and parking outside the hotel. There was a man he'd never seen before in reception, who gave him a friendly nod and handed over the key. Lindman went up to his room, took off his shoes and stretched out on the bed. He could hear a vacuum cleaner in the room next door. He sat up. Why not leave straightaway, today? He wouldn't get all the way to Borås, but he could stop somewhere en route. Then he lay down again. He didn't have the energy to organise a trip to Mallorca. The idea of going back to his flat in Allégatan depressed him. He'd only sit there, on edge, worrying about what was in store.

He couldn't make up his mind. The vacuum cleaner went quiet. At 1 p.m. he thought he'd better have some lunch, even though he didn't feel hungry. There must be a library somewhere in Sveg. He'd be able to sit there and study everything he could lay his hands on about radiotherapy. The doctor in Borås had explained it to him, but he seemed to have forgotten everything. Or maybe he hadn't been listening? Or couldn't bring himself to think about what it involved?

He put his shoes on again, and looked for a clean shirt. He opened the top of his suitcase that was perched on the rickety table next to the bathroom. He wasn't sure why, but something was different. He told himself he was imagining things, but he knew that wasn't true. He'd learnt from his mother how to pack a suitcase. He could fold up shirts so that they wouldn't crease, and he'd become fussy about planning his packing in minute detail.

He told himself again that he was imagining things. But no! Somebody had disturbed the contents of his case. Not much, but enough for him to notice it.

He went through all that was in it. Nothing was missing. Nevertheless, he was certain: somebody had been through his case while he'd been in Östersund. It could have been a chambermaid with itchy fingers, of course. But he didn't believe that. Somebody had been in his room and searched his case.

CHAPTER 8

Lindman stormed down to reception. When the usual girl, now back on duty, smiled at him, his anger fizzled away. It must have been the chambermaid. She had probably bumped into the case, and it had fallen. The rest was his imagination. After all, nothing was missing. He just smiled, put his key on the desk and went out. He paused on the steps, and wondered what he should do. It seemed that he was incapable of making the simplest of decisions. He ran his tongue over his teeth. The lump was still there. I'm carrying death in my mouth, he thought. If I survive this, I swear that I shall always keep a close watch on my tongue. He shook his head at such an idiotic idea, and decided to find out where Elsa Berggren lived. True, he'd promised Larsson that he wouldn't talk to her, but that didn't mean he couldn't find out where she lived. He went back into reception. The girl was on the phone, and he scrutinised the wall map of the town. He found the street on the other side of the river, in an area called Ulvkälla. There was another bridge, an old railway bridge: that was the one to use for crossing the river.

As he left the hotel, there was a thick layer of cloud over Sveg. He crossed the street and stopped at the window of the local newspaper. He read the pages they had displayed about the murder. A few hundred metres along Fjällvägen, he came to the old railway bridge. It was an arched bridge, and he stopped in the middle and looked down into the brown water. When he got to the other side, he turned left for Elsa Berggren's house. It was a white-painted wooden house in a well-tended garden. There was a free-standing garage in the grounds. The doors were wide open, but there was no car inside. As he walked past, he thought he saw a twitch in one of the curtains on the ground floor of the two-storey house. He kept on walking. A man was standing in the middle of the road, staring at the sky.

"Is it going to snow?" he said.

Lindman liked the dialect. There was something friendly about it, almost innocent. "Could be," he said. "But isn't it a bit early? It's only just turned November."

The man shook his head. "It can snow here in September, June even." The man was quite old. His face was wrinkled and he could have done with a shave. "Are you looking for somebody?" he said, making no attempt to conceal his curiosity.

"I'm just visiting. And thought I'd take a walk."

Lindman made up his mind on the spot. He'd told Larsson he wouldn't talk to Berggren, but he hadn't promised not to talk *about* her. "A nice house," he said, pointing to the house he'd just passed.

The man nodded. "Elsa takes good care of her house. The garden too. Do you know her?"

"No."

The man looked at him, as if he were waiting for the next step. "The name's Björn Wigren," he said eventually. "The longest trip I've ever made was to Hede, once upon a time. Everybody travels the world nowadays. Not me. I lived on the other side of the river when I was a boy. I suppose I'll have to go back over the river one of these days. To the cemetery."

"My name's Stefan. Stefan Lindman."

"Just visiting, you say?"

"Yes."

"Do you have relatives here?"

"No. I'm just passing through."

"And you've come out for a walk?"

"That's right."

The conversation petered out. Wigren's curiosity was natural, not aggressive at all. Lindman tried to think of a way of leading the conversation towards Elsa Berggren.

"I've lived here in my house since 1959," the man said. "But I've never known a stranger to take a walk here. Not at this time of year."

"There's always a first time."

"I could offer you a coffee," said Wigren. "If you'd like one? My wife's dead. The young have flown the nest."

"A coffee would be nice."

They went in through the gate. Had Wigren been standing in the street specifically to catch somebody who could share his loneliness?

His house was a bungalow. On a wall in the entrance hall was *The Gypsy Woman*, her breast bared. There were also several trophies, including a pair of elk antlers. Lindman counted 14 points, and wondered whether that was a lot or something less impressive. On the kitchen table was a thermos flask, and a plate covered by a napkin. Wigren produced a second cup, and invited Lindman to sit.

"We don't need to talk," he said, surprisingly. "You can drink coffee with a stranger and not say a word."

They drank a cup of coffee and each of them ate a cinnamon bun. A clock on the kitchen wall sounded at the quarter hour. Lindman asked himself how people had managed to communicate with each other before coffee had penetrated as far as Sweden.

"I gather you're retired," Lindman said – and realised at once what a stupid thing that was to say.

"I've worked in the forest for 30 years," Wigren said. "Sometimes I think about how hard we worked – not that anybody has the slightest idea about that nowadays. We loggers were slaves under the thumb of the big forestry companies. I don't think people realise what a blessing it was when the power saw was invented. But then I got back ache and packed it in. I spent my last few years making roads. I don't know if I was any use to them. I spent most of my time minding a machine and sharpening skates for schoolchildren. I did do one useful thing while I was allegedly helping to build roads. I learnt English. Sat there night after night, wrestling with books and tapes. I was on the point of giving up several times, but I stuck at it. Then I retired, and two days after my final working day, my wife died on me. I woke up in the morning, but she was already cold. That was 17 years ago. I was 82 last August."

Lindman raised an eyebrow. He found it hard to believe.

"I'm not having you on," Wigren said, seeing Lindman's surprise. "I am 82 years old, and I'm in such good health that I'm counting on scoring 90 at least, and maybe more. Whatever difference that will make."

"I've got cancer," Lindman said. "I don't know if I'll even make 40." The words came out of the blue.

Wigren raised an eyebrow. "It's a bit unusual to tell somebody that you've got cancer, when you don't know each other."

"I've no idea why I said that."

Wigren produced the plate with buns. "You said it because you needed to say it. If you want to say more, I'm all ears."

"I'd rather not."

"OK, we'll draw a line under that. If you want to say anything, OK. If you don't, that's also OK."

Lindman saw how he could turn the conversation in the direction he wanted.

"If somebody wanted to buy a house around here like the one we mentioned before, for example, how much would it cost?"

"Elsa's house, you mean? Houses are cheap around here. I keep my eye on the adverts. Not in the papers, on the Internet. I reckoned I ought to find out how to sort that out. It took time, but I think I got there in the end. I've got plenty of time, after all. I have a daughter who works for the council in Gävle. She came here and brought her computer with her, and showed me what to do. Now I chat with a fellow in Canada, called Jim – he's 96 and also worked in the forests. There's no limit to what those computer things can do. We're busy trying to set up a site where old loggers and lumberjacks can chat to each other when they feel like it. What are your favourite web addresses?"

"I'm afraid I don't know much about that, I don't even have a computer."

The man on the other side of the table looked worried.

"You must get yourself one. Especially if you're ill. There are loads of folk all over the world with cancer. I've seen that with my own eyes. I once looked up spinal cancer, which is the worst thing I can possibly imagine. I got 250,000 matches." He paused. "Needless to say, I've no intention of talking about cancer," he said. "As you said yourself."

"It's not a problem. Besides, I don't have cancer of the spine. At least, not as far as I know."

"I wasn't thinking."

Lindman returned to the question of house prices. "A house like Elsa's – what would it cost?"

"Two or three hundred thousand, no more. But I don't think Elsa has any intention of selling."

"Does she live alone?"

"I don't think she's ever been married. She can be a bit stand-offish at times. After my wife died, I thought I might make a move for her, but she wasn't interested."

"What sort of age is she?"

"Seventy-three, I think."

So. More or less the same as Molin, Lindman thought.

"Has she always lived here?"

"She was here when we built our house. That was in the late '50s. She must have lived in that house for 40 years."

"What did she do?"

"She said she'd been a teacher before she came here. No comment."

"What do you mean by that?"

"Who retires at the age of 40 or less? Something fishy there, don't you think?"

"She must have had some means of support?"

"She inherited her parents' estate. That's when she moved here. Or so she says."

Lindman tried to keep up. "So she wasn't born here? She must have been an incomer?"

"Skåne, I think she came from. Eslöv? Can that be somewhere down there where Sweden drifts to a halt?"

"That's right. And so she came here. Why here? Had she any family in Norrland?"

Wigren looked hard at him. "You're talking like a police officer. Some people might even suppose that you were interrogating me."

"I'm curious, like everybody else. You have to ask why somebody would move here from southern Sweden unless they were going to get married or had found their dream job," Lindman said, sensing that he might be making a serious mistake not telling the truth.

"I wondered about that as well. My wife too. But you don't ask questions if you don't have to. Elsa is nice, and helpful. She baby-sat for us when we needed it. And I still have no idea why she moved here. She didn't have any relatives in these parts." Wigren fell silent. Lindman waited. He had the impression that there was more to come.

"You might well think it's a bit odd," said Wigren when he eventually got round to saying something. "I've been living next-door to Elsa

84

for a whole generation. Even so, I've no idea why she bought this house in Ulvkälla. But there's another thing that's even odder."

"What?"

"All these years I never set foot in her house. Nor did my wife while she was alive. Nor the children while they were growing up. I don't know anybody who's ever been inside her house. Let's face it, that's a little strange."

Lindman agreed. There was something about Berggren's life that was reminiscent of Molin's. Both came from elsewhere, and both led isolated lives. The question is whether what I think is true of Molin, that he was running away from something, applied also to Berggren. She was the one who had bought the house on his behalf. But why? How had they got to know each other? Did they have anything else in common?

"Did you never see anyone arrive at the house?"

"Nobody has ever seen anyone set foot inside her house, nor come out again, for that matter."

Lindman decided it was time to move on. He looked at his watch. "I'm afraid I've got to go now," he said. "But thank you for the coffee."

They headed for the front door. Lindman pointed to the 14-pointed antlers.

"I shot that beast when I belonged to a group of hunters from around Lillhärdal."

"Is that big?"

Wigren burst out laughing. "The biggest I ever shot. It wouldn't have found its way onto my wall if it wasn't. When I die, it will fetch up on the rubbish dump. None of my children want it. We could be in for some snow tonight," he said at the door. Then he turned to face Lindman. "I don't know why you've been asking all these questions about Elsa, but I'm not going to say anything. One of these days though, you'll come and join me here in the kitchen and tell me what's going on."

Lindman nodded. He'd been right not to have underestimated Wigren.

"Good luck with the cancer," the old man said in farewell. "What I mean is, I hope you recover."

*   *   *

85

Lindman walked back the way he'd come. There was still no car on Berggren's drive, or in the garage. He glanced at the windows. No movement of the curtains. When he crossed the bridge he stopped again and gazed down into the water. The fear he felt at the thought of his illness came and went in waves. He could no longer stop himself thinking about what was in store for him. What he was doing here. Wandering about the periphery of the investigation of Molin's murder was a form of therapy which had only a limited effect.

In the centre of the town he found the public library in the Community Centre. There was a large stuffed bear in the foyer, staring at him. He had a sudden urge to attack it in a trial of strength. The thought made him burst out laughing. A man carrying a bundle of papers looked up at him in surprise.

Lindman located the shelves with medical literature, but when he sat down with a book with information on all varieties of cancer, he couldn't bring himself to open it. It's too soon, he thought. One more day. But not more. Then I will have to come to terms with my situation, instead of trying to bury it under my pointless efforts to find out what happened to Molin.

When he left the Community Centre, he again felt a wave of indecision. Annoyed, he started marching back to the hotel. On the way, he decided to stop at the wine shop. He hadn't been told by the doctor in Borås that he shouldn't drink alcohol. No doubt he shouldn't, but just now, he didn't care. He bought two bottles of wine. As he emerged into the street, his phone rang. He put his bag down on the pavement and answered it. It was Elena.

"I was wondering why you hadn't phoned me."

Lindman immediately felt guilty. He could hear that she was hurt and disappointed.

"I don't feel too good," he said, apologetically.

"Are you still in Sveg?"

"Where else could I be?"

"What are you doing there?"

"I don't know. Maybe I'm waiting to go to Molin's funeral."

"Do you want me to come? I could take some time off work."

He nearly said yes, and yes, he did want her to come. "No," he said. "I think it's better for me to be on my own."

She didn't ask again. They talked for a while without anything being said. Afterwards, he wondered why he hadn't told her the truth. Why hadn't he told her that he missed her? That he didn't want to be on his own? It was as if he understood less and less about himself. And all because of the accursed lump in his mouth.

He walked into the hotel with his bottles. The girl was in reception, watering the flowers.

"Have you got everything you need?" she said.

"Everything's fine," he said.

She fetched his key, still holding the watering can.

"I can't believe how grey everything looks," she said. "Early November. And the worst is yet to come. All that ghastly winter."

She went back to her plant pots. Lindman returned to his room. The suitcase was where he had left it. He put the carrier bag on the table. It was a few minutes past three. It's too early, he thought. I can't sit here drinking wine midway through the afternoon.

He stood motionless, gazing out of the window. Then he made up his mind. He would drive to the lake where he'd discovered the traces of a camp, but he'd go to the far side, to the forestry roads Larsson had talked about. He didn't expect to find anything, but it would help to pass the time.

It took him an hour to find one of the forestry roads. On the map the lake was called Stångvattnet. It was long and narrow, widest at the point where the forestry road ended with a space big enough for lorries to turn in. He got out of the car and walked the few metres to the water's edge. It was starting to grow dark already. He stood still and listened. The only sound was a faint rustling in the trees. He tried to remember if there had been any mention in the material he'd read in Östersund of the weather on the day of Molin's murder. He couldn't remember anything. It seemed to him that even if the wind were blowing towards the house it would have been possible to hear a shot fired from that direction. But what evidence was there to suggest that anybody had been here that day? None. None at all.

He remained by the water until darkness fell. A few ripples danced over the surface of the lake, then everything was still again. This was the first time in his life that he had been alone in a forest. Apart from that day when he and Molin had been chasing an escaped murderer outside Borås, and he'd witnessed his colleague's fear. So, why did Molin move here? Because he wanted a refuge, a nest he could crawl into and hide? Or was there some other reason?

He thought about what Wigren had said. That nobody ever visited Berggren. That didn't prevent Molin being visited by her, though. There were two questions he ought to have asked Wigren: Did Berggren go out at night? Did she still like dancing? Two questions that could have given him a lot of answers.

It struck him that it was Molin who had once taught him this simple truth. If you ask the right question at the right time, you can get a lot more answers than you were looking for.

There was a scraping noise in the darkness behind him. He gave a start. Then all was quiet again. A branch falling, he thought, or an animal.

He didn't have the energy to think about Molin or Berggren any more. There was no point. From tomorrow he would devote all his strength to understanding what was happening to himself. He would leave Härjedalen. He had no business to be here. It was Larsson's job to unravel the tangled web of information and find a motive and a murderer. He needed all his energy to prepare himself for radiotherapy. He stood there in the darkness a while longer. The trees about him were like soldiers standing guard. The black water was like a moat. For a moment he felt invulnerable.

When he got back to the hotel, he rested for an hour, drank a couple of glasses of wine, then went down to the dining room. The test drivers had gone. The girl from reception was in her waitress outfit again. She plays all the roles, he thought. Perhaps that's the only way the hotel can make itself pay?

He sat at his usual table. He read the menu and saw to his disappointment that it was the same as yesterday. He closed his eyes and jabbed his index finger onto the sparse column showing the main courses. It was elk steak again. He had just begun eating when he heard someone come into the dining room behind him. He turned and saw a woman walking towards his table. She stopped and eyed him up and down. Lindman couldn't help observing that she was strikingly attractive.

"I don't want to disturb you," she said, "but a policeman in Öster-sund told me that one of my father's old colleagues was here."

Lindman didn't understand at first. Then it dawned on him: the woman was Molin's daughter.

CHAPTER 9

Veronica Molin was one of the most beautiful women Lindman had ever met. Before she had sat down, before even she'd had time to say who she was, he'd imagined her naked. He thought back to the files he'd read in Larsson's office and remembered that in 1955 Molin had had a daughter, christened Veronica. The woman standing at his table now, wearing expensive scent, was therefore 44, seven years older than he was. If he hadn't known that, he would have guessed she was his age.

He stood up, introduced himself, shook hands, and expressed his condolences.

"Thank you." Her voice was strangely flat. It didn't belong with her beauty. She reminds me of somebody, he thought. One of those celebrities forever appearing in the papers or on television. But he couldn't remember who it was. He invited her to join him.

The girl from reception came over to their table. "Now you won't have to eat alone," she said to Lindman. He just managed to avoid telling her to go to hell.

"If you prefer to be on your own," Veronica Molin said, "then, of course, you must be."

He noticed that she was wearing a wedding ring. This depressed him, just for a moment. It was an absurd reaction, unreasonable, and soon passed. "Not at all," he said.

She raised an eyebrow. "Not at all, what?"

"I don't at all want to be on my own."

She sat down, consulted the menu, but put it down again immediately.

"Could I have a salad?" she said. "And an omelette? Nothing else."

"No problem," the girl said.

Lindman wondered if she also did the cooking.

Veronica Molin ordered a mineral water. Lindman was still trying to remember who she reminded him of.

"I misunderstood the situation," she said. "I thought it was here in Sveg that I was going to meet the police, but it is in Östersund. I'll be going there tomorrow."

"Where have you come from?"

"Cologne. That's where I was when the news of my father's death reached me."

"Do you live in Germany, then?"

She shook her head. "In Barcelona. Or Boston. It depends. But I was in Cologne. It was very strange and frightening. I'd just got back to my room. The Dom Hotel, it's called, next to the enormous cathedral. The church bells started ringing at the same time as the phone rang, and a man from somewhere a long way away told me that my father had been murdered. He asked if I'd like to talk to a clergyman. I flew to Stockholm this morning, the soonest I could organise my affairs, and then on here. But, apparently, I ought to have gone to Östersund."

Her mineral water arrived and she fell silent. Somebody in the bar burst out laughing, loud and shrill. Lindman thought it sounded like a man trying to imitate a dog. Then it came to him who she reminded him of. An actress in one of those soap operas that go on and on. He tried to remember her name, but he couldn't.

Veronica Molin was serious and tense. Lindman wondered how he would have reacted if he'd been in a hotel somewhere and been told over the telephone that his father had been murdered.

"I'm really very sorry about what happened," he said. "A completely pointless murder."

"Aren't all murders pointless?"

"Of course. But some have a motive that one can understand, despite everything."

"Nobody could have had any reason to kill my father," she said. "He had no enemies. He wasn't rich."

But he was scared, Lindman thought, and perhaps that fear was at the root of what happened. Her food arrived on the table. Lindman had a vague sense that the woman sitting opposite him had the upper hand. She had an assurance that he lacked.

"I gather you and he used to work together."

"Yes, in Borås. I started my police career there. Your father helped to put me on the right lines. He left a big gap when he retired."

That makes it sound as if we were close friends, he thought. It isn't true. We were never friends. We were colleagues.

"Needless to say, I wondered why he'd moved up here to Härjedalen," he said after a while.

She saw through him immediately. "I didn't think he had told anyone where he was going to move to."

"Perhaps I remember wrongly. But I'm curious, naturally. Why *did* he move here?"

"He wanted to be left in peace. My father was a recluse. So am I."

There's no answer to that, thought Lindman. She hadn't only given him a reply, she'd nipped the conversation in the bud. Why is she sitting at my table if she doesn't want to talk to me? He could feel himself getting irritated.

"I've nothing to do with the murder investigation," he said. "I came here because I was off work."

She put down her fork and looked at him. "To do what?"

"Maybe to attend the funeral. Assuming it will take place here. Once the medical people release the body."

She didn't believe him, he could see that, and that increased his irritation.

"Were you often in contact with him?"

"Very seldom. I'm a consultant for a computer firm that operates all over the world. I'm nearly always travelling. I used to send him a postcard once or twice every year, maybe phoned him at Christmas. But that was about it."

"It doesn't sound as if you had a very good relationship."

He looked hard at her. He still thought she was beautiful, but she radiated coldness and remoteness.

"What kind of relationship I had with my father is hardly anybody else's business. He wanted to be left in peace. I respected that. And he respected the fact that we were two of a kind."

"You have a brother as well, I believe?"

Her response was firm and outspoken.

"We avoid speaking to each other unless it's absolutely necessary. The best way of describing that relationship is that it is close to open enmity. Why that should be is no business of anybody else either. I've been in touch with a firm of funeral directors who will take care of everything. My father will be buried here in Sveg."

That was the end of the conversation.

Lindman ran his tongue over his teeth. The lump was there.

They ordered coffee. She asked if he'd mind if she smoked. He said that it was fine and she lit a cigarette and blew smoke rings towards the ceiling. Then she looked at him.

"Why did you come here, really?" she said.

Lindman gave her part of the truth. "I'm on sick leave. I had nothing else to do."

"The policeman I spoke to in Östersund said you were helping with the investigation."

"One gets upset when a colleague is murdered, naturally. But my visit here is of no significance. I've just spoken to a few people, that's all."

"Who?"

"Mainly the police officer you'll be meeting in Östersund tomorrow. Giuseppe Larsson. And Abraham Andersson."

"Who's he?"

"Your father's nearest neighbour, even if he does live quite a long way away."

"Had he anything interesting to say?"

"No. But if anybody was going to notice something, it would have been him. You can talk to him, if you like."

She stubbed out her cigarette, crushing the butt as if it were an insect.

"Your father changed his name," Lindman said. "From Mattson-Herzén to Molin. That was a few years before you were born. At about the same time he asked to be discharged from the army and moved to Stockholm. When you were two, there was another move, to Alingsås. You can hardly be expected to remember anything about the time in Stockholm. A two-year-old doesn't have a conscious memory. But there's one thing I wonder about. What did he do in Stockholm?"

"He had a music shop." She could see that he was surprised. "As you say, I don't recall anything about it. But I heard later. He tried running a shop and opened one in Solna. It went well in the early years. He opened a second one in Sollentuna. But things went rapidly downhill from there. My first memories are from Alingsås. We lived outside the town in an old house that never got sufficiently warm in the winter." She paused and lit another cigarette. "I wonder why you want to know all this."

"Your father is dead. That means that all questions are important."

"Are you suggesting that somebody killed him because he once owned a music shop?"

Lindman didn't answer and moved instead to the next question.

"Why did he change his name?"

"I don't know."

"Why would anybody want to change their name from Herzén to Molin?"

"I simply don't know."

Lindman suddenly had the feeling that he ought to be careful. He wasn't sure where the feeling came from, but it was certainly there. He was asking questions and she was answering, but at the same time something quite different was going on. Veronica Molin was finding out how much he knew about her father.

He picked up the coffee pot and asked if she would like a refill. She said no.

"When we worked together I had the impression that your father was worried. In fact, that he was scared. What of, I've no idea, but I can remember his fear still, though it's more than ten years since he retired."

She frowned. "What should he have been scared of?"

"I don't know. I suppose I'm asking you."

She shook her head. "My father wasn't the frightened type. On the contrary, he was brave."

"In what way?"

"He was never afraid of doing things. Never afraid of refusing to do things."

Her mobile phone rang. She apologised, and answered. The conversation took place in a foreign language. Lindman wasn't sure if it was Spanish or French. When it was over she beckoned the girl from reception and asked for her bill.

"Did you go out to see the house?" Lindman said.

She looked at him for a while before answering. "I have a good memory of my father. We were never close, but I've lived long enough to know what sort of a relationship some children can have with their parents. I don't want to spoil the image of my father by seeing the place where he was killed."

Lindman understood. Or at least, he thought he did.

"Your father must have been very fond of dancing," he said.

"Why on earth should he have been?"

Her surprise seemed genuine.

"Somebody said so," Lindman said.

The girl from reception came with two bills. Lindman tried to take them both, but she insisted on taking hers.

"I prefer to pay my own way."

The girl went to get some change.

"What exactly does a computer consultant do?" Lindman said.

She smiled but didn't reply.

They went their separate ways in reception. Her room was on the ground floor.

"How are you going to get to Östersund?" he said.

"Sveg is only a little place," she said, "but I managed to hire a car even so. Thanks for your company."

He watched her walk away. Her clothes, her shoes, everything about her, looked expensive. Their conversation had restored some of his lost energy. The question was: what should he do with it? He didn't suppose there was much in the way of night life in Sveg.

He decided to go for a walk. What Björn Wigren had told him made him think. There was a connection between Berggren and Molin that he wanted to know more about. The curtain had been moved. He was certain of it.

He fetched his jacket and left the hotel. It was chillier than the previous night.

He took the same road as he'd taken earlier in the day. Stopped on the bridge. Listened to the water flowing beneath him. He met a man walking his dog. It was like meeting a ship with no lights far out on a black sea. When he reached the house, he stood in the shadows, away from the glow of the street lights. There was a car on the drive now, but it was too dark to see what make it was. There was a light on upstairs, behind drawn curtains. He stood motionless.

He didn't know what he was waiting for. But he stood there never-theless.

The man approaching moved very quietly. He'd been watching Lindman for some time before deciding that he'd seen enough. He came diagonally from behind, keeping all the time in the shadows. Johansson had no idea who the man was. He looked in good condi-tion. He eyed him warily.

"Hello," he said. "I was wondering what you're doing here."

Lindman was startled. The man had moved so quietly, he'd had no idea there was anybody there.

"Who are you, asking me these questions?"

"Erik Johansson. I'm a police officer. I am asking myself just what you are doing here."

"I'm looking at a house," said Lindman. "I'm in a public place, I'm sober, I'm not creating a disturbance, I'm not even having a pee. Is it forbidden to stand looking at a pretty house?"

"Not at all. But the lady who lives there was made nervous and tele-phoned. When people get nervous, I'm the one they contact. I thought I'd find out who you were. People are not used to strangers standing in the street staring at them. Not at night, in any case."

Lindman took out his wallet and produced his police ID. He'd moved a couple of metres so that he was in the glow from the street light. Johansson grinned.

"So it's you," he said, as if he'd known Lindman of old but only just remembered.

"Stefan Lindman."

Johansson scratched his forehead. Lindman noticed that he was only wearing a thin vest under his jacket.

"Both of us being police officers doesn't improve matters. Larsson told me you were here. But I couldn't know it was you outside Elsa's house."

"It was Elsa who bought Molin's house for him," Lindman said. "No doubt you knew that?"

"I didn't know that at all."

"I found that out from an estate agent in Krokom. I thought Larsson might have mentioned that."

"All he said was that you were here on a visit and that you used to work with Molin. He certainly didn't say anything about you spying on Elsa."

"I'm not spying," Lindman said. "I went out for a walk. I don't know why I stopped."

He realised that it was an idiotic answer. He'd been standing there for ages.

"We'd better move on," Johansson said. "Otherwise Elsa will start wondering."

Johansson's car was parked in a nearby side street. It wasn't a blue and white police car, but a Toyota with a dog grille in front of the luggage space.

"So you went out for a walk," Johansson said, again. "And just happened to land up outside Elsa's house?"

"Yes."

Johansson looked worried.

"It's probably best if we don't say anything about this to Larsson," he said. "He'd no doubt be a bit worried if we did. I don't think they're all that thrilled in Östersund to have you spying on people."

"I'm not spying."

"No, you said that. But it's a bit odd that you should be standing here at Elsa's house. Even if she was the one who bought Molin's cottage for him."

"Do you know her?"

"She's always lived here. Nice and friendly. Takes an interest in children."

"Meaning?"

"She runs dancing classes in the Community Centre. Or used to. The children learned how to dance. I don't know if she still does it."

Lindman nodded, but didn't ask any questions.

"Are you staying at the hotel? I can give you a lift."

"I'd rather walk," Lindman said. "But thanks for the offer. I haven't noticed a police station in Sveg."

"We're in the Community Centre."

"Can I call in tomorrow morning? Just to see how things are here. And to have a chat."

"Of course."

Johansson opened his car door.

"I'd better give Elsa a ring and tell her everything's OK."

He got into the car, said goodbye and closed the door. Lindman waited until the car was out of sight before walking away.

He stopped on the bridge for the fourth time. The link, he thought. It's not just that Berggren and Molin knew each other. There's more to it than that. But what? He started walking slowly, waiting for his thoughts to fall into a pattern. Molin had used Berggren to find a house for him. They already knew each other. Maybe Molin had moved to Härjedalen to be close to her?

At the end of the bridge he paused again. Another thought had struck him. He ought to have considered it earlier. Berggren had noticed him in the street, despite the fact that he'd avoided the light of the street lamps. That could only mean that she was keeping watch over the street. That she either expected or feared that somebody would come. He was certain of it. She couldn't possibly have seen him by chance.

He set off again, more quickly now. It seemed to him that the interest Berggren and Molin shared in dance could not have been a coincidence.

The reception was closed by the time he got back to the hotel. As he walked up the stairs, he wondered if Veronica Molin was asleep. Assuming she was still called Molin.

He unlocked his door and switched on the light. On the floor, pushed under the door, was a message. He picked it up and read it. "Phone Giuseppe Larsson in Östersund. Urgent."

CHAPTER 10

It was Larsson himself who answered.

"I couldn't find your mobile number," he said. "I must have left it at the office. I phoned the hotel, but they said you were out."

Lindman wondered if Johansson had phoned Larsson after all, to tell him about their meeting outside Berggren's house.

"I went for a walk. There's not much else to do here."

Larsson chuckled. "I think they show films sometimes at the Community Centre."

"I need to keep moving."

Lindman could hear that Larsson was talking to somebody. The volume of the television set behind him was turned down.

"I thought I'd entertain you with something we heard from Umeå today. A paper signed by Dr Hollander. You might well ask why he didn't mention it in the first preliminary report he sent us, but these pathologists have their own way of doing things. Have you got a moment?"

"I have all the time in the world."

"He says he's found three old entry wounds."

"What does he mean by that?"

"That Molin had been shot at some time. Did you know that?"

"No."

"Not just one bullet. Three. And Dr Hollander takes the liberty of deviating from strict protocol. He considers that Molin was fantastically lucky to have survived. He actually used that word, 'fantastic good fortune'. Two of the bullets hit him in the chest just beneath his heart, and the third in his left arm. On the basis of the scars and other things I don't understand, Hollander concludes that Molin received these wounds when he was a young man. He can't tell whether all three bullets came at the same time, but it seems likely."

Larsson started sneezing. Lindman waited.

"Red wine always does that to me," he said. "I'm sorry, but I couldn't resist the temptation tonight. I'm being punished for it."

"There was nothing about bullet wounds in the files, was there?"

"No. But I phoned Borås and spoke to a friendly man who laughed nearly all the time."

"Inspector Olausson."

"That's the one. I didn't mention that you were here, I simply asked if he knew that Molin had been shot. He didn't. Which enables us to draw a simple conclusion."

"That it happened before he joined the police?"

"Even earlier than that. When the old regional council offices were reformed, the police took over their archives and personnel details. It would have been documented when the police force was nationalised and Molin became an employee of His Majesty the King."

"So it must have happened while he was in the army."

"That's more or less the conclusion I'd come to. But it takes time to get at military archives. What we should be asking ourselves even now is what might have happened if it turns out that he *wasn't* wounded while he was a soldier."

Larsson paused.

"Does this change the picture?"

"It changes everything *in* the picture. Or rather, we don't have a picture any more. I don't think we're going to find out who did this for quite a long time. My experience tells me that it's going to take a long time, because we're going to have to dig deep. What does your experience tell you?"

"That you might be right."

Larsson started sneezing again.

"I thought you'd want to know this," Larsson said when he came back on the phone. "Incidentally, I shall be meeting Molin's daughter tomorrow."

"She's staying here in the hotel."

"I thought you might meet her. What's she like?"

"Reserved. But she's a very good-looking woman."

"I have something to look forward to, then. Have you spoken to her?"

"We had dinner together. She told me something I didn't know, about those missing years in the mid-'50s. She says Molin owned a couple of music shops in the Stockholm area, but he went bankrupt."

"I suppose there's no reason why she should lie about that?"

"Hardly. But you'll meet her tomorrow anyway."

"I'll certainly ask her about the bullet wounds. Have you decided how long you're going to stay?"

"Perhaps tomorrow as well. Then I'm off. But I'll stay in touch."

"Make sure you do."

Lindman put the phone down and slumped onto the bed. He felt tired. Without even taking off his shoes, he stretched out and fell asleep.

He woke up with a start and checked his watch. 4.45. He'd been dreaming. Somebody was chasing him. Then he was surrounded by a pack of dogs that were tearing at his clothes and biting him all over his body. His father was there somewhere, and Elena. He went to the bathroom and rinsed his face in cold water. It wasn't difficult to interpret the dream. The illness I have, the cells multiplying out of control, they are like a pack of wild dogs careering around inside me. He undressed and burrowed into the bedclothes, but didn't manage to get back to sleep.

It was always in the early morning, before dawn, that he felt most defenceless. He was 37, a police officer trying to lead a decent life. Nothing remarkable, a life that was never more than ordinary. There again, what was ordinary? He was rapidly approaching middle age and didn't have any children. Now he was having to fight an illness that might overcome him. In which case the end of his life wouldn't even be ordinary. It would mean that he would never be able to demonstrate his true worth.

He got up at 6 a.m. They wouldn't start serving breakfast for another half-hour. He took some clean clothes from his suitcase. Thought that he ought to shave, but didn't bother. By 6.30 he was in reception. The dining room door was ajar. When he peeped in he was surprised to see that the girl from reception was sitting on a chair, drying her eyes with a napkin. Hastily, he withdrew. She'd obviously been crying. He went back up the stairs and waited. The doors were opened. The girl was smiling.

"You're early," she said.

As he ate his breakfast, he wondered why she'd been crying, but it was none of his business. We all have our private miseries, he thought. Our packs of dogs to do battle with.

By the time he'd finished, he'd made up his mind. He would go back to Molin's house. Not because he thought he might find anything new, but to go again in his mind through what he now knew. Or didn't know. Then he'd leave everything to sort itself out. He wouldn't stay in Sveg waiting for a funeral that he didn't want to go to anyway. Just now, this was the last thing he wanted to submit himself to. He'd go back to Borås, repack his bag and hope to find a cheap package holiday to Mallorca. I need a plan, he thought. If I don't have a plan, I won't be able to cope with what's in store for me.

He left the hotel at 7.15. There'd been no sign of Molin's daughter. The girl in reception smiled as she always did when he handed in his room key. Something must have happened, but it wasn't likely that she'd been told she had cancer.

He drove west through the autumn and the silence. Occasionally a few drops of rain spattered against the windscreen. He switched on the radio and half-listened to the news. The New York stock exchange had gone up, or was it down? He couldn't hear. As he passed Linsell he saw some children with satchels waiting for the school bus. Most house roofs there had satellite dishes. He thought back to his own childhood in Kinna. The past became almost tangible. He looked at the road and thought about all the boring journeys he'd made through central Sweden while he was assistant to the motocross rider who'd hardly ever won a race. He was so lost in thought that he missed the turning to Rätmyren. He went back, and parked in the same place as last time.

There were fresh tyre marks in the gravel. Perhaps Veronica Molin had changed her mind? He got out of the car and filled his lungs with crisp, chilly air. A wind was gusting through the treetops. This is what Sweden's all about, he thought. Trees, wind, cold. Grass and moss. A lonely person in the middle of a forest. Only that person doesn't usually have cancer of the tongue.

He walked slowly round the house and made a list of all he now knew

102

about the death of Herbert Molin. There was the campsite, the place to which somebody had rowed across the lake, pitched a tent, and then abandoned it. Larsson's news about the bullet wounds. Lindman stopped in his tracks. What had Larsson said? Two wounds in the chest and one in the left arm. So Molin had been hit from in front. Three shots. He tried to imagine what could have happened, but failed.

Then there was Berggren, an invisible shadow behind a curtain. If his suspicions were correct, she was on guard. Against what? Johansson had described her as a friendly person who gave dancing lessons for children. That was another link: dancing. But what did it mean? Did it mean anything at all? He continued his circuit round the smashed-up house. Wondered why the police hadn't made a better job of boarding up the broken windows. Bits of torn plastic flapped in front of the gaping holes. Veronica Molin had turned up unexpectedly. A beautiful woman who'd heard the news of her father's death, in a hotel room in Cologne, while on her travels around the world. Lindman, who had been all round the house by now, thought back to the time he'd been chasing, with Molin, the escaped murderer from Tidaholm. His fear. "I thought it was somebody else." Lindman paused again. Unless Molin had been the victim of a madman, there must have been a crucial starting point. Fear. The flight to the forests of Härjedalen. A hiding place at the end of a side road that Lindman had great difficulty in finding.

That was as far as he got. Molin's death was a riddle: he'd managed to find a few loose threads that led to a centre that was still a vacuum. He went back to his car. The wind was getting stronger. He was about to open his car door when he had the feeling he was being watched. He spun round. The forest was empty. The dog pen was abandoned. The torn plastic was flapping against the window frames. He got into his car and drove away, certain that he would never return.

He parked outside the Community Centre and went in. The bear was still glaring at him. He found his way to the police offices and bumped into Johansson, who was on his way out.

"I was going to have a coffee with the library staff," he said. "But that can wait. I have news for you."

They went to his office. Lindman sat in the visitor's chair. Johansson had cheered up the décor with a devil-mask hanging on the wall.

"I bought it in New Orleans ages ago. I was drunk at the time and no doubt paid far too much for it. I thought it would look good hanging here. A reminder of the forces of evil that conspire to make things difficult for the police."

"Are you the only one on duty today?"

"Yes," said Johansson cheerfully. "There should really be four or five of us, but people are off sick or on study leave or maternity leave. I'm the only one left. It's impossible to get stand-by staff."

"How do you manage?"

"I don't. But at least people who phone here during working hours don't get fobbed off with an answering machine."

"But Berggren phoned you in the evening, didn't she?"

"There's a special emergency number. Lots of people in town know it."

"Town?"

"I call Sveg a town. It makes it a bit bigger that way."

The telephone rang. Lindman looked at the mask and wondered what the news was that Johansson had promised him. The call was from someone who had found a tractor tyre on a road. Johansson seemed to be a man blessed with a fund of patience. He eventually replaced the receiver.

"Elsa Berggren rang this morning. I tried to get hold of you at the hotel."

"What did she want?"

"She wanted to invite you round for coffee."

"That sounds odd."

"No more odd than you staking out her house."

Johansson stood up. "She'll be at home now," he said. "Go round straightaway. She's going shopping later on. By all means come back here and tell me what she said, if it's of any interest. But not this afternoon or this evening. I'm off to Funäsdalen. I have a spot of police business to see to, and then I'm going to play poker with some mates. We may be in the middle of a murder investigation, but that doesn't prevent us from leading as normal a life as possible."

Johansson went off for his coffee. Lindman paused to have another look at the bear.

Then he drove to Ulvkälla and parked outside the white house. He saw Wigren in the street, no doubt looking for somebody he could invite for a cup of coffee in his kitchen.

She opened the door before he could ring the bell. Lindman didn't know what to expect, but certainly not the elegantly dressed lady in the doorway. She had long, black hair, obviously dyed, and she was heavily made up around her eyes.

"I thought you might as well come in," she said. "Instead of standing out there in the street."

Lindman stepped into the hall. He'd got further than Wigren had managed in 40 years. She led him into the living room that was at the back of the house, facing the garden. In the background Lindman could see the wooded hills rising towards Orsa Finnmark.

The room was expensively furnished. There were no prints of bare-breasted gypsy girls on Berggren's walls. She had original oil paintings instead, and it seemed to Lindman that she had good taste. She excused herself and disappeared into the kitchen. He sat on the sofa to wait.

He stood up again immediately. There were several photographs in frames in a bookcase. One of the pictures was of two girls sitting on a park bench. It had been taken several decades ago. In the background was a house with a sign outside. Lindman peered to see if he could make out what was on it. It didn't look like Swedish, but it wasn't clear enough to be sure. He sat down again. Berggren came in with coffee and biscuits.

"A man appears and stands staring at my house," she said. "Naturally, I'm surprised. And worried as well. After what happened to Herbert things will never be the same again in Sveg."

"I'll tell you why I was there," Lindman said. "I used to work with Herbert Molin. I'm also a police officer."

"Erik told me that."

"I'm on sick leave and was kicking my heels. So I came here. I happened to speak to an estate agent in Krokom who told me you had bought Herbert's house on his behalf."

"He asked me to. He phoned before he retired. He wanted me to help him."

"So you knew each other?"

She looked dismissively at him. "Why else would he ask me to help him?"

"I'm trying to understand who he was. I've realised that the man I used to work with was not who I thought he was."

"In what way?"

"In many ways."

She stood up and adjusted a curtain in one of the windows.

"I knew Herbert's first wife," she said. "We were at school together. So I also got to know Herbert, to some extent. That was when he lived in Stockholm. Then I lost contact with her after they divorced. But not with Herbert." She returned to her chair. "That's all there is to it. And now he's dead. And I'm sad about that."

"Did you know that his daughter Veronica's here?"

She shook her head.

"No, I didn't know that. But I don't expect her to pay me a visit. It was Herbert I knew, not his children."

"Did he move here because you were here?"

She looked him straight in the eye. "That is something that concerned only him and me. And now it concerns only me."

"Of course."

Lindman took a sip of coffee. Berggren was not telling him the truth. The disappearing wife was plausible, but there was something about what she said that didn't add up. Something he ought to be able to work out. He put down his cup, which was blue with a gold edge.

"Have you any idea who could have killed him?"

"No. Have you?"

Lindman shook his head.

"An old man who wanted to live in peace," she said. "Who on earth would want to kill him?"

Lindman looked at his hands. "There must have been somebody who did," he said.

There was only one other question he wanted to ask.

"I find it strange that you haven't spoken to the police in Östersund. The ones who are in charge of the investigation."

"I've been waiting for them to contact me."

Lindman was now certain. The woman was not telling him the whole truth.

"I've been thinking a lot about why Herbert came here," he said. "Why would anybody want to live such a lonely life?"

"It's not lonely up here," Berggren said. "There's lots you can do if you want to. For instance, I'm going to a concert in the church tonight. There's an organist coming here from Sundsvall."

"I heard from Erik Johansson that you give dancing lessons."

"Children should learn how to dance. If nobody else teaches them, I can. But I don't know if I've got the strength to go on for much longer."

Lindman decided not to ask any questions about Molin's interest in dancing. Larsson was the man to ask those questions, nobody else.

A telephone rang somewhere in the house. She excused herself and left the room. Lindman stood up and made a rapid choice between the balcony door and a window, then unfastened the catch on a window, making sure it held tight and didn't open. Then he sat down again. She returned a minute later.

"I won't impose on you any longer," Lindman said, getting to his feet. "Thank you for the coffee. It's not often you get coffee as strong as that."

"Why should everything have to be weak?" she said. "Everything is weak nowadays. Coffee, and people as well."

Lindman had left his jacket in the hall. As he put it on, he looked round to see if the house had a burglar alarm. He could see no sign of one.

He drove back to the hotel, thinking over what Berggren had said about weak coffee and weak people. The girl in reception seemed to be her cheerful self again. There was a notice board next to the desk. On it was a yellow poster advertising an organ concert in the church that evening, starting at 7.30. The programme consisted exclusively of music by Johann Sebastian Bach.

Shortly after 7.00 that evening Lindman went to the church. He took up a position beyond the church wall. He could hear the organist rehearsing. At 7.25, Berggren arrived and walked into the church.

Lindman hurried back to the hotel and got into his car. He drove to the river and parked on the other side of the bridge. Then he approached Berggren's house from the back. He was counting on the

107

concert lasting for at least an hour. He checked his watch: 7.41. There was a narrow path around the back of the white house. He had no torch with him, but he felt his way cautiously forward in the dark. There was a light on in the room where he had had his coffee. He paused when he came to the garden fence and listened. Then he jumped over and ran to the house wall, crouching low. He stood up and felt the underside of the window. Berggren had failed to notice that he had unhooked the catch. He opened it carefully, hoisted himself up and, taking careful stock of its position, lifted down the vase of flowers on the windowledge.

Here he was, breaking into Berggren's house just as he had into Molin's house a few days earlier.

He wiped the soles of his shoes with a handkerchief. It was 7.45. He looked round the room. He had no idea what he was looking for. Perhaps some indication that he had been right, that Berggren hadn't been telling the truth. He knew that a lie could be exposed by an object. He left the living room, glanced into the kitchen and then continued into what appeared to be a study. This is the last place I'll search, he decided. First he wanted to look in the upper floor. He ran up the stairs. The first room seemed to be a guest room. He walked into Berggren's bedroom. She slept in a large double bed. There was a pale blue, fitted carpet. He looked into the bathroom. Bottles were lined up in neat rows in front of the mirror.

He was about to go downstairs to the study when he had the idea of opening the double doors of the wardrobe. The hangers were tightly packed. He ran his hand over the clothes. They all seemed to be of high quality. At the furthest left of the hangers, something caught his eye. He pulled some dresses to one side to get a closer look.

A uniform. It was several seconds before he realised what it was – a German army uniform. On the shelf above was an army hat. He took it down and saw the skull. Hanging in Berggren's wardrobe was an SS officer's uniform.

CHAPTER 11

Lindman didn't bother to search Berggren's study. He left the house in Ulvkälla as he'd entered it, replacing the vase exactly as it had been, closing the window carefully behind him. It had started snowing – heavy, wet flakes. He drove back to the hotel, poured himself a glass of wine and tried to make up his mind whether or not to phone Larsson right away. He hesitated to do so. He'd promised not to contact Berggren. Now he'd not only spoken to her, he'd broken into her house. This was not the kind of thing to discuss on the telephone, he thought. Larsson will understand that. We need to be sitting face to face, with plenty of time.

He switched on the television and zapped his way through the channels. Eventually opted for an old Western with faded colours. A man with a rifle was crawling around among some rocks in a studio landscape, trying to avoid some other men coming towards him on horseback. Lindman turned the sound down and took out his notepad. He tried to make a summary of what had happened since he came to Sveg. What did he know now that he hadn't known before? He tried to construct a plausible hypothesis of the reason for Molin's death. He made it simple, as if he were reading a story to himself.

At some point a man called Herbert Molin – probably at that point called Mattson-Herzén – is shot three times. He survives. At some point this man also runs a music shop. He also has a particular association with dancing. Perhaps it's just that dancing has been a passion for him all his life? The way that other people are mad about picking mushrooms or fishing for salmon in Norwegian rivers?

There's a woman called Elsa Berggren in his life. When Molin retires he asks her to find him a house deep in the forests of Härjedalen, not far from where she lives herself. He never goes

109

to visit her, however. That is confirmed by the best possible witness – an inquisitive neighbour. In Elsa Berggren's wardrobe, deep in a corner, is an SS uniform.

And somebody may have come paddling over a lake of water and set up camp not far from Molin's house, perhaps with the intention of taking his life.

In Lindman's head that's where the story ended. With a man paddling over a lake who then disappears without trace.

But there were other bricks to build into the story. The bloodstained footprints that formed the basic steps of the tango. Molin's fear. The fact that he'd changed his name. A downmarket move, it seemed to Lindman. In all probability there were very few people in Sweden called Mattson-Herzén. But plenty called Molin. He thought that there could only be one explanation. The change of name was a hiding place. The man was covering his tracks. But what tracks? And why? If he'd thought that Mattson-Herzén was too long and awkward, he could simply have called himself Mattson.

He read through what he'd written, then turned over the page and wrote down two dates. Born 1923, died 1999. Then he returned to the notes he'd made when he'd been shut away in Larsson's office. In 1941, when Molin is 18, he does his military service. War is raging all around neutral Sweden. He's posted to the coastal defence forces. Lindman's notes were not complete, but he remembers that Molin had been stationed on a small island in the Östergötland archipelago, guarding one of the main sea channels to Sweden. Lindman assumed he'd remained with the coastal defences until the end of the war, by which time he'd been commissioned. Seven years later he applies for a discharge, tries his hand at being a shop owner, and is then employed first in some council offices and subsequently in the police force.

From a military family, Lindman had noted. His father was a cavalry officer based in Kalmar, his mother a housewife. So to start with, Molin does not stray far from the family tradition. He tries a career as an army officer, but then changes course.

Lindman put down his pad and filled his wine glass. The man crawling around in the rocks not far from Hollywood had now been captured by the men on horseback. They were about to hang him. The man with the rope round his neck seemed strangely unconcerned about his fate. The colours were still very pale.

If the circumstances surrounding Molin's death had been a film, Lindman thought, it would now be necessary for something to happen. Otherwise the audience would become bored. Even police officers can become bored. But that doesn't mean they give up the search for an explanation and a murderer.

He reached for his pad again. As he did so the man in the film was getting away in highly improbable circumstances. Lindman tried to develop a few plausible theories. The first, the most obvious one, was that Molin had been the victim of a madman. Where he'd come from and why he'd been equipped with a tent and some tear gas was impossible to explain, of course. The madman scenario was bad, but it had to be formulated even so.

The second theory had to do with an unknown connection between the murder and something that lay concealed in Molin's past. As Veronica Molin had pointed out, her father didn't possess a fortune. Money could hardly be the reason for his death, even if his daughter had made it sound as if it were the only conceivable motive for murdering anybody. But police officers acquire enemies, Lindman thought. Nowadays it was not uncommon for police officers to receive death threats, for bombs to be placed under prosecutors' cars. Somebody bent on revenge could wait for as long as it took to get their own back. This meant that patient searches through the archives would be essential.

There was a third possibility. Something connected with Berggren. Had the uniform in her wardrobe anything to do with Molin? Or had Berggren something in her past linked with Hitler's Germany?

According to Björn Wigren, Berggren and Molin were about the same age. Berggren could have been born a year or so later, around 1924 or 1925. So she would have been 15 when war broke out, and 21 when it ended. Lindman shook his head. That didn't fit. But Berggren has a father, and perhaps also an elder brother. He made more notes. Berggren lives alone, has an income from an unknown source, is on her guard. He made another note: Molin and Berggren. According to her own account she had known Molin since his first marriage. When she said that, he'd had a strong feeling that she wasn't telling the truth.

That was as far as he could get. He put down the pad. He'd talk to Larsson the following day. That would mean he'd have to drive back to Östersund. Once he'd done that, he could return to Borås. As he was getting ready for bed he wondered if he should ask Elena whether there was any chance of her being able to take a week off work and fly south with him. But he wasn't sure if he'd be able to cope with that. The choice between having her company and being alone would be a hard one to make.

He went to the bathroom, opened his mouth and stuck out his tongue. The lump was not visible, but it was there. He studied his face and thought that he looked pale. Then in his mind's eye he put on the uniform he'd seen in Berggren's wardrobe. Tried to remember the ranks they'd had in the SS – Rottenführer Lindman, Unterscharführer Lindman.

He took off the invisible peaked cap and washed his face. By the time he left the bathroom the Western had almost finished. The man who had escaped the lynching party was sitting with a big-breasted woman in a log cabin. Lindman reached for the remote control and switched off.

He dialled Elena's number. She answered almost immediately.

"I'm leaving here tomorrow. I might even be back home by tomorrow evening."

"Don't drive too fast, will you?"

"That's all, really. I'm tired out. We can talk when I get home."

"How's it going?"

"How's what going?"

"You, your health."

He said he didn't have the strength to discuss how he was feeling, and Elena understood.

He drank another glass of wine before settling down in bed. I've one more visit to make, he thought as he was falling asleep. I have one more person to see before I talk to Larsson, and then I can put all of this behind me.

He woke up before dawn with excruciating pains in one of his cheeks. He was also running a temperature. He lay still in the darkness and tried to wish away the pain by sheer will power. But it didn't work. When he got out of bed, he felt another stab in his cheek. He found a tube of headache tablets and dissolved two in a glass of water. He wondered if he'd been lying awkwardly during the night. But he knew that the pain was coming from the inside. The doctor had warned him. He might suddenly find himself in pain. He emptied the glass and lay down again, hoping the pain would go away. But things got no better. Seven a.m. passed but he was in too much pain to go down for breakfast.

After another hour, he couldn't stand it any longer. He looked up the telephone number for the hospital in Borås, and had a stroke of luck. His doctor answered as soon as he was put through. He described the pain he was in. She said she would write him out a prescription and phone it to the chemist in Sveg. If that didn't ease the pain, he was to phone her again. Lindman went back to bed. The doctor had said she would ring Sveg straightaway. He decided to try to put up with the pain for another hour. Then he would drive to the chemist's. He lay still in bed. All he could think about was the pain. At 9 a.m. he got up, dressed and went downstairs. The girl in reception wished him a good morning. He smiled and left his key on the desk.

He collected his tablets and took the first dose immediately. Then he went back to the hotel. The girl handed him his key.

"Are you unwell?" she said.

"Yes, I'm in a bit of pain," he said. "But it'll pass."

"You haven't had any breakfast. Would you like something in your room?"

"Just coffee, please. And some extra pillows."

He waited until she arrived with a tray and two more pillows.

"Give me a call if there's anything you need."

"You were upset last night," he said. "I hope you feel better now."

She didn't seem surprised. "I noticed you in the doorway," she said. "It was just a momentary weakness. Nothing more."

When she was gone, Lindman lay down on the bed and wondered what a "momentary weakness" entailed. It occurred to him that he didn't know her name. He took another tablet.

After a while the pain began to ease. He looked to see what it said on the box. "Doleron". There was a red warning triangle on the packet. He noticed he was feeling drowsy, but he also thought that there is no greater happiness in life than the ebbing away of acute pain.

He stayed in bed for the rest of the day. The pains came and went. He dozed off and again dreamed of the pack of wild dogs. It was late afternoon before it became clear that the pain was going away rather than just becoming more bearable. Although he hadn't eaten anything all day, he wasn't hungry. Shortly after 4 p.m. his mobile rang. It was Johansson.

"How did it go?" Lindman said.

"How did what go?"

"The poker game in Funäsdalen."

Johansson laughed. "I won 19 kronor. After four hours. I thought you were going to get in touch with me?"

"I'm not so well today."

"Nothing serious, I hope?"

"Just a bit of pain. But I talked to Elsa Berggren."

"Did she have anything interesting to say?"

"Not really. She claimed she'd known Molin for a long time."

"Had she any idea about why he was murdered?"

"She found it incomprehensible."

"I thought as much. Will you be calling in tomorrow? I forgot to ask how long you were staying."

"I'm leaving tomorrow. But I can call in even so."

"About 9 a.m. would be convenient."

He switched off his phone. The pain had more or less gone now.

He dressed and went down to reception. He left his key on the desk and opened the hotel door. The snow had melted. He went for a walk through the little town. Went into Agardh's Hardware and bought some disposable razors.

Last night he'd made up his mind to visit Abraham Andersson. He wasn't sure he felt up to it. It was dark. He wondered if he'd be able to find the house. But Andersson had said there was a sign to Dunkärret. He went back to the hotel and got into his car. I'll go for it, he thought. Tomorrow morning I'll call on Johansson. Then I'll drive to Östersund and talk to Larsson. I can be back in Borås by nightfall.

Before leaving Sveg he stopped at a petrol station and filled his tank. When he went to pay he noticed a stand with pocket torches next to the counter. He bought one and put it in the glove compartment.

He set off in the direction of Linsell, waiting all the time to see if

114

the pains were coming back. For now at least they were leaving him in peace. As he drove, he kept a look out for signs of animals by the side of the road. He slowed down as he passed the turn-off to Molin's house. For a moment he wondered if he ought to go there, but decided it would be inappropriate. He pressed ahead, wondering what Molin's daughter and her brother planned to do with the property. Who would buy a house in which someone had been so savagely murdered? The repercussions of that killing would haunt the region for a long time to come.

He passed Dravagen, kept going towards Glöte until he saw the sign, "Dunkärret 2". The road was bumpy and narrow. After about a kilo-metre it divided into two. Lindman kept to the left as the other road appeared to be more or less unused. About another kilometre and he was there. Andersson had put up a sign of his own with the name "Dunkärr". The house lights were on. Lindman switched off the engine and got out of the car. A dog started barking. Lindman walked up a slope. The house was quite high up, surrounded by darkness. He wondered what drove people to live in such isolated places. What could a person find in all this darkness, apart from a hiding place? He could see the dog now. It was running back and forth along a line stretched between a tree and the house wall. There was a kennel by the tree. It was a Norwegian elkhound, the same breed as Molin's. Lindman wondered who had buried the dead dog. The police? He walked up the steps to the front door and knocked hard. The dog started barking again. After a while he knocked again harder. He tried the door. It was unlocked. He opened it and shouted into the house. Perhaps Andersson was one of those people who go to bed early? He looked at his watch. 8.15. Too early. He stepped into the hall and shouted again.

Suddenly he was on his guard. He didn't know why. He had the feeling that all was not as it should be. He went into the kitchen. There was an empty coffee cup on the table, and next to it a programme for the Helsingborg Symphony Orchestra. He shouted again, but there was no answer. He went from the kitchen into the living room. There was a music stand next to the television, and a violin on a sofa. He frowned. Then he went upstairs and looked everywhere, but found no-one. Something was definitely wrong.

Lindman went back outside and shouted yet again. The dog

continued barking, running back and forth on its line. He walked towards it. The dog stopped barking and started wagging its tail. He stroked it cautiously. Not much of a guard dog, he thought. Then he went back to the car and collected the torch. He shone it around, feeling all the time that something was very much amiss. Andersson's car was parked beside an outhouse. Lindman checked and found it was unlocked. He looked inside and saw the keys in the ignition. The dog barked again, then all was silent. There was a rustling of wind through the trees in the darkness. He pricked up his ears, then shouted again. The dog answered him with a bark. Lindman went back to the house. He felt the rings on the cooker. They were cold. A telephone rang. Lindman gave a start. The telephone was on a table in the living room. He picked up the receiver. Somebody was trying to send a fax. He pressed the start button and put down the receiver. It was a hand-written note from somebody called Katarina saying, "The Monteverdi sheet music has come."

Lindman went back outside. Now he was certain that something was wrong.

The dog, he thought. It knows. He went back to the house and took a lead hanging from the wall.

The dog jerked at the line when he approached, then stood quite still while he attached the lead to its collar and released it from the line. Immediately it began dragging him towards the forest behind the house. Lindman switched on his torch. The dog was heading for a path into the pine trees. Lindman tried to hold it back. I shouldn't be doing this, he thought, not if there's a madman loose in the forest.

The dog turned off the path. Lindman followed, restraining it as much as he could. It was rough ground, and he kept stumbling in the undergrowth. The dog forged ahead.

Then it stopped, raised one of its front paws and sniffed the air. He shone his torch among the trees. The dog put down its paw. Lindman pulled at the lead. It resisted, but the lead was long enough for Lindman to tie it round a tree trunk.

The dog was staring intently at some rocks just visible through a dense clump of pine trees. Lindman went towards the trees and walked round them. He made out a path leading to the rocks.

He stopped. At first he wasn't sure what he'd seen. Something white, shining. Then, to his horror, he realised that it was Andersson. He was naked, tied to a tree. His chest was covered in blood. His eyes were open and staring straight at Lindman. But the gaze was as lifeless as Abraham Andersson himself.

PART II

The man from Buenos Aires /
October–November 1999

CHAPTER 12

When Aron Silberstein woke up he didn't know who he was. There was a belt of fog between dream and reality that he must find his way through to discover if he really was Aron Silberstein, or if at that moment he was Fernando Hereira. In his dreams his two names often switched. Every time he woke up, he experienced a moment of great confusion. This morning was no exception, when he opened his eyes and saw light seeping through the canvas. He slid his arm out of his sleeping bag and looked at his watch. It was 9.03. He listened. All quiet. The night before he'd turned off the main road after passing through a town called Falköping. Then he'd driven through a little hamlet with a name something like Gudhem and found a cart track leading into the forest, and there he'd been able to pitch his tent.

And that was where he had just woken up, feeling that he had to force his way out of his dreams. It was raining, a thin drizzle with occasional drops pecking against the canvas. He put his arm back into his sleeping bag to keep warm. Every morning he was overcome by the same yearning for warmth. Sweden was a cold country in the autumn. He'd learnt that during his long stay.

Soon it would all be over. He would drive to Malmö. He'd return his rented car, get rid of the tent and spend a night in a hotel. Early the next day he would make his way to Copenhagen and in the afternoon board a plane that would take him home to Buenos Aires by way of Frankfurt and São Paulo.

He settled down in the sleeping bag and closed his eyes. He didn't need to get up yet. His mouth was dry and he had a headache. I overdid it last night, he thought. I drank too much, more than I needed to, in order to get to sleep.

He was tempted to open his rucksack and take out one of the bottles inside it, but he couldn't risk being stopped by the police. Before leaving Argentina he'd been to the Swedish Embassy in Buenos Aires to find out about the traffic laws in Sweden. He had discovered that there was zero tolerance when it came to alcohol. That had surprised him as he'd read in a newspaper article some time ago that Swedes were heavy drinkers and were often drunk in public. He resisted the temptation to drink spirits this morning. At least he wouldn't smell of alcohol if the police were to stop him.

Light trickled in through the canvas. He thought about the dream he'd had during the night. In it he was Aron Silberstein again. He was a child and his father Lukas was still with him. His father was a dancing master and he received his pupils at home in their Berlin flat. It was during that last horrific year – he knew because in the dream his father had shaved off his moustache. He'd done that a couple of months before the catastrophe. They were sitting in the only room that didn't have broken windows. Just the two of them, Aron and his father: the rest of the family had disappeared. And they waited. They said nothing, just waited, nothing else. Even now after 54 years it seemed to him that his childhood was one long, drawn-out wait. Waiting and terror. All the awful things that happened outside in the streets, when the sirens sounded and they scurried down into the shelter, had never affected him. What would come to dominate his life was the waiting.

He crawled out of his sleeping bag. Took out an aspirin and the water bottle. He looked at his hands. They were shaking. He put the pill in his mouth and washed it down. Then he crawled out of the tent for a pee. The ground was cold and wet under his bare feet. One more day and I'll be away from all this, he thought. All this cold, the long nights. He crawled back into the tent, down into the sleeping bag and pulled it up to his chin. The temptation to take a swig from one of the bottles of spirits was there all the time, but he would wait. Now that he'd come as far as this he was determined not to take any unnecessary risks.

The rain grew heavier. Everything went as it was destined to go, he told himself. I waited for more than 50 years for that moment to come. I'd almost, but only almost, given up the hope of finding the explanation for what had ruined my life, and how to avenge it. Then the unexpected happened. By some totally incredible coincidence somebody turned up and was able to supply the piece of the jigsaw that enabled me to discover what had happened. A chance meeting that ought to have been inconceivable.

He decided that as soon as he got back to Buenos Aires he would go to the cemetery where Höllner was buried and put a flower on his grave. But for him he would never have been able to carry out his mission. There was some kind of mysterious, possibly even divine justice that enabled him to meet Höllner before he died, and find out the answers to the questions he'd been asking for so long. Discovering what happened that day when he was only a child had put him in a state of shock. Never before had he drunk as much as he did for some time after that meeting. But then, when Höllner died, he'd forced himself to sober up and reduce his drinking so that he could go to work again and devise a plan.

And now it was all over.

As the rain pattered on the canvas, he ran through what had happened. First, the meeting with Höllner, whom he'd met by pure chance in La Cābana. That was two years ago. Even then Höllner was showing signs of the stomach cancer that would soon kill him. It was Filip Monteiro, the old waiter with the glass eye, who had asked him if he would consider sharing a table one night when the restaurant was very full. He'd been seated at a table with Höllner.

They knew immediately that they were both immigrants from Germany – they had similar accents. He had expected to discover that Höllner was one of the large group of Germans who came to Argentina via the well-organised lifelines that helped Nazis flee the Third Reich, which was supposed to last for a thousand years but which now lay in ruins. At first Silberstein hadn't given his real name. Höllner might easily have been one of those who entered the country on false papers; perhaps he'd landed in Argentina from one of the U-boats that were sailing up and down the coast of Argentina in the spring of 1945. He might also have been assisted by one of the Nazi groups that operated from Sweden, Norway and Denmark. Or he might have come later, when Juan Peron opened his political arms to welcome German immigrants without asking any questions about their past. Silberstein knew that Argentina was full of Nazis who had gone to ground, war criminals who lived in constant fear of being arrested. People who had never renounced their beliefs, and still had a bust of Hitler in a prominent position at home. But Höllner was not one of those. He'd referred to the war as the catastrophe it was. His father had been a high-ranking Nazi, but Höllner himself was one of the many German immigrants who had come to Argentina in search of a future they thought they could never find in the ruins of Europe.

They had shared a table at La Cābana. Silberstein could still remember that they'd ordered the same meal – a meat stew the chefs at La Cābana made better than anybody else. Afterwards they'd walked home together, as they lived in the same neighbourhood, Silberstein in Avenida Corrientes and Höllner a few blocks further on. They arranged to meet again. Höllner explained that he was a widower, whose children had returned to Europe. Until recently he had been running a printing business, but now he'd sold it. Silberstein invited him to visit the workshop where he restored old furniture. Höllner accepted the invitation, and then it became the norm for him to visit Silberstein in the mornings. He seemed never to tire of watching Silberstein painstakingly re-upholstering an old chair brought in by some member of the Argentinian upper classes. They would occasionally go out to the courtyard for a coffee and a smoke.

They'd compared their lives, as old people do. And it was while they were doing so that Höllner asked in passing if Silberstein happened to be related to a certain herr Jacob Silberstein from Berlin, who had escaped being deported with his fellow-Jews in the 1930s, and then avoided all other forms of persecution during the war because he was the only person who could give Hermann Goering a satisfactory massage to ease his back pains. Feeling that history had caught up with him at a stroke, Silberstein told him that the masseur Jacob Silberstein was his uncle. And that it was thanks to the special privileges enjoyed by Jacob that his brother Lukas, Silberstein's father, had also evaded deportation. Höllner explained that he himself had met Jacob Silberstein because his own father had also been massaged by him.

Silberstein had immediately closed his workshop and posted a notice on the door to the effect that he wouldn't be back until the following day. Then he'd accompanied Höllner to his home, not far from the harbour in a badly maintained block of flats. Höllner had a small flat overlooking the rear courtyard. Silberstein could remember the strong scent of lavender, and all the awful watercolours of the Pampas painted by Höllner's wife. They'd talked long into the night about the amazing coincidences, how their paths had crossed in Berlin so many years ago. Höllner was three years younger than Silberstein. He was only nine in 1945, and his memories were fuzzy. But he remembered the man who was fetched by car once a week to give his father a massage. He even remembered thinking that there was something remarkable about it, something remarkable and also a little dangerous, in that a Jew (whose name he didn't know at that time) was still there in Berlin. And, more-over, a man being protected by no less a person than the terrifying Reichsmarschall Goering. But when he recounted what he remembered about Jacob Silberstein's appearance and his gait, Silberstein knew that there could have been no misunderstanding: Höllner was talking about his uncle.

The key reference was to an ear, his left ear, that Jacob Silberstein had disfigured as a child, cutting himself on a shattered window pane. Silberstein broke into a sweat when Höllner described the ear he remembered so vividly. There was no doubt at all, and Silberstein was so touched that he felt obliged to embrace Höllner.

Now, lying in his tent, he remembered all that as if it had happened only yesterday. Silberstein checked his watch. 10.15. He changed iden-tity again in his thoughts. Now he was Fernando Hereira. He had landed in Sweden as Hereira. He was an Argentinian citizen on holiday in Sweden. Nothing else. Least of all Aron Silberstein who arrived in Buenos Aires one spring day in 1953 and had never been back to Europe since. Not until now, when he finally had an opportunity to do what he'd been longing to do all those years.

He dressed, broke camp and drove back to the main road. He stopped for lunch outside Varberg. His headache had cleared up by now. Two more hours and he'd be in Malmö. The car hire company was next to the railway station. That was where he'd collected the car 40 days earlier, and that was where he would return it. No doubt he'd be able to find a hotel nearby. Before then he would have to get rid of the tent and the sleeping bag. He'd dumped the camping stove, saucepans and plates in a rubbish bin at a lay-by in Dalarna. He'd thrown all the cutlery into a river he'd driven over. He'd keep a look-out for a suitable place to off-load the rest of his stuff before he got to Malmö.

He found what he was looking for a few kilometres north of Helsingborg: a skip behind a petrol station where he'd stopped to fill up for the last time. He buried the tent and the sleeping bag under the cardboard boxes and plastic bottles that had already filled the skip. Then he took out a plastic bag lying at the top of his rucksack. It contained a bloodstained shirt. Although he'd been wearing overalls that he'd burnt while still up there in the forest, Molin had managed to cover his shirt in blood. How it had happened was still a mystery. Just as big a mystery as why he hadn't burnt the shirt when he'd disposed of the overalls.

Deep down, though, he knew the answer. He'd kept the shirt so that he could look at it and convince himself that what had happened was real, not simply a dream. Now he didn't need it any longer. The time for remembering was in the past. He dug the plastic bag as deep into the skip as he could. As he did so, his mind turned again to Höllner, the pale man that he'd met at La Cābana. Had it not been for him, he wouldn't be here now, shedding the last physical traces of a journey to Sweden during which he'd taken a person's life, and sent a final horrific greeting to the equally horrific past by means of some blood-soaked footprints he'd left behind on a wooden floor.

From now on the only traces would be inside his head.

He returned to his car and sat at the wheel without starting the engine. A question was nagging away at the back of his mind. It had been there ever since the night he'd attacked Molin's house. A question regarding an unexpected discovery he'd made about himself. He had felt frightened on the way to Sweden. He'd spent the whole of the long flight wondering how he would manage to achieve the mission he'd set himself. A mission comprising a single task: killing a man. So far in his life he had never been anywhere near close to harming another human being. He hated violence, he was scared stiff of being assaulted himself. But there he was, on his way to another continent to kill a man in cold blood. A man he'd met six or seven times before, when he was 12 years old.

As it turned out, it was not at all difficult.

That was what he couldn't understand. It frightened him, and forced him to think back to all that had happened over 50 years ago, the starting point that led to the deed he had now performed. Why had it been so easy? It ought to be the hardest thing there is, killing another human being. The thought depressed him. He'd been convinced that it would be difficult. All the time he'd worried that when the moment came, he would hesitate, and afterwards be overcome by remorse; but his conscience had remained at peace.

He sat in the car for ages, trying to understand. In the end, when his urge to drink something very strong got the better of him, he started the engine and drove away.

He continued towards Malmö. After a while he could see on his right a long bridge linking Sweden to Denmark. He drove into the city and had no difficulty finding the car hire company. When he paid the bill, he was surprised at how much they'd charged him. He said nothing, of course, and paid in cash, though he'd left them his credit card number when he rented the car. He hoped the documentation recording that Fernando Hereira had rented a car in Sweden would disappear in the depths of some archive.

Back on the street, he found that there was a cold wind blowing in from the sea, but it had stopped raining. He set off towards the city centre and stopped at a hotel in a side street off the first square he came to. No sooner had he entered his room than he stripped down and took a shower. While he was living in the forest he'd forced himself to take a dip in the freezing lake once a week and try to rinse all the filth away. Now, as he stood under his shower in Malmö, he thought that at last he could wash off all the ingrained dirt.

Afterwards, he wrapped himself in a bath towel and sat down with the last of the bottles in his rucksack. Freedom! He took three large swigs, and felt the warmth spreading over his body. The previous night he'd drunk too much. That had annoyed him. Tonight the only thing he needed to worry about was getting to the airport the next day.

He stretched out on the bed. He was thinking more clearly now that he had brandy flowing through his veins. What had happened was rapidly becoming a memory. His aim now was to get home to his workshop. His whole life revolved around that. The cramped work-shop behind the house in Avenida Corrientes was the cathedral he attended every morning. And his family, of course. His children had flown the nest. His daughter Dolores had moved to Montevideo and would soon give him his first grandchild. Then there was Rakel, who was still studying to be a doctor. And Marcus, the restless dreamer of the family, who longed to become a poet, although he was earning his living at the moment as a researcher for a radical programme on Argentinian television. He loved his wife, Maria, and his children. Nevertheless, it was his workshop that was the mainspring of his life. He would soon be back there. August Mattson-Herzén was dead. Now there was a chance that all the events that had been haunting him since 1945 might leave him in peace.

He stayed on the bed for a while. Occasionally he reached out for the brandy bottle. Every time he took a swig he made a silent toast to Höllner. But for him, nothing of this would have happened. But for Höllner, he would never have been able to find out who killed his father. He stood up and tipped the contents of his rucksack onto the floor. He bent down and picked up the diary he'd been keeping for the 43 days he'd spent in Sweden, one page for every day. In fact he had got as far as page 45. He'd started writing on the flight to Frankfurt, and then on the flight to Copenhagen. He went back to the bed, switched on the bedside lamp and leafed through the pages. Here was the whole story. He'd written it thinking he might give it to his children, but they wouldn't get it until after his death. What he'd written was the history of his family. And he'd tried to explain why he'd done what he had done. He'd told his wife he was going on a journey to Europe to meet some furniture makers who could teach him something new. In fact, he had embarked on a journey into his past. In the diary he described it as a door that had to be closed.

Now, as he lay thumbing through what he'd written, he began to have doubts. His children might not understand why their father had made such a long journey to take the life of an old man who lived in seclusion in a remote forest.

He dropped the book on the floor and took another swig of brandy. That was the last one before he dressed and prepared to go out for a meal. He would have something to drink with his food. What was left in the bottle would see him through the night and the next day.

He was feeling tipsy now. If he'd been at home in Buenos Aires,

Maria would not have said anything, but looked accusingly at him. He didn't need to worry about that now. Tomorrow he'd be on his way home. This evening was for him alone, and his private thoughts.

He left the hotel at 6.30. The strong, cold wind almost bowled him over. He had been thinking of going for a walk, but the weather forced him to abandon that idea. He looked round. Further down the street was a restaurant sign, swaying in the wind. He set off in that direction, but hesitated when he got there. There was a television set high in a corner showing an ice hockey match. He could hear the commentary from the street. Some men were sitting at a table, drinking beer, watching the game. He suspected the food wouldn't be especially good, but on the other hand, he couldn't face more of the cold. He sat at an empty table. At the next table was a man staring in silence at his almost empty beer glass. The waitress came with a menu, and he ordered beef steak with Béarnaise sauce and chips. And a bottle of wine. Red wine and brandy was what he drank. Never beer, never anything else at all.

"I hear that you speak English," said the man with the beer glass.

Silberstein nodded. He hoped to goodness the man at the next table wouldn't start talking to him. He wanted to be at peace with his thoughts.

"Where do you come from?" the man said.

"Argentina," Silberstein said.

The man looked at him, his eyes glassy. "*Entonces, debe hablar español*," he said.

His pronunciation was almost perfect. Silberstein looked at him in surprise.

"I used to be a sailor," the man said, still speaking Spanish. "I lived in South America for some years. That was a long time ago, but when you learn a language properly, it stays with you."

Silberstein agreed.

"I can see you want to be left in peace," the man said. "That suits me fine. So do I."

He ordered another beer. Silberstein tasted his wine. He'd ordered the house wine. That was an error. But he hadn't the energy to send it back. All he was really interested in was staying tipsy.

A loud roar filled the premises. Something had happened in the ice

129

hockey match. Players dressed in blue and yellow embraced each other. The food arrived. To his surprise, it was good. He drank more wine. He felt calm now. All the tension had faded away, and was being replaced by a vast and liberating vacuum. Mattson-Herzén was dead. He had achieved what he had set out to do.

He'd finished eating when he glanced at the television screen. There was evidently a break in the match. A woman was reading the news. He almost dropped his glass when the dead man's face appeared on the screen. He couldn't understand what the woman said. He sat motionless, and could feel his heart pounding. For a moment, he half-expected his own face to appear there as well. But the face that did appear was not his own, but another old man. A face he recognised.

He turned to the man at the next table, who seemed to be lost in thought.

"What are they saying on the news?" he said.

The man turned to the television and listened. "Two men have been murdered," he said. "First one, and then another. Up in Norrland. One was a policeman, the other played the violin. They think they were killed by the same murderer."

The picture on the screen disappeared, but he knew now that his eyes had not deceived him. The first man was Mattson-Herzén, or Molin, and the second one was the man he'd once seen visiting him.

Silberstein put down his glass and tried to think straight. *The same murderer*. That wasn't true. He had killed the man who called himself Molin, but not the other man.

He sat quite still. The ice hockey match had started again.

CHAPTER 13

The night of November 3, 1999 was one of the longest Stefan Lindman had ever endured. When dawn finally broke, faint light creeping over the wooded hills, it felt as though he were in a weightless vacuum. He'd stopped thinking long ago. Everything happening around him seemed surreal, a nightmare. A nightmare that began when he'd walked round the trees and found Andersson's body.

He had forced himself to feel for traces of a pulse, which he knew had stopped for ever. The body was still warm — at any rate, rigor mortis had not yet set in. That could mean that whoever shot him was still in the vicinity. The light from Lindman's torch had shown where the shot blast had hit him, just over his heart. He'd almost fainted. It was a big hole. Andersson had been executed from close quarters, with a shotgun.

The dog had started howling as soon as Lindman tied it up. His first thought was that it might have found the scent of the killer, who might be very close. Lindman had raced back to it, scratching his face badly on tree branches. Somewhere along the way he'd also lost his mobile phone, which had been in his shirt pocket. He'd taken the dog back to the house, and rung the emergency number. Lindman had mentioned Larsson's name and from then on, the man on duty in Östersund had asked no unnecessary questions. He'd asked if Lindman had a mobile, was told he'd dropped it somewhere, and said he would ring the number to help him to find it. Now it was beginning to get light; his telephone was still lost, and he had not heard it ringing. He had the feeling all the time that the killer was close by. He'd crouched low as he ran to his car, and reversed into a dustbin as he turned to drive to the main road and give directions to the first of the police cars. The man in Östersund said they would be coming from Sveg.

The first to arrive was Johansson. He had a colleague with him, Sune

Hodell. Lindman led them to Andersson's body, and both officers drew back in horror. Then time had dragged as they waited for daylight. They set up their base in Andersson's house. Johansson had been in constant telephone contact with Östersund. At one point he'd come into the living room where Lindman was lying down on the sofa with a nose-bleed, and announced that Larsson was on his way from Östersund. The cars from Jämtland turned up soon after midnight, and were closely followed by the doctor. Johansson had got through to him in a hunting lodge north of Funäsdalen. He'd contacted colleagues in the neighbouring provinces of Hälsingland and Dalarna to tell them what had happened. Once during the night Lindman had heard him talking to the Norwegian police in Rorös. The forensic team had rigged up a floodlight in the forest, but the investigation had been marking time, waiting for the light of morning.

At 4 a.m. Larsson and Lindman had been alone in the kitchen.

"Rundström will be here as soon as it gets light," Larsson said. "Plus three dog handlers. We'll bring them in by helicopter, that's the easiest way. But he's bound to wonder what you're doing here. I need to have a good explanation to give him."

"Not *you*," Lindman said. "*I* need a good explanation myself."

"Well, what is it?"

Lindman thought for a while before answering. "Maybe it was that I wanted to know if he'd remembered anything," he said, eventually. "Concerning Molin."

"And you stumbled upon a murder? Rundström will understand that, but he's going to think it odd even so."

"I'm getting out of here very soon," Lindman said.

"OK. But not before we've talked through what happened here."

Then one of Larsson's colleagues had appeared and reported that the Helsingborg police had informed Andersson's wife. Larsson went off to talk to somebody, possibly fru Andersson, on one of the many mobile phones that seemed to be ringing constantly. Lindman wondered how it had been possible to conduct a criminal investigation in the days before mobile phones, and then he wondered about what mechanisms come into play when a murder investigation gets under way. There are set routines that have to be followed, procedures where everybody knows exactly what to do. But beyond the routines, what happens then?

Lindman thought he could see what was going on inside Larsson's mind, and he was having similar thoughts himself. Or at least, trying to have. He was handicapped by the image that kept recurring in his mind's eye. Andersson tied to a tree trunk with a rope. The enormous entry wound. A blast or more than one blast from a shotgun at close quarters.

Andersson had been executed. An execution squad had appeared in the darkness, held a court-martial, carried out the sentence, and then disappeared as discreetly as it had arrived. This is no straightforward little murder either, Lindman thought several times as the night progressed. But if it isn't, what is it? There has to have been a link between Molin and Andersson. They form the base of a triangle. At its missing tip is somebody who turns up under cover of night, not once but twice, and kills two old men who, on the face of it, have nothing in common.

At that point all the doors slammed shut. This is the heart of the investigation, he thought. There is some invisible connection between the two men, a link that is so fundamental that somebody kills both of them. This is what Larsson is thinking about while he's going through the routines and waiting for the dawn that never seems to come. He's trying to see what is hidden under the stones.

Lindman stayed close to Larsson throughout the night. He followed him when they hurried back and forth between the scene of the crime and the house they'd made their headquarters. He'd been surprised by how lightly Larsson seemed to be approaching his work. Despite the horrific image of a man messily shot and tied to a tree, he heard Larsson's cheerful laughter several times. There wasn't a trace of callousness or cynicism about him, just that liberating laughter that helped him to endure all the horror.

Morning came at last, and a helicopter sunk down onto the patch of grass behind the house. Out jumped Rundström and three dog handlers with Alsatians tugging eagerly at their leads. The helicopter took off again at once and was soon out of sight.

In the morning light, all the activities that had gone so slowly during the hours of darkness changed character. The officers who had been working non-stop since they arrived on site were tired and their faces as grey as the sky, but now their tempo increased. After giving Rundström a brief summary, Larsson and the dog handlers gathered round a map of the area and divided the search between the three of them. Then they left for the place where the body was now being released from the tree.

The first dog found Lindman's mobile straightaway. Somebody had stepped on it during the night and the battery wasn't functioning. Lindman put it into his pocket and the thought struck him: who would inherit it if he didn't survive the cancer?

After an hour or so of silent and steady work, Rundström summoned all the police officers to the house to go through the case so far. By then two more cars had arrived from Östersund with more equipment for the forensic team. Then the helicopter had returned and collected Andersson's body. Later it would be taken by car from Östersund to the coroner's office in Umeå.

Before the meeting started, Rundström had gone over to where Lindman was sitting in his car and asked him to join in. As yet he hadn't enquired how Lindman had been the one to discover Andersson's body.

The officers huddled in the sizeable kitchen. They were tired and cold. Larsson was leaning against a wall, pulling hairs out of one of his nostrils. Lindman thought he looked older than his 43 years. His cheeks were sunken, his eyelids heavy. He sometimes gave the impression of not being with it, but Lindman thought it was more likely that his mind was working overtime. His concentration was directed inwards. Lindman supposed that Larsson was looking for the answer to the question every investigation leader asks himself over and over: what is it that we can't see?

Rundström opened the meeting by talking about road blocks. They had been set up on all the major access roads. Before the police had arrived in Särna, there had been a report of a car driving at high speed, south towards Idre. This was an important sighting. Rundström asked Johansson to talk to colleagues in Dalarna.

Then he turned to Lindman. "I don't know if all present know who you are," he said. "We have a colleague from Borås here, who used to work with Herbert Molin. I think it will be best if you explain the circumstances in which you came to discover Abraham Andersson's body."

Lindman described what had happened when he'd driven to Dunkärret from Sveg. Rundström asked him a few questions. What he wanted to know was the timing of various points. Lindman had been experienced enough and had the presence of mind to check his watch both when he arrived at the house and when he discovered the body. The meeting was short. The forensic team were keen to get back to work as the weather forecast threatened sleet later in the day. Lindman went outside with Larsson.

"There's something that doesn't fit," Larsson said. "You have suggested that the reason for Molin's death may well be found in his past. That sounded reasonable to me. But where do we stand now? Andersson has never been a police officer. He and Molin didn't know each other until they happened to settle in the same remote spot. That sinks your theory, I'd have thought."

"It must be looked into, though, surely? Molin and Andersson may have had something in common that we don't yet know about."

Larsson shook his head. "Of course we shall look into it. But I don't buy it even so." He burst out laughing. "Police officers shouldn't believe anything, I know. But we do. From the very first moment we arrive at the scene of a crime we start forming possible conclusions. We make nets without knowing how big the mesh should be. Or what fish we are hoping to catch, not even what kind of water we're going to put them in. The sea or a mountain lake? A river or a tarn?"

Lindman had some difficulty in following Larsson's imagery, but it sounded convincing.

One of the dog handlers emerged from the forest. Lindman could see from the state of the dog that it had really been stretching itself.

"Nothing," said the handler. "And besides. I think Stamp's ill."

"What's the matter with him?"

"He brought up his food. He's probably caught a virus."

Lindman turned to look at Andersson's Norwegian elkhound: it was standing motionless on its line, staring at the place where the voices of the forensic officers could be heard.

"What's going on here in the forest?" Larsson said. "I don't like it.

It reminds me of a shadow moving in the dusk. You don't know if its real or imagined."

"What kind of a shadow?"

"The kind we're not used to up here. Molin was the victim of a well-planned attack. Andersson was executed. I don't get it."

Their conversation was interrupted by Johansson. "We can forget about the car at Särna. It was a man in a hurry to get his wife to the maternity hospital."

Larsson muttered something inaudible in reply. Johansson went back to the house.

"What do you think?" Larsson said. "What's really happened?"

"I'd use the same word you did. An execution. Why take a man into the forest, tie him to a tree and then shoot him?"

"If it happened in that order. But of course, that's what I've been wondering," Larsson said. "Why go to that trouble? There's also a similarity with the murder of Molin. Why go to the trouble of planting those bloodstained tango steps on the floor?" He provided the answer himself. "A message. But to whom? We've talked about this before. The murderer sends a greeting. To us or to somebody else? And why does he do it? Or why do *they* do it? We don't know if there's more than one murderer." Larsson looked up at the overcast sky. "And are we dealing with a madman? And is this the last? Or will there be more?"

They went back to the house. Rundström was on the phone. The forensic unit had started searching Andersson's house. Rundström put the phone down and pointed at Lindman.

"We should have a word," he said. "Let's go outside."

They went to the back of the house. The clouds scuttling across the sky were getting darker.

"How long are you thinking of staying?" Rundström said.

"I had intended leaving today. Now I suppose it will have to be tomorrow."

Rundström looked at him quizzically. "I have a feeling there's something you haven't told me. Am I right?"

Lindman shook his head.

"There wasn't anything between you and Molin that you ought to tell us about?"

"Nothing."

Rundström kicked at a stone.

"It's probably best for you to let us look after the investigation now. Best you keep out of it."

"I haven't the least intention of getting involved in your work."

Lindman could feel himself getting annoyed. Rundström wrapped his words in a sort of casual friendliness. Lindman was irritated because he didn't speak plainly.

"Let's leave it at that, then," Rundström said. "It's good that you found him, of course. So that he didn't need to be tied up there until someone else found him."

Rundström walked off. Lindman noticed Larsson standing in a window, watching him. Lindman beckoned to him.

"You're leaving, then?"

"Tomorrow."

"I'll get in touch with you later today."

"Call me at the hotel. My mobile's not working."

Lindman drove off. After a very few kilometres he felt sleepy. He turned onto a forestry track, switched off the engine and reclined the seat.

When he woke, he was enclosed by silent, white walls. It had started snowing while he was asleep, and the car windows were already covered. He sat and held his breath. Could this be what death is like? A white room with pale light filtering through the walls? He readjusted his seat and felt stiff all over. He'd had a dream, he knew that, but he couldn't remember what it had been about. Something to do with Andersson's dog, perhaps? Hadn't it started to chew one of its own legs? He shuddered at the thought. Whatever it was he'd dreamt, he'd rather forget about it. He looked at his watch: 11.15. He'd been asleep for more than two hours. He opened the door and got out for a pee. The ground was white, but it had stopped snowing already. There was no movement in the trees. No wind. Nothing, he thought. If I stood still I'd soon turn into a tree.

He drove back to the main road. He'd return to Sveg, have something to eat, then wait for Larsson to phone. Nothing more. He'd tell Larsson about his visit to Berggren. About the Nazi uniform in her wardrobe. He hadn't had an opportunity to do so during the night, and he wasn't going to leave until he'd passed on everything that might help Larsson in his investigation.

He came to the turning to Molin's house. He had no intention of stopping. Even so, he stamped so hard on the brakes that he skidded on the slippery surface. Why did he stop? One last visit, he thought. One final, short visit, that's all. He drove up to the house and got out. There were animal tracks on the white ground. A hare, he thought. He searched his memory to recall the pattern of those bloodstained footprints. He reproduced them on the white ground. Tried to picture Molin and his doll. A man and a doll dancing the tango in the snow. At the edge of the forest an Argentinian orchestra is playing. What instruments make up an Argentinian tango orchestra? Guitar and violin? Bass? Accordion, perhaps? He didn't know. It wasn't important. Molin had been dancing with death without knowing it. Or maybe he did know that death was there in the forest, waiting for him? He kept an eye on movements in the shadows even when I knew him, or at least thought I knew him. An elderly policeman who had never particularly distinguished himself. Even so he made time to talk to me, a raw young constable who knew nothing about what it was like having a drunk throw up all over you, or a drunken woman spitting at you, or a raving psychopath trying to kill you.

Lindman looked hard at the house. It seemed different, now that the ground was white. He turned his attention to the shed. He'd been in there the first time, but then he'd been more interested in the house. He opened the door. It was one room with a concrete floor. He switched on the light. There was a stack of firewood along one wall. On the opposite wall was a bench, shelves full of tools and a metal locker. Lindman opened it, thinking that there might be a police uniform inside, but there was only a set of dirty overalls and a pair of rubber boots. He closed the locker and looked round the room again. What does it have to say? he asked himself. The stack of firewood tells us that Molin knew how to build the perfect wood stack, but not much else. He turned his attention to the shelves of tools. What did they have to say for themselves? Nothing unexpected.

Lindman recalled that when he was a child his father had a tool shed in Kinna. It looked just like this one. Molin had everything he needed for minor repairs to the house and his car. There was nothing that didn't fit the pattern, no tool that suggested an unexpected story. He resumed his tour of the shed.

In one corner was a pair of skis with poles. Lindman took one of the skis to the doorway. The binding was worn. So, Molin had used them. Maybe he'd skied over the lake when it was covered in ice and the weather was good? Because he enjoyed it? Or because he needed the exercise? Or to go fishing through the ice? He put the ski back. What was this? Something unexpected. Another pair of skis, shorter, possibly ladies' skis. Now he could envisage two people gliding over the frozen lake, in glitteringly clear winter weather. Molin and Berggren. What did they talk about when they were out skiing? Or perhaps you didn't talk when you were skiing? Lindman didn't know because he hadn't skied since he was a child. He continued his search. In another corner was a broken sledge, some coils of steel wire and some roof tiles.

Something caught his eye. He looked more closely. It took him almost a minute to realise what it was. The tiles were lying haphazardly. Here was something that didn't fit into the pattern. Molin solved jigsaw puzzles, he stacked firewood with a feeling for symmetry and order. The same applied to the tools. They were all neatly arranged. But not the tiles. They weren't orderly in the same way as the rest. He bent down and removed them, one by one.

Underneath was a sheet of metal sunk into the concrete floor. A lid, locked. Lindman stood up and fetched a crowbar from among the tools. He forced it into the crack between the floor and the edge of the lid, and used all his strength to lever it open. It gave way suddenly, and Lindman fell over, banging his head against the wall. His hand was bloodstained when he rubbed his head. There was a box of rags under the tool shelves. He wiped his forehead and held a rag pressed against his head until the bleeding stopped.

Then he looked into the hole in the floor. There was a package inside. When he lifted it, he could see it was something wrapped in an old, black raincoat. Molin was very close to him now. He had hidden something under the floor that he didn't want anyone else to see. Lindman put the package on the bench, apologising silently to Molin, then moved the tools out of the way. The package was tied with thick string. Lindman untied the knots and removed the raincoat.

There were three objects: a black notebook, some letters tied with red ribbon, and an envelope.

He started by opening the envelope. It contained three photographs. He was not surprised by what he saw. He'd known, ever since that visit to Berggren's. Deep down, he'd known, and here was the confirmation. There were three black and white photographs. The first was of four young men with their arms round one another's shoulders. They were looking straight at the camera. One of the four was Herbert Molin, at that time August Mattson-Herzén. The background was unclear, but it could have been a house wall. The second photograph was of Molin alone. It was taken in a studio, the name of which was at the bottom of the picture.

The third photograph was also of Molin as a young man. Here he was standing beside a motorcycle and sidecar. He was holding a rifle. He was smiling at the camera. Lindman laid the photographs side by side. They also had this in common: Molin's clothes. His uniform. It was the same as the one in Berggren's wardrobe.

CHAPTER 14

There was a story about Scotland.

It was in the middle of the diary, slotted like an unexpected parenthesis into the account Molin had written of his life. In May 1972, Molin has a fortnight's holiday. He takes a ferry from Göteborg to Immingham on the east coast of England. He takes a train to Glasgow and arrives late in the afternoon of May 11. He books into Smith's Hotel, which, according to his description of it, is "close to some museums and a university", but he doesn't visit the museums. The next day he rents a car and continues his journey northwards. His diary says that he passes through Kinross, Dunkeld and Spean Bridge. He drives for a long way that day, as far as Drumnadrochit on the western shore of Loch Ness, where he stays the night. He doesn't look for the monster, however.

Early on the morning of May 13, he drives on along the lochside and reaches his destination in the afternoon: the town of Dornoch, situated on a peninsula east of the Highlands. He books into the Rosedale Hotel near the harbour, and notes in his diary that "the air here is different from that in Västergötland". He doesn't explain in what way it is different. Now he has reached Dornoch, it's the middle of May 1972, and so far he has made no mention of why he's here. Just that he will meet "M.". And he does in fact meet "M." that same evening. "Long walk through the town with M.," he writes. "Strong wind, but no rain." He makes the same note for each of the next seven days. "Long walk through the town with M." Nothing more. The only thing he finds worth remembering is that the weather changes. It seems always to be windy in Dornoch, but sometimes it's "pouring down", sometimes the weather is "threatening", and just once, on Thursday, May 18, "the sun is shining" and it's "rather warm". A few days later he drives back the same way as he came. It is not clear whether it's the same rented car, or whether he has dropped off the first one and rented another. On the other hand, when he comes to pay his bill at the

Rosedale Hotel, he's surprised that "it didn't cost more". After a few more days, having been forced to spend an extra 24 hours in Immingham due to "the ferry's engine breaking down", he returns to Göteborg and then Borås. By May 26 he's back at work.

The passage about Scotland was a mysterious insertion in the middle of a diary with large time gaps. Sometimes several years pass without Molin applying pen to paper, usually a fountain pen, although occasionally he used a pencil to write his journal. The trip to Scotland, to the town of Dornoch, is an exception. He goes there to meet somebody called "M.". They go for walks. Always in the evening. It is not clear who "M." is, nor what they talk about. They go for walks, that's all. On one occasion, Wednesday, May 17, Molin allows himself to make one of the extremely few personal comments to be found in his diary. "Woke up this morning fully rested. Realise I ought to have made this journey ages ago." That's all. "Woke up this morning fully rested." It is a significant comment in many ways, because elsewhere in the diary there are many references to how difficult he finds it to sleep. But in Dornoch he sleeps soundly, and realises he ought to have come here ages ago.

It was afternoon by the time Lindman had read this far. When he found the package in the shed, his first thought was to take the diary to his hotel in Sveg. Then he'd changed his mind, and for the second time he entered Molin's house by climbing in through the window. He'd brushed the jigsaw puzzle pieces to one side on the table in the living room, and replaced them with the diary. He wanted to read it there, in the ruined house, with the spirit of Herbert Molin close at hand. He set out the three photographs beside the diary. Before opening it, he untied the red ribbon around the letters. There were nine of them. They were from Molin to his parents in Kalmar, dated between October 1942 and April 1945. All of them were written in Germany. Lindman decided to work his way through the diary first.

It started with notes from Oslo on June 3, 1942. Molin recorded the fact that he'd bought the diary in a stationery shop in Stortingsgatan, Oslo, with the intention of "noting down significant events in my life". He'd crossed the border into Norway to the west of Idre in northern Dalarna, on a road passing through Flötningen. The road had been recommended by a certain "Lieutenant W. from Stockholm whose job it is to ensure that those who wish to join the German army can find the way there through the mountains". It was not explained how he travelled from the border to Oslo, but the fact is that he's there now, it's June 1942, he buys a notebook and starts to keep his diary.

Lindman paused at this point. It was 1942, and Molin was 19. In fact, his name at that time was August Mattson-Herzén. He started keeping his diary when he was passing through a life-changing phase. Nineteen years of age, and he decides to enlist in the German army. He wants to fight for Hitler. He's left Kalmar, and somehow or other got in touch with a Lieutenant W. in Stockholm who has something to do with recruitment for the German military. But does young August go off to war with or without the blessing of his parents? What are his motives? Is he fighting Bolshevism? Or is he just a mercenary bent on adventure? It is not clear. All that emerges is that he is 19 years of age and is in Oslo.

Lindman read on. On June 4 Mattson-Herzén records the date then starts writing something that he crosses out. Nothing more until June 28. He notes in capital letters, in bold, that he's "been enlisted", and that he was to be taken to Germany as early as July 2. His notes exude triumph. He's been accepted by the German army! Then he records that he buys an ice cream. Walks down the main street and looks at pretty girls who "embarrass me when I catch their eye". This is the first comment of a personal nature in the diary. He licks an ice cream and eyes the girls. And is embarrassed.

The next note is hard to decipher. After a while Lindman realises why. Mattson-Herzén is on a train, which is shaking. He's on his way to Germany. He writes that he is tense, but confident. And that he's not alone. He's accompanied by another Swede who has joined the Waffen-SS, Anders Nilsson from Lycksele. He notes that "Nilsson doesn't have much to say for himself, and that suits me. I'm pretty reserved myself." They are accompanied by some Norwegians, but he doesn't record their names. The rest of the page is empty – apart from a large brown stain. Lindman imagined Mattson-Herzén spilling coffee onto his diary, then putting it away in his rucksack so as not to spoil it.

His next note is from Austria. It's October by now. "October 12, 1942. Klagenfurt. I've almost finished basic training for the Waffen-SS. In other words, I'm about to become one of Hitler's elite soldiers, and I'm determined to make the most of it. Wrote a letter that Erngren will take back to Sweden: he's been taken ill, and has been discharged."

Lindman turned to the pile of letters. The first one was dated October 11, from Klagenfurt. He noted that it had been written with the same pen Molin is using for his diary – a fountain pen that occasionally produced large blots. Lindman went over to one of the windows to read it. A bird flew off through the trees.

Dear Mother and Father!

I realise you may have been worried because I haven't written before now. Father's a soldier himself, and no doubt knows it's not always easy to find time and a place to sit down with pen and paper. I just want to assure you, dear Mother and Father, that I am well. I came from Norway via Germany to France, where the basic training took place. And now I'm in Austria for weapons training. There are a lot of Swedes here, and also Norwegians, Danes, Dutchmen and three boys from Belgium. Discipline is strict, and not everybody can cope with it. I've kept my nose clean so far and even been praised by a Captain Stirnholz who's in charge of part of the course here. The German army, and especially the Waffen-SS that I now belong to, must have the best soldiers in the world. I have to admit that we're all waiting impatiently for the moment when we can get out there and start doing some good. The food is generally fine, but not always. But I'm not complaining. I don't know when I'll be able to come to Sweden. One is not entitled to any leave until one has been active for a certain length of time. Of course, I'm longing to see you again, but I grit my teeth and do my duty. And that is the great task of fighting for the new Europe and the defeat of Bolshevism.
Love from
Your son August.

The paper had turned yellow and become brittle. Lindman held it up to the light. The watermark, the German eagle, was very obvious. He stayed in the window. August Mattson-Herzén leaves Sweden, sneaks over the border into Norway and joins the Waffen-SS. His motive is clear from the letter he sent to his parents. August is no mercenary. He joins the German war effort, fights for Nazism, in order to contribute to the emergence of a new Europe that requires the elimination of Bolshevism. At the age of 19, the boy is already a convinced Nazi.

Lindman returned to the diary. By the beginning of January 1943, Mattson-Herzén finds himself deep in Russia, on the Eastern Front. The optimism that had been in the diary to start with has changed into doubt, then despair, and finally fear. Lindman was struck by an extract from the winter:

14 March. Location unknown. Russia. Freezing cold as ever. Scared stiff every night of losing a body part. Strömberg killed by shrapnel yesterday. Hyttler has deserted. If he's caught, they'll either shoot him or hang him. We are dug in and expecting a counter-attack. I'm frightened. The only thing that keeps me going is the thought of getting to Berlin and taking some dancing lessons. I wonder if I'll ever make it.

He's dancing, Lindman thought. He's in some trench or other and he survives by dreaming about how he might be gliding around a dance floor.

Lindman examined the photographs. Mattson-Herzén is smiling. No sign of fear there. His smile is that of a real smooth operator. The fear is hidden behind these pictures, in photographs that were never taken. Unless he'd chosen not to keep any that betrayed his fear. So as not to remember.

Molin's life can be split down the middle, Lindman thought. There is a decisive watershed, before the fear and with the fear. It creeps up on him in the winter of 1943 when he tries to survive on the Eastern Front. He's 20 at the time. It could be the same fear as I'd detected in the forest near Borås. The same fear, more than 40 years later.

Lindman read his way through the book. It was starting to grow dark. The chill seeped in through the broken windows. He took the book into the kitchen, closed the door, covered the windows with a blanket from the bedroom, and carried on reading.

In April 1943, Mattson-Herzén writes for the first time that he wants to go home. He's afraid of dying. The soldiers are engaged in

145

a remorseless and depressing retreat, not only from an impossible war, but also from an ideology that has collapsed. The circumstances are horrendous. Occasionally, he writes about the corpses on all sides, body parts shot to pieces, the eyeless faces, the slit throats. He is constantly searching for a way out, but he can't find one. On the other hand, he realises what is not a solution. Later in the spring he is given execution duties. They are going to shoot a Norwegian and two Belgian deserters who had been captured. This is one of the longer diary entries.

"May 19, 1943. Russia. Or possibly Polish territory. Was ordered by Captain Emmers to be part of an execution platoon. Two Belgians and the Norwegian Lauritzen were to be shot for desertion. They were hustled into a ditch, we stood on the road. Difficult to shoot downwards. Lauritzen was crying, tried to crawl away through the mud. Captain Emmers ordered him to be tied to a telegraph pole. The Belgians were silent. Lauritzen was screaming. I aimed for the heart. They were deserters. Military law applies. Who wants to die? Afterwards we were all given a glass of brandy. It's spring in Kalmar now. If I close my eyes I can see the sea. Will I ever make it to home?"

Lindman could feel the young man's fear resonating from the text. He shoots deserters, considers it to be a fair sentence, is given a glass of brandy and dreams of the Baltic Sea. But fear is creeping up on him all the time, forcing its way into his brain and giving him no peace. Lindman tried to imagine what it must have been like, lying in a trench somewhere on the Eastern Front. Sheer hell, no doubt. In less than a year his naïve enthusiasm had turned to terror. Nothing now about the new Europe: now it's a question of survival. And hoping he'll get back to Kalmar one day.

But it goes on until the spring of 1945. Mattson-Herzén has returned to Germany from Russia. He's wounded. In the entry for October 19, 1944 Lindman sees the explanation for the bullet wounds found by the pathologists in Umeå. It is not exactly clear what had happened, but at some point in August 1944 he is shot. He survives by some kind of miracle, but the message that emerges from his diary notes is not one of gratitude. Lindman observes that something new is starting to happen to Mattson-Herzén. What characterises the contents of his diary is no longer fear. Another emotion has crept in. Hate. He expresses his anger at what is happening, and speaks of the necessity to be "ruthless" and to have no hesitation in "allotting punishment". Although he recognises that the war is lost, he does not lose belief in the righteousness of the cause, the justification of the aims. Hitler may have let them down, but not as much as all those people who failed to understand that the war was a crusade against Bolshevism. These are the people Mattson-Herzén starts to hate in the course of 1944. This emerges very clearly from one of the letters he writes to Kalmar. It is dated January 1945, and as usual there is no sender's address. He'd evidently had a letter from his parents, anxious about his welfare. Lindman wondered why Mattson-Herzén hadn't saved the letters he'd received, only the ones he'd sent. Perhaps the explanation was that his own letters were a sort of complement to the diary. It was always his own voice doing the talking, his own hand holding the pen.

Dear Mother and Father!

I'm sorry I haven't written for so long, but we have been constantly on the move and are now not far from Berlin. You have no need to worry. The war is a sad tale of suffering and sacrifice, but I've come through comparatively unscathed and been very lucky. I've seen a lot of my former comrades killed, but I have never lost heart. I do wonder, however, why more young Swedes, and older ones come to that, have not rallied to the German flag. Do people in my homeland fail to see what is at stake? Have they not realised that the Russians are going to subjugate everyone who fails to resist? Ah well, I shall not try you with my thoughts and my anger, but I am sure, dear Mother and Father, that you understand what I mean. You didn't prevent me from joining up, and you, Father, said that you would have done the same if you'd been younger and didn't have a gammy leg. I must close now, but at least you know I am still of this world and continuing the struggle. I often dream about Kalmar. How are Karin and Nils? How are Aunt Anna's roses faring? I think about all sorts of things in quiet moments, but there are not so many of them.

Your loving son,
August Mattson-Herzén.
Now promoted to Unterscharführer.

Mattson-Herzén's motives were now clearer than ever. He'd been encouraged by his parents to fight for Hitler against Bolshevism. When he went to Norway, it was not as some kind of adventurer. He had set himself a mission. Towards the end of 1944, possibly in connection with the wounds he had suffered, he had been promoted. What exactly was an "Unterscharführer"? What was the Swedish equivalent? Was there an equivalent?

Lindman read on. The entries became less frequent and shorter, but Mattson-Herzén stayed in Germany until the end of the war. He is in Berlin as the city falls, street by street. He describes how he saw a Russian tank from close quarters for the first time. He notes that on several occasions he was close to "falling into the clutches of the Russians, in which case I would have had to rely on the mercy of the good Lord". No Swedish names crop up by now, nor are there any Danish or Norwegian ones. He is now the only Swede among German comrades. The last wartime entry in his diary is dated April 30.

"April 30. I'm fighting for my life now, fighting to escape alive from this living hell. All is lost. Swapped my uniform for clothes taken from a dead German civilian. That's more or less the same as deserting, but everything is crumbling on all sides now. I shall try to escape over a bridge tonight. Then we shall just have to see what happens."

It is not clear what happened next, but Mattson-Herzén did survive and did manage to get back to Sweden. A year passes before he makes the next entry in his diary. He is in Kalmar by then. His mother had died on April 8, 1946. He writes on the day of her funeral: "I shall miss Mother. She was a good woman. The funeral was beautiful. Father fought to hold back his tears, but managed to keep composed. I think about the war all the time. Shells whistle past my ears even when I'm sailing in Kalmar Bay."

Lindman read on. The entries became shorter and sparser still. He notes that he has got married. That his wife gives birth to children. But he writes nothing about changing his name. Nor is there any mention of the music shop in Stockholm. One day in July 1955, for no apparent reason, he starts a poem. He crosses it out, but it is still possible to read the words:

Morning sun in Kalmar Bay
The birds are twittering in the trees
Today will be a lovely day

Perhaps he couldn't think of anything to rhyme with "trees", Lindman thought. "Bees" would have worked. Or "breeze". He took a pen from his pocket and wrote in a notepad: "With white clouds scudding in the breeze." It would have been a very bad poem. Perhaps Molin had enough sense to realise the limits of his poetic gifts.

Molin – he is now Molin – moves to Alingsås, and then to Borås. Ten days in Scotland produce an unexpected outburst of writing. To find anything like it Lindman would have to go back to the first months in Germany when Molin's optimism is intact.

After Scotland everything reverts to normal. He seldom takes up his pen, and then merely notes individual events, with no personal comment.

Lindman became more attentive as he came to the end of the diary. Before that, Molin had noted when he did his last day's work at the police station, and when he moved to Härjedalen. One particular entry aroused Lindman's curiosity:

"March 12, 1993. Greetings card from the old portrait painter Wetterstedt, congratulating me on my birthday."

On May 2, 1999 he makes his last entry: "May 2, 1999. +7 degrees. My master jigsaw puzzle maker Castro in Barcelona has died. Letter from his widow. I realise now that he must have had a hard time these last few years. An incurable kidney disease."

That is all. The diary is far from full. The book Molin bought in a stationer's in Oslo in June, 1942, has been with him for the rest of his life, but is incomplete. If a diary can ever be finished. When he started writing he was young, a convinced Nazi, on his way from Norway to Germany and the war. He eats ice creams and is embarrassed when Norwegian girls look him in the eye. Fifty-seven years later he writes about the death of a jigsaw puzzle maker in Barcelona. Six months later, he is dead himself.

Lindman closed the book. It was almost pitch dark outside. Is the solution in this diary or elsewhere? he asked himself. I can't answer that question. I don't know what he left out, only what he wrote. But

I now know a few things about Molin that I didn't know before. He was a Nazi, he fought for Hitler's Germany in the Second World War. He also travelled to Scotland and went for a lot of long walks with somebody he called "M.".

Lindman packed the letters, photographs and the diary into the raincoat again. He left the house the same way as he'd come in, through the window. Just before opening the car door he paused. A vague feeling of sorrow had come over him. About the life Herbert Molin had led. But he realised that some of the sorrow was directed at himself. He was 37 years of age, childless, and was carrying an illness that could send him to his grave before he made 40.

He drove back to Sveg. There was little traffic on the roads. Shortly before Linsell he was overtaken by a police car heading for Sveg, then another. What had occurred the previous night seemed strangely distant and unreal. Yet it was less than 24 hours since he'd made the horrific discovery. Molin had made no mention of Abraham Andersson in his diary. Nor Elsa Berggren. His two wives and two children he mentioned only in passing, briefly and factually.

Reception was deserted when he entered the hotel. He leaned over the desk and took his key. When he came up to his room he examined his suitcase. Nobody had touched it. He must have imagined it.

He went down to the dining room shortly after seven. Larsson still hadn't phoned. The girl emerged from the swing doors and smiled as she produced the menu.

"I saw you'd taken your key," she said. Then she became serious. "I hear something else has happened. That another old man has been killed somewhere near Glöte."

"That's right."

"This is awful. What's going on?"

She shook her head in resignation, not expecting an answer, and gave him the menu.

"We've changed today," she said. "I wouldn't recommend the veal cutlets."

Lindman chose elk fillet with Béarnaise sauce and boiled potatoes. He had just finished eating when the girl came through the swing doors and announced that he was wanted on the phone. He went up the steps to reception. It was Larsson.

"I'll be staying overnight, at the hotel," he said.

"How's it going?"

"Nothing tangible to go on."

"The dogs?"

"They haven't found a thing. I expect to be there in an hour. Will you keep me company while I have supper?"

Lindman said he would.

At least I've something I can give him, he thought when the call was finished. I've no idea what the relationship was between Molin and Andersson, but I can open a door for Larsson even so. In Berggren's house there was a Nazi uniform. And Molin had been very careful to withhold his past from the world. There is a possibility, Lindman thought, that the uniform in Berggren's wardrobe belonged to Molin. Even if he had exchanged his uniform for civilian clothes to escape from the burning ruins of Berlin.

CHAPTER 15

Larsson was exhausted by the time he arrived at the hotel. Even so he happily laughed as he sat down at the dining-room table. The kitchen would be closing shortly. The girl who alternated between the dining room and reception was setting tables for breakfast. There was only one other guest, a man at a table next to the wall. Lindman supposed he must be one of the test drivers, although he looked rather old to be test-driving cars in hostile conditions.

"When I was younger, I often used to go out for meals," Larsson said, by way of explanation for his laughter. "Now it only happens when I'm forced to spend the night away from home. When there's some violent crime or something similarly unpleasant to sort out."

As he ate, he told Lindman what had happened during the day. What he had to say could be summed up in a single word. Nothing.

"We're marking time," he said. "We can find no tracks. Nobody saw anything, although we've traced four or five people who drove past that evening. What Rundström and I are wondering now is if there really is a link between Andersson and Molin. And if there is, what could it be?"

When he'd finished eating he ordered a pot of tea. Lindman ordered coffee. Then he told Larsson about his visit to Berggren's, how he'd got into her house, and his discovery of the diary in Molin's shed. He moved his coffee cup to one side and set out the letters, the photographs and the diary for Larsson to see.

"You've really overstepped the mark," Larsson said, clearly irritated. "I thought we'd agreed that you wouldn't continue poking your nose in."

"I can only say I'm sorry."

"What do you think would have happened if Berggren had caught you?"

Lindman had no answer to that.

"It mustn't happen again," Larsson said after a while. "But it's better if we don't say anything to Rundström about your evening visit to the lady in question. He tends to be a bit touchy about things like that. He wants everything to go by the book. And as you have already seen, he is not best pleased when outsiders start interfering in his investigations. I say 'his investigations' because he insists on regarding cases of violent crime as his own personal business."

"Johansson might tell him about it? Even though he said he would keep it to himself?"

Larsson shook his head. "Erik's not all that keen on Rundström," he said. "One should never underestimate antagonisms between individuals and also between provinces. Being junior to big brother Jämtland doesn't go down well in Härjedalen. That kind of problem afflicts the police force as well."

He poured himself another cup of tea from the pot, and examined the photographs.

"What you have uncovered makes for a very mysterious story," he said. "So Molin belonged to the Nazi party and went to fight for Hitler. Unterscharführer? What on earth was that? Was he mixed up with the Gestapo? Concentration camps? What was it they put over the entrance to Auschwitz? 'Arbeit macht frei.' Horrific stuff."

"I don't know much about Nazism," Lindman said, "but I imagine that if you were a Hitler supporter you didn't shout it from the rooftops. Molin changed his name. This might tell us why. He was covering his tracks."

Larsson had asked for his bill, and paid it. He took out a pen and wrote MOLIN on the back of it.

"I think better when I write things down," he said. "August Mattson-Herzén becomes Herbert Molin. You've spoken of his fear. It could be that he was scared that something in his past would catch up with him. You talked to his daughter, I suppose?"

"She said nothing about her father having been a Nazi. But then, I didn't ask her about that, of course."

"It's like having a criminal in the family. You'd rather not talk about them."

"That was my thinking. Do you wonder if Andersson was another one with a past?"

"Let's see what we find in his house," Larsson said, writing down ANDERSSON. "The forensic unit were going to take a few hours' rest, then carry on through the night."

Larsson drew an arrow with two tips between the two names, Andersson and Molin. Then he drew a swastika followed by a question mark next to Andersson's name.

"We'll have a serious chat with fröken Berggren first thing tomorrow morning," he said, writing her name and drawing an arrow between it and the other two. Then he crumpled the bill up and put it in the ashtray.

"We?"

"We can say that you are in attendance as my extremely private assistant, unauthorised." Larsson laughed aloud, then turned serious again. "We have two horrific murders to deal with," he said. "I couldn't care less about Rundström. Nor do I care whether everything goes by the book. I want you to be there. Two people listen better than one."

They left the dining room. The man was still sitting at his table. They parted in reception, agreeing to meet the next morning at 7.30.

That night Lindman slept like a log. When he woke he realised he'd been dreaming about his father. They'd been looking for each other in the woods. When the young Stefan finally found him in his dream, he'd felt boundlessly relieved and happy.

Larsson had slept badly, however. He'd got up as early as 4 a.m. and by the time he wished Lindman good morning in reception, he'd already been to Andersson's house. Nothing had changed. They had no clues to point to who had killed Andersson, and perhaps also Molin.

As they were about to leave the hotel Larsson turned to the girl in reception and asked if she'd seen his bill from last night's dinner. It was only when he'd got to bed that he'd realised he'd need it for his expenses claim. She said she hadn't seen it.

"Didn't I leave it on the table?" Larsson said.

"You crumpled it up and put it in the ashtray," Lindman said.

Larsson shrugged. They decided to walk to Berggren's house. There wasn't a breath of wind, and the clouds had melted away. It was still dark as they walked to the bridge that would take them over the river to Ulvkälla. Larsson pointed to the white-painted district court-house.

154

"There was a nasty incident here a few years ago that wasn't widely reported. A violent assault. Two of those found guilty boasted of being neo-Nazis. I can't remember what they said their organisation was called. 'Keep Sweden Swedish', something like that. Maybe it doesn't exist any longer?"

"Nowadays they call themselves 'WAR'," Lindman said.

"What does that stand for?"

"White Aryan Resistance."

Larsson grimaced. "Very nasty stuff. I suppose we thought we'd buried Nazism once and for all, but apparently it's alive and kicking, even if most of 'em are shaven-headed urchins running wild in the streets."

They crossed over the bridge.

"There used to be trains here when I was little," Larsson said. "The Inland Railway. You could get from Östersund to Orsa via Sveg. You changed there. Or was it Mora? I did that trip with Grandma when I was little. Nowadays the train only runs in the summer. The Italian singer Mum saw in the People's Park came here on that train. No planes or limousines in those days. She was at the station to wave goodbye to him. She even has a picture of it. Blurred and wobbly. Taken with a common or garden box camera. She guards it like the crown jewels. She must have been madly in love with him."

They had reached Berggren's house.

"Did you warn her that we were coming?" Lindman said.

"I thought we'd give her a surprise."

They went through the gate. Larsson rang the bell. The door opened almost immediately, as if she'd been expecting them.

"Giuseppe Larsson, Östersund CID. I think you've already met Lindman. We have quite a few questions to ask you. It's to do with the investigation into the death of Herbert Molin. You knew him, I believe?"

We, indeed, Lindman thought. I don't intend asking any questions. He looked at Larsson, who winked at him as they stepped into the hall.

"I suppose this must be important, since you've come so early in the morning?"

"It certainly is," Larsson said. "Where can we sit down? This is going to take quite a while."

Lindman noticed that Larsson was much more brusque than he'd expected. He wondered what his own approach would have been, if he'd been the one asking the questions. They went into the living room. Berggren didn't ask them if they'd like coffee. Larsson proved to be a man who didn't beat about the bush.

"You have a Nazi uniform in one of your wardrobes," he said as an opening gambit.

Berggren stiffened. Then she looked at Lindman. Her eyes were cold. Lindman could see that she'd immediately suspected him, without being able to understand how he'd managed to get into her bedroom.

"I don't know if it's against the law to possess a Nazi uniform," Larsson said. "I am pretty sure it's illegal to appear in public wearing it. Can you fetch it for us?"

"How do you know that I have a uniform in my wardrobe?"

"That's a question I have no intention of answering, but you must understand that it's of relevance to two current murder investigations."

She looked at them in astonishment. It seemed to Lindman that her surprised expression was genuine. He could see that she knew nothing about the murder at Glöte. He was surprised by this. Almost two days had passed, but still she knew nothing about it. She can't have been watching television, he thought. Or listening to the radio. Such people do exist, I suppose, although there aren't many of them.

"Who else has been killed – besides Herbert Molin?"

"Abraham Andersson. Does that name mean anything to you?"

"Yes, he lived not far from Herbert. What has happened?"

"All I can tell you so far is that he's been murdered."

She stood up and left the room.

"No harm in being direct," Larsson said, softly. "But she obviously didn't know that Andersson was dead."

"The news was released long ago, surely?"

"I don't think she's making it up."

She came back with the uniform and cap. She put them down on the sofa. Larsson leaned forward to examine them.

"Who do they belong to?"

"Me."

"But I hardly think you were the one who wore them?"

"I don't think I need answer that question. Not merely because it's idiotic."

"Not just at the moment, but we could take you to Östersund for a quite different kind of questioning. It's up to you."

She thought for a while before answering. "It belonged to my father. Karl-Evert Berggren. He's been dead for many years now."

"So he fought in the Second World War, in the German army, is that right?"

"He was a member of the volunteer corps known as the Swedish Company. He was awarded two medals for bravery. I can show them to you if you wish."

Larsson shook his head. "That's not necessary. I take it you know that Molin was also a Nazi in his youth, and was a volunteer in the Waffen-SS during the war?"

She sat up straight, but she didn't ask how they knew that. "Not 'used to be'. Herbert was just as convinced a National Socialist the day he died as he was as a young man. He and my father fought side by side. Even if my father was much older than Herbert, they remained good friends all their lives."

"And you?"

"I don't think I need to answer that question. There is no law that requires one to declare one's political persuasion."

"If that persuasion, as you call it, involves an association with a group that can be linked with violence and a crime known as racial agitation, it is a question that can be justified."

"I am not a member of any organisation," she said, obviously angered. "What would it be? That band of idiots who run around the streets with shaven heads and desecrate the Hitler salute?"

"Let me rephrase the question. Were you of the same political views as Herbert Molin?"

Her reply came with no hesitation. "Of course. I grew up in a family well aware of race. My father was one of the founders of the National Socialist Workers' Party in 1933. Sven-Olof Lindholm, our leader, often came to visit us. My father was a doctor and an officer in the territorial army. We lived in Stockholm in those days. I still remember my mother taking me with her on demonstrations in support of the National Socialist women's organisations. I have been giving the Hitler salute since I was ten. My parents could see what was happening. Jews flocking into the country, degeneration, moral decay. And the threat of Communism. Nothing has changed. Now Sweden is being undermined by indiscriminate immigration. The very thought of mosques being built on Swedish soil makes me feel sick. Sweden is a society that is rotting away. And nobody is doing anything about it."

Her outburst had set her off trembling. Lindman was nauseated, and wondered where all this hatred could have come from.

"What you have just said was not exactly uplifting," Larsson said.

"I stand by every single word. Sweden is a social concept that barely exists any longer. One has to feel nothing but loathing for the people who have allowed this to come to pass."

"So Molin's moving up here was no coincidence?"

"Of course not. In times like this when everything is falling apart, those of us who maintain the old ideals have a responsibility to help one another."

"So there is an organisation, despite what you said?"

"No. But we know who our real friends are."

"You keep it all secret, though?"

She snorted with disgust as she answered. "Being faithful to the land of our fathers seems to be a criminal offence nowadays. If we are to be left in peace, we have to keep quiet about our views."

"Nevertheless, somebody tracked down your friend, and killed him, isn't that so?"

"What has that got to do with his patriotic views?"

"You said it yourself. You are forced to hide away and conceal your idiotic ideals."

"There must have been some other reason for Herbert's death."

"What, for instance?"

"I didn't know him well enough to know."

"But you must have wondered?"

"Of course, but I find it impossible to understand."

"These last few months. Did anything unexpected happen? Did he behave in any way differently?"

"He was just the same as he always was. I used to visit him once every week."

"He didn't mention anything that was worrying him?"

"No, nothing."

Larsson paused. It seemed to Lindman that Berggren was telling the truth.

"What happened to Abraham Andersson?" she said.

"He was shot. It seems to have been an execution. Did he belong to your organisation – which isn't an organisation, of course?"

"No. Herbert used to talk to him occasionally, but they never discussed politics. Herbert was very cautious. He had very few real friends."

"Have you any idea who might have killed Abraham Andersson?"

"I didn't know the man."

"Can you tell me who was closest to Molin?"

"I suppose that must have been me. And his children. His daughter at least. His relationship with his son had been broken off."

"By the father or by the son?"

"I don't know."

"Anybody else? Have you ever heard of anybody by the name of Wetterstedt, from Kalmar?"

She hesitated before answering. Larsson and Lindman exchanged glances. She had been surprised to hear the name Wetterstedt.

"He sometimes referred to a person of that name. Herbert was born and grew up in Kalmar. Wetterstedt was related to a former Minister of Justice, I believe, the one who was murdered some years ago. He may have been a portrait painter, but I'm not sure."

Larsson had taken out his notebook and written down what she said. "Is that all?"

"Yes. But Herbert was not a man to say anything more than the bare essentials. People have their integrity, don't you agree?"

Larsson looked up at Lindman.

Then he said: "I have one more question. Did you and Molin do an occasional twirl when you visited him?"

"What on earth do you mean by that?"

"I wondered if you used to dance together?"

For the third time she looked startled. "We did, as a matter of fact."

"Tango?"

"Not only that. But often, yes. We also did some of the old-fashioned dances, ones that are dying out. The ones that require some technique and a certain elegance. How do they dance nowadays? Like monkeys?"

159

"I suppose you know that Molin had a sort of doll that he used to dance with?"

"He was a passionate dancer. Very skilled. He practised a lot. When he was young, I believe he dreamed of becoming a professional dancer, but instead he did his duty and answered the call to arms."

Lindman was struck by her high-flown language. It was as if she were trying to make time go backwards, to the '30s and '40s.

"May I take it that there were not many people who knew that Molin was a dancer?"

"He did not have many friends. How many times do I need to tell you that?"

"How far back do you remember his interest in dancing went?"

"I think it was aroused during the war. Perhaps shortly before."

"Why do you think that?"

"He once said so."

"What did he say?"

"What I've just told you. Nothing more. The war was harrowing, but he did have leave occasionally. The German armed forces took good care of their troops. They were granted leave whenever possible, and everything was paid for them."

"Did he often talk about the war?"

"No. But my father did. They once had a week's leave at the same time. They went to Berlin together. My father told me that Herbert wanted to go out dancing every evening. I believe that Herbert went to Berlin to go dancing whenever he was allowed to leave the front."

"Have you anything to say to us that you think could be of assistance in apprehending his murderer?"

"No, I do not, but I want you to find the guilty person, even if they will not receive any punishment worthy of the name. In Sweden the powers that be protect the criminal, not the victim. Naturally, it will emerge that Herbert remained faithful to his old ideals, and he will be condemned, despite the fact that he is dead."

"That will be all for the time being. But you will be called for further talks."

"Am I suspected of some crime?"

"No."

"Will you kindly tell me how you knew about my father's uniform?"

"Some other time," Larsson said, getting up. "I have to say that your opinions verge on the unacceptable."

"Sweden is already beyond redemption," she said. "When I was young one often came across police officers who were politically aware and who shared our beliefs. That is now a thing of the past."

She closed the door behind them. Larsson couldn't get away from her house fast enough.

"That's what I call a really nasty person," he said when they came to the gate. "I was sorely tempted to box her ears."

"There are more people than you would imagine who share her views," Lindman said.

They walked back to the hotel in silence. Larsson suddenly stopped short.

"What did she actually say? About Molin?"

"That he'd always been a Nazi."

"And what else?"

Lindman shook his head.

"What she actually said was that Molin remained a person with the same views until the day he died. I haven't read his diary in detail, but you have. One might well ask what he actually got up to during the war. And one might well wonder if there are not a lot of people who would have been glad to see him dead."

"I doubt that," Lindman said. "The war ended 54 years ago. That's an awfully long time to wait."

"Maybe," Larsson said. "Maybe."

They set off again. As they were passing the district court, Lindman said: "What happens if we turn the whole business upside down? We are assuming everything started with Molin, since he was murdered first. What if we approach it from the other side? If we started concentrating on Andersson?"

"Not 'we'," Larsson said. "'I'. Obviously I'll keep that possibility open. But it's most unlikely. Andersson moved here for reasons very different from Molin's. He didn't hide himself away. He mixed with his neighbours and was a completely different personality."

They returned to the hotel. Lindman had been annoyed by Larsson's remark. He was excluded again.

"What are you going to do now?" Larsson said.

Lindman shrugged. "I have to get out of here."

Larsson hesitated before asking, "How are you?"

"I was in pain one day, but I'm OK now."

"I try to imagine what it must be like, but I can't."

They were standing outside the hotel entrance. Lindman watched a house sparrow pecking away at a dead worm. I can't imagine it myself either, he thought. I still think the whole business is a nightmare, and that I won't in fact have to turn up at the hospital in Borås on November 19 to start the radiotherapy.

"Before you leave, I'd like you to show me that place where the tent was pitched."

Lindman thought that he'd prefer to leave Sveg as soon as possible, but he could hardly say no.

"When?" he asked.

"How about now?"

They got into Larsson's car and set off in the direction of Linsell.

"There's no end to the forests in this part of the country," Larsson said, suddenly breaking the silence. "If you stop here and walk ten metres into the trees, you're in a different world. Perhaps you know that already?"

"I've tried it."

"Somebody like Molin would find it easier to live with his memories in the forest," Larsson said. "Where there's nothing to disturb him. Where time stands still, if you like. Was there really no uniform where you found that diary? He might have got kitted up and gone into the depths of the forest to make the Hitler salute, then goose-stepped along the paths."

"He wrote in his diary that he deserted. Exchanged his uniform for civvies that he took off a corpse, with Berlin in flames all around him. If I understand his diary correctly, he became a deserter the day Hitler committed suicide in his bunker. But we can assume that Molin didn't know anything about that."

"I think they withheld news of his suicide for some days," Larsson said. "Then somebody gave it out on the radio that the Führer had fallen in action. Mind you, it could be that my memory is a bit hazy."

They turned on to the road to Molin's house. Bits of the police tape used to cordon off the scene of crime were fluttering from low branches.

"We ought to clean up when we leave a place," Larsson said, not pleased by what he saw. "We've handed the house over to Molin's daughter now. Have you met her?"

"Not since we spoke at the hotel the other evening."

"A very self-confident young lady," Larsson said, disapprovingly. "I wonder how much she really knows about her father's past. That's something I intend discussing with her, in any case."

"Surely she can't not know."

"I expect she's ashamed of it. Who wouldn't be if their father was a Nazi?"

They got out of the car. Listened to the rustling of the trees. Then Lindman led the way down to the lake and along the shore to the campsite. He saw straightaway that somebody had been there. He stopped in his tracks. Larsson stared at him in surprise.

"What's the matter?"

"I think somebody's been here since I was here last."

"Has something changed?"

"I can't tell yet."

Lindman studied the place where the tent had been pitched. Superficially, everything seemed the same. Even so, he was certain somebody had been there since. Something was different. Larsson said nothing. Lindman walked around the clearing in the trees, examining the site from different angles. He walked round a second time. Then the penny dropped. He had sat on the fallen tree trunk. As he looked round, he'd had a broken twig in his hand. He'd left it on the ground in front of him when he'd stood up to leave, but it wasn't there any more. It was lying by the side of the path down to the water.

"Somebody has been here," Lindman said. "Somebody has been sitting on this log." He pointed to the twig. "Can you take finger prints from a twig?"

"I wouldn't be surprised," Larsson said, taking a plastic bag from his pocket. "We can always try. Are you sure?"

Lindman was certain. He remembered where he'd left the twig. It had definitely been moved. He could picture somebody sitting there on the log, just as he'd done, bending down to pick up the twig, then tossing it away.

"In that case we'll call in a dog team," Larsson said, taking out his mobile.

Lindman turned to look into the forest. He had the feeling that there might be somebody there, very close. Somebody keeping an eye on them. He also had the nagging feeling that there was something he ought to remember. Something to do with Larsson. But what? He couldn't put a finger on it.

Larsson was listening to what they were saying on the phone. Asking questions, asking for a dog team to be mobilised, and then finishing the call.

"Very odd," Larsson said.

"What is?"

"Andersson's dog has disappeared."

"What do you mean disappeared?"

"What I say. Vanished. There's no sign of it. And the place is crawling with police."

They looked at each other, amazed. A bird clattered up from a branch and flew off over the lake. They watched it until it was gone from view.

CHAPTER 16

Silberstein lay on top of a hill with a view of Abraham Andersson's house, aiming his binoculars down at the surrounding area. He counted three police cars, two vans and three private cars. From time to time, somebody wearing overalls would come out of the forest. He gathered that it was there, among the trees, that Andersson had been killed; but he hadn't been able to go there yet. He would make that excursion after nightfall, if possible.

He scanned the house and cars again. A dog, of the same race as the one he'd been forced to kill at Molin's place, was tied to a line running between the house and a tree at the edge of the forest. He wondered if the dogs might have come from the same litter, or at least have the same parents. Thinking of the dog whose throat he'd slit made him feel sick. He put the binoculars down, lay on his back and breathed deeply. He could smell the damp moss. Clouds sailed overhead.

I'm mad, he thought. I could have been in Buenos Aires, instead of here in the Swedish wilderness. Maria would have been glad to see me. We might even have made love? In any case, I'd have slept soundly, and the following morning I'd have been able to open my workshop again. No doubt Don Antonio has been phoning, getting crosser by the day, that the chair he sent me three months ago still isn't ready.

If he hadn't happened to sit down at a table with a Swedish sailor in a restaurant in Malmö, a sailor who understood and could speak Spanish, and if that damned television set hadn't been on and shown the face of an old man who'd been murdered, he wouldn't have needed to abandon his plan. He would have been looking forward to an evening at La Cābana.

Above all, he wouldn't have needed to be reminded of what had happened. He'd thought it was all over, at long last, the business that had dogged him all his life. When he'd returned to his hotel room he'd sat on the edge of the bed until he'd reached a decision. He didn't drink a drop that night. At dawn he took a taxi to the airport some way out of town, where a friendly woman had helped him to buy a ticket to Östersund. A hire car was waiting for him. He drove into town and once again bought a tent and a sleeping bag, a camping stove and the other things he needed for making meals, some more warm clothes and a torch. At the System wine shop he bought enough wine and brandy to last him a week. Finally he went to the bookshop in the square and bought a map – he'd thrown away the one he'd had before, just as he'd dumped his pans, stove, tent and sleeping bag. It was as if the nightmare was starting over. In Dante's purgatory there was a level where men were tortured by everything repeating itself. He tried to remember what sins they'd committed, but he couldn't.

Then he drove out of town and stopped at a petrol station where he bought every local paper he could find. He sat in the car and looked for everything they'd written about the dead man. It was front-page news in all the local papers. He didn't understand the words, but there was a name mentioned after a reference to Abraham Andersson. Glöte. He guessed that must be the place where Andersson had lived, and where he'd been murdered. There was another name, Dunkärret, but that wasn't on the map. He got out of the car and spread the unwieldy map over the bonnet and set about making a plan. He didn't want to get too close. There was also a risk that the police might have set up road blocks.

He decided on a place called Idre. He judged it to be far enough from Andersson's house. He was tired when he arrived, and pitched his tent at the end of a forest track where he felt safe. He left the tent, after covering it with leaves and branches he'd laboriously gathered. Then he drove north towards Sörvattnet, turned off for Linsell, and had no difficulty in finding the road marked by a sign saying "Dunkärret 2". But he didn't take that road; instead he continued towards Sveg.

Just before the road leading to Molin's house he'd passed a police car. About a kilometre further on he'd driven into the trees along a track that was almost completely overgrown. He'd surveyed the area thoroughly during the three weeks he'd spent observing Molin. He had compared himself to an animal that needed many exits from its den.

Now he parked his car and walked along the familiar track. He didn't think the place would be guarded, but even so he kept stopping and listening. Eventually, he could glimpse the house through the trees. He waited for 20 minutes. Then he walked up to the house and the spot where he'd left Molin's dead body. The forest floor was trodden down. The remains of red and white police tape hung from trees. He wondered if the man he'd killed had been buried yet. Perhaps the police doctors were still examining the body? He wondered if they'd realise that the lashes on Molin's back had been made by a bull-whip used by cowboys on the Pampas. He approached the house and heaved himself up until he could see into the living room. The bloodstained footsteps had dried into the floor, but could still be made out. The woman who came to clean for Molin had obviously not been back.

He took his usual path to the lake. That was the path he'd used the night he decided he'd been waiting long enough. The other woman, the one who used to visit Molin and dance with him, had been there the previous day. If they followed their usual custom, it would be a week more before she came again. Moreover, the other man, the one called Andersson, had also been there the day before. He'd followed Andersson home, and from behind some trees had watched as he closed all the shutters and locked the shed and gave every sign of being about to go away. He could still remember the feeling of having decided that the time had come. It had been raining that day. The clouds had dispersed by evening and he'd gone to the lake for a swim in the cold water, so that his head would be clear when he made the fateful decision. Afterwards he'd snuggled up in his sleeping bag, in order to restore his body heat. All the weapons he'd acquired when he'd made his break-in on the way to Härjedalen were spread out on a plastic sheet beside him.

The time had come. Even so he was held back by a strange reluctance. It was as if he'd been waiting so long, he didn't know what would happen when the waiting was over. As so often before, his mind went back to the events of the last year of the war, when his life fell to pieces and could never wholly be restored. He'd often thought of himself as a sailing ship with a broken mast and shredded sails. That was how his life had been, and nothing would be fundamentally changed by what he was about to do. He'd harboured the thought of revenge all his adult life, and he'd sometimes hated that feeling more than he hated the man responsible. Still, it was too late now. He couldn't return to Buenos Aires without doing what he'd come here to do. He made up his mind after swimming in the dark lake. That night he launched his attack, carried out his plan.

He walked along the undulating shore of the lake, keeping his ears pricked all the time. The only sound was the rustling of the wind through the trees around him. When he came to the place where he'd pitched his tent, he decided that violence had not warped him, despite everything. He was basically a kind man who couldn't bear to see suffering. Violence to another human being would be unthinkable in any other circumstances. What he'd done to Molin was a closed book the moment he'd left his naked body at the edge of the forest.

Violence has not poisoned me, he thought. All the hatred that built up inside me over those years deadened my senses. I was the one who lashed Molin's skin into bloody strips, but at the same time, it wasn't me.

He'd sat down on the fallen trunk and fiddled with a pine twig. Had the hatred left him now? Would he be in peace for the years he had left to live? He had no way of knowing, but that was his hope. He would even light a candle for August Mattson-Herzén in the little church he passed every time he went to his workshop. He might even drink a toast to him, now that he was dead.

He stayed in the forest until the light faded. A thought he'd had when living in his tent here, that the forest was a cathedral and the trees were columns supporting an invisible roof, had returned. He felt cold, but he felt serenely calm. If he'd had a towel with him, no doubt he'd have jumped into the cold water and swum out until he could no longer touch the bottom.

He walked back to his car through the gloaming and drove into Sveg. Something remarkable happened then: he had dinner in a hotel dining room, and at another table were two men talking about Molin and Andersson. At first he thought he was imagining things. He couldn't understand Swedish, but the names had cropped up over and over again. After a while he went out to reception and, as there was nobody around, he looked in the hotel ledger and found that two of the hotel guests were described as "CID Inspectors". He returned to the dining room, but neither of them evidenced the slightest interest in him. He listened intently and picked up some other names, including "Elsa Bergén" or something of the sort. Then he watched one of the policemen write something on the back of his bill; when they left, he crumpled the bill up and dropped it in the ashtray. Silberstein waited until the waitress was in the kitchen, then picked up the crumpled bill and left the hotel. In the light of his torch, he tried to decipher what was written on the back of the bill. The most important thing was the name of the third person, Berggren, called Elsa, obviously a woman. Linking the three names – Molin, Andersson and Berggren – were arrows forming a triangle. Next to Andersson's name was a swastika and a large question mark.

He drove to Linsell and then continued as far as Glöte. He parked the car behind some log stacks and picked his way through the trees until he came to the vicinity of Andersson's house, then climbed up the hill where he was now lying. He had no idea what he thought he might discover, but he realised that he had to be very close to the place where it had happened if he were ever going to get an answer to the question he kept asking himself: who killed Andersson? And was it indirectly his fault because he'd killed Molin? He needed the answers to those questions before he could return to Buenos Aires. If he didn't have them, he would be haunted by the anxiety for the rest of his life. Molin would have had the last laugh after all. His mission to cleanse himself from all hatred would have turned back on him with full force.

He used his binoculars to watch the police officers coming and going between the edge of the forest and the house. They would assume that it was the same person who had killed both Molin and Andersson. There are only two people who know that is not true, he thought. One of them is me, and the other is whoever killed Andersson. They are looking for one person when they ought to be looking for two.

He realised now, he'd come back to make clear, somehow or other, that he wasn't the one who had killed Andersson. The police officers he'd been observing through his binoculars were following a trail that would lead them astray. Of course, he couldn't be certain what the men around the edge of the forest were thinking, but there is always a certain logic to fall back on, it seemed to him. I don't know, but I suspect there aren't very many violent crimes up here. People are few and far between, they don't say much and they seem to get on well with one another. Like Molin and Andersson, for instance: they appeared to have got on OK. Now they were both dead. He had killed Molin. But who killed Andersson? And why? The man who was his closest neighbour?

He put down his binoculars and rubbed his eyes. The effects of the alcohol had started to leave his body now. His mouth was still dry, and his throat hurt every time he swallowed, but he seemed to be able to think clearly again. He stretched out in the damp moss. His back ached. Clouds sailed over his head. A car engine came to life below, and he heard it reverse, turn, then drive away.

He relived again what had happened. Could there be a connection between Molin and Andersson that he didn't know about? There were a lot of unanswered questions. Was it coincidence that Molin had chosen to live in the vicinity of Andersson? Who had arrived there first? Did Andersson come from those parts? Had Andersson too fought for Hitler? Was he too one of those people who had done terrible things and escaped punishment? The thought struck him as most unlikely, but not impossible.

He heard a car approaching, and sat up. Through his binoculars he watched a man emerge from a car that wasn't painted blue and white and didn't have POLICE written on its sides. He tried to hold the binoculars steady. It was the policeman he'd seen in the restaurant, the one who'd written on the back of the bill. So he was right so far. This man was involved in both cases – he wasn't looking only for the killer of Abraham Andersson, he was hunting the man who'd killed Herbert Molin.

It was a strange experience, using his binoculars to observe a police officer who was trying to find him. He felt an impulse to run away, but his desire to find out what had happened to Andersson was stronger than the urge to save his own skin. He couldn't leave until he knew if he was indirectly responsible for the murder.

He put down the binoculars, and rubbed the back of his neck, which was feeling stiff. This was a very strange situation, it seemed to him. No matter who had killed Andersson, the murderer must have had a motive that had nothing to do with him. If he'd gone to a different restaurant, if there hadn't been a television set or a sailor who spoke

Spanish, he wouldn't have made this long journey back to where – a few kilometres down the road – he himself had committed murder. He raised his binoculars again and watched the man walk over to the dog and pat it on the head. Then he disappeared into the forest.

Silberstein focused on the dog. A thought started to evolve in his mind. He put down the binoculars and lay on his back. I must tell them they are on the wrong track, he thought. I can only do that by announcing that I'm still here. Not tell them who I am, nor that I killed Molin, nor why. I have to indicate only that it was somebody else who killed Andersson. My only chance is to put a spanner in their works, to make them stop and think about what actually happened.

The dog. The dog can help me, he thought.

He stood up, did some exercises to ease the stiffness in his body, then set off into the forest. He had always lived in cities, but even so, he had a good sense of direction and was good at finding his way in the countryside. It took him less than an hour to find his way back to his car. He had taken with him some food and some bottles of water. He was tempted by the thought of a glass of wine or brandy, but he knew he was capable of resisting the temptation. There was a job to be done. He couldn't put that at risk by getting drunk. He ate enough to satisfy his hunger, then curled up on the back seat of the car. He could rest for an hour before going back and still be there by midnight. To ensure that he woke up in time, he set the alarm on his watch.

He closed his eyes and immediately he was back in Buenos Aires. He wondered whether to choose the bed in which Maria was already asleep, or the mattress at the back of his workshop. He chose the latter. The sounds that filled his ears were no longer those from the trees. Now he was hearing the noise from the streets of Buenos Aires.

The alarm on his wristwatch was ringing. He switched it off, got out of the car, opened the boot and took out his newly acquired torch, then set off.

The last part of the way, he was guided by the beams from the spot-lights mounted in the forest. The light shining up from the trees reminded him of the war. One of his earliest memories was peeping out through cracks in the black-out curtains, when nobody was around to see him, and watching the anti-aircraft defences searching for enemy bombers flying in over Berlin at night. He'd always been terrified that a bomb would fall on their house and kill his parents. In his imagination, he himself always survived; but that only made his fear more acute. How would he be able to go on living if his parents and brothers and sisters were no longer alive?

He banished any such thoughts and, being careful to shield the light, used his torch to locate his binoculars, which were in a plastic bag to protect them from the damp. He sat on the moss, leaning against a tree trunk, and focused on the house. There was light coming from all the windows on the ground floor. The door opened occasionally and someone went in or came out. There were only two cars parked outside now. Before long two men got into one of the cars and drove off. By then somebody had also switched off some of the lights in the forest. He continued scanning the house with his binoculars, until he found what he was looking for. The dog was sitting quietly, at the edge of the light coming from one of the windows. Somebody had placed a food bowl beside it.

He looked at his watch. 10.30. He should be on his way home from La Cãbana, where he'd dined with a customer. That is what Maria believed, at least. He pulled a face at the thought. Now that he was so far from home, it worried him that he lied so often to Maria. He had never dined with any of his customers at La Cãbana nor at any other restaurant. He didn't dare tell her the truth: that he didn't want to eat with her, answer her questions, listen to her voice. My life has slowly grown narrower and become a path strewn with lies. That is another price I've had to pay. The question is, will I be honest with Maria in future, now that I've killed Molin? I love Maria, but at the same time, I recognise that I actually prefer to be on my own. There's a split inside me, between what I do and what I want to do. That split has been there since the catastrophe happened in Berlin. What can I do but accept that most things have already been lost and will never be recovered?

Time passed. A snowflake floated from the sky. He held his breath and waited. A snowfall was the last thing he wanted. It would make it impossible for him to carry out his plan. Luckily, there was only the occasional single flake.

172

At 11.15 one of the policemen came out onto the steps for a pee. He whistled to the dog, but it didn't react. Just as he was finishing, another man came out with a cigarette in his hand. It dawned on him that there were only two officers in the house, two men keeping guard.

Still he waited until it turned midnight. The house was quiet. Sometimes he thought he could hear the sound of a television or perhaps a radio, but he wasn't sure. He shone his torch on the ground and made sure he hadn't forgotten anything. Then he started making his way down the back of the hill. He really ought to carry out his plan now, but he couldn't resist the temptation to see the place where Andersson had been murdered. There could be somebody there standing guard, somebody he hadn't seen. It was a risk. But he felt he had to take it.

When he came close to the edge of the trees he switched off his torch. He moved very slowly, feeling his way forward on hands and feet, half-expecting the dog to bark at any moment. He went back into the trees at the other side of the house. Now he was assisted by the light from the spot lights.

There was no guard. There was nothing at all, in fact. Just a tree on which the police had attached various markers. He plucked up courage and walked right up to the trunk. At about chest height some of the bark had been split open. He frowned. Had Andersson been standing by a tree trunk when he was murdered? In that case he must have been tied to it? And that meant it was an execution. He broke out into a cold sweat and swung round, but there was nobody there. I was after Mattson-Herzén, he thought. Then somebody appeared behind Andersson, and now I have the feeling there is somebody behind me as well. He moved out of the light and made himself invisible. Tried to think straight. Had he set in motion a struggle between different forces over which he had no control? Had he stumbled into something he knew nothing about, when he decided to take his revenge? His head was filled with questions and fear. For some minutes he came very close to doing exactly the same as the man who became Molin had done: running away, disappearing, hiding, and forgetting what had happened – not to some forest in his case, but to Buenos Aires. He should never have come back, but it was too late now. He wouldn't go home until he'd found out what happened to Andersson. This is Molin's revenge on me, he thought, and he felt furious. If it had been possible, he wouldn't have hesitated to kill him all over again.

Then he forced himself to be calm. He took a few deep breaths and imagined waves breaking on a beach. After a while he checked his watch. 1.15 a.m. It was time now. He went back towards the house. He could hear music coming from inside, and the sound of voices conducting a quiet conversation. Presumably the radio was on, and two weary police officers were talking to stay awake. He walked towards the dog and called to it in a low voice. It growled but wagged its tail. He stopped short of the light coming from the window. The dog came up to him in the shadows. He stroked it. It seemed worried, but was still wagging its tail.

Then he released the lead from the running line and led the dog away. They left no tracks in the darkness.

CHAPTER 17

Lindman had seen it many times before. A police officer receives some unexpected information and reacts instinctively by reaching for the telephone. But Larsson was already holding a telephone, and it wasn't necessary to call anybody in any case. Both of them realised that the first thing to do was to work out the significance of the dog. It could lead to some kind of breakthrough in the investigation, but it could also be a red herring – the most likely explanation.

"I suppose there's no chance that it simply ran away?" Lindman said.

"Evidently not."

"Isn't it possible that somebody stole it?"

Larsson shook his head doubtfully. "From under the noses of several police officers? I don't think that's what happened."

"It's hardly likely that the murderer has returned to collect the dog."

"Unless we're dealing with a lunatic. Let's face it, we can't rule that out."

They sat quietly, exploring the various possibilities.

"We'll have to wait," Larsson said, eventually. "We must be careful not to get carried away by this dog business. In any case, it might turn up again before long. Dogs usually do."

Larsson put his mobile back in his jacket pocket and started walking to Molin's house. Lindman stayed where he was. It was several hours since he'd last thought about his illness, felt the creeping terror about when the severe pains might return. As he watched Larsson walking away, he felt as if he'd been abandoned.

Once when he was very young he'd been taken by his father to a football match at Ryavallen in Borås. It was a Swedish Premier League match, very important in some way or other, maybe crucial for the championship. He remembered that the opposition was IFK Göteborg. His father had said, "We've got to win this one", and as they drove from Kinna to Borås he kept repeating the mantra, "We've got to win this one". When they parked outside the ground, his father bought him a yellow and black scarf. It sometimes seemed to Stefan that his interest in football had been awoken by that yellow and black scarf rather than by the match itself. The teeming mass of people had frightened him, and he'd clung onto his father's hand as they walked towards the turnstiles. In the middle of that seething crowd, he'd concentrated on just one thing: holding tightly to his father's hand. That was the difference between life and death. If he let go, he'd be hopelessly lost among all these expectant would-be spectators queuing to get in. And then, just before they came to the turnstiles, he'd glanced up at his father and seen a face he didn't recognise. He didn't recognise the hand either, now that he looked closely. Without realising, he'd let go of his father's hand for a couple of seconds and taken hold of the wrong one. He was panic-stricken, and burst into tears. People looked round to see what had happened. The stranger didn't seem to have noticed that a boy in a yellow and black scarf had taken hold of his hand, and now snatched it away, as if the boy were about to pick his pocket. At the same moment, his father appeared again. The panic subsided, and they passed through the turn-stile. They had seats at the top of the stand on one of the long sides, giving an overall view of the pitch, and they'd watched the yellow-and-blacks battling with the blue-and-whites over the light brown ball. He couldn't remember the result. IFK Göteborg had probably won, in view of his father's silence all the way home to Kinna. But Stefan had never forgotten that brief moment when he'd let go of his father's hand, and felt utterly lost.

He remembered that incident as he watched Larsson walk off through the trees.

Larsson turned. "Aren't you coming?"

Lindman drew his jacket tighter around him, and hurried after him.

"I thought you might prefer me not to be there. What with Rundström."

"Forget Rundström. As long as you're here, you're my personal assistant."

They left Rätmyren behind. Larsson was driving fast. When they arrived at Dunkärret, Larsson immediately started shouting at one of the police officers there. He was a man in his fifties, small and very thin, by the name of Näsblom. Lindman gathered that he was stationed at Hede. Larsson was furious when he couldn't get a straight answer to his question about precisely when the dog had disappeared. Nobody seemed to be sure.

"We gave it some food last night," Näsblom said. "I keep dogs myself, so I brought some dog food from home."

"Obviously you can get a refund for that if you submit an invoice," Larsson said. "But when did the dog disappear?"

"It must have been after then."

"Even I can work that out. When did you realise it was no longer there?"

"Just before I phoned you."

Larsson looked at his watch. "OK, you gave the dog some food last night. When?"

"About 7.00."

"It's now 1.30 in the afternoon. Don't you feed dogs in the morning as well?"

"I wasn't here then. I went home this morning, and didn't come back until this afternoon."

"But you must have seen if the dog was still there when you left?"

"I'm afraid I didn't."

"But you keep dogs yourself . . ."

Näsblom looked at the empty running line. "Obviously, I ought to have noticed. But I didn't. I suppose I thought it must have been in its kennel."

Larsson shook his head in resignation.

"What's easier to notice?" he said. "A dog that's disappeared, or one that hasn't?"

He turned to Lindman. "What do you think?"

"If a dog is there, maybe you don't think about it, but if it isn't there, I suppose you ought to notice."

"I'll go along with that. What do you think?"

The last question was directed at Näsblom.

"I don't know, but I think the dog had gone by this morning."

"But you're not sure?"

"No."

"You've talked to your colleagues, no doubt. None of them saw it disappear, or heard anything?"

"Nobody noticed anything at all."

They walked over to the running line, with no dog attached.

"How can you be certain that it didn't just break loose?"

"I looked at the lead and the way it was attached to the running line when I fed it. It was a very sophisticated system. It couldn't possibly have broken loose."

Larsson studied the running line.

"It was dark by 7.00 last night," he said. "How come you could see anything at all?"

"There was light enough from the kitchen window," Näsblom said. "I could see."

Larsson turned his back firmly on Näsblom.

"What have you to say about this?" he said to Lindman.

"Somebody came here during the night and took the dog away."

"Anything else?"

"I don't know a lot about dogs, but if it didn't start barking, it must have been somebody it recognised. Assuming it was a guard dog, that is."

Larsson nodded, absent-mindedly. He was studying the forest that surrounded the house.

"It must have been important," he said after a while. "Somebody comes here in the dark and fetches the dog. A murder has been committed here, the place is sealed off. Even so, somebody takes the dog away. Two questions occur to me straightaway."

"Who and why?"

Larsson agreed.

"I don't like this," he said. "Who apart from the killer could have taken the dog away? Andersson's family lives in Helsingborg. His wife is in a state of shock and has said she isn't going to come here. Have any of Andersson's children been here? We'd have known if they had, surely. If it wasn't a lunatic or a sick animal rights supporter or somebody who makes a living from selling dogs, it must have been the murderer. That means he's still here somewhere. He stayed around after murdering Molin, and didn't leave after killing Andersson. You could draw several conclusions from that."

"He might have come back, of course," Lindman said.

Larsson looked at him in surprise. "Why should he come back?

Because he'd forgotten there was somebody else he needed to kill? Or because he'd forgotten the dog? It doesn't add up. The man we're dealing with – always assuming it is a man and that he's operating on his own – plans what he does, detail by detail."

Lindman could see that Larsson was thinking along the right lines. Even so, there was something nagging away at him.

"What are you thinking?"

"I don't know."

"You always know what you're thinking. It's just that you're sometimes too lazy to spell it out."

"I suppose the bottom line is that we don't know for sure that the same person murdered Molin and Andersson," Lindman said. "We think it was, but we don't know."

"It goes against common sense and all my experience to think that two incidents like this would take place at almost the same time and in the same place without there being a common murderer and a common motive."

"I agree. But even so, the unexpected does happen occasionally."

"We'll find out sooner or later," Larsson said. "We'll dig deep into the lives of both these men. We'll eventually find a link between them."

While they were talking Näsblom had slunk away into the house. He came back now, and approached hesitantly. Lindman could see that he had great respect for Giuseppe Larsson.

"I thought I might suggest that I could fetch one of my own dogs and put him on the scent."

"Is it a police dog?"

"It's a hunting dog. A mongrel. But it might be able to pick up a scent."

"Shouldn't we rather bring in one of our own dogs from Östersund?"

"They say not."

Larsson looked at Näsblom in astonishment.

"Who says not?"

"Chief Inspector Rundström. He thought it was unnecessary. 'The bloody dog has run away, no doubt,' he said."

"Go and fetch your Fido," Larsson said. "It's a good idea. But you ought to have had it the moment you noticed that Andersson's dog had gone walkies."

The dog Näsblom fetched picked up a scent immediately. It set off at full speed from the running line between the house wall and the tree, dragging Näsblom along behind it, and the two of them disappeared into the forest.

Larsson was discussing the house-to-house operation currently being undertaken in the district with one of the officers whose name Lindman didn't know. Lindman listened at first, but then moved away. He could see it was time for him to leave. His trip to Härjedalen was over. It started when he opened a newspaper in the hospital café in Borås and saw the photograph of Herbert Molin. Now he'd been in Sveg for a week. Neither he nor anybody else knew yet who had killed Molin and probably also Andersson. Perhaps Larsson was right in thinking there was a link between the two murders? Lindman wasn't convinced. On the other hand he knew now that at one time in his life Molin had fought for the Germans on the Eastern Front, that he had been a Nazi, maybe was to the very last moment of his life, and that there was a woman who shared his opinions, Berggren, who had helped him to find the house in the forest.

Molin had been on the run. He had retired from his post in Borås and crept into a lair where someone had finally found him. Lindman was certain that Molin knew somebody was looking for him. Something happened in Germany during the war, he was sure of *that*. Something not recorded in the diary. Or it could be in a code that I can't read. Then there's the week in Scotland and the long walks with "M.". Somehow or other this must all be linked with what happened in Germany.

But now I'm going to leave Sveg. Giuseppe Larsson is a very experienced police officer. He and his team will solve the case eventually. He wondered if he would live long enough to learn the solution. He found this hard to cope with now. The treatment he would start receiving in a week or so might not suffice. The doctor had said they could try cytoxins if radiotherapy and operative treatment didn't achieve the desired result. There were lots of other drugs they could try. Having cancer was no longer a death sentence, she insisted. OK, he thought, but it's not the same as being cured. I might be dead a year from now. I have to cope with that, no matter how hard it might be.

He was overwhelmed by fear. If only he could, he'd run away.

Larsson came over to him.

"I'm leaving now," Lindman said.

Larsson looked hard at him. "You've been a big help," he said. "And obviously, I wonder how you feel."

Lindman shrugged, but said nothing. Larsson held out his hand.

"Would you like me to keep in touch and let you know how things are progressing?" he said.

What did he really want? Apart from getting well again? "I think it's better if I get in touch with you," he said. "I don't know how I'll feel once the radiotherapy starts."

They shook hands. It seemed to Lindman that Giuseppe Larsson was a very likeable man. Although he didn't really know anything about him.

Then it dawned on him that his car was in Sveg.

"Obviously, it ought to be me driving you to your hotel," Larsson said. "But I feel I ought to hang around here for a while and wait for Näsblom to come back. I'll ask Persson to stand in for me."

Persson didn't have much to say for himself. Lindman contemplated the trees through the car windows, and thought that he would have quite liked to meet Veronica Molin one more time. He'd have liked to ask her some questions about her father's diary. What had she known about her father's past? And where was Molin's son? Why hadn't he put in an appearance?

Persson dropped him off outside the hotel. The girl in reception smiled when he walked in.

"I'm leaving now."

"It can get cold as evening draws in," she said. "Cold, and quite slippery."

"I'll drive carefully."

He went up to his room and packed his things. The moment he closed the door, he couldn't remember what the room looked like. He paid his bill without checking the details.

"How's it going?" she said when he'd handed over the money. "Are you going to catch the murderer?"

"I certainly hope so."

Lindman left the hotel. He put his case in the boot and was just about to get behind the wheel when he saw Veronica Molin come out of the hotel entrance. She walked up to him.

"I heard you were about to leave."

"Who told you that?"

"The girl in reception."

"That must mean you asked after me."

"Yes."

"Why?"

"I wanted to hear how things were going, of course."

"I'm not the one to ask about that."

"Inspector Larsson thought you were. I spoke to him on the phone a few minutes ago. He said you might still be around. I guess I got lucky."

Lindman locked the car door and accompanied her back to the hotel. They sat down in the dining room, which was empty.

"Inspector Larsson said he'd found a diary. Is that right?"

"That's correct," Lindman said. "I've glanced through it. But it belongs to you and your brother, of course. Once they release it. At the moment it's an important piece of evidence."

"I didn't know my father kept a diary. It surprises me."

"Why's that?"

"He wasn't the type to write anything when it wasn't strictly necessary."

"Lots of people keep a secret diary. I bet practically everybody has done so at some stage in their lives."

He watched her taking out a packet of cigarettes. She lit one, then looked him in the eye.

"Inspector Larsson said the police are still struggling to find any leads. They haven't found anything specific. Everything seems to suggest that the man who killed my father also murdered the other man."

"Who you didn't know?"

She looked up at him. "How could I have known him? You're forgetting that I hardly even knew my father."

It seemed to Lindman that he might as well not beat about the bush. He should ask her the questions he'd already formulated.

182

"Did you know your father was a Nazi?"

He couldn't tell if the question had come as a surprise or not.

"What do you mean by that?"

"Can that mean so very many different things? I read in his diary that as a young man he left Kalmar and crossed the border into Norway in 1942 to enlist with the German army. He fought for Hitler until the end of the war in 1945. Then he returned to Sweden. Married, then your brother and you were born. He changed his name, divorced, remarried and then divorced again: but all the time he was a Nazi. If I'm not much mistaken, he remained a convinced Nazi until his dying day."

"Is that what he wrote in his diary?"

"There were some letters as well. And photographs. Your father in uniform."

She shook her head. "This comes as a hideous shock."

"He never spoke about the war?"

"Never."

"Nor about his political views?"

"I didn't even know he had any. There was never any talk of politics when I was growing up."

"You can express your views even when you're not discussing specific political questions."

"How?"

"You can reveal your view of the world and your fellow men in a lot of different ways."

She thought for a while, then shook her head. "I can remember from when I was a child that he said several times that he wasn't interested in politics. I had no idea he held extremist views. He concealed them pretty well, if what you say is right, that is."

"It's all crystal clear in his diary."

"Is that all it's about? Didn't he write anything about his family?"

"Very little."

"That doesn't really surprise me. I grew up with the impression that we children were nothing more than a nuisance as far as Father was concerned. He never really bothered about us, he just pretended to."

"By the way, your father had a woman friend here in Sveg. I don't know if she was his mistress. I don't know what people do to keep themselves occupied when they've turned 70."

"A woman here in Sveg?"

He regretted having mentioned that. It was information she ought to have had from Larsson, not from him, but it was too late now.

"Her name is Elsa Berggren and she lives on the south bank of the river. She was the one who found his house for him. She shares his political views too. If you can call Nazi views political, that is."

"What else could they be?"

"Criminal."

It seemed as if it had suddenly dawned on her why he was asking these questions.

"Do you think my father's opinions might have had something to do with his death?"

"I don't think anything. But the police have to keep all options open."

She lit another cigarette. Her hand was shaking.

"I don't understand why nobody's told me this before now," she said. "Why haven't I heard that my father was a Nazi, nor about that woman?"

"They'd have told you sooner or later. A murder investigation can sometimes take a long time. Now they have two dead men for whom they have to find a murderer. Plus a vanished dog."

"I was told the dog was dead?"

"That was your father's dog, but now Abraham Andersson's dog has gone missing."

She gave a shudder, as if she were starting to feel cold.

"I want to get away from here," she said. "Even more than before. I'll get round to reading that diary eventually, but first I must see to the funeral. Then I'll be off. And I'll have to get used to the idea that not only did my father merely pretend to care about me, he was also a Nazi."

"What'll happen to the house?"

"I've spoken to an estate agent. Once the estate inventory has been drawn up it will be sold. That's if anybody will have it."

"Have you been there?"

She nodded. "I went there, in spite of everything. It was worse than I could ever have imagined. Most especially those footprints."

Lindman looked at his watch. He ought to leave now, before it was too late.

"I'm sorry you're leaving."

"Why?"

"I'm not used to being all by myself in a little hotel in the back of beyond. I wonder what it's like to live here."

"Your father chose to do so."

She accompanied him out into reception.

"Thank you for making the effort," she said.

Before leaving, Lindman phoned Larsson to hear whether they'd found the dog. He heard that Näsblom had tagged on behind the excited dog for half an hour through the forest, but the trail had disappeared on a dirt track somewhere in the middle.

"Somebody will have picked it up in a car that was waiting there," Larsson said. "But who? And where did they go?"

He drove south, over the river and into the forest. Occasionally he would ease back on the accelerator when he realised he was driving too fast. His head was empty. The only thought that arose sporadically in his mind was what had happened to Andersson's dog. Shortly after midnight he stopped at a hot dog stall in Mora that was just shutting up shop. When he'd finished eating, he felt too tired to go any further. He drove into the nearby car park and curled up on the back seat. When he woke up his watch said 3 a.m. He went out into the dark for a pee. Then he continued driving south through the night. After a few hours he stopped again to sleep.

By the time he woke up it was 9 a.m. He walked round and round the car to stretch his legs. He would be home in Borås by nightfall. When he'd come as far as Jönköping, he would phone Elena and give her a surprise. An hour or so later, he'd be pulling up outside her house.

But after passing Örebro, he turned off again. His mind was clearer now, and he'd started thinking back to his conversation with Veronica Molin the night before. She hadn't been telling the truth.

There was that business about her father. If she'd known he was a Nazi or not. She had only pretended to be surprised. She'd known, but tried to hide the fact. He couldn't put his finger on how he knew she wasn't telling the truth. And there was another question he couldn't answer either: Had she known about Berggren, for all that she claimed she hadn't?

Lindman pulled up and got out of the car. This has nothing to do with me, he thought: I have my illness to worry about. I'll go back to Borås and admit that I've been missing Elena all the time I've been away. Then, when I feel like it, I'll phone Larsson and ask how the case is going. That's all.

Then he made up his mind to go to Kalmar. Where Molin had been born, under the name of Mattson-Herzén. That's where it had all begun, in a family that had been adherents of Hitler and National Socialism. There should be a man there by the name of Wetterstedt. A portrait painter. Who knew Molin.

He rummaged around in the boot and came up with a tattered map of Sweden. This is madness, he thought; even so, he worked out the best route to Kalmar. I'm supposed to be going to Borås. But he knew he couldn't let go now. He wanted to know what had happened to Molin. And Andersson. Perhaps also what lay behind the disappearance of the dog.

He reached Kalmar by evening. It was November 6. In two weeks time he would have started his radiotherapy. It had started raining a few miles north of Västervik. The water glistened in the beam from his headlights as he drove into the town and looked about for somewhere to stay.

CHAPTER 18

Early the following day Lindman walked down to the sea. He could just make out the Öland bridge through the fog that had settled over the Kalmarsund. He went to the water's edge and stood contemplating the sea as it lapped against the shore. The long car journey was still taking its toll on his body. Twice he'd dreamt that big lorries were heading straight for him. He'd tried to get out of the way, but it had been too late and he'd woken up. His hotel was in the middle of town. The walls were like cardboard, and he'd been forced to listen to a woman nattering away on the phone. After an hour of that, he'd felt justified in thumping on the wall – soon afterwards the conversation came to an end. Before dropping off to sleep, he'd lain in bed and stared up at the ceiling, wondering why he'd come to Kalmar. Could it be that he was trying to put off his return to Borås for as long as possible? Had he grown tired of being with Elena but didn't want to admit it? He didn't know, but he was not sure that his detour to Kalmar was exclusively due to curiosity about Herbert Molin's past.

The forests of Härjedalen were already a part of his own past. All that mattered now was himself, his illness and the 13 days remaining until he was due to start his therapy. Nothing else had any importance. Stefan Lindman's 13 days in November. How will I look back on them ten or 20 years from now, always assuming I live that long? He tried to avoid answering the question, and wandered back towards town, leaving the water and the fog behind him. He found a café, went in, ordered a cup of coffee and borrowed a telephone directory.

There was only one Wetterstedt in the Kalmar district. Emil Wetterstedt, artist. He lived in Lagmansgatan. Lindman turned the pages until he found a map of the area: he located the street straight-away. In the centre of town, only a couple of blocks from the café. He took out his mobile phone – then he remembered that it didn't work. If I can get hold of a new battery, I should be able to use it again, he thought. Or I could go to his flat. Ring the doorbell. But what would I say? That I was a friend of Herbert Molin's? That would be a lie: we were never friends. We worked together at the same police station in the same police district. We once went looking for a murderer together. That's all. He gave me some useful advice now and then, but whether that advice really was as good as I'm claiming it to be, I can't possibly say. I can hardly arrive and announce that I've come to have my portrait painted. Another thing: Wetterstedt is no doubt an old man, about the same age as Molin. An old man who doesn't much care about the world any longer.

He kept sipping at his coffee. When he'd finished working his way through his ideas one by one, he'd ring Wetterstedt's doorbell, say that he was a policeman and say that he would like to talk to him about Herbert Molin. What happened next would depend on how Wetterstedt reacted.

He drained his cup and left the café. The air felt different from the air he'd been breathing in Härjedalen. It had felt dry up there, whereas the air he was breathing now was damp. All the shops were still closed, but as he walked to the house where Wetterstedt lived, he saw one that sold mobile phones. Perhaps the old portrait painter was a late riser.

The block of flats in Lagmansgatan was three storeys high, with a grey façade. No balconies. The front door was unlocked. From the names next to the bells, he saw that Wetterstedt lived on the top floor. There was no lift. The old man must have strong legs, he thought. A door slammed somewhere. It echoed through the stairwell. By the time he reached the top of the three flights he was out of breath. He was surprised that his condition seemed to have so deteriorated.

He rang the bell and counted silently to 20. Then he rang again. He couldn't hear any ringing noise inside the flat. He rang a third time. Still no reply. He knocked on the door, waited, then hammered on it really hard. The door behind him opened. In the doorway was an elderly man in a dressing gown.

"I'm looking for herr Wetterstedt," Lindman said. "It seems he's not at home."

"He spends the autumn at his summer place. That's when he takes his holidays."

The man in the doorway looked at Lindman with an expression of utter contempt. As if it was the most natural thing in the world to take a holiday in November. And that a pensioner still had a job to take a holiday from.

"Where is his summer place?"

"Who are you? We like to keep an eye on people who come sauntering about this building. Are you going to commission a portrait?"

"I want to speak to him about an urgent matter."

The man eyed Lindman up and down.

"Emil's summer place is on Öland. In the south of the island. When you've gone past Alvaret you see a sign that says Lavender. And another sign informing you that it's a private road. That's where he lives."

"Is that the name of the house? Lavender?"

"Emil talks about a shade of blue tending towards lavender. In his opinion it's the most beautiful shade of blue there is. Impossible for a painter to reproduce. Only nature can create it."

"Thank you for your help."

"You're welcome."

Lindman started for the stairs, but stopped.

"Just one more thing. How old is herr Wetterstedt?"

"He's 88, but he's pretty spry."

The man closed his door. Lindman walked slowly down the stairs. So, I have a reason to cross over the bridge, into the fog, he thought. I, too, am on a sort of involuntary holiday, with no aim other than filling in time until November 19.

He went back the way he'd come. The shop selling mobile phones was open. A young man yawned and diffidently produced a battery that fitted Lindman's mobile. He paid, and even as he did so the phone bleeped to indicate that he had messages. Before leaving Kalmar, he sat in his car and listened to them. Elena had called three times, sounding increasingly resigned and curt. There was a message from his dentist, reminding him it was time for his annual check-up. That was all. Larsson hadn't phoned. Lindman hadn't really expected him to, although he'd hoped he would. None of his colleagues had tried to contact him, but he hadn't expected that either. He had virtually no close friends.

He put the phone on the passenger seat, drove out of the car park and started looking for a road leading to the bridge. The fog was thick as he drove over the water. Perhaps this is what it's like to die, he thought. In the old days people imagined a ferryman coming with a boat to row you over the River Styx. Now it might be a bridge you have to cross, into the fog, and then oblivion.

He came to Öland, turned right, passed some sort of zoo and continued southwards. He drove slowly. Very few cars were coming in the opposite direction. He could see no countryside, only fog. At one point he stopped in a lay-by and got out. He heard a foghorn sounding in the distance and what may have been the sound of waves. Apart from that, it was silent. It felt as if the fog had seeped into his head and blanketed his mind. He held one hand in front of his face. It, too, was white.

He drove on, and almost missed the sign for "Lavender 2". It reminded him of another sign he'd been looking for recently, "Dunkärret 2". Sweden is a country where people live two kilometres from the main road, he thought.

The dirt road he turned into was full of potholes and evidently little used. It was dead straight, and disappeared into the fog. Eventually he came to a closed gate. On the other side was an ancient Volvo 444 and a motorcycle. Lindman switched off his engine and clambered out. The bike was a Harley-Davidson. Lindman knew a bit about motorbikes, thanks to the time when he'd chauffeured the motocross buff around Sweden. This wasn't one of the standard Harley-Davidson models. It was a home-made one-off, a valuable specimen. But did a man aged 88 really drive around on a Harley-Davidson? He'd have to be very fit to manage that. Lindman opened the gate and continued along the path. There was still no sign of a house. A figure emerged from the mist, walking towards him. A young man with close-cropped hair, nattily dressed in a leather jacket and a light-blue open-necked shirt. Obviously he had been working on his fitness.

"What are you doing here?" The voice was shrill, almost a shriek.

"I'm looking for Emil Wetterstedt."

"Why?"

"I want to talk to him."

"Who are you? What makes you think he wants to talk to you?"

Lindman bristled at the cross-examination. The youth's voice was hurting his eardrums.

"I want to talk to him about Herbert Molin. Perhaps I should mention that I'm a police officer."

The boy stared at him. His jaws worked away at a wad of chewing gum. "Wait here," he said. "Don't shift from this spot."

He was swallowed up by the fog. Lindman followed him, slowly. After only a few metres a house came into view. The boy disappeared through the front door. It was a whitewashed house, long and narrow, with a wing jutting out from one of the gable ends. Lindman waited. He wondered what the countryside was like here, how far it was from the sea. The door opened again and the boy approached.

"I thought I told you to stay put!" he shrieked in that shrill voice of his.

"You can't always have what you want, sonny," Lindman said. "Is he going to receive me, or isn't he?"

The boy gestured to Lindman that he should follow him. There was a smell of paint in the house. All the lights were on. Lindman had to bow his head when he entered through the door. The boy showed him into a room at the back of the house. One of the long walls was a picture window.

Emil Wetterstedt was sitting in an armchair in a corner. He had a blanket over his knees, and on a table next to his chair was a pile of books and a pair of glasses. The boy positioned himself behind the armchair. The old man had thin white hair and a wrinkled face, but the eyes he directed at Lindman were very bright.

"I don't like being disturbed when I'm on holiday," he said.

His voice was the very opposite of the boy's. Wetterstedt spoke very softly.

"I shan't take much of your time."

"I don't accept commissions for portraits any more. In any case, your face is too round to inspire me. I prefer longer, thinner faces."

"I haven't come here to ask you to paint my portrait."

Wetterstedt shifted his position. The blanket over his legs fell to the floor. The boy darted forward to put it back.

"Why have you come, then?"

"My name's Stefan Lindman. I'm a police officer. I spent some years working alongside Herbert Molin in Borås. I don't know if you've been informed that he's dead."

"I have been told that he's dead. Do you know who did it?"

"Not yet."

Wetterstedt gestured towards a chair. Somewhat reluctantly, the boy moved it into place.

"Who told you that Molin was dead?"

"Does it matter?"

"No."

"Is this an interrogation?"

"No. Just a chat."

"I'm too old for chats. I gave that up when I reached 60. I'd done enough talking in my life by then. Nowadays I neither speak, nor listen to what anybody else has to say. Apart from my doctor. And a few young people."

He smiled, and nodded at the boy standing guard behind his chair. Lindman started to wonder what was going on. Who was this boy, whose assignment seemed to be to keep guard over the old man?

"You say you've come here to talk to me about Herbert Molin. What do you want to know? And come to that, what really happened? Was Herbert murdered, can that be right?"

Lindman decided to get straight to the point. As far as Wetterstedt was concerned, it didn't matter that Lindman was not officially connected to the murder investigation.

"We don't have any specific clues pointing either to a motive or to a killer," he said. "That means we have to dig deep. Who was Herbert Molin? Can we find a motive hidden in his past? Those are the sort of questions we're asking ourselves, and others. People who knew him."

Wetterstedt did not react. The boy made no secret of his dislike of Lindman.

"It was actually Herbert's father I knew. I was younger than he was, but older than Herbert."

"And Axel Mattson-Herzén was a Captain in the Cavalry?"

"An honourable rank that ran in the family. One of his ancestors fought in the battle of Narva. The Swedes won, but the forefather fell. That tragedy gave rise to a family tradition. Every year, they celebrated the victory at Narva. I remember the family had a big bust of King Karl XII on a table. There were always fresh flowers in a vase next to it. I still remember that clearly."

192

"You were not related?"

"Not directly. But I did have a brother who also got into hot water because of all this."

"The Minister of Justice?"

"Just so. I always advised him against going in for politics. Especially as his views were way out."

"He was a Social Democrat."

Wetterstedt looked Lindman in the eye. "I said his views were way out. Perhaps you know that he was murdered by a madman. They found his body on a beach somewhere near Ystad. I never had any truck with him. We had no contact at all for the last 20 years of his life."

"Was there any other bust on that table? Alongside the one of Karl XII?"

"What do you mean? Who?"

"Hitler."

The boy standing behind the chair came to life. It was a momentary reaction, but Lindman noticed. Wetterstedt remained calm.

"What are you trying to suggest?"

"Molin volunteered to fight in Hitler's army during the war. We've also discovered that his family were Nazis. Is that right?"

Wetterstedt responded without hesitation. "Of course it's right. I, too, was a Nazi," he said. "We don't need to play games, herr Policeman. How much do you know about my past?"

"Only that you were a portrait painter, and were in contact with Molin."

"I was very fond of him. He displayed great courage during the war. Everybody with a grain of common sense sided with Hitler. The choice was between watching the relentless advance of Communism, or putting up some resistance. We had a government in Sweden we could trust only so far. Everything was set up."

"Set up for what?"

"For a German invasion." It was the boy who answered. Lindman looked at him in astonishment.

"But not everything was in vain," Wetterstedt said. "I'll soon have painted my last portrait and be gone, but there's a younger generation that applies common sense to what is going on in Sweden, in Europe, indeed in the world at large. We can be happy that Eastern Europe has collapsed. Not a pretty sight, but uplifting even so. On the other hand, the situation here in Sweden is worse than ever. Everything going to the dogs. No discipline. We don't have borders any more. Anybody can get in wherever they like, whenever they like, no matter what their motives. I fear the national character of Sweden has been lost for ever. Nevertheless, one has to keep plugging away."

Wetterstedt paused and turned to Lindman with a smile.

"As you have seen, I stand up for my opinions. I've never attempted to conceal them, nor ever had any regrets. Obviously, there have been folk who've preferred not to acknowledge me in the street, and some who have even spat at me. But they were insignificant beings. My brother, for instance. I've never been short of commissions for portraits. Rather to the contrary, in fact."

"What do you mean by that?"

"That there has never been a shortage of people in this country of ours who have respected me for standing up for my opinions. People with the same views as mine, but who have preferred not to make their opinions public, for various reasons. I could understand them, at times. At others, I've thought they were cowards. But I've painted their portraits, even so."

Wetterstedt indicated that he wanted to stand up. The boy moved smartly to assist him, and gave him a walking stick. Lindman wondered how Wetterstedt coped with the stairs at his flat in Kalmar.

"There's something I'd like to show you."

They went out into the corridor, paved with stone flags. Wetterstedt paused and looked at Lindman.

"Did you say your name was Lindman?"

"Stefan Lindman."

"If I'm not much mistaken, your accent suggests you come from Västergötland?"

"I was born in Kinna, not far from Borås."

Wetterstedt nodded thoughtfully. "I've never been to Kinna," he said. "I've been through Borås. But I feel most at home on Öland or in Kalmar. I've never understood why folk want to travel around so much." Wetterstedt tapped his walking stick hard on the floor.

It occurred to Lindman that only a few days earlier he'd heard another old man, Björn Wigren, say something similar about not wanting to travel. They kept on until they came to a room with no furniture at all. There was a curtain on one of the walls. Wetterstedt moved it to one side with his walking stick. Behind it were three oil paintings in oval, gilded frames. The one in the middle was of Hitler, in profile. On the left was a portrait of Goering, and on the right one of a woman.

"This is where I keep my gods," Wetterstedt said. "I painted this one of Hitler in 1944, when everybody, including his generals, had started to turn their backs on him. This is the only portrait I've ever painted exclusively from photographs."

"So you actually met Goering?"

"In Sweden and in Berlin as well. For some time in the inter-war years he was married to a Swede by the name of Karin. I met him then. In May 1941 I was called by the German Legation in Stockholm. Goering wanted to have his portrait painted, and I'd been chosen to do it. That was a great honour. I'd painted Karin, and he'd been pleased with that. So I went to Berlin and did a portrait of him. He was very kind. On one occasion it was the intention that I should meet Hitler at some reception or other, but something cropped up and got in the way. That is the biggest regret of my life. I was so close, but in fact I never got near enough to shake his hand."

"Who's the woman?"

"My wife. Teresa. I painted her portrait the year we married, 1943. If you have eyes to see, you'll appreciate that the picture is full of love. We had ten years together. She died of an inflamed heart muscle. If that had happened today, she'd have survived."

Wetterstedt signalled to the boy, who drew the curtain shut. They returned to the studio.

"Now you know who I am," Wetterstedt said, having settled in the armchair again, and had the blanket spread over his knees. The boy had resumed his position behind the old man.

"You must have had some reaction to the news that Herbert Molin was dead. A retired police officer, murdered in the forests of Härjedalen. You must have wondered what happened?"

"I thought it had to be the work of a madman, obviously. Perhaps one of the many criminals who enter Sweden and commit crimes they are never punished for."

Lindman was getting impatient with the views that Wetterstedt kept expressing.

"It was no madman. The murder was carefully planned."

"Then I really don't know."

The answer came quickly and firmly. A little too quickly, Lindman thought. Too quickly and too firmly. He continued his line of questioning, cautiously.

"Something might have happened a long way in the past, something that took place during the war, for example."

"Such as?"

"That's what I'm asking."

"Herbert Molin was a soldier. Full stop. He would have told me if anything exceptional had happened. But he never did."

"Did you meet often?"

"We haven't met at all for the last 30 years. We kept in touch through letters. He wrote letters, and I replied with picture postcards. I've never liked letters. Neither receiving them nor writing them."

"Did he ever mention that he was scared?"

Wetterstedt drummed his fingers in irritation on his armrest.

"Of course he was scared. Just as I am scared. Scared at what's happening to this country of ours."

"But there wasn't anything else he was frightened of? Something to do with him, personally?"

"What could that have been? He chose to conceal his political identity. I can understand that, but I don't think he was afraid of being exposed. He wasn't fearful of papers landing up in the wrong hands."

The boy coughed and Wetterstedt shut up immediately. He's said too much, Lindman thought. The boy is his minder.

"What papers are you referring to?"

Wetterstedt shook his head in vexation. "There are so many papers in the world nowadays," he said, avoiding the question. Lindman waited for more, but nothing came. Wetterstedt started drumming his fingers on the armrest again.

"I'm an old man. Conversations tire me. I live in an extended twilight zone. I don't expect anything. I'd like you to leave now, and leave me in peace."

The boy behind the chair grinned cheekily. It was clear to Lindman that most of the questions he had would be unanswered. The audience granted him by Wetterstedt was at an end.

"Magnus will see you out," Wetterstedt said. "You don't need to shake hands. I'm more frightened of bacteria than I am of people."

The boy whose name was Magnus opened the front door. The thick layer of fog was still enveloping the landscape.

"How far is it to the sea?" Lindman said, as they walked to the car.

"That's not a question I'm required to answer, is it?"

Lindman stopped in his tracks. He could feel the anger rising inside him.

"I always thought that little Swedish Nazis had shaven heads and Doc Marten boots. I now realise they can look exactly like normal people. You, for example."

The boy smiled. "Emil has taught me how to deal with provocation."

"Just what are your fantasies? That there's a future for Nazism in Sweden? Are you going to hunt down every immigrant that sets foot in Sweden? That would mean kicking out several million Swedes. Nazism is dead, it died with Hitler. Just what do you think you're doing? Licking an old man's arse? A man who had the doubtful privilege of shaking Goering by the hand? What do you think he can teach you?"

They'd come to the car and the motorbike. Lindman was so angry, he'd broken out into a sweat.

"What do you think he can teach you?" he asked again.

"Not to make the same mistake as they made. Not to lose faith. Now clear off."

Lindman turned his car and drove away. In his rear-view mirror he saw the boy watching him.

He drove slowly back to the bridge, thinking over what Wetterstedt had said. He could be dismissed as a political idiot. His views were not dangerous any more. They were but vague memories of a terrible time that was history. He was an old man who'd chosen never to understand, just like Molin and Berggren. The boy Magnus was another kettle of fish. He plainly believed that Nazi doctrines were still very much alive.

Lindman reached the bridge. He was about to cross it when his mobile rang. He pulled into the side, switched on his warning lights, and answered.

"Giuseppe here. Are you back in Borås yet?"

Lindman wondered if he ought to say something about his meeting with Wetterstedt, but decided to say nothing for the time being.

"I'm nearly there. The weather's been pretty awful."

"I wanted to phone you to say that we've found the dog."

"Where?"

"Somewhere we'd never have guessed."

"Where?"

"Guess."

Lindman tried to think. But he couldn't raise a thought.

"I don't know."

"In Molin's dog pen."

"Are you saying it was dead?"

"No, as lively as they come. A bit short of food, though."

Larsson laughed, merrily, at the other end of the line. "Somebody collects Andersson's dog during the night, and our men on duty are so tired they don't notice anything. Then whoever was responsible for kidnapping this dog dumps the animal in Molin's pen. Mind you, it wasn't tied to the line. What have you to say to that?"

"That there is somebody not a thousand miles away from where you are who's trying to tell you something."

"Quite right. The question is: what? The dog is a message. A sort of bottle thrown into the sea with a note inside it. But what? To whom? Think about that, and get back to me. I'm going home to Östersund now."

"It's pretty remarkable."

"I'll say it's pretty remarkable. And frightening. Now I'm convinced that what we've got to so far is just the tip of an iceberg."

"And you still think you're looking for the same murderer?"

"Yes, that's for sure. Keep in touch. And drive carefully!"

There was a crackling noise in the telephone, then it went dead. A car passed. Then another. I'm going home now, he thought. Emil Wetterstedt had nothing new to tell me. But he did confirm what I already knew. Molin was a Nazi who never reformed. One of the incurables.

He drove onto the bridge, intending to go back home to Borås, and before he reached the mainland, he had changed his mind.

CHAPTER 19

He dreamt that he was walking through the forest to Molin's house. The wind was blowing so hard that he could scarcely keep his balance. He had an axe in his hand and was frightened of something behind him. When he came to the house he stopped at the dog pen. The strong wind had dropped altogether, as if somebody had snipped through a sound tape in his dream. In the pen were two dogs, both hurling themselves in a frenzy at the wire netting.

He gave a start and was jerked out of his dream. It wasn't the dogs breaking through the wire netting, but a woman standing in front of him, tapping him on the shoulder.

"We don't like people to be asleep in here," she said sternly. "This is a library, not a sun lounge."

"I'm very sorry."

Lindman looked dozily round the reading room. An elderly man with a turned-up moustache was reading *Punch*. He looked like a caricature of a British gentleman. He was glaring disapprovingly at Lindman. Lindman pulled towards him the book he had fallen asleep over, and checked his watch. 6.15. How long had he been asleep? Ten minutes, perhaps, surely not more. He shook his head, forced the dogs out of his mind and pored over the book again.

He had made up his mind coming back over the bridge. He would make a nocturnal visit to Wetterstedt's flat. He couldn't bear the thought of another night at the hotel, though. He would simply wait until night fell, then go into the flat. Until then, all he could do was wait. He parked his car within walking distance of Lagmansgatan, and found an ironmonger's, where he'd bought a screwdriver and the smallest jemmy he could find. Then he'd picked out a cheap pair of gloves at a gents' outfitters. He wandered around the town until he felt hungry, ate at a pizzeria and read the local newspaper, the *Barometer*. After two cups of coffee he'd tried to make up his mind whether to go back to his car and sleep for an hour or two, or to continue his walk. Then it occurred to him that he would do well to go to the local library. He'd asked for assistance, and in the section devoted to history he'd found what he was looking for. A fat volume on the history of German Nazism, and a thinner book on the Hitler period in Sweden. He soon discarded the big tome, but the smaller one had captured his attention.

It was lucidly written, and after less than an hour's reading he realised something that he hadn't grasped before. Something Wetterstedt had said, and maybe also Berggren: that in the '30s and up to around 1943 or 1944, Nazism had been much more widespread in Sweden than most people nowadays were aware of. There had been various branches of Nazi parties that squabbled between themselves, but behind the men and women in the parades there had been a grey mass of anonymous people who had admired Hitler and would have liked nothing more than a German invasion and the setting up of a Nazi regime in Sweden. He found astonishing information about the government's concessions to the Germans, and how exports of iron ore from Sweden had been crucial in enabling the German munitions industry to satisfy Hitler's constant demand for more tanks and other war materials. He wondered what had happened to all that history when he was a schoolboy. What he vaguely remembered from his history classes was a very different picture: a Sweden that had succeeded – by means of extremely clever policies and by skilfully walking the tightrope – in staying out of the war. The Swedish government had remained strictly neutral and thus saved the country from being crushed by the German military machine. He'd heard nothing about quantities of home-grown Nazis. What he was now discovering was an entirely different picture, one which explained Molin's actions, his delight at crossing the border into Norway and looking forward to going on to Germany. He could envisage young Mattson-Herzén, his father and mother, and Wetterstedt and the grey mass of people hovering between the lines of the text, or in the blurred background of the photographs of demonstrations by Nazis in Swedish streets.

That was when he must have fallen asleep and started dreaming about the frenzied dogs.

The *Punch* man stood up and left the reading room. Two girls, heads almost touching, sat whispering and giggling. Lindman guessed that they probably came from the Middle East. That made him think about what he'd been reading: about how Uppsala students had protested against Jewish doctors who'd been persecuted in Germany seeking asylum in Sweden. They had been refused entry.

He went downstairs to the issuing counter. There was no sign of the woman who'd woken him up. He found a toilet, and washed his face in cold water. Then he returned to the reading room. The giggling girls had left. There was a newspaper lying on the table where they'd been sitting. He went to investigate what they'd been reading. It was in Arabic script. They'd left behind a faint perfume. It reminded him that he ought to phone Elena. Then he sat down to read the last chapter, "Nazism in Sweden after the war." He read about all the factions and various more or less clumsily organised attempts to set up a Swedish Nazi party that would carry real political weight. Behind all those small groups and local organisations that kept coming and going, changing their names and symbolically scratching one another's eyes out, he could still sense the grey mass assembling at the blurred periphery. They had nothing to do with the little neo-Nazi boys with shaven heads. They were not the ones who robbed banks, murdered police officers or beat up innocent immigrants. He was clear about the difference between them and the weirdos who demonstrated in the streets and shouted the praises of Karl XII.

He put the book to one side, and wondered where the boy who kept watch over Wetterstedt fitted in. Was there in fact some kind of organisation that nobody knew about, where the likes of Molin, Berggren and Wetterstedt could make propaganda for their views? A secret room where a new generation, to which the boy standing behind Wetterstedt's chair belonged, could be admitted? He thought about what Wetterstedt had said, about "papers landing up in the wrong hands". The boy had reacted, and Wetterstedt had clammed up immediately.

He returned the books to their places on the shelves. It was dark when he left the library. He went to his car and phoned Elena. He couldn't put it off any longer. She sounded pleased when she heard his voice, but also cautious.

"Where are you?" she said.

"I'm on my way."

"Why is it taking so long?"

"Troubles with the car."

"What kind of troubles?"

"Something to do with the gear box. I'll be back by tomorrow."

"Why do you sound so irritable?"

"I'm tired."

"How are you feeling?"

"I haven't the strength to go into that now. I just wanted to ring and tell you that I was on my way."

"You must realise that I am worried."

"I'll be in Borås tomorrow, I promise."

"Can't you tell me why you sound so irritable?"

"I've already said that I'm tired."

"Don't drive too fast."

"I never do."

"You always do."

The connection was cut off. Lindman sighed, but made no attempt to phone again. He switched his mobile off. The clock on the dashboard suggested it was 7.25 p.m. He wouldn't dare to break into Wetterstedt's flat before midnight. I ought to go home, he thought. What will happen if I'm caught? I'll be sacked and disgraced. A police officer breaking into a property is not something a prosecutor would turn a blind eye to. I wouldn't only be putting my own future on the line, I'd be creating trouble for all my colleagues. Larsson would think he'd been visited by a lunatic. Olausson in Borås would never be able to laugh again.

He wondered if what he really wanted was to be caught. If he was intent on an act of self-destruction. He had cancer, and so he had nothing to lose. Was that the way it was? He didn't know. He drew his jacket closer around him, and closed his eyes.

When he woke up it was 8.30. He hadn't dreamt about the dogs again. Again he tried to convince himself that he should get out of Kalmar as quickly as possible. But in vain.

The last lights in the windows of the flats in Lagmansgatan went out. Lindman stood in the shadows under a tree, looking up at the façade of the block of flats. It had started raining and a wind was getting up. He hurried across the street and tried the front door. To his surprise, it was still open. He slipped into the dark entrance hall and listened. He had his tools in his pocket. He switched on his torch and crept up the stairs to the top floor. He shone his torch onto the door of Wetterstedt's flat. He'd remembered correctly. Earlier in the day when he'd been waiting for somebody to answer the door, he'd noticed the locks. There were two, but neither of them was a safety lock. That surprised him. Shouldn't a man like Wetterstedt take as many safety precautions as possible? If Lindman's luck was out, it would be fitted with an alarm, but that was a risk he would have to take.

He pushed the letter box open and listened. He couldn't be absolutely certain that there was nobody in the flat. It was all quiet. He took out the jemmy. The torch was small enough for him to hold in his teeth. He knew he could only make one attempt. If he didn't manage to open the door straightaway he would have to leave. In the first few months of his police career he had learnt the basic techniques used by burglars to force open a door. Just one try, no more. One single unexpected noise would generally pass unnoticed, but if it happened again there was a serious risk that somebody would hear and become suspicious. He crouched down, put the jemmy on the floor and pushed the screwdriver as far into the crack between the door and the frame as it would go. He prised it back and forth, and the crack widened. He pressed the screwdriver further in, then pulled it up as far as the lower of the two locks. He picked up the jemmy and forced it in at a point between the two locks, and pressed his knee against the screwdriver to widen the opening as far as possible. He was starting to sweat from the effort. He still wasn't satisfied. If he forced it now there was a risk that only the frame would split and the locks would hold fast. He pressed hard against the screwdriver once more and this time managed to push the jemmy further in between the door and the frame. He got his breath back before testing the jemmy again. It was impossible to push it any further in.

He wiped his brow. Then he forced the jemmy with all his might, simultaneously pressing hard against the screwdriver with his knee. The door gave way. The only noise was a creaking and the thud of the screwdriver landing on his shoe. He switched off his torch and listened, ready to flee if necessary. Nothing happened. He opened the door carefully and pulled it to behind him. There was a stuffy, closed-in smell in the flat. He had a vague feeling that it reminded him of his aunt's house near Värnamo, where he'd been to visit her several times as a child. A smell of old furniture. He switched on his torch, careful not to point it at a window. He had no plan and didn't know what he was looking for. If he'd been an ordinary burglar it would have been easier. He'd have been looking for objects of value, and trying to find likely hiding places. He examined a pile of newspapers on a table. Nothing suggested that Wetterstedt subscribed to a morning paper that would be delivered in the early hours.

He walked slowly round the flat. It was just three rooms, plus kitchen and bathroom. Unlike the spartan furniture and fittings at the summer cottage, Wetterstedt's town flat was overflowing with furniture. He glanced into the bedroom, then continued to the living room, that evidently also served as a studio. There was an empty easel, and an escritoire against one wall. He opened a drawer.

Old pairs of glasses, packs of playing cards, newspaper cuttings. "The portrait painter Emil Wetterstedt celebrates his 50th birthday." The photograph had faded, but Lindman recognised Wetterstedt's piercing eyes gazing straight at the photographer. The text was full of deference. "The nationally and internationally well-known portrait painter who never left his home town Kalmar, in spite of many chances to establish himself elsewhere . . . Rumours abounded of an offer to settle on the Riviera with famous and rich clients." He returned the cutting, thinking that it wasn't very well written. Wetterstedt had said that he didn't like writing letters, only brief messages on postcards. Perhaps he'd written the newspaper text himself, and it had turned out so badly because he wasn't used to writing. Lindman searched through the drawers. He still didn't know what he was looking for. He moved on to the third room, a study, and went to the desk. The curtains were drawn. He took off his jacket and hung it over the desk lamp before switching it on.

There were two piles of paper on the desk. He looked through the first one. It consisted of bills, and brochures from Tuscany and Provence. He wondered if Wetterstedt in fact enjoyed travelling, despite claiming not to. He replaced the pile, and drew the second one towards him. It was mainly crossword puzzles, torn out of newspapers. They were all solved, with no crossings out or alterations. He might not care for letter-writing, but he knew his words.

At the bottom of the pile was an envelope, already opened. He took out an invitation card printed in a typeface reminiscent of rune stones. It was a reminder. "On November 30 we meet as usual at 1300 hours in the Great Hall. After lunch, reminiscences and music, there will be a lecture given by our comrade, Captain Akan Forbes, on the subject of his years fighting to keep Southern Rhodesia white. This will be followed by our A.G.M." It was signed by the "Senior Master of Ceremonies". Lindman looked at the envelope. It was postmarked Hässleholm. He moved the desk lamp closer and read the text again. What exactly was this an invitation to? Where was this Great Hall? He put the card back in its envelope and replaced the pile.

Then he went through the drawers, which were unlocked. All the time he was listening for the slightest noise from the landing. In the bottom left-hand drawer was a brown leather box file. It filled the drawer. Lindman took it out and laid it on the desk. There was a swastika impressed on the leather. He opened it carefully as the side was split. It contained a thick bundle of typewritten sheets. They were carbon copies, not originals. The paper was thin. The text was written on a typewriter with a letter "c" that was slightly higher than the other letters. They seemed to be some kind of accounts. At the top of the first page was a handwritten heading: "Comrades, departed and deceased, who continue to fulfil their commitments". Then followed long lists of names in alphabetical order. In front of every name was a number. Lindman moved carefully on to the next page: another long list of names. He glanced through them without recognising any. They were all Swedish names. He turned to the next page.

Under the letter D, after Karl-Evert Danielsson, the same hand as had written on the first page had noted: "Now deceased. Pledged an annual subscription for 30 years." Annual subscription to what? Lindman wondered. There was no reference to the title of an organisation, just this list of names. He could see that many had died. In some places there was a handwritten note that future subscriptions had been specified in a will, in others that "the estate will pay" or "paid by the son or daughter, no name given". He turned back to the letter

B. There she was, Berggren, Elsa. He turned to the letter M. Sure enough, there was Molin, Herbert. He returned to the beginning. The letter A. No Andersson, Abraham. He moved on to the end. The last name was Öxe, Hans, numbered 1,430.

Lindman closed the file and replaced it in the drawer. Were these the papers Wetterstedt had referred to? A Nazi old comrades association, or a political organisation? He tried to work out what he had stumbled upon. Somebody ought to take a look at this, he thought. It ought to be published. But I can't take the file with me because there would be no way I could have got it without having broken into this flat. He turned off the desk lamp and sat in the dark. The air was heavy with the disgust he was feeling. What stank was not the old carpets or the curtains – it was the list of names. All these living and dead individuals paying their subscriptions, in person or via their trustees, their sons or daughters – to some organisation that declined to reveal its name – 1,430 persons still adhering to a doctrine that ought to have been done away with once and for all. But that wasn't the way it was. Standing behind Wetterstedt had been a boy, a reminder that everything was still very much alive.

He sat there in the dark, making up his mind that it was time for him to set off for home. But something held him back. He took out the file once more, opened it and turned to the letter L. At the bottom of a page was the name "Lennartsson, David. Subscription paid by the wife." He turned the page.

It was like being on the receiving end of a punch, he reflected afterwards, on his way to Borås, driving far too fast through the darkness. He had been totally unprepared. It was as if somebody had crept up on him from behind. But there was no room for doubt. It was his father's name there at the top of the page: "Evert Lindman, deceased, subscriptions pledged for 25 years." There was also the date of his father's death seven years ago; and there was something else that removed any possible doubt. He recalled as clear as day sitting with one of his father's friends, a solicitor, going through the estate. There had been a gift, written into the will a year or so before his father died. It was not a large sum, but striking nevertheless. He had left 15,000 kronor to something calling itself the Strong Sweden Foundation. There was a bank giro number, but no name, no address. Lindman had wondered about that donation, and what kind of a foundation it was. The solicitor assured him that there was no ambiguity, his father had been very firm on the point; Lindman had been devastated by the death of his father, and lacked the strength to think any more about it.

Now, in Wetterstedt's stuffy flat, that donation had caught up with him. He couldn't close his eyes to facts. His father had been a Nazi. One of the type that kept quiet about it, didn't speak openly about their political opinions. It was incomprehensible, but true nevertheless. Lindman now realised why Wetterstedt had asked about his name, and where he came from. He knew something Lindman didn't know: that his own father was among those Wetterstedt admired above all others. Lindman's father had been like Molin and Berggren.

He closed the drawer, pushed back the desk lamp, and noticed that his hand was shaking. Then he checked everything meticulously before leaving the room. It was 1.45 a.m. He needed to get away fast, away from what was hidden in Wetterstedt's desk. He paused in the hall, and listened. Then he opened the door, and went out, shutting it as tightly after him as he could.

At that very moment there came the sound of the front door opening or closing. He stood motionless in the darkness, holding his breath and keeping his ears pricked. No sound of footsteps on the stairs. Someone might be standing down there, hidden in the dark, he thought. He kept on listening, and also checked to make sure he'd remembered to take everything with him. The torch, the screwdriver, the jemmy. All present and correct. He went down one floor, tentatively. The lunacy of the whole undertaking had now hit him like a freezing cold shower. Not only had he committed a pointless break-in, he'd also unearthed a secret he'd infinitely rather not have known anything about.

He paused, listened, and then switched on the staircase lights. He walked down the last two flights to the front door. He looked round when he emerged into the street. No-one. He hugged the wall of the block of flats to the end, then crossed the street. When he reached his car he looked round again, but could see no sign of anybody having followed him. Nevertheless, he was quite sure. He wasn't imagining things. Someone had left the building as he was closing the damaged door to the flat.

He switched on the engine and backed out of his parking place. He didn't see the man in the shadows writing down his registration number.

He drove out of Kalmar, on the Västervik road. There was an all-night café there. An articulated lorry was parked outside. When he went into the café, he noticed the driver immediately, sitting with his head against the wall, sleeping with his mouth open. Nobody here will wake you up, he thought. An all-night café's not like a library.

The woman behind the counter gave him a smile. She had a name badge: she was called Erika. He poured himself a cup of coffee.

"Are you a lorry driver?" she said.

"Afraid not."

"Professional drivers don't need to pay for coffee during the night."

"Maybe I ought to change jobs," he said.

She declined his offer to pay. He took a good look at her and decided she had a pretty face, in spite of the stark light from the fluorescent tubes on the ceiling.

When he sat down, he realised how exhausted he was. He still couldn't come to terms with what he'd found in Wetterstedt's desk drawer. He would have to face up to that later, but not now.

He drank his coffee, decided against a refill. He was in Borås by 9.00, by way of Jönköping. He'd stopped twice and taken a nap. On both occasions he'd been woken by headlights in his face.

He undressed and stretched out on the bed. I got away with it, he thought. Nobody will be able to prove that I broke into Wetterstedt's flat. Nobody saw me. Before going to sleep, he tried to work out how many days he'd been away. He couldn't make it add up. Nothing added up.

He closed his eyes and thought about the woman who hadn't charged him for his coffee. He had already forgotten her name.

CHAPTER 20

He had disposed of the tools on the road home, but when he woke up after a few hours of restless sleep, he began to wonder if he'd only imagined it. The first thing he did was to go through his pockets. No sign of the tools. Somewhere not far from Jönköping, at the coldest and darkest time of the night, he had stopped for a sleep. Before driving away from the lay-by, he'd buried the jemmy and the screwdriver under the moss. He remembered exactly what he'd done, but even so, he couldn't help wondering. He seemed to be unsure of everything now.

He stood in the window, looking down over Allégatan. He could hear fru Håkansson playing the piano in the flat downstairs. This was a regular occurrence, every day except Sunday. She played the piano from 11.15 to 12.15. Always the same piece, over and over again. There was a detective inspector at the police station who was interested in classical music. Once, Lindman had tried to hum the tune for him, and the inspector had said without hesitation that it was Chopin. Lindman had later bought a record containing that particular mazurka. For some time when he was working nights and sleeping during the day he would try to put the record on simultaneously with fru Håkansson's playing, but he had never managed to get the two versions synchronised.

She was playing now. In my chaotic world, she's the only thing that is unchanging, he thought. He looked into the street. The self-discipline he had hitherto taken for granted didn't exist any longer. It had been sheer idiocy to break into Wetterstedt's flat. Even if he'd left no trace behind, even if he'd taken nothing other than a piece of knowledge he would have preferred to be without.

He finished his breakfast and collected the dirty washing he was going to take to Elena's. There was a laundry room in the basement of the flats where he lived, but he hardly ever used it. Then he fetched a photo album he kept in a bureau, and sat with it on the living-room sofa. His mother had collected the pictures and given him the album as a 21st birthday present. He remembered how, when he was very small, his father had taken photographs with a box camera. Then he'd bought more modern models, and the last pictures in the book had been taken by a Minolta SLR camera. It had always been his father taking the pictures, never his mother, although he'd used the self-timer whenever practical. Lindman studied the pictures, his mother on the left and his father on the right. There was always a hint of stress in his father's face, as if he had only just come into the picture before it was taken. It often went wrong. Lindman remembered once when there was only one exposure left on the film and his father had stumbled as he hurried away from the camera. He leafed through the album. There were his sisters side by side, and his mother staring straight at the lens.

What do my sisters know about their father's political views? Presumably nothing. What did my mother know? And could she have shared his opinions?

He started again and worked his way slowly through the album, one picture at a time.

1969, he's seven. His first day at school. Colours starting to fade. He remembered how proud he was of his new, dark-blue blazer.

1971, he's nine. It's summer. They've gone to Varberg, and rented a little cottage on the island of Getterön. Bath towels among the rocks, a transistor radio. He could even remember the music being played when the picture was taken: "Sail along, silvery moon". He remembered because his father had said what it was called just before pressing the self-timer. It was idyllic there among the rocks, his father, mother, himself and his two teenaged sisters. The sun was bright, the shadows solid, and the colours faded, as usual.

Pictures only show the surface, he thought. Something quite different was going on underneath. I had a father who led a double life. Perhaps there were other families in cottages on Getterön that he would visit and involve in discussions on the Fourth Reich that he must have hoped would come to pass sooner or later. When Lindman was growing up, in the '60s and '70s, there had never been any mention of Nazism. He had a vague memory of classmates at school hissing "Jewish swine" at some unpleasant person who wasn't in fact Jewish at all. There were swastikas drawn on the lavatory walls at school, and the caretaker would be furious and try to scrub them off. Even so, he certainly couldn't recall any symptoms of Nazism.

The pictures slowly brought memories to life. The album was made up of stepping stones that he could jump along. In between were other memories that had not been photographed, but which came to mind even so.

He must have been twelve years old. He'd been hoping for a new bike for ages. His father wasn't mean, but it took some time to convince him that the old one simply wasn't up to it any more. In the end his father gave in, and they drove to Borås.

They had to wait their turn in the shop. Another man was buying a bike for his son. He spoke broken Swedish. It took some time to complete the deal, and the man and the boy went off with the new bicycle. The shop owner was about the same age as Stefan's father. He apologised for the delay.

"Those Yugoslavians. We're lumbered with more and more of 'em."

"What are they doing here?" his father said. "They should be sent back. They've no business to be in Sweden. Haven't we got enough problems with all the Finns? Not to mention the gypsies. We should send the whole lot packing."

Lindman could remember it well. It wasn't a wording made up in retrospect: that was exactly what his father said. And the shop assistant didn't react to the last comment: "We should send the whole lot packing." He might have smiled or nodded, but he didn't say anything. Then they'd bought the bicycle, fixed it to the roof of the car and driven back to Kinna. The memory was crystal clear, but how had he reacted at the time? He'd been full of enthusiasm about the long hoped-for bike. He remembered the smell of the shop – rubber and oil. Nevertheless, he remembered something else he'd felt at the time – not that his father thought the gypsies and Yugoslavs ought to be sent packing, but the fact that his father had expressed an opinion. A political opinion. That was so unusual.

When he was growing up, nothing had ever been discussed among the family apart from insignificant matters. What to have for dinner, whether the lawn needed mowing, what colour they ought to choose for the kitchen table cloth they were going to buy. There was one exception: music. That was something they could talk about.

All his father listened to was old-fashioned jazz. Lindman could still remember the names of some of the musicians his father had tried in vain to persuade him to listen to and admire. King Oliver, the cornet player who had inspired Louis Armstrong. He'd played with a handkerchief over his fingers, so that other trumpeters wouldn't be able to work out how he'd managed to produce his advanced solos. And then there was a clarinettist called Johnny Dodds. And the outstanding Bix Beiderbecke. Time and time again Lindman had been forced to listen to these scratchy old recordings, and he'd pretended to like what he heard. Pretended to be as enthusiastic as his father wanted him to be. If he did that, he might stand a better chance of getting a new ice hockey set, or something else he badly wanted. In reality, he preferred to listen to the same music as his sisters. Often the Beatles, but more usually the Rolling Stones. His father had accepted that as far as music was concerned, his daughters were a lost cause; but he thought that his son might just be saved.

When he was younger, his father had played the music he admired. There was a banjo hanging on the living-room wall. Occasionally he would take it down and play. Just a few chords, no more. It was a Levin with a long neck. A real beauty, his father had insisted, dating from the 1920s. There was also a picture of his father playing in the Bourbon Street Band – drums, base, trumpet, clarinet and trombone. Plus his father on the banjo.

They'd often discussed music at home – but nothing that might fuel his father's furious outbursts that were rare, but real. As Lindman grew up, he was constantly worried about the possibility of his father bursting into a fit of rage.

When they went to Borås to buy a bicycle, his father had expressed an opinion that went a long way beyond deploring the stupidity of listening to pathetic pop music. What he said had to do with people, and their right to exist. "We should send the whole lot packing." The memory grew in Lindman's consciousness as he recalled the incident.

And there was an epilogue.

He'd been sitting in the passenger seat. In the side mirror, he could see the bike handlebars sticking out from the roof.

"Why do gypsies have to be sent packing?" he'd said.

212

"Because they're inadequate, as people," his father had told him. *"They're inferior. They're not like us. If we don't keep Sweden for the Swedes, everything will fall apart."*

He could still hear those words, as clear as a bell. He also remembered feeling worried about what his father had said. Not about what might happen to the gypsies if they hadn't the wit to flee the country. It was more to do with himself. If his father was right, he'd be bound to think the same thing, that the gypsies ought to be sent packing.

His memories drifted away. There was nothing left of the rest of the journey. It was only when they got back home and his mother came out to admire the new bicycle that his memory started to work again.

The telephone rang. He gave a start, put the album down and answered.

"Olausson here. How are you?"

He'd expected to hear Elena's voice. He was instantly on his guard.

"I don't know how I am. I just go through the motions, waiting for the treatment."

"Can you call in at the station? Are you up to it?"

"What about?"

"A minor matter. When can you be here?"

"Five minutes from now."

"Let's say half an hour, then. Come straight up to my office."

Lindman hung up. Olausson hadn't laughed. Kalmar has caught up with me already, he thought. The forced door, the police in Kalmar asking questions, another policeman, a colleague from Borås, paying an unexpected visit. Does he know anything about the break-in? Let's phone our colleagues in Borås and ask.

That's what must have happened. It was nearly 2 p.m. That meant the police in Kalmar would have had time to search the flat and talk to Wetterstedt. He was sweating. He was sure there was nothing to link him to the affair, but he'd have to talk to Olausson without being able to mention anything about the contents of the brown leather box file in the desk drawer.

The telephone rang again. This time it was Elena.

"I thought you were going to come here?"

"I have a few things to see to. Then I'll come."

"What sort of things?"

He was tempted to put down the receiver.

"I have to go to the police station. We can talk later. Bye."

He hadn't the energy to cope with questions just now. It would be hard enough inventing something plausible enough to convince Olausson.

He stood in the window and rehearsed the story he'd made up about his activities the previous day. Then he put on his jacket and headed for the police station.

He paused to greet the girls in reception. Nobody asked him how he was. That convinced him that everybody in the building knew he had cancer. The duty officer, Corneliusson, also came out to the desk for a brief chat. No questions, no cancer, nothing. Lindman took the lift up to Olausson's floor. The door of his office was ajar. He knocked. Olausson shouted "Come!" Every time Lindman entered his room, he wondered what tie he would be faced with. Olausson was notorious for ties with strange patterns and odd colour combinations. Today, however, it was an unremarkable dark blue. Lindman sat down. Olausson burst out laughing.

"We caught a burglar this morning. He must be one of the thickest people alive. You know that radio shop in Österlånggatan, next to the square? He'd broken in through the back door, but he must have been so sweaty that he took his coat off and hung it up. And he forgot it when he left. In one of the pockets was a wallet with his driving licence and some visiting cards. The bastard had his own visiting cards! 'Consultant', godammit. All we had to do was pop round to his address and take him in. He was in bed asleep. Forgotten all about his coat."

Lindman thought he'd better take the initiative when Olausson said nothing more.

"What did you want?"

Olausson picked up some faxed sheets from his desk.

"Just a bagatelle. We received this earlier on from our colleagues in Kalmar."

"I've just come from there, if that's what you were wondering."

"Precisely. I gather you went to see somebody called Wetterstedt on Öland. I seem to recognise that name, incidentally."

"His brother, one-time Minister of Justice, was murdered some years ago in Skåne."

"Ah yes, that's right. What happened?"

"The murderer was a teenager. I remember reading in the paper about a year ago that he committed suicide."

Olausson looked thoughtful.

"Has something happened?" Lindman said.

"Evidently there's been a burglary at Wetterstedt's flat in Kalmar. During the night. One of the neighbours claims you were there yesterday. His description of you corresponds closely to the one Wetterstedt gave the police."

"I was there yesterday morning, trying to find Wetterstedt. An old man in the flat next door told me he was at his summer place on Öland."

Olausson put the fax down. "I knew it."

"Knew what?"

"That there'd be a straightforward explanation."

"Explanation of what? Is somebody suggesting I did the break-in? I found Wetterstedt and spoke to him at his summer cottage."

"They were just asking what you were doing there. That's all"

"Is that all, then?"

"More or less."

"Am I under suspicion?"

"Not at all. You were looking for Wetterstedt, and he wasn't there. Is that it?"

"I thought maybe the bell wasn't working, so I hammered on the door. I also wondered if Wetterstedt might be hard of hearing. He's well over 80, after all. The neighbour heard me rapping on the door."

"And then you went to Öland?"

"Yes."

"Then you drove home."

"Not straightaway. I didn't leave until evening. I spent a few hours in the library, then I stopped for an hour or two near Jönköping to get some sleep, in the car. Let's face it, if I'd intended going back that night and breaking into the flat, I'd hardly have attracted attention to myself by belting on the door, would I?"

"I imagine not."

215

Olausson was retreating now. Lindman had managed to steer the conversation his way. Nevertheless, he was worried. Someone might have seen his car. And there was that business with the front door opening as he was about to leave the flat.

"Obviously, nobody for a minute thinks that you broke into the flat. We want to answer our colleagues' questions as soon as possible, that's all."

"Well, I've answered them."

"You didn't notice anything that might give them a lead?"

"Such as what?"

Olausson burst out laughing. "I've no idea."

"Neither have I."

Lindman could see that Olausson believed him. He was amazed at how easy it had been to lie. Now it was time to steer the conversation in another direction.

"I hope nothing valuable was stolen from Wetterstedt's place."

Olausson picked up the fax. "According to this, nothing at all was stolen. Which seems rather remarkable, given that Wetterstedt claims there was quite a bit of valuable art in the flat."

"Not many junkies are *au fait* with the art market. Prices, and which artists are in demand by the collectors and fences, that's a bit off their patch."

Olausson carried on reading. "There was evidently a fair amount of jewellery and cash lying around. The kind of stuff that would interest your usual burglar. But none of it was taken."

"Maybe they were frightened off?"

"Assuming there was more than one. The way the door was forced suggests a thief who knows what he's doing. Not an amateur." Olausson lay back in his chair. "I'll phone Kalmar and tell them I've spoken to you. I'll tell them you couldn't think of anything that might be of use to them."

Olausson stood up and opened the window. Until then Lindman hadn't noticed how stuffy it was in the room.

"There's something wrong with the ventilation all over the police station," Olausson said. "Officers are complaining about allergy attacks. Down in the cells they are moaning about headaches. Nothing gets done, though, because there's no money."

Olausson sat down again. Lindman noticed that he'd put on weight. His stomach was hanging out over his trousers.

"I've never been to Kalmar," Olausson said. "Nor Öland. They say it's beautiful around there."

"If you hadn't asked me to come in, I'd have phoned you anyway. There was a reason why I went to see Wetterstedt. It had to do with Herbert Molin."

"What exactly?"

"Herbert Molin was a Nazi."

Olausson stared at him in astonishment. "A Nazi?"

"Long before he joined the police, when he was a young man, he fought as a volunteer in Hitler's army. And he never abandoned those opinions. Wetterstedt had known him when he was young, and they'd stayed in contact. Wetterstedt was a very unpleasant person."

"You mean to say you went to Kalmar to speak to him about Herbert?"

"It's not forbidden, is it?"

"No, but I'm a good deal surprised to hear it."

"Did you know anything about Molin's past? Or his views?"

"Not a thing. I'm flabbergasted."

Olausson leant forward over his desk. "Has that anything to do with his murder?"

"It could have."

"What about the other man, the second who was murdered up there? The violinist?"

"There's no apparent connection. At least, there wasn't when I left. Molin moved to Härjedalen because he knew a woman up there. She helped him to buy a house. She's also a Nazi. Her name's Elsa Berggren."

Olausson shook his head. The name meant nothing to him. Lindman could tell that Kalmar was forgotten now. If Olausson had vaguely suspected Lindman of being responsible for the break-in, he'd forgotten all about it.

"The whole thing sounds incredible."

"I couldn't agree more. There's no doubt about it, though: we had an out-and-out Nazi working for the police here in Borås, for years."

"He was a good policeman, all the same, irrespective of his politics."

217

Olausson stood up to signal that the interview was at an end. He accompanied Lindman as far as the lift.

"Needless to say, I wonder how you are. Health-wise."

"I'm due back at the hospital on the 19th. Then we'll find out."

The lift door slid open.

"I'll talk to Kalmar," Olausson said.

Lindman got into the lift. "I suppose you didn't know either that Molin was a passionate dancer?"

"Good lord no. What kind of dancing?"

"Preferably the tango."

"There's obviously a lot that I didn't know about Herbert Molin."

"I suppose that's true of all of us. None of us knows much more than we find on the surface."

The lift door closed. Olausson had no time to comment. Lindman left the police station. When he emerged into the street, he wasn't sure what to do next. Kalmar wasn't going to be a problem. Not unless somebody had seen him that night. That was hardly likely.

He stopped, unable to make up his mind what to do. For some reason, his reaction was annoyance, and he swore out loud. A woman walking past gave him a wide berth.

Lindman went back to his flat and changed his shirt. He looked at his face in the mirror. As a child he'd always looked like his mother. The older he became, the more he began to resemble his father. Somebody must know, he thought. Somebody must be able to tell me about my father and his politics. I must get in touch with my sisters. But there's somebody else who must know. My father's friend, the solicitor who drew up his will. He didn't even know if the solicitor was still alive. Hans Jacobi, that was his name. It sounded Jewish, but Lindman recalled that Jacobi was fair-haired, tall and burly, a tennis player. He looked him up in the phone book. Sure enough, there he was. Jacobi & Brandell, Solicitors.

He dialled the number. A woman answered, reciting the name of the firm.

"I'd like to speak to herr Hans Jacobi."

"Who's speaking, please?"

"My name is Stefan Lindman."

"Herr Jacobi has retired."

"He was a good friend of my father's."

"Yes, I remember. But herr Jacobi's an old man now. He retired over five years ago."

"I phoned mainly to discover if he is still alive."

"He's not well."

"Does he still live in Kinna?"

"His daughter's looking after him, at her home near Varberg."

"I'd like to get in touch with him."

"I'm sorry, I'm not allowed to tell you his address or telephone number. Herr Jacobi has asked that callers be advised that he wishes to be left in peace. When he finished here, he did exactly what one ought to do."

"Which was what?"

"He passed all his work on to his younger colleagues. Mainly to his nephew, Lennart Jacobi. He's a partner."

Lindman thanked the woman, and hung up. It wouldn't be difficult to track down the address in Varberg. But was he really justified in pestering an old, ailing man with questions about the past? He couldn't make up his mind and left it until tomorrow. Right now there was something else that needed doing. Something more important.

Shortly after 7 p.m. he parked outside the block of flats in Norrby where Elena lived. He looked up at her window. Without Elena, I am nothing at the moment, he thought. Nothing at all.

CHAPTER 21

Something had disturbed Silberstein during the night. At one point he'd been woken by the sound of the dog rubbing against the side of the tent. He'd hissed at it, and it stopped. Then he'd fallen asleep again and dreamt about La Cābana and Höllner. It was still dark when he next woke up. He lay motionless, listening. The watch he'd hung from one of the tent poles said 4.45. He wondered what had disturbed him, if it was something inside himself, or whether there was something out there in the autumn night. Although there was a long time to go before dawn he couldn't lie there in his sleeping bag any longer. The darkness was full of questions.

If things turned out badly for him and he was tried for the murder of Herbert Molin, he would be found guilty. He had no intention of denying what he had done. If all had gone according to his original plan, he would have returned to Buenos Aires and would never have been traced. The murder would have been filed away in the Swedish police archives and never solved.

Several times, especially while he was waiting for the right moment, in his tent by the lake, he'd considered writing a confession that he would ask a solicitor to send to the Swedish police after his death. It would be a story going back to 1945, and would describe simply and clearly what had happened. If he were arrested now, though, he would also be accused of a murder he hadn't committed.

He crawled out of the sleeping bag and dismantled the tent while it was still dark. The dog was wagging its tail and tugging at its lead. With the aid of his torch he made a thorough search of where the tent had been standing, making sure that he had left no trace. Then he drove off with the dog in the back seat. When he came to a crossroads with a sign pointing to Sörvattnet he stopped. He lit the inside light and unfolded the map. What he wanted to do most of all was to go back south, leave all the darkness behind, phone Maria and tell her he was on his way home. But he knew he couldn't do that, his life would be intolerable if he didn't find out what had happened to the man called Andersson. He took a road east to Rätmyren. He parked on one of the forestry roads he knew from before, and cautiously approached Molin's house. The dog by his side was quiet. When he was sure the house was deserted, he put the dog inside the pen, closed the gate, hung the lead on the fence and went back into the woods. That will give the police something to worry about, he thought, as he made his way back to where he'd parked the car. It was still dark.

The gravel crunched under the tyres when he drove off the main road to study the map again. It wasn't far to the Norwegian border, but that's not where he was going. He set off again, heading north, and passed through Funäsdalen before turning into a smaller road and driving into the darkness to see where it would take him. He was climbing steeply now, perhaps he was in the mountains already. He could well be, if he'd read the map correctly. He drew up, switched off the engine and sat back to wait for daylight.

When dawn began to break, he set off again, climbing all the time. He noticed several chalets tucked among the rocks and bushes. He must be in some kind of holiday village. There were no lights anywhere. He kept on going until he came to a gate blocking the road. He got out of the car to open it, and continued along the track after closing the gate behind him. He realised that if they came after him, he'd be cornered. But he didn't care. All he wanted was to keep on going until the track petered out. Then he would have to make a decision.

Eventually the road came to an end and he could go no further. He got out of the car and filled his lungs with the chilly air. The light seemed to be grey. He looked round: mountain-tops, in the distance a long valley, and beyond that more mountains. A path led into the trees. He followed it. After a few hundred metres he came to an old wooden chalet. Nobody had been along that path for ages, he could see that. He went up to the chalet and peered in through the windows. The front door was locked. He tried to imagine where he would have hidden a key if the chalet had been his. There was a broken plant pot in front of one of the flat stones forming part of the steps up to the front door. He bent down and lifted the pot. No key. Then he felt underneath the stone, and there it was, fastened to a lump of wood by a piece of ribbon. He unlocked the door.

The chalet hadn't been aired for a considerable time. It comprised a big living room, two small bedrooms and a kitchen. The furniture was made of light-coloured wood. He ran his fingers over one of the chair arms, and thought how attractive some of this light-coloured wooden furniture would look in his dingy home in Buenos Aires. Tapestries were hanging on the walls, with embroidered texts that he couldn't understand. He went into the kitchen. The chalet had mains electricity, and there was a telephone. He picked up the receiver and listened to the dialling tone. He looked in the big freezer. It was full of food. What could that mean? Was the chalet only empty for a short time? He had no way of knowing. He took out some packets of deep-frozen hamburgers and put them in the sink. Then he turned on a tap over the sink, and water came gushing out.

He sat down by the telephone and dialled the long number to Maria in Buenos Aires. He'd never quite managed to work out the time difference. He could hear it ringing at the other end. He wondered who would be paying for this international call from his cottage in the mountains.

Maria answered. As usual, she sounded impatient, as if he'd interrupted her when she was doing something important, like cleaning or preparing food. If she had any time to herself, she used to play complicated games of patience. He'd tried in vain to decipher the rules. He had the impression that she cheated. Not to solve the patience, but to make it last as long as possible.

"It's me," he said. "Can you hear me all right?"

She spoke loud and quickly, as she always did when she was nervous. I've been away for too long, he thought. She's started to suspect that I've left her, and will never come back home.

"Where are you?" she said.

"I'm still in Europe."

"Where?"

He thought about the map he'd been studying in the car, trying to come to a decision.

"Norway."

"What are you doing there?"

"I'm looking at furniture. I'll be coming home soon."

"Don Batista's been asking for you. He's upset. He says you promised to renovate an antique sofa for him. He wanted to give it to his daughter as a wedding present in December."

"Tell him it will be ready in time. Has anything else happened?"

"What do you expect to have happened? A revolution?"

"I don't know. I'm only asking."

"Juan has died."

"Who?"

"Juan. The old porter."

She was speaking more slowly now, but still far too loudly, as if that was necessary because Norway was so far away. He suspected that she wouldn't even be able to point to it on a map. It also struck him that she was never closer to him than when she was talking about somebody who'd died. He was not surprised to hear that the old caretaker was dead. He'd had a stroke a few years back, and since then had only been able to shuffle round the courtyard, looking at all the work that needed doing, but he no longer had the strength to do it.

"When's the funeral?"

"It's already been. I sent flowers from both of us."

"Thank you." There was a swishing and crackling in the receiver. "Maria, I'll soon be back home. I miss you. I haven't been unfaithful to you, but this journey has been very important. I feel as if I'm moving around in a dream, as if I'm really back in Buenos Aires. I had to make this trip as there was something I needed to see that I'd never seen before. Not just this foreign furniture in such light colours, but also something inside myself. I'm starting to get old, Maria. A man of my age ought only to make journeys by himself. To find out who he really is. I'll be a different person when I get back."

"What do you mean, a different person?" She sounded worried.

He knew that Maria was always worrying in case something changed. He wished he hadn't said that.

"I'll be changed for the better. I shall have dinner at home in future. I'll very seldom dine at La Cābana and leave you alone."

She didn't believe him and was silent again.

"I've killed a man," he said. "A man who committed a terrible crime, a long time ago, when I still lived in Germany."

Why had he said that? A confession made over the phone from a chalet in the mountains in the Swedish province of Härjedalen to a cramped, damp flat in Buenos Aires. A confession to somebody who didn't understand what he was talking about, and was even less able to imagine him doing harm to any other person. It was probably because he couldn't bear any more not having shared his secret with someone else, even if it was only Maria, who wouldn't understand what he said.

"When are you coming home?" she said, again.

"Soon."

"They've put the rent up again."

"Think of me in your prayers."

"Because they've raised the rent?"

"Don't worry about the rent. Just think of me. Every morning and every night."

"Do you think of me when you say your prayers?"

"I don't say any prayers, Maria, you know that. You're the one who does that job in our household. I'll have to stop now. I'll ring again later."

"When?"

"I can't say. Goodbye, Maria."

He put the phone down, and it at once occurred to him that he ought to have told her he loved her, even if he didn't. After all, she was the one who was always around, she'd be the one who held his hand when he was dying. He wondered if what he'd told her had sunk in.

He stood up and went over to one of the low windows. It was light outside now. He looked at the mountains, and in his mind's eye he could also see Maria, sitting in the plush red armchair next to the little table with the telephone.

He needed to get back home.

He made some coffee and opened the front door to let in some air. If anybody were to come along the path to the house, he knew what he would say. He'd tell them he'd killed Molin, but not the other man. But nobody would come, he was convinced of that. He was alone here. He could make this little chalet his base while he tried to find out what had happened to Andersson.

There was a framed photograph on a shelf. Two children were sitting on the stone slab under which he'd found the key, smiling at the camera. He took it down and looked at the back. He could just about make out a date: 1998. It also said "Stockholm". He searched for the name of the owner of the cabin. He found an invoice from an electrical shop in Sveg addressed to a man by the name of Frostengren with a home address in Stockholm. That persuaded him that he need have no fear of being disturbed. The chalet was a long way off the beaten track, and November was not a month for hikers or skiers. The only thing he'd have to avoid was being seen when he joined the main road. He'd also better keep an eye on the other cottages whenever he left or returned, to make sure that they were all shut up for the winter.

He spent the rest of the day in the chalet. He slept a lot, dreamlessly, and woke up without feeling restless. He drank coffee, grilled a hamburger and occasionally went out to look at the mountains. At about 2 p.m. it started raining. He switched on the light over the table in the living room and sat by the window to work out what to do next.

There was only one obvious and absolutely incontrovertible starting point: Aron Silberstein or Fernando Hereira, whichever he happened to be at the time, had committed murder. If he'd been a believer, like Maria, that would have ensured eternal hell. He was not a believer, however; as far as he was concerned there were no gods, apart from those he occasionally created for himself in moments of weakness, and then only fleetingly. Gods were for the poor and weak. He was neither poor nor weak. Even as a child he'd cultivated a thick skin, which had become part of his nature as the years went by. He was unsure if he was first and foremost a Jew, or a German emigrant to Argentina. Neither the Jewish religion and traditions, nor the Jewish community had given him any assistance in life.

He had visited Jerusalem once, in the late 1960s. It was after the first of the wars with Egypt, and it was in no sense a pilgrimage. He'd made the journey out of curiosity and perhaps as a penance for his father, an apology for not yet having traced the man who killed him. Staying at the same hotel as Silberstein in Jerusalem was an old Jewish gentleman from Chicago, an orthodox believer, and they'd often taken breakfast together. Isak Sadler was a friendly man. With a friendly smile that did not disguise the fact that he was still astonished at how it happened, he told Silberstein about how he survived a concentration camp. When the US troops arrived to liberate them, Sadler was so emaciated that he'd had to use his last reserves of strength to let the Americans know he was still alive and shouldn't be buried. After that it seemed only natural that he should go to America and spend the rest of his life there. One morning they'd spoken about Eichmann, and discussed the principle of revenge. It had been a depressing time for Silberstein. He'd grown resigned by the end of the 1960s, and supposed that he would never be able to trace the man who'd killed his father.

However, his conversations with Sadler had given him the inspiration to take up the search once more. Sadler had argued very strongly that the execution of Eichmann had been appropriate. The hunt for German Nazis must continue for as long as there was the slightest hope of finding alive any of those who had been associated with the horrendous crimes.

When he returned from Jerusalem, Silberstein had cared no more about his Jewish origins, but he'd resumed his search and received assistance from Simon Wiesenthal in Vienna, although it led to nothing. He didn't know it at the time, but he would have to wait until Höllner appeared before he found the clue he'd been looking for.

He sat in the chalet belonging to the man called Frostengren, gazing at the mountains and valleys. He'd managed to find a needle in a haystack, and when the moment of truth came, he hadn't hesitated. Molin was dead. Everything had gone according to plan up to that point. Then they'd found the other man, murdered in the woods outside his own house.

There were similarities between the two deaths, as if whoever killed Andersson had imitated what Silberstein had done with Molin. Two old men who lived on their own. Both had a dog. Both were killed in the open. Yet more important were the differences. He couldn't tell how much the police had noticed, but he could see the differences because he had had nothing to do with Andersson's death.

Silberstein looked at the mountains. Clouds of mist drifted down to the valley. He was close now to a decision. Whoever killed Andersson had tried to make it look as if the same murderer had come back to strike again. This raised an intriguing question: who knew so much about the way Molin died? Silberstein did not know what had been in the newspapers, and he had no idea what the police had revealed at the press conferences they'd presumably held.

There was another "why" that he was trying to find an answer to. The person who killed Andersson must have had a motive. A spring was wound up, it seemed to him. When Molin died, it triggered some mechanism that meant Andersson had to be killed as well. Why, and by whom? He spent the whole day analysing these questions from different points of view. He made lots of meals, not because he was especially hungry, but to quell his nervousness. He couldn't help worrying that somehow or other, he was responsible for what happened to Andersson. Was there a secret between the two men? Was there a risk that Andersson might reveal it after Molin's death? That must have been it. Something he hadn't known about. Molin's death meant that somebody had been put in danger, and therefore Andersson had to die as well, to prevent the secret coming out.

He opened the door and went outside. It smelt of damp moss. Clouds were drifting past, very low. Clouds move in complete silence. He walked slowly round the wooden chalet, then again.

Another person had appeared in the place where Molin and Andersson lived their lives. A woman. He'd seen her three times, when she came to visit Molin. He'd followed them when they went for walks on forest tracks. Once, during her second visit, they'd gone towards the lake and he'd been afraid they might discover his tent. Luckily they turned back before they came to the last bend. He'd followed them through the trees, like a boy scout or one of those Red Indians he'd read about as a child, in the books by Edward S. Ellis. Sometimes they talked, and very occasionally they'd laughed.

After their walks they'd gone back to the house, and he'd heard the sound of music. The first time he'd scarcely been able to believe his ears when he heard somebody singing in Spanish, Argentinian Spanish, with the characteristic intonation different from that in any other Spanish-speaking country. After the music, which usually lasted between half an hour and an hour, everything had been quiet. He wondered if they'd been making love. Afterwards Molin had accompanied her to where she'd parked her car. They had shaken hands, never embraced. Then she'd driven away.

He guessed that woman must have been Elsa Berggren. That was the name with those of Molin and Andersson on the back of the bill the police officer had crumpled up and dropped into the ashtray. He still wasn't sure what the implications were. Was Berggren another old Nazi who'd withdrawn to Härjedalen?

He gazed over the hills and tried to work out a possibility. A triangle of Molin, Berggren and Andersson. He didn't know if Berggren also knew Andersson. Andersson and Berggren had been mere extras in the drama he'd come up to the forests to enact.

He walked round the house one more time. He thought he could hear an aeroplane in the distance, then only the wind swishing along the sides of the mountains.

There was no other explanation, it seemed to him, but that there was some kind of link, a secret, between the three of them, just as the policeman had written on that bill. Molin was dead, so Andersson had to die as well. That left only the woman. She must be the one with the key to all this.

He went back inside. He'd taken another packet of hamburgers out of the freezer, and they were thawing on the draining board. He would have to speak to the Berggren woman to find out what had happened.

In the evening, he worked out his plan. He had drawn the curtains and put the table lamp on the floor so that no light would seep out into the surrounding darkness. He sat at the table until midnight. By then he knew what he was going to do. It would be risky, but he had no choice.

Before going to bed he dialled a telephone number in Buenos Aires. The man who answered was in a hurry. He could hear the hum of conversation in the background.

"La Cābana," the man shouted. "Hello?"

Silberstein replaced the receiver. The restaurant was still there. Before long he'd be back at his table, next to the window overlooking the side street leading into Avenida Corrientes.

Next to the telephone was a directory in which he found Elsa Berggren's number and a town address. He checked the map of Sveg in the phone book and saw that it was a street on the south side of the river. He breathed a sigh of relief: he wouldn't need to go looking for her house in the forest. The risk of being seen by somebody else would be greater, of course. He wrote the address on a scrap of paper, then put the directory back where he'd found it.

He slept uneasily. He felt shattered when he woke. He stayed in bed all day, only getting up occasionally to eat some of the food he'd taken out of the freezer.

He stayed in Frostengren's chalet for three more days, by which time he could feel his strength returning. On the morning of the fourth day he cleaned the place, and waited until the afternoon before locking up and replacing the key under the stone. When he came to his car, he consulted the map again. Although it was hardly likely that the police would have set up road blocks, he decided not to take the shortest route to Sveg. Instead, he drove north towards Vålådalen. When he came to Mittådalen he turned off towards Hede and came to Sveg just as it was getting dark. He parked on the edge of the little town where there were shops and two petrol stations, and also an information board and a map. He found his way to fröken Berggren's house. She lived in a white house surrounded by a large garden. There was a light on downstairs. He took a good look around, then returned to his car when he'd seen enough.

He still had a lot of hours to fill in. He went into a supermarket, found himself a woollen hat big enough for it to be pulled down over his face, then joined the longest of the check-out queues, where the girl seemed to be the one most under pressure. He gave her exactly the right amount, and was sure as he left the store that nobody would remember what he looked like nor how he was dressed. When he got back to the car he used a knife he'd taken from Frostengren's chalet to make holes in the hat for him to see through.

By 8 p.m. there was not much traffic. He drove over the bridge and parked where his car was invisible from the road. Then he went on waiting. To pass the time, he re-upholstered in his head the sofa that Don Batista wanted to give his daughter as a wedding present.

He set off at midnight. He took with him a small axe that he had taken from the chalet. He waited until a heavy lorry had gone past, then he hurried over the road and along the path down by the river.

CHAPTER 22

Lindman stormed out of Elena's home in a fury at 2 a.m. Even before he reached the street his rage had subsided, but he couldn't bring himself to go back, for all that he really wanted to. He got into his car and drove into town, but he avoided Allégatan: he didn't want to go home, not yet at least. He pulled up at the Gustav Adolf church and switched off the engine. The place was deserted and dark.

What had actually happened? Elena had been pleased to see him. They'd sat in the kitchen and shared a bottle of wine. He'd told her about his journey and the sudden pains he'd had in Sveg. He'd told her the bare minimum about Molin and Andersson and Wetterstedt: Elena wanted to know what *he'd* been doing. She was very concerned about him, and her eyes betrayed her worry. They'd sat up for a long time, but she shook her head when he asked if she was tired. No, she wanted to hear everything about what he'd been up to while he was away. We shouldn't always insist on sleeping, she said, not when there were more important things to do. Even so, after a while they'd started clearing away before going to bed. After washing the glasses, she'd asked him in passing if he couldn't have phoned her a bit more often, despite everything. Hadn't he realised how worried she'd been?

"You know I don't like telephones. We've been through that lots of times."

"There's nothing to stop you ringing, saying hello and hanging up."

"Now you're annoying me. You're pressurising me."

"All I'm asking is why you don't phone me more often."

He grabbed his jacket and stormed out. He regretted it by the time he was dashing downstairs. He knew he shouldn't drive. If he'd been caught in a police check, he'd have been drunk in charge. I'm running away, he thought. All the time I'm running away from November 19. I go wandering around the forests in Härjedalen, I break into a flat in Kalmar and now I drive when I've been drinking. My illness is dictating my actions, or rather my fear, and it's so strong that I can't even be with the person I'm closest to in the whole world, a woman who is totally honest and showing that she loves me.

He took out his mobile and dialled her number.

"What happened?" she asked.

"I don't know. I'm sorry. I didn't mean to hurt you."

"I know that. Are you coming back?"

"No. I'll sleep at home."

He didn't know why he'd said that. She didn't say anything.

"I'll phone you tomorrow," he said, trying to sound cheerful.

"We'll see," she said wearily, and hung up.

He switched off his mobile and remained sitting there in the darkness. Then he left the car and walked back to Allégatan. He wondered if this is what death looked like, a solitary figure walking through the night.

He slept badly and got up at 6 a.m. No doubt Elena would be awake already. He ought to phone her, but he didn't feel up to it. He forced himself to eat a substantial breakfast, then went to fetch his car. There was a squally wind blowing, and he felt the cold. He drove south out of Borås. When he came to Kinna he left the main road and drove into the town itself. He stopped outside the house where he'd grown up. He knew that the man who lived there now was a potter who had made his studio in what used to be his father's garage and workshop. The house looked deserted in the early morning light. The branches of the tree where Lindman and his sisters used to have a swing were swaying in the strong wind. He suddenly thought that he could see his father come out of the door and walk towards him, but instead of his usual suit and grey overcoat he was wearing the uniform that hung in Berggren's wardrobe.

Lindman drove back to the main road and didn't stop again until he came to Varberg. He had a coffee at the café opposite the railway station, and borrowed their phone book to look up Anna Jacobi's number. The address was in a suburb to the south of the town. Perhaps he ought to phone first, but then Anna Jacobi or whoever answered might say that the old man didn't want to or wasn't well enough to be visited. He eventually found the place, after several wrong turnings.

The house looked as if it had been built around the turn of the century, and stood out from the other houses which were all modern. He opened the gate and walked down the long gravel path to the front door, which was under a veranda roof. He hesitated before ringing the bell. What am I doing? he thought. What do I expect Jacobi to tell me? He was my father's friend. Superficially, at least. What my father really thought about Jews I can only imagine, and fear the worst. Nevertheless, he was one of the small group of well-to-do people who lived in Kinna in those days. That must have been the most important thing as far as my father was concerned, keeping the peace in that little group. I'll never know what he really thought about Jacobi.

He decided to take the Strong Sweden Foundation as his starting point, which was the reason why his father had made a pledge in his will. He'd asked about it once before. Now he was coming to ask again, and if necessary he would say it had to do with Molin's death. I've already been in Olausson's office and lied through my teeth to him. I can hardly make matters any worse. He rang the doorbell.

After the second ring, the door was opened by a woman in her forties. She looked at him from behind a pair of strong spectacles that magnified her pupils. He introduced himself and explained what he wanted.

"My father doesn't receive visitors," she said. "He's old and ill and wants to be left in peace."

Lindman could hear the sound of classical music from inside the house.

"My father listens to Bach every morning. In case you're wondering. Today he asked for the third Brandenburg Concerto. He says it's the only thing that keeps him going. Bach's music."

"I have something important to ask him about."

"My father stopped dealing with anything remotely connected with work a long time ago."

"This is personal. He once drew up a will for my father. I spoke to your father about it in connection with my father's estate. Now the matter of a pledge in the will has come up again, in connection with a difficult legal case. I won't pretend that it doesn't have great significance for me personally as well."

She shook her head. "I've no doubt that what you want to ask is important, but the answer has to be no even so."

"I promise not to stay for more than a couple of minutes."

"The answer is still no. I'm sorry."

She took a step back, preparing to close the door.

"Your father is old, and he'll soon be dead. I'm young, but I might die soon as well. I have cancer. It would make it easier for me to die if I'd been able to ask my questions."

Anna Jacobi stared at him from behind her thick glasses. She was using a very strong perfume that irritated Lindman's nose.

"I assume that people don't tell lies about fatal diseases."

"If you like I can give you the telephone number of my doctor in Borås."

"I'll ask my father. If he says no, I shall have to ask you to leave."

Lindman agreed and she shut the door. He could still hear the music. He waited. He was beginning to think she'd closed the door for good when she came back.

"Fifteen minutes, no more," she said. "I'll be timing you."

She ushered him into the house. The music was still there, but the volume had been turned down. She opened the door of a large room with bare walls, and a hospital bed in the middle.

"Speak into his left ear," she said. "He can't hear anything in his right one."

She closed the door behind him. Lindman suspected he'd heard a trace of weariness or irritation in her voice when she referred to her father's deafness. He went up to the bed. The man in it was thin and hollow-cheeked. In a way he reminded Lindman of Emil Wetterstedt. Another skeletal figure, waiting to die.

Jacobi turned his head to look at him. He gestured to a chair at the side of the bed.

"The music is nearly finished," he said. "Please excuse me, but I regard it as a serious crime to interrupt the music of Johann Sebastian Bach."

Lindman sat on the chair and waited. Jacobi had turned up the volume with a remote control, and the music echoed round the room. The old man lay listening, with his eyes closed. When the music stopped he pressed the remote control with trembling fingers, and put it on his stomach.

"I shall die soon," he said. "I think it has been a great blessing to

233

live after Bach. I have my own way of measuring time, and I divide history into the age before Bach and the age after him. An author whose name I've forgotten has written poems about that. I am being granted the enormous privilege of spending my last days to the accompaniment of his music."

He adjusted his head on the pillows.

"Now the music has finished and we can talk. What was it you wanted?"

"My name is Stefan Lindman."

"My daughter has already told me that," Jacobi said, impatiently. "I remember your father. I drew up his will. That was what you wanted to discuss, but I don't know how you can expect me to remember the terms of an individual will. I must have drawn up at least a thousand during my 47 years as a practising solicitor."

"It was to do with a donation to a foundation called Strong Sweden."

"I might remember. But I might not."

"It transpires that the foundation is part of a Nazi organisation here in Sweden."

Jacobi drummed with his fingers on his quilt. "Nazism died with Hitler."

"It appears that a lot of people in Sweden still support this organisation. And the fact is that young people are joining it."

Jacobi looked hard at him. "Some people collect stamps. Others collect matchbox labels. I regard it as not impossible that there are some people who collect obsolete political ideals. People have always wasted their lives doing pointless things. Nowadays people drop dead while gaping at all those trivial and degrading television series that go on for ever."

"My father pledged money to this organisation. You knew him. Was he a Nazi?"

"I knew your father as a proud and patriotic Swede. No more than that."

"And my mother?"

"I didn't have much contact with her. Is she still alive?"

"No, she died some time ago."

Jacobi cleared his throat. "Precisely why have you come here?"

"To ask if my father was a Nazi."

"What makes you think I could answer that question?"

"There are not many people still alive who can. I don't know anybody else."

"I've already given you my answer, but of course, I wonder why you have come to disturb me and ask me your question."

"I discovered his name in a membership list. I didn't know he'd been a Nazi."

"What sort of membership list?"

"I'm not sure, but it contained more than a thousand names. Many of them were already dead, but they were continuing to pay their subscriptions by leaving money for that purpose in their wills, or by way of their surviving relatives."

"But the association or organisation . . . what did you say it was called? Strong Sweden?"

"It seems to be some sort of foundation that is a part of a bigger organisation. What that is, I don't know."

"Where did you find all this?"

"I'm afraid I can't tell you that for the time being."

"But your father was a member?"

"Yes."

Jacobi licked his lips. Lindman interpreted that as an attempt to smile.

"In the 1930s and '40s Sweden was teeming with Nazis. Not least in the legal profession. It wasn't only the great master Bach who came from Germany. In Sweden, ideals – be they literary, musical or political – have always come from Germany. Until the period following the Second World War. Things changed then, and all the ideals started coming from the USA. However, just because Hitler led his country to a catastrophic defeat doesn't mean that ideas about an Aryan superman or hatred of Jews died out. They survived among the generation that had been indoctrinated when they were young. It's possible that your father was one of them, perhaps your mother also. No-one can be certain that those ideals will not rise again, like a phoenix."

Jacobi fell silent, short of breath after the effort he'd made. The door opened and in came Anna Jacobi. She gave her father a glass of water.

"Your time's up," she said.

Lindman stood up.

"Have you received the answer you were looking for?" asked Jacobi.

"I'm trying to work it out," Lindman said.

"My daughter said you were ill."

"I've got cancer."

"Terminal?"

Jacobi asked the question in an unexpectedly jocular tone, as if, despite everything, he could be happy that death wasn't the exclusive priority of old men who spent the last of their days listening to Bach.

"I hope not."

"Of course. Still, death is the shadow we can never get away from. One day that shadow turns into a wild beast that we can no longer keep at bay."

"I hope to be cured."

"If not, I recommend Bach. The only medicine worth taking. It provides comfort, eases a bit of the pain and gives a certain degree of courage."

"I shall remember that. Thank you for your time."

Jacobi didn't answer. He had closed his eyes. Lindman left the room.

"I think he's in pain," his daughter said, at the front door. "But he refuses to take painkillers. He says he can't listen to music if he's not thinking straight."

"What illness is he suffering from?"

"Old age and despair. That's all."

Lindman shook hands and said goodbye.

"I hope things turn out OK for you," she said. "That you'll be cured."

Lindman went back to his car. He had to duck into the wind. What do I do now? he wondered. I go to see an old man close to death and try to find out why my father was a Nazi. I discover only that he was a proud and patriotic Swede. I can get in touch with my sisters and ask what they knew, or I can see how they react when I tell them. But then what? What can I do with the answers I get? He got into the car and looked across the street. A woman was struggling to steer a pram into the wind. He watched her until she was out of sight. This is all that's left to me, he thought. An isolated moment in my car, parked in a street in a suburb south of Varberg. I'll never come back here, I'll soon have forgotten the name of the street and what the house looked like.

He took out his mobile to phone Elena. There was a message for him. Larsson had rung. He called his number.

"Where are you?" he said.

It struck Lindman that in the age of the mobile telephone, this had become the standard greeting. You started by asking where people were.

"I'm in Varberg."

"How are you?"

"Not too bad."

"I just wanted to tell you about the latest developments. Have you got time?"

"I have all the time in the world."

Larsson laughed. "Nobody has that. Anyway, we've made a bit of progress regarding the weapons used. In Molin's case there was a whole arsenal. Shotgun, tear gas canisters, God only knows what else. They must have been pinched from somewhere or other. We've been chasing up reported cases of weapons thefts, but we still don't know where they came from. But one thing we do know. It was a different gun that killed Andersson. The forensic boys have no doubt about that. It means we're now faced with something we weren't really expecting."

"Two different murderers?"

"Exactly."

"It could still be the same one even so"

"It could. But we can't ignore the other possibility. And I can tell you something else as well. Somebody reported a burglary in Säter yesterday. The owner had been away for a week. When he got back home he found that he'd been burgled and a gun had been stolen. He reported it to the police, and we found out about it when we started making enquiries. It could have been the gun used to kill Andersson. It's the right calibre. But we have no tabs on the thief."

"How was the break-in done? The way they do it always says something about the burglar."

"A front door forced, neat and tidy. The same applies to the gun cupboard. Not an amateur, in other words."

"Somebody getting himself a gun, with a specific job in mind?"

"That's more or less the way I see it."

Lindman tried to envisage the map.

"Am I right in thinking that Säter is in Dalarna?"

"The road from Avesta and Hedemora goes through Säter to Borlänge and then up to Härjedalen."

"Somebody drives up from the south, gets himself a gun on the way, then keeps on going until he comes to Andersson's house."

"That's what could have happened. We don't have a motive, though. And the murder of Andersson really worries me if it transpires that we have a different murderer. We might well ask ourselves what on earth's going on. Is this the beginning of something that's got some way to go yet before it's finished?"

"You think there could be more acts of violence in store?"

Larsson roared with laughter again.

"Acts of violence. Police officers do have a special way of expressing themselves. I sometimes think that's why the criminal is generally one step ahead. He calls a spade a spade, but we have to find some round-about way of describing it."

"All right, but what you are expecting is more murders?"

"If we have two different weapons, there's an increased likelihood that we could have two different murderers. Are you driving or are you standing still, by the way?"

"I'm parked."

"In that case, I'll tell you a bit more about the way we're thinking. The first thing, of course, is the dog. Who took it and then put it in Molin's pen? And why? We now know that it was taken from Andersson's house by car. We haven't a clue why."

"It might be a macabre joke."

"Could be. But the folks up here aren't all that inclined to go in for what you call macabre jokes. People are most upset and indignant. That's obvious when we knock on doors and talk to people. They really are keen to help."

"It's very strange that nobody seems to have seen anything."

"We've had a few vague reports, a car that somebody might have seen, that sort of thing. Nothing definite. Nothing to give us a clear lead."

"What about Berggren?"

"Rundström took her to Östersund. Spent a whole day questioning her. She stuck to the same story. The same disgusting opinions, but very clear on key matters. She's no idea who might have killed Molin.

She'd only met Andersson once, very briefly, when she was visiting Molin and Andersson happened to call in. We've even given her house the once-over to see if she had any weapons. Nothing. I think she'd tell us if she was frightened of somebody coming after her as well."

There was a grating noise in the telephone. Lindman shouted "Hello" several times before Larsson's voice returned.

"I'm starting to think that this is going to take time. I'm worried."

"Have you found any link between Andersson and Molin?" Lindman said.

"We're ferreting away. According to Andersson's widow, he only ever mentioned Molin as a neighbour, one of several. We've no reason to suspect that isn't true. That's about as far as we've got."

"What about the diary?"

"What about it precisely?"

"His journey to Scotland. The person referred to as 'M.'."

"I can't see why we should give that priority."

"I just wondered."

Larsson sneezed comprehensively. Lindman held his mobile at arm's length, as if the germs might fly through the ether and attack him.

"Sorry about that. The usual autumn cold. I always catch one about now."

Lindman took a deep breath, then told him about his experiences in Kalmar and on Öland. He said nothing about the break-in; but he stressed Wetterstedt's Nazi views. When he'd finished there was so long a silence at the other end, he started to wonder if he'd been cut off.

"I'll suggest to Rundström that we should bring in the national CID," Larsson said, eventually. "They have a section that specialises in terrorists and neo-Nazis. I can't believe that what we're up against here can be traced back to a few skinheads, but you never know."

Lindman said he thought it was a sensible move, and then he wound up the call. He felt hungry. He drove into Varberg and found a restaurant. When he got back to the car he found it had been burgled. Instinctively he felt in his jacket pocket. His mobile was still there. But the car radio had been stolen. And the central locking system was broken. He cursed as he climbed into the driving seat. He ought to report it to the police, but he knew the thief would not be caught and that the police would devote no more than a strictly rationed portion of time to the case. The police were overworked everywhere. He also knew that the excess on his insurance policy was such that he might just as well buy a new radio. There was the problem of the central locking, but he had a friend who helped the police with car repairs on the side.

He set off for Borås. He could feel the wind buffeting the car. The countryside looked grey and desolate. Autumn is setting in, winter is approaching, he thought. And November 19 was approaching too. If only time could be cut off, and he could advance to the day after the beginning of his treatment.

He had just driven into Borås when his phone rang. He wondered if he ought to answer. It was bound to be Elena. There again, he couldn't keep her waiting any longer. One of these days she'd get fed up with the way he was forever running away, always putting his own needs before hers. He pulled in to the side and answered.

It was Veronica Molin.

"I hope I'm not disturbing you. Where are you?"

"In Borås. You're not disturbing me."

"Have you got time?"

"I have time. Where are you?"

"In Sveg."

"Waiting for the funeral?"

Her reply seemed hesitant. "Not only that. I got your number from Inspector Larsson. The policeman who claims to be investigating the murder of my father."

She'd made no attempt to conceal her contempt. That angered him.

"Larsson is one of the best police officers I've ever come across."

"I didn't mean to offend you."

"What do you want?"

"I want you to come here."

Her response had been swift and definite.

"Why?"

"I think I know what happened, but I don't want to discuss it over the phone."

"You shouldn't be talking to me. You should phone Larsson. I've got nothing to do with the investigation."

"Just at the moment you are the only person I know who can possibly help me. I'll pay for your flight here, and all the rest of your costs. But I want you to come. As soon as possible."

"Are you saying you know who killed your father?"

"I think so."

"And Andersson?"

"That has to have been somebody else. But there's another reason why I want you to come. I'm frightened."

"Why are you frightened?"

"I don't want to talk about that on the phone either. I want you to come here. I'll be in touch again in a couple of hours."

The phone went dead. Lindman drove home and went back to his flat. He still hadn't phoned Elena. He thought over what Veronica Molin had said. Why didn't she want to talk to Larsson? And what could she possibly be frightened of?

He waited in his flat. Two hours later, the phone rang again.

CHAPTER 23

Lindman landed at Östersund airport at 10.25 a.m. the following day. When Veronica Molin phoned him the second time he'd been determined to say no. He was not going to come back to Härjedalen and there was nothing he could do to help her. He was also going to inform her tersely and clearly that it was her obligation to talk to the local police, if not to Giuseppe Larsson then to someone else, Rundström perhaps.

When the call came, however, nothing went according to plan. She came straight to the point, asking him if he wanted to go or not. He said yes. Then when he'd started asking his various questions, she'd been evasive and said she didn't want to discuss it over the telephone. She'd rung off after they'd agreed to meet in Sveg the following day. He'd asked her to book a room for him, preferably Number 3 as before.

He went to the window and looked out at the street. He wondered what was making him act the way he did. The fear digging at him, the illness he was trying to keep at bay? Or was it Elena that he couldn't cope with? He didn't know. The day he heard he had cancer, everything had been put out of joint. On top of everything else he was all the time thinking about his father. It's not Molin's past that I'm tracking down, he told himself. It's my own past, the truth about something I didn't know until I broke into Wetterstedt's flat in Kalmar.

He'd called Landvetter airport, checked flight times and booked a ticket. Then he'd phoned Elena, who was subdued and non-committal. He went to her flat at 7.15 and stayed until next morning when he'd been forced to go home, throw some clothes into a bag and then drive the 40 kilometres to Landvetter. They had made love during the night, but it was as if he hadn't really been there. Perhaps she had not noticed, she hadn't said anything. Nor had she asked why he had suddenly to go back to Härjedalen. When they said goodbye in her hall, he could feel her trying to envelop him in her love. He'd tried to suppress his worries, but as he drove back to Allégatan through the deserted streets he didn't feel that he'd succeeded. Something was happening inside him, like a cloud of mist creeping up on him and threatening to choke him. He was in a panic, afraid that he was losing Elena, forcing her to desert him for her own sake.

When he walked down the aeroplane steps at Frösön he felt the fierce cold. The ground was white with frost. He rented a car – Veronica Molin would pay for it. He had intended going straight to Sveg, but changed his mind when he drove onto the bridge from Frösön to Östersund. It was unacceptable not to tell Larsson that he'd come back. What reason should he give? Veronica Molin had contacted him confidentially, but he didn't want to keep it from Larsson. He had enough problems already.

He parked outside the National Rural Agency, but stayed in the car. What should he say to Larsson? He couldn't tell him the whole truth. On the other hand, he didn't want to tell a complete lie even if he had become quite good at it lately. He could come out with a half truth. Say that he couldn't cope with being in Borås, that he preferred to be somewhere else until the radiation therapy actually started. Someone with his illness had the right to be restless and to change his mind.

He went to reception and asked for Larsson. The girl recognised him from his earlier visit, smiled, and said that Larsson was in a meeting but it would be over soon. Lindman took a seat and thumbed through the local paper. The murder investigation was front-page news. Rundström had held a press conference the previous day. It was largely concerned with the weapon, and there was a new appeal for witnesses. No reference to what the police already knew. Nothing about certain makes of car or individuals moving around in the area. The article implied that the police were marking time, and had nothing to go on. Larsson appeared in reception at 11.30 a.m. He was unshaven and looked tired and worried.

"I ought to say that I'm surprised to see you, but nothing surprises me at the moment." He looked more resigned than Lindman had seen him before. They went to his office, and he closed the door behind them. Lindman said what he'd made up his mind to say, that he'd come

243

back because he couldn't settle in Borås. Larsson eyed him sternly.

"Do you go ten-pin bowling?" Larsson said.

"Do I go *bowling*?"

"I do, when I feel restless. I sometimes find it difficult to cope too. Don't underestimate bowling. It's best to play with a few friends. The skittles you knock over can either be your enemies, or problems you can't solve and which are getting you down."

"I've never tried it."

"Take it as a friendly suggestion. Nothing more."

"How's it going?"

"I saw you reading the local rag. We've just had a meeting of the investigative team. Wheels are turning, routines are being followed, everybody's ferreting away for all they're worth. Nevertheless, what Rundström told the reporter is true: we're getting nowhere."

"Are there two murderers?"

"Presumably. That's what the evidence suggests."

"That needn't mean that the crimes have different motives."

Larsson agreed. "That's what we thought. And then there is the business of the dog. I don't think it's a macabre joke: I think it's a conscious effort to tell us something."

"What, for example?"

"I don't know. The fact that we realise that somebody is trying to tell us something has created a sort of constructive chaos. We're forced to accept that there aren't any simple answers – not that we ever thought there were."

Someone laughed outside in the corridor. Then it was quiet again.

"There was a sort of fury about it all," Larsson said. "About both murders. In Molin's case an insane fury. Somebody drags him round in a bloodstained tango, lashes him to death and leaves him in the forest. There was anger behind the death of Andersson as well. More controlled. No dead dogs. No bloodstained dance. But an ice-cold execution. I wonder if these two crimes, displaying such different temperaments, can possibly have been hatched in the same brain. Molin's murder was meticulously planned. Not least your discovery of the campsite makes that clear. But Andersson's is different. So far I can't quite work out how."

It was obvious that Larsson wanted to know Lindman's opinion.

"If the murders are linked, and if it's the same murderer, I suppose we have to assume that something happened subsequently that made it necessary for him to kill Andersson."

"I agree. My colleagues don't. Or it could be that I haven't been able to express myself clearly enough. Anyway, I still think the most likely explanation is two different murderers."

"It's strange that nobody's reported anything. The whole community must be as alert as they are fearful."

"I've been playing this game for many years, but I can't ever remember knocking on so many doors and making so many appeals without hearing so much as a squeak in response. Generally speaking, there's always somebody peering out from behind their curtains and noticing something different from the usual village routine."

"Not hearing anything is also significant, of course. You're dealing with people who know exactly what they're doing. Even when a plan goes wrong they can still find a way out very fast, in cold blood."

"You're saying 'them'."

"I'm wavering between one murderer and some kind of plot involving more than one."

There was a knock on the door. A young man in a leather jacket and with highlights in his dark hair marched in before Larsson had time to respond. He nodded to Lindman and put a bundle of papers down on the desk.

"The latest from the house-to-house operation."

"Well?"

"A mixed-up old crone from Glöte claims the murderer lives in Visby."

"Why?"

"Mostly because the Swedish Lottery has its HQ there. She reckons the Swedish nation is being attacked by mad gamblers. Half the population is running around and killing off the other half to make it easier for them to submit their lottery coupons. That's your lot."

The door closed behind him.

"He's new," Larsson said. "New, confident, and dyes his hair. He's a recruit of the type that goes out of his way to stress that he's young and the rest of us are ancient. He'll be OK when he grows up."

He stood up.

245

"I like talking to you," he said. "You listen, and you ask the questions I need to hear. I'd like to carry on a bit longer, but I have an appointment with the forensic boys that can't wait."

Larsson went with him as far as reception.

"How long are you thinking of staying?"

"I don't know."

"The same hotel in Sveg?"

"Is there another one?"

"A good question. I don't know. There should be a B & B, I suppose."

Lindman remembered a question he'd almost let slip. "Have they released Molin's body for burial yet?"

"I can find out, if you like. I'll be in touch."

Driving to Sveg, he remembered what Larsson had said about ten-pin bowling. He stopped just north of Överberg and got out. It was dead calm and chilly. The ground under his feet was hard. I'm giving way to self-pity, he thought. I'm locking myself up in gloom and doom, and it's not doing me a bit of good. I'm usually a cheerful type, not at all like the man I seem to be at present. Larsson is quite right when he goes on about bowling. I don't need ever to aim a single bowl at a row of skittles, but I have to take seriously what he's trying to tell me. I'm trying to convince myself that I'm going to overcome this illness, but at the same time I'm doing my best to play the rôle of a man on death row, beyond hope.

By the time he got to Sveg, he was wishing he'd never come. He had to resist the urge to drive past the hotel, return to Östersund and fly back to Borås and Elena as quickly as possible. He parked and went into the hotel. The girl in reception seemed pleased to see him.

"I thought you wouldn't be able to drag yourself away," she chuckled.

Lindman laughed. It sounded far too shrill and loud. Even my laughter is telling lies, he thought.

"I've given you your old room," the girl said. "Number 3. There's a message for you from fröken Molin."

"Is she in?"

"No. She said she'd be back around 4 p.m."

He went up to his room. It was as if he'd never left. He went into the bathroom, opened his mouth wide and stuck out his tongue.

246

Nobody dies of tongue cancer, he thought. It will turn out all right. I'll take my course of radiation therapy, and I'll be right as rain. Everything will be as right as rain. There'll come a time when I look back on this period of my life as a mere interlude, a sort of nightmare, nothing more.

He consulted his address book and found the telephone number of his sister in Helsinki. He listened to her recorded message, and left one of his own, with his mobile phone number. He didn't have in his book the number of his other sister, who was married and lived in France, and he couldn't be bothered to chase it up. Nor was he sure he would be able to spell her name correctly.

He looked at the bed. If I lie down I'll die, he thought. He took off his shirt, moved a table out of the way and started doing press-ups. He felt like giving up when he got as far as 25, but he forced himself to go on to 40. He sat on the floor and took his pulse. 170. Far too high. He decided he'd have to start exercising. Every day, regardless of the weather, regardless of how he felt. He rummaged through his bag. He'd forgotten his trainers. He put on his shirt and jacket and went out. He found his way to the one sports shop in Sveg. There was a very limited selection of trainers, but he found a pair that fitted him. Then he went to the pizzeria for a meal. He could hear a radio in the background. He pricked up his ears when he heard Larsson's voice. He was making another appeal, asking the public to get in touch with the police if they had noticed anything unusual, or had any information, etc., etc. They really are in a mess, Lindman thought. He wondered if the murders would ever be solved.

He went for a walk after his meal. North this time, past a museum comprising several old houses, and then past the hospital. He walked fast, so as to exert himself. He heard music playing in his mind's ear. It was some time before he realised it was the music he'd heard at Jacobi's. Johann Sebastian Bach. He kept going until he'd left Sveg far behind him.

He took a shower, then went down to reception. Veronica Molin was waiting for him. He noticed again what a good-looking woman she was.

"Thank you for coming," she said.

"The alternative was ten-pin bowling."

She looked at him in surprise, then laughed.

"I'm glad you didn't say golf. I've never understood men who play golf."

"I've never touched a golf club in my life."

She looked round reception. Some test drivers had just come in, declaring in loud voices that it was high time for a beer.

"I don't normally invite men to my room," she said, "but at least we can be left in peace there."

Her room was on the ground floor, at the end of the corridor. It was different from Lindman's – bigger, for a start. He wondered what it must be like for somebody used to staying in five-star hotels all over the world to adjust to the simplicity of a hotel in Sveg. He remembered her saying that she'd heard about her father's death in a room with a view of the cathedral in Cologne. From the window in this room she could see the River Ljusnan and beyond it the wooded hills of Härjedalen. Perhaps this view is as beautiful, he thought, and in its way as impressive as Cologne Cathedral.

There were two armchairs in the room. She'd switched on the bedside lamp and directed it away from them, so that the room was dimly lit. He smelled her perfume. He wondered how she would react if he were to tell her that what he most wanted to do just now was to remove all her clothes and make love to her. Would she be surprised? She was no doubt aware of the effect she had on men.

"You asked me to be here," he said. "I'd like to hear what you have to tell me. Which said, this conversation shouldn't be taking place. You ought to be talking to Inspector Larsson, or one of his colleagues. I have nothing to do with the investigation."

"I know. But I want to talk to you even so."

Lindman could see that she was agitated. He waited.

"I've been trying to understand," she said. "Who would have had any reason for killing my father? It was beyond all comprehension at first. It seemed as if somebody had raised his hand and brought it crashing down on my father's head for no reason. I could see no motive at all. I was stunned. I don't usually react like that. In my work I come up against crises every day, crises that can develop into commercial catastrophes if I don't stay absolutely calm and make sure

I'm influenced by nothing but the facts in whatever I do. The feeling passed. I was eventually able to think rationally again. And I started remembering." She looked at him. "I read that diary," she said. "What was in it came as a shock."

"You mean you knew nothing about his past?"

"Nothing at all. I told you that."

"Have you spoken to your brother?"

"He didn't know anything either."

Her voice was strangely toneless. Lindman felt an odd sensation of uncertainty. He concentrated harder, leaned forward so that he could see her face more clearly.

"Naturally, it was a bolt from the blue to discover that my father had been a volunteer in Hitler's army. Not just paying lip service to it, but very much an active Nazi. I was ashamed. I hated him. Mainly because he'd never said anything."

Lindman wondered if he was ashamed of his own father. He didn't think he'd come that far yet. He was in a very peculiar situation, though. He and the woman opposite him had made the same discovery about their fathers.

"Anyway, it dawned on me that there might be an explanation in that diary for why he was killed."

A lorry rumbled past in the street outside. Lindman waited eagerly for what was coming next.

"How well do you remember what was in it?" she asked.

"Pretty well. Not all the detail and dates, of course."

"He describes a journey to Scotland."

Lindman remembered that. The long walks with "M.".

"It was a long time ago. I wasn't very old, but I do remember my father going to Scotland to see a woman. I think her name was Monica, but I'm not sure. He'd met her in Borås and she was also a police officer, but quite a bit younger, I think. There'd been some kind of an exchange between Sweden and Scotland. They fell in love. My mother knew nothing about it. Not then at least. Anyway, he went to meet her. And he cheated her."

"How?"

She shook her head impatiently. "I'm telling this at my own pace. It's difficult enough as it is. He tricked her out of some money. I don't know what he told her, of course, but he borrowed money off her, large sums of money. And he never paid it back. My father had a weakness. He was a gambler. Mainly on horses. Cards as well, I think. Anyway, he lost. All her money went down the drain. She demanded the money back. There was nothing about it in writing, apparently. He refused. She came to Borås once, that's how I know about this. She appeared at the door one evening. It was winter. My mother was at home, and my father and me. I don't know where my brother was. Anyway, there she was at the door and, although he tried to prevent her, she forced her way into the house and told my mother everything, and she yelled at my father, threatening to kill him if he didn't return the money. I'd learnt enough English to be able to understand what they were saying. My mother collapsed and my father was wild with rage, or maybe it was fear. She promised she'd kill him in the end, no matter how long it took. I remember distinctly what she said."

"So you're suggesting that after all those years she came here to exact vengeance?"

"That must be what happened."

Lindman shook his head. It seemed to him grossly improbable. In his diary Molin had described the Scotland trip in a way that didn't fit in at all with what he'd just heard.

"You have to tell the police about your theory. They'll look into it. For myself, I can't believe it."

"Why not?"

"It simply doesn't sound credible."

"Aren't most violent crimes incredible?"

Someone walked past in the corridor. They waited until all was quiet again.

"I have a question that you have to answer," Lindman said. "Why don't you want to tell this to Inspector Larsson?"

"I want to and I shall tell him, but I wanted your advice first."

"Why me?"

"Because I had confidence in you."

"What kind of advice do you think I can give you?"

"How can I prevent the truth about my father from coming out? That he was a Nazi?"

"If it has nothing to do with the murder, there's no reason for the police or the prosecution service to make any such information public."

"I'm frightened of reporters. I've had them after me before and I never want to go through that again. I was involved in the complicated merger of two banks in Singapore and England. Something went wrong. The reporters came after me because they knew that I was one of those most involved."

"I don't think you need to worry. Which said, I don't agree with you."

"About what?"

"That the truth shouldn't be told about your father. The old form of Nazism is dead. And yet it's still alive, and growing, in new forms. If you turn over the right stones, they come teeming out. Racists, supermen. All the creatures who look for inspiration from the rubbish dumps of history."

"Can I at least prevent the diary from being published?"

"Presumably. But there may be others who decide to dig deeper."

"What do you mean, others?"

"Me, perhaps."

She leaned back in her chair. Her face disappeared in the shadows. Lindman regretted what he'd said.

"But I shan't be digging into it. I'm a police officer, not a journalist. You don't need to worry on that score."

She stood up. "You made a long journey for my sake," she said. "And I am afraid it wasn't necessary. I could have asked you over the telephone. The trouble is that for once, I've lost a little of my usual presence of mind. My work is sensitive. My employers might abandon me if I were tainted by rumours. After all, the man lying dead in the forest was my father. My belief is that the woman called M. is behind it all. I have no idea who would have killed the other man."

Lindman gestured to the phone. "You should call Inspector Larsson."

He stood up.

"When are you leaving?" she said.

"Tomorrow."

"Can't we have dinner together? That's the least I can do for you."

"I only hope they've changed the menu."

"7.30?"

"That suits me fine."

*   *   *

She was reserved and distant during dinner. Lindman could feel himself getting cross. Partly because she'd persuaded him to make this absurdly unnecessary journey on account of her exaggerated anxiety, and partly because he couldn't avoid being attracted by her.

They said goodbye in reception, with hardly a word exchanged. She said she would send a cheque to his office in Borås to cover his costs, and went to her room. Lindman fetched his jacket and went out. He'd asked if she'd phoned Larsson. She said she had, but that she couldn't get through, and would try again.

As he walked through the deserted town, he thought about what she'd said. The story about the woman in Scotland could conceivably be true, but he refused to believe that after all those years she'd come to Sweden to take her revenge. It didn't make sense.

Without realising it, he'd reached the old railway bridge. He thought it was time to return to the hotel, but something made him keep walking. He crossed the bridge and turned into Berggren's street. There was light in two of the ground floor windows. He was about to walk past when he thought he noticed a shadowy figure disappearing rapidly round one of the gable walls. He frowned. Stood still, peering into the darkness. Then he opened the gate and approached the house. He stopped to listen. Not a sound. He pressed himself against the wall and peered round the corner. Nobody there. He must have been imagining things. He crept round to the back of the house, keeping to the shadows. Nobody there either.

He never heard the footsteps behind him. Something struck the back of his neck. He was on the ground and the last he felt was a pair of hands tightening round his throat. Then nothing. Only darkness.

PART III

The woodlice / November 1999

CHAPTER 24

Lindman opened his eyes. He knew immediately where he was. He sat up slowly, took a deep breath and looked around in the darkness. Nothing to be seen, nor was there a sound. He felt the back of his neck. There was some blood, and it hurt when he swallowed. Still, he was alive. He couldn't say how long he'd been unconscious. He raised himself up, clinging on to the drainpipe on the house wall. He was thinking clearly again, despite the pain in his throat and at the back of his neck. So his eyes hadn't deceived him. There had been some-body moving in the shadows at the back of the house, somebody who'd seen him, and tried to kill him.

Something must have happened. Why was he still alive? Whoever had tried to throttle him must have been disturbed and been forced to let go. Mind you, there was another possibility. His attacker might have intended to stop him, but not to kill him. He let go of the drain-pipe, and listened. Still not a sound.

A faint light reached him from one of the windows. Something must have happened in that house, he thought. Just as something happened in Molin's house, and later in Andersson's. Now I'm standing outside my third house. He wondered what to do, and had no problem in making up his mind. He took out his mobile and phoned Larsson's number. His hand was shaking, and he pressed the wrong buttons twice. When he did get through, a girl answered.

"This is Daddy's telephone."

"Can I speak to Giuseppe, please?"

"Good grief, he went to bed ages ago. Do you realise what time it is?"

"I have to talk to him."

"Who are you?"

"Stefan."

"Are you the one from Borås?"

"Yes. You must wake him up. This is important."

255

"I'll give him the telephone."

While he waited Lindman moved a few paces from the house and stood in the shadow of a tree. Then he heard Larsson's voice, and was able to explain briefly what had happened.

"Are you hurt?" Larsson said.

"The back of my neck is bleeding and it hurts a lot when I swallow, otherwise it's OK."

"I'll try to get hold of Johansson. Where exactly are you?"

"At the back of the house. By one of the gables. Under a tree. Something may have happened to Berggren."

"You said you disturbed someone leaving the place, is that right?"

"I think so."

Lindman waited for a long silence.

"Let's keep the line open," Larsson said at last. "Ring her doorbell and stay at the door. If there's no sign of her, wait until Erik gets there."

Lindman walked round to the front of the house and rang the bell. The outside light was on. He held the phone to his ear all the time.

"What's happening?" Larsson said.

"I've rung. Twice. Nothing."

"Ring again. Knock."

Lindman tried the door handle. It was locked. He knocked loudly. Every time he rapped on the door he felt pain in the back of his neck. Then he heard footsteps.

"Someone's coming now."

"You can't be certain it's her. Be careful."

Lindman took a couple of paces back from the door. The door opened. It was Elsa Berggren. She was still dressed. Lindman could see from her face that she was scared.

"It's her all right. She's opened," Lindman said into the telephone.

"Ask her if anything's happened."

Lindman asked.

"Yes," she said. "I've been attacked. I've just phoned Inspector Johansson. He said he'd come."

Lindman reported what she'd said to Larsson.

"But she's not injured?"

"Not as far as I can see, at least."

"Who attacked her?"

"Who was it that attacked you?"

"He was wearing a hood. When I dragged it off him I caught sight of his face. I've never seen him before."

Lindman passed this on.

"It sounds very strange. A masked man? What do you make of it?"

Lindman looked her in the eye as he replied.

"I think she's telling the truth. Even if the truth sounds incredible."

"Wait there with her until Erik comes. I'll get dressed and drive over. Ask Erik to phone me when he turns up. OK, Roger and out."

Lindman stumbled as he walked in through the door. He felt dizzy and was forced to sit down. Then he saw that he had blood on one of his hands. He told her what had happened. She went to the kitchen and came back with a wet cloth.

"Turn round. I can stand the sight of blood."

She pressed the cloth gently against the back of his neck.

"That's enough, thank you," he said, getting slowly to his feet.

A clock somewhere struck a quarter hour. They went into the living room. A chair was lying on its back, and a glass dish had shattered. She wanted to tell him what had happened, but he told her to wait.

"Inspector Johansson's the one who should listen to what you've got to say. Not me."

Johansson arrived just as the invisible clock was striking the next quarter hour.

"What's happened?" he said.

Then he turned to Lindman.

"I didn't even know you were still here."

"I came back. But that's irrelevant. This story didn't start with me, it started in here."

"That's as maybe," Johansson said, "but to make things easier perhaps you can explain how you came to be involved."

"I was out walking, and thought I saw somebody acting suspiciously in the garden. I went to investigate and was knocked down. Almost strangled, come to that."

Johansson leaned over Lindman.

"You've got bruises on your neck. Are you sure you don't need a doctor?"

"Quite sure."

Johansson sat down, gingerly, as if frightened that the chair might collapse under him.

"How many times in succession is this?" he said. "That you've taken a walk past fröken Berggren's house, I mean. The second? Third?"

"Is that important now?"

Johansson's ponderous approach was beginning to irritate Lindman.

"How do I know what's important? But let's hear what fröken Berggren has to say."

Berggren was sitting on the edge of the sofa. Her voice was different, she could no longer conceal her fear. Lindman noticed that she was trying to do so, nevertheless.

"I'd just left the kitchen and was on my way up to bed when there was a knock on the door. I thought that was odd, because I rarely, if ever, have visitors. When I opened the door, I had the safety chain on – but he flung himself at it so violently that it gave way. He told me to be quiet. I couldn't see his face because he was wearing a sort of hood. A woollen hat with holes in it for his eyes. He dragged me into the living room and threatened me with an axe, and started asking me who'd killed Abraham Andersson. I tried to keep calm. I was sitting here, on the sofa. I could see that he was getting nervous. He raised his axe, and so I made a run at him. That was when the chair fell over. I pulled the hood off him, and he ran out of the house. I'd just phoned you when there was a belting on the door. I looked out of the window and saw that it was you," she said, turning to Lindman.

"Did he speak Swedish?" Lindman said.

Johansson growled. "I'm the one asking questions here. I thought Rundström had made that clear to you. But answer anyway. Did he speak Swedish?"

"Broken English."

"Was it a Swede pretending to be a foreigner?"

She thought before answering. "No," she said. "Not Swedish. I think he might have been an Italian. Or a southern European, in any case."

"Can you describe what he looked like? How old was he?"

"It all happened very quickly. But he was old, not what I had expected. Greying hair, going bald, brown eyes."

"And you've never seen him before?"

Her fear was starting to turn to anger. "I don't mix with that sort of person. You ought to know that."

"I do know that, Elsa, but I have to ask you. How tall was he? Was he thin or fat? What was he wearing, what did his hands look like?"

"Dark jacket, dark trousers, I didn't notice his shoes. No rings on his fingers." She stood up and walked to the door. "I'd say he was about this height, neither fat nor thin." She marked a place on the frame with her hand.

"One eighty," Johansson said, turning to Lindman. "What do you think?"

"All I saw was a moving shadow."

Berggren sat down again.

"He threatened you," Johansson said. "How exactly?"

"He asked questions about Abraham Andersson."

"What kind of questions?"

"Only one, I suppose. Who killed Andersson?"

"Nothing else? Nothing about Molin?"

"No."

"What exactly did he say?"

"'Who killed herr Abraham?' Or 'Who killed herr Andersson?'"

"You said he threatened you."

"He said he wanted the truth. Otherwise there'd be trouble. Who killed Abraham? That's all. I told him I didn't know."

Johansson shook his head and looked at Lindman. "What do you make of all this?"

"I am surprised that he didn't ask about the motive. *Why* was Abraham Andersson murdered?"

"But he didn't. He only asked who'd done it. He obviously thought I knew. Then I realised he was actually implying something different. That was when I got really scared. He thought that I had killed him."

Lindman felt his dizziness coming and going in waves. He tried to concentrate. He could see that Berggren's account of the attack was crucial. The important thing was not what the man had asked her, but what he *hadn't* asked her. There was only one explanation: he knew the answer. Lindman had broken into a sweat. The man in the shadows who'd tried to strangle him, either to kill him or just to render him unconscious, could be playing the central role in the drama that started with Molin's murder.

Johansson's mobile rang. It was Larsson. Lindman could hear that he was worried in case Larsson was driving too fast.

"He's already through Brunflo," Johansson said. "He wants us to wait here for him. Meanwhile I'm to write up what you've said. We must start searching for this man."

Lindman stood up.

"I'm going out. I need some air."

Once outside, Lindman began searching his memory for something to do with what Berggren had said. He returned to the back of the house, avoiding any footprints there might be. He tried to picture the face she'd described. He knew he'd never seen the man before. Nevertheless, it was as if he recognised him. He hammered at his forehead in an attempt to stir his memory. It had something to do with Larsson.

Dinner at the hotel. They'd sat there eating. The waitress had been to-ing and fro-ing between the kitchen and the dining room. There'd been another person there that evening. A man on his own. Lindman hadn't noticed his face. But there was something else about him. It eventually dawned on him what it was. The man hadn't said a single word to the waitress, despite the fact that he'd summoned her several times. That man had been in the dining room when first Lindman and then Larsson had arrived, and he was still there when they left.

He racked his brains. Larsson had scribbled things on the back of the bill, then crumpled it up and dropped it in the ashtray as they left. There was something about that bit of paper. He couldn't remember what. And the man on his own at the nearby table; he hadn't said a word. And somehow he answered the description Berggren had given.

He went back into the house. It was 1.20. Berggren was on the sofa, very pale.

"He's making coffee," she said.

Lindman went to the kitchen.

"I can't think straight without coffee," Johansson said. "Would you like some? To be frank, you look awful. I wonder if you shouldn't see a doctor, no matter what you say."

"I want to talk to Larsson first."

"I'm sorry if I sounded a bit brusque earlier on. The police here in Härjedalen sometimes feel they are being patronised and trampled all over. That goes for Giuseppe as well. Just so that you know."

"I understand."

"No, you don't. But never mind."

He handed Lindman a cup of coffee. Lindman was trying to remember what Larsson had scribbled on that bit of paper.

It wasn't until about 5 a.m. that he had an opportunity of asking Larsson about what had happened that evening in the dining room. Larsson arrived at Berggren's house at 1.50. Once he'd taken stock of the facts, he'd gone with Johansson and Lindman to the police station. An officer had been posted to keep watch over Berggren's house. The description they had of the attacker was too imprecise to be sent out and trigger a nationwide alert. On the other hand, reinforcements would arrive from Östersund the next morning. They'd mount yet another house-to-house operation. Somebody must have seen something, was Larsson's conviction. The man must have had a car. There can't be all that many English-speaking southern Europeans in Sveg at this time of year. People occasionally came from Madrid or Milan to hunt elk, and the Italians are ardent mushroom pickers, of course. The only thing is, we're not in the mushroom-picking or elk-hunting seasons. Somebody must have seen him. Or a car. Or something.

At 5.30 Johansson left to cordon off Berggren's garden. Larsson was tired and irritable. "He ought to have done that right away. How can we carry out correct police procedures if people don't follow the routines?"

Larsson had his feet on the desk.

"Can you remember that dinner we had at the hotel?" Lindman said.

"Very well."

"There was a man in the dining room as well. Do you remember him?"

"Vaguely. Next to the kitchen door, if I remember rightly."

"To the left."

Larsson looked at him, his eyes weary. "Why do you ask?"

"He said nothing. That could mean that he didn't want to let us know that he was a foreigner."

261

"Why the hell shouldn't he want to do that?"

"Because we were police officers. We used the word 'police' again and again during dinner. The word is similar in most languages. What's more, I think he looked a bit like the description Berggren tried to give us."

Larsson shook his head. "It's too circumstantial, too far-fetched."

"Possibly. But even so. You sat there doodling on a piece of paper when you'd finished eating."

"It was the bill. I asked about it the next day, but it had disappeared. The waitress said she hadn't seen it."

"That's the point. Where did it go?"

Larsson stopped rocking back and forwards in his chair.

"Are you saying that man took the bill after we'd left?"

"I'm not saying anything. I'm just thinking aloud. One question is: what did you write?"

Larsson tried to remember. "Names, I think. Yes, I'm sure. We were talking about the three of them: Molin, Andersson and Berggren. We were trying to find a link." Larsson sat up with a start. "I wrote down their names, and I joined them with arrows. They made a triangle. I think I drew a swastika at the side of Andersson's name."

"Nothing else?"

"Not that I remember."

"I might be wrong, of course," Lindman said, "but I think I saw a big question mark after the swastika."

"You could be right."

Larsson stood up and leaned against the wall. "I'm listening," he said. "I'm starting to catch on to the way you're thinking."

"The man is in the hotel dining room. He hears that we are police officers. When we leave, he pinches the bill you left behind. Now a few assumptions. If he takes the bill, he does so because he has an interest. And if he has an interest it can only be because he's involved."

Larsson raised a hand. "Involved? – How?"

"That takes us on to the next assumption. If this is the man who came to see Berggren last night and tried to strangle me, we ought to ask ourselves at least one more important question."

"Which is?"

"A question about the question he asked Berggren: 'Who killed Andersson?'"

262

Larsson shook his head in annoyance. "You've lost me."

"I'm suggesting that this question leads us to another question, the crucial one, the one he didn't ask."

The penny dropped. It was as if Larsson started breathing again.

"Who murdered Molin?"

"Exactly. Shall I go on?"

Larsson nodded.

"You could draw various conclusions. The most likely is that he didn't ask the question about Molin because he already knew the answer. It means that in all probability, he was the one who killed Molin."

Larsson raised both arms. "Hang on, you're going far too fast. We need a bit of time to sort ourselves out up here in Jämtland. So, we're looking for two murderers. We've already reached that conclusion. The question is: are we looking for two different motives?"

"Maybe."

"It's just that I find it difficult to take all this in. We're in a place where crime of this kind is rare. Now we have two cases, one on top of the other, but not committed by the same man. You have to accept that all my experience rebels against such a conclusion."

"There always has to be a first time. I think it's time you started thinking new thoughts."

"Let's hear them!"

"Somebody makes his way here to the forest and kills Molin. It's carefully planned. A few days later Andersson dies as well. He's killed by somebody else. For some reason we don't know, the man who killed Molin wants to know what happened. He'd been camping beside the lake, but had gone away after dragging Molin's dead body to the edge of the forest. He comes back, because he needs to know what happened to Andersson. Why was he murdered? He picks up a scrap of paper left on a restaurant table by a police officer. What does he find there? Not two names, but three."

"Berggren?"

"It seems to him that she must know the answer, so he tries to put pressure on her. She attacks him when he gets threatening. He runs away, but I happen to be there. You know the rest."

Larsson opened a window and left it ajar.

263

"Who is this man?"

"I don't know. But we can make another assumption. And it could prove that I'm right."

Larsson said nothing, but waited for what was coming next.

"We think we know the murderer camped by the lake. Once he's killed Molin, he goes away. But then he comes back again. He's not going to put up his tent in the same place. So the question is: where's he living?"

Larsson looked doubtful.

"You mean he might have booked into a hotel?"

"That possibility could be worth following up."

Larsson checked his watch. "When's breakfast?"

"They start serving at 6.30."

"That means we might be in luck. Let's go."

A few minutes later they were in the hotel reception. The girl at the desk looked at them in surprise.

"Two early birds looking for breakfast?"

"Breakfast can wait," Larsson said. "Have you a guest list for last week? Do you have your customer records in a ledger, or on loose sheets of paper?"

The girl looked worried. "Has something happened?"

"This is a routine enquiry," Lindman said. "Nothing to worry about. Have you had any foreigners staying here in the last week or so?"

She thought for a moment. "There were four Finns here for two nights last week, Wednesday and Thursday."

"Nobody else?"

"No."

"He might have booked in somewhere else, of course," Larsson said. This isn't the only place to stay in Sveg."

He turned to the girl. "When we had dinner here, quite late, you may remember another customer in the dining room. What language did he speak?"

"English. But he came from Argentina."

"How do you know?"

"He paid by credit card. He showed me his passport."

She went into a back room and eventually came back with a Visa counterfoil. They read the name. Fernando Hereira. Legible even in the signature.

Larsson grunted with pleasure. "We've got him," he said. "Always assuming it is him."

"Has he been here before?" Lindman said.

"No."

"Did you see what make of car he had?"

"No."

"Did he say where he'd come from? Or where he was going to?"

"No. He didn't say much at all. He was friendly, though."

"Could you describe him?"

The girl thought for a moment. Lindman could see she was trying hard.

"I've got such an awful memory for faces."

"But you must have seen something. Did he look like one of us?"

"Not at all."

"How old was he?"

"Sixty, perhaps."

"Hair?"

"Grey hair."

"Eyes?"

"I wouldn't remember that."

"Was he fat or thin?"

"I don't think he was fat."

"What was he wearing?"

"A blue shirt, I think. And a blazer, I'm not sure."

"Can you remember anything else?"

"No."

Larsson shook his head and sat down on one of the brown sofas in the reception area, with the Visa slip in his hand. Lindman joined him. By now it was 6.25 a.m. on November 11. Eight days to go before Lindman was due to report to the hospital in Borås. Larsson yawned and rubbed his eyes. Neither of them spoke.

A door leading to the bedrooms opened. Lindman looked up and saw Veronica Molin.

CHAPTER 25

Silberstein watched the dawn approaching. For a while it was like being at home. The light was the same as he'd often seen as the sun rose over the horizon and spread its rays over the plains to the west of Buenos Aires, but after a few minutes, the feeling had gone. He was in the Swedish mountains, not far from the Norwegian border. He'd gone straight back to Frostengren's chalet after the botched visit to the Berggren woman. The man he'd seen behind the house, and had no choice but to knock down and frighten with a pretended attempt to throttle him, was one of the police officers he'd seen at the hotel when he'd been having dinner. He couldn't understand what the man was doing there at night. Was the woman's house being guarded after all? He'd kept a careful watch on it before knocking on the door and pushing his way in.

He forced himself to consider the possibility that he had squeezed too hard and that the policeman was dead.

He'd driven fast through the night, not because he was afraid somebody might be chasing him, but because he could no longer control his craving for alcohol. He'd bought both wine and spirits in Sveg, as if he'd anticipated a disaster. Now he accepted that he could no longer do without alcohol. The only restriction he would apply was that he would not open any of the bottles until he got back to the chalet.

It was 3 a.m. by the time he drove the last difficult stretch up to Frostengren's chalet. It was pitch dark on all sides as he made his way to the door. The moment he was inside, he opened a bottle of wine and downed half of it. Calm gradually settled in him. He sat at the table next to the window, without moving a muscle, without a thought in his head, and steadily drank. Then he drew the telephone towards him and dialled Maria's number. There was a buzzing and scraping in the line, but her voice sounded very close even so. He could almost smell her breath through the receiver.

"Where are you?" she asked.

"I'm still here."

"What can you see through your window?"

"Darkness."

"Is what I'm afraid of true?"

"What are you afraid of?"

"That you'll never come back?"

The question worried him. He took another drink of wine before answering.

"Why shouldn't I come back?"

"I don't know. You are the only one who knows what you're doing and why you aren't here. You're lying to me, Aron. You're not telling me the truth."

"Why should I lie to you?"

"You haven't made this journey to look at furniture. There's some other reason. I don't know what it is. Perhaps you've met another woman. I don't know. The only one who knows is you. And God."

He realised that what he'd told her before hadn't sunk in – that he'd killed a man.

"I'll be home soon."

"When?"

"Soon."

"I still don't know where you are."

"I'm high up in the mountains. It's cold."

"Have you started drinking again?"

"Not very much. Just so that I can sleep."

The connection was cut. When Silberstein dialled the number again, he couldn't get through. He tried several times without success. Then he prepared to wait for the dawn. Things had now entered the crucial stage, that was clear. The Berggren woman had seen his face when she pulled the hood off. He hadn't expected that, and he had panicked. He ought to have stayed there, put the hood on again and forced her to tell him what he was certain she knew. Instead he'd fled and run into the policeman.

Although he was filling his body with alcohol, he was still able to think during the long wait for the dawn. He always experienced a moment of great insight before he became intoxicated. He had learnt how much he could drink, and how quickly, while still being in control of his thoughts, and he needed to think clearly now. The end game was starting. Nothing had turned out as he'd thought it would. Despite all his planning, all his meticulous preparations. It was all Andersson's fault. Or rather, it was because somebody had killed him. It had to be the woman. The question was: why? What forces had he set in motion when he killed Molin?

He carried on drinking, but held his intoxication in check. He found it hard to accept that a woman in her seventies could have murdered Andersson. She must have had an accomplice. In which case, who? And if the police thought she was the murderer, why hadn't they arrested her? He couldn't find any answers, and started all over again. The woman had said that she didn't know who killed Andersson. He was sure from the start that she wasn't telling the truth. When she heard that Molin was dead, she drove under cover of darkness to Andersson's house and killed him. Was it revenge? Did she think Andersson had killed Molin? What was between these people that he couldn't work out? The police must have seen that there was a link. He still had the crumpled restaurant bill with the three names on the back of it.

He was beginning to think that revenge was a sort of boomerang that was now on its way back and would soon hit his own head. It was a matter of guilt. He was indifferent with regard to Molin. Killing him had been necessary, something he owed to his father. But Andersson wouldn't have died if he hadn't whipped Molin to death. The question now was: did he have an obligation to avenge the death of Abraham Andersson? Thoughts buzzed around in his head all night. Occasionally he went outside and gazed at the starry sky. He wrapped himself in a blanket while he waited. Waited for what? He didn't know. For something to go away. His face was known now. The woman had seen it. The police would start putting two and two together and work out where he was. Sooner or later they'd find his name on the credit card receipt at the hotel. That had been the one thing that had scotched his careful planning: running out of ready cash. The police would come looking for him, and they would assume *he*'d killed Andersson. And now that he might have killed a police officer – even by accident – they would commit all their resources to hunting him down.

He kept coming back to that chance encounter. Had he squeezed the policeman's neck too hard? When he let go and walked away, he was convinced that he hadn't overdone it. Now he wasn't so sure. He ought to get away, as far away as possible, but he knew he wouldn't do that, not until he found out what had happened to Andersson. He could not go back to Buenos Aires until he had the answers to his questions.

Dawn broke. He was tired. From time to time he nodded off as he sat looking at the mountains. He couldn't stay here: he had to move on, or they'd find him soon enough. He stood up and started wandering round the house. Where should he go? He went outside for a pee. It was slowly getting light, the thin, grey mist he was familiar with from Argentina. Only it wasn't so cold there. He went back inside.

He'd made up his mind. He gathered together his belongings, the bottles of wine, the tinned food, the crispbread. He didn't bother about the car. That could stay where it was. Perhaps somebody would find it tomorrow, perhaps he'd get a start. He left the house at about 9 a.m. and headed straight up the mountain. He stopped after only a hundred metres and off-loaded some of his luggage. Then he set off again, uphill all the time. He was drunk, kept stumbling, falling over and scratching his face on the rough ground. Even so he kept on until he could no longer see the chalet.

By noon he hadn't the strength to go any further. He pitched his tent in the lee of a large rock, took off his shoes, rolled out his sleeping bag and lay down, with a bottle of wine in his hand.

The light seeping through the canvas turned the interior of the tent into something resembling a sunset. He thought about Maria as he emptied the bottle, how much she meant to him. Then he snuggled down and fell asleep.

When he woke up, he knew he had one more decision to make.

At 10 a.m. there was to be a meeting in Johansson's office. The forensic unit were already in Berggren's house, and a dog team was trying to sniff out traces of the man who had attacked both Berggren and Lindman. Lindman had slept for a couple of hours at the hotel, but Larsson woke him soon after 9 a.m., telling him he must attend the meeting.

"You're involved in these murder investigations whether you or I like it or not. I've spoken to Rundström. He thinks you ought to be there. Not formally, of course. But we can forget the rule book, given the circumstances."

"Any new clues?"

"The dog headed straight for the bridge. That's where he must have parked his car. The forensic boys reckon they've got a pretty good print of his tyres. We'll see if it matches any of the casts we made at the Molin and Andersson sites."

"Have you had any sleep?"

"Too much to see to. I've brought in four men from Östersund, and we've called in a couple of Erik's boys who were off duty. There are a lot of doors we have to knock on. Let's face it, somebody must have seen something. A swarthy-featured man speaking broken English. It's impossible to live without talking to other people. You fill your tank with petrol, you eat, you shop. *Someone* must have seen him. He must have spoken to someone, somewhere."

Lindman said he would be there. He got out of bed, and felt the back of his neck. It was tender. He'd taken a shower before going to bed. As he was getting dressed, he thought about his meeting with Veronica Molin a few hours before. They'd breakfasted together as he was on his way into the hotel. Lindman had told her what had happened during the night. She'd paid close attention without asking any questions. Then he'd begun to feel sick and excused himself. They'd agreed to meet later in the day, when he felt better. He'd fallen asleep the moment he'd crawled into bed.

When he was woken by Larsson's call, he felt fine. He examined his face in the bathroom mirror and was overcome by a feeling of unreality that he had no defence against. He burst into tears, flung a towel at the mirror and staggered out of the bathroom. I'm dying, he thought. I've got cancer. It's incurable, and I'm going to die.

His mobile was ringing in the jacket he'd dropped on the floor. Elena. He could hear the buzz of voices behind her.

"Where are you?" she said.

"In my room. And you?"

"At school. I had the feeling I ought to phone you."

"Everything's OK here. I miss you."

"You know where I am. When are you coming home?"

"I have to report to the hospital on the 19th. I'll be back some time before then."

"I dreamt last night that we went to England. Can't we do that? I've always wanted to see London."

"Do we have to fix it now?"

"I'm just telling you about a dream I had. I thought it might be good to have something we could both look forward to."

"Of course we'll go to London. If I live that long."

"What do you mean by that?"

"Nothing. I'm just tired. I have to go to a meeting now."

"I thought you were supposed to be on sick leave?"

"They asked me to stay on."

"There was something in the paper here yesterday about the murders. And a picture of Herbert Melin."

"Molin. Herbert Molin."

"I have to go now. Phone me tonight."

Lindman promised to call. He put the phone down. Where would I be without Elena? he thought. Nowhere.

When they met for the meeting Rundström surprised Lindman by giving him a friendly handshake. Johansson took off a pair of muddy rubber boots, a dog handler from Östersund asked angrily if somebody by the name of Anders had been in touch. Larsson tapped the table with his pen and started the meeting. He made a brisk and clear summary of what had happened the night before.

"Berggren has asked us to wait until this evening before questioning her in any more detail," he said. "That seems reasonable. In any case, we have lots of other things that are just as pressing."

"We have some footprints," Johansson said. "From inside Elsa's house, and from the garden. Whoever it was that broke in and then tapped Lindman on the head was rather careless. We have footprints from the Molin and Andersson murders. That will be a priority for the forensic boys now, establishing whether there's a match. That and the tyre tracks."

Larsson agreed. "The dogs picked up a scent," he said. "It went as far as the bridge. Then what happened?"

The dog handler answered. He was middle-aged, and had a scar across his left cheek. "It went cold."

"No finds?"

"Nothing."

"There's a car park there," Johansson said. "In fact, it's just the grass verge that's been concreted over. Anyway, the scent petered out. We can assume that his car was parked there. Especially if we bear in mind that it's not easy to see anything there in the dark. The street lighting is pretty poor just there. It's by no means unheard of, especially in summer, for people to park there and do a bit of cuddling in the back seat." Chuckles from all round the table. "Occasionally we find ourselves lumbered with more intricate problems based on happenings there," he said. "The kind of thing that used to take place off remote forest tracks and kept the magistrates busy with paternity suits."

"Somebody must have seen this man," Larsson said. "The name on his credit card was Fernando Hereira."

"I've just been talking to Östersund," said Rundström, who'd been quiet until now and let Larsson chair the meeting. "They've triggered a computer search and come up with a Fernando Hereira in Västerås. He was arrested for VAT evasion some years ago – but he's over 70 now, so we can probably take it that he's not the man we're after."

"I don't know any Spanish," Larsson said, "but I have an idea that Fernando Hereira would be quite a common name."

"Like mine," Johansson said. "Every other bastard's called Erik, up here in Norrland at least, and in my generation."

"We don't know if it's his real name," Larsson said.

"We can chase him up through Interpol," Rundström said. "As soon as we have some fingerprints, that is."

Several phones started ringing at once. Larsson proposed a ten-minute break and stood up. He also indicated to Lindman that they should go out into the corridor. They sat down in the reception area. Larsson eyed the stuffed bear up and down.

"I saw a bear once," he said. "Not far from Krokom. I'd been sorting out a few moonshiners, and was driving back to Östersund. I remember I was thinking about my father. I'd always thought it was that Italian crooner, but when I was twelve my Mum told me it was some chancer from Ånge, who disappeared the moment he heard

Mum was pregnant. All of a sudden, there was this bear, by the side of the road. I slammed on the brakes, and thought: 'For Christ's sake! That can't be a bear. It's just a shadow. Or a big rock.' But it was a bear all right. A female. Her fur was very shiny. I watched her for a minute or so, then she lumbered off. I remember thinking: 'This simply doesn't happen! And if it does, it's a once-in-a-lifetime affair.' A bit like getting a royal flush at poker. They say Erik was dealt one 25 years ago. The rest of the deal was rubbish, there were only five kronor in the pot and everybody else discarded."

Larsson stretched and yawned. Then he was serious again.

"I've been thinking about our chat," he said. "That stuff about having to think again. I have a problem with the fact that we might be looking for two different killers. It seems so unlikely. Such a metropolitan way of looking at things, if you take my meaning. Out here in the wilds, things generally happen in accordance with a simpler pattern. There again, I can see that a lot of the evidence suggests you might be right. I talked to Rundström about it, before the meeting."

"What did he say?"

"He's a right bastard with both feet on the ground, never believes anything, never guesses, always sticks to the facts. He shouldn't be underestimated. He catches on fast, possibilities and pitfalls."

Larsson watched a group of children.

"I've tried to map things out in my head," he said when the last of the children had filed into the library. "A man speaking broken English turns up here and kills Molin. That rubbish his daughter goes on about – owing money to some woman in the UK: I don't believe that for a moment. What you suggest could be right, especially if you read that awful diary – that the motive can have its source a long time ago, during the war. The brutality, the fury we've witnessed might suggests revenge. So far so good. That means we are after a killer who was very clear about what he was undertaking. But then he hangs around. That's what I can't work out. He ought to be running away as fast as he can."

"Have you uncovered any links at all with Andersson?"

"Nothing. Our colleagues in Helsingborg have talked to his wife. She claims that Abraham told her everything. He'd mentioned Molin now and then. They were worlds apart. One played classical music and wrote pop songs as a hobby. The other was a retired police officer. I don't think we're going to work out how all this hangs together until we find the bastard who knocked you out. How's your head, by the way."

"It's OK, thanks."

Larsson stood up. "Andersson wrote a song called 'Believe me, I'm a girl'. Erik remembers it. That pseudonym 'Siv Nilsson'. He had a record by some dance band or other – Fabians, or something of the sort. All very odd. He played Mozart one day, made up pop music the next. Erik reckons the pop songs were utter rubbish. I suppose that's life. Mozart on Monday, drivel on Tuesday."

They went back to the conference room where the rest of them were assembled, but the meeting never got going again. Rundström's mobile rang. He answered, then raised his hand.

"They've found a rental car in the Funäsdalen mountains," he said.

They gathered round the wall map. Rundström pointed to the spot.

"There. The car was abandoned."

"Who found it?" It was Larsson who asked.

"A man called Elmberg, he has a summer place there. He'd gone to check that his cottage was OK. Somebody had been there, and he thought it was a bit odd at this time of year. Then he found the car. He suspects the chalet where the car's parked has been broken into too."

"Did he see anybody?"

"No. He didn't hang around. I suppose he was thinking Molin and Andersson. But he did notice a few other things. The car had an Östersund number plate. Plus he saw a foreign newspaper on the back seat."

"Let's go," Larsson said, putting on his jacket.

Rundström turned to Lindman.

"You'd better come too. I mean, you more or less saw him. Assuming it was him."

Larsson asked Lindman to drive because he had calls to make from his mobile.

"Forget the speed limit," Larsson said. "As long as you keep us on the road."

Lindman listened to what Larsson was saying on the phone. A helicopter was on its way. And dogs. They were about to drive through Linsell when Rundström phoned: a shop assistant in Sveg had told the police that she'd sold a knitted woollen hat the previous day.

"Unfortunately the girl can't remember what he looked like, nor does she know if he said anything," Larsson said, with a sigh. "She can't even remember if it was a man or a woman. All she knows is that she sold a bloody woollen hat. Come on! Some people keep their eyes in their arse."

There was a man waiting for them just north of Funäsdalen. Elmberg, he said he was. They hung around until Rundström and another car arrived. Then they continued a couple of kilometres along the main road before turning off.

It was a red Toyota. None of the police officers there could distinguish between Spanish, Portuguese or Italian. Lindman thought the newspaper on the back seat, *El País*, was Italian. Then he looked at the price and realised that Ptas meant pesetas, hence Spain. They continued on foot. The mountain towered above them. There was a chalet where the final steep ascent started. It looked like an old shepherd's hut that had been modernised. Rundström and Larsson reconnoitred, and decided there was nobody there. Both were armed, however, and they approached the front door with care. Rundström shouted a warning. No reply. He shouted again. His words died away with a ghostly echo. Larsson flung the door open. They ran in. A minute later Larsson emerged to say that the chalet was empty, but that somebody had been there. They would now wait for the helicopter with the dog team. The forensic unit that had been sifting the evidence at Berggren's house had broken off and were on their way.

The helicopter came in from the north-east and landed in a field above the chalet. The dogs and dog handlers disembarked. The handlers let the dogs sniff at an unwashed glass Larsson had found. Then they set off into the mountains.

CHAPTER 26

Larsson called off the search at around 5 p.m. Mist had come rolling in from the west, and that together with the gathering darkness made it pointless to go on.

They'd started walking towards the mountain at 1 p.m. All approach roads were being watched. The dogs kept losing the scent, then finding it again. They started out heading due north, then branched off along a ridge heading west before turning north again. They were on a sort of plateau when Larsson called off the operation, after consulting Rundström. They'd set off in line, then spread out as they walked along the ridge. It had been easy going to start with, not too steep. Even so, Lindman soon noticed that he was out of condition, but he didn't want to give up, certainly not be the first to do so.

But there was something else about this walk up the mountain. At first it was just a vague, imprecise feeling, but eventually it turned into a memory and became steadily clearer. He'd been up this mountain before. It happened when he was seven or eight, but he'd repressed it.

It was late summer, a couple of weeks before school started again. His mother was away – her sister, who lived in Kristianstad, had been unexpectedly widowed and his mother had gone there to help her. One day his father announced that they were going to pack the car and go on holiday. They would head north, live in a tent, and do it on the cheap. Lindman had only a vague recollection of the car journey. He'd been squashed in the back seat with one of his sisters and all the luggage that for some reason his father had not secured on the roof. He was also fighting against car sickness. His father didn't deem it necessary to stop just because one of the children was going to be sick. He couldn't remember if he and his sisters survived without vomiting: that part of his recollection had gone for ever.

Lindman was the last in line. Thirty metres in front of him was

Johansson, who occasionally answered calls on his walkie-talkie. The memory unfolded with every step he took.

If he was eight then, it was 29 years ago. 1970, August 1970. On their way up to the mountains they'd spent a cramped night in the tent, and Stefan had to clamber over the rest of the family to go outside for a pee. The next day they'd come to a place that Lindman seemed to remember was Vemdalsskalet. They'd pitched their tent behind an old wooden cabin not far away from the mountain hotel.

He was surprised that he'd been able to lose the memory of that holiday. So he'd been here before, in these very parts. Why had he chosen not to remember? What had happened?

There was a woman somewhere in that memory. She'd appeared just after they'd pitched the tent. His father had seen her on the other side of the road, and had gone to greet her. Stefan and his sisters watched as their father shook hands with the woman and started talking, out of earshot. Stefan remembered asking his sisters if they knew who she was, but they'd hissed at him to be quiet. That was a part of his recollection that raised a smile. His youth was marked by his sisters always telling him to be quiet, never listening to what he said, looking at him with a degree of contempt that indicated he would never be included in their games or their circle of friends, that he was too small, too stupid.

His father came back to join them, the woman as well. She was older than he was, with stripes of grey in her hair; and she was wearing the black and white uniform of a waitress. She reminded him of somebody, he now thought. And then the penny dropped: Elsa Berggren. Even if it wasn't her. He could remember a smile, but also something off-putting, a ruthless streak. They'd stood next to the tent, and she hadn't been surprised by their arrival. Stefan remembered being rather worried – worried that his father would never go back to Kinna, and that his mother would stay in Kristianstad. The rest of the meeting with the unknown woman now fell into place. His father told them that her name was Vera, that she was from Germany, and then she'd shaken hands with them all in turn, first his sisters and then him.

Lindman stopped. Johansson was over to his left, and cursed as he tripped. The helicopter came clattering in at a low altitude and started circling over the valley below. He started walking again. There's another door to open yet, he thought. They'd walked on the mountain all those years ago as well. No really long treks, always within easy distance from the hotel.

An unusually hot August evening in the mountains. He couldn't see where his sisters were, but Vera and his father were in deckchairs next to the wooden cabin. They were laughing. Stefan didn't like what he saw, and went away, to the back of the cabin. There was a door there, and he opened it. He'd no idea if it was allowed, but now he was inside Vera's house. Two cramped rooms and a low ceiling. Some photographs standing on a bureau. He strained his eyes to conjure up those pictures. A wedding photo. Vera and her husband wearing a uniform.

He recalled it now, as clear as day. The man in an army uniform, Vera dressed in white, smiling, a garland of flowers in her hair, or maybe it was a bridal crown. Next to the wedding photograph was another picture in a frame. A picture of Hitler. At that moment the door opened. Vera was there, with his father. She said something in German, or possibly Swedish with a German accent, he couldn't remember. But she'd been angry, he remembered that all right. His father had led him away and boxed his ears.

That was it. The memory ended as the box on the ears landed. He had no recollection of the drive back to Kinna. Nothing about being squashed in the back seat, of feeling car sick. Nothing at all. A picture of Hitler, a box on the ears, nothing else.

Lindman shook his head. Thirty years ago his father had taken the children and visited a German woman who worked at a hotel in the mountains. Just under the surface, as on a photograph behind another photograph, was the whole of the Hitler era. It was as Wetterstedt had said: nothing had completely gone away, it had simply taken on new forms, new means of expression, but the dream of white supremacy was still alive. His father went to see a woman called Vera, and boxed his son's ears when he saw something he shouldn't have seen. Was there anything else? He searched his memory, but his father had never made any reference to it. After the box on the ears there was nothing more.

The helicopter circled round once more then flew off. Lindman let his gaze wander over the mountain, but all he actually saw were two photographs standing in a room with a low ceiling.

Soon after that the mist came down and they turned back. They came to the chalet at about 6 p.m. The helicopter dropped two of the dog handlers, then disappeared in the direction of Östersund. The pilot had brought with him baskets containing sandwiches and coffee. Rundström seemed to be forever talking into his walkie-talkie when he wasn't on the telephone. Lindman kept to the periphery. Larsson listened to a report from one of the forensic officers who had searched the chalet, and made notes. Then he poured himself a cup of coffee and came over to Lindman.

"Well, we've found out a few things at least," he said.

He balanced his cup on a stone and flicked through his note–book.

"The owner is a Kurt Frostengren and lives in Stockholm. He usually comes here in the summer, over Christmas and New Year, and a week in March for some skiing. The house is empty for the rest of the year. Apparently he inherited it from a relative. Someone has broken in and set up his HQ here, then gone away. He knows Berggren has seen his face. He must be aware of the possibility that we might have put two and two together and realised that he read the back of my bill in the restaurant. There is a cold-blooded side to the man that we mustn't underestimate. He knows we'll go looking for him. Especially after he attacked you and Berggren."

"Where's he heading for?"

Larsson thought before replying. "I'd formulate the question differ-ently. Why is he still here?"

"There's something still to do."

"The question is: what?"

"He wants to know who murdered Andersson. We've already talked about that."

Larsson shook his head. "Not only that. He wants more than that. He intends killing whoever murdered Andersson." There was no other explanation. But he had one more question for Lindman.

"Why is it so important for him?"

"If we knew that, we'd know what this whole business is about."

They stood gazing into the mist.

"He's hiding," Larsson said. "He's clever, our man from Buenos Aires."

Lindman looked at him in surprise. "How do you know he's from Buenos Aires?"

Larsson took a piece of paper out of his pocket. A torn piece of newspaper, the crossword from *Aftonbladet*. Something like a doodle was in the margin, crossed out but originally written quite firmly.

"541," Larsson said. "54 is Argentina. And 1 is Buenos Aires. The paper is dated June 12, when Frostengren was here. He saved newspapers for making fires. The numbers have been written by somebody else. It must be Fernando Hereira. The newspaper in the car is Spanish, not from Argentina, but the language is the same. It can't be easy to find newspapers from Argentina in Sweden, but it's comparatively easy to find Spanish ones."

"Is there a full telephone number in Argentina?"

"No."

Lindman thought for a moment.

"So, he's been sitting up here in the mountains, and made a phone call to Argentina. Can't the call be traced?"

"We're doing that now. Frostengren's phone has its own line and you can dial direct. If Hereira had used a mobile, we could have traced that without difficulty."

Larsson bent down to pick up his coffee.

"I keep forgetting that we're looking for not one but perhaps two cold-blooded murderers," he said. "We're beginning to get an idea of who Hereira might be and how he goes about things, but what about the other one? The one who killed Andersson, who's he?"

The question remained unanswered in the mist. Larsson left Lindman and went to talk to Rundström and the remaining dog handler. Lindman looked at the Alsatian. It was exhausted. It lay with its neck pressed against the damp earth. Lindman wondered if a police dog could feel disappointment.

Half an hour later Larsson and Lindman returned to Sveg. Rundström would stay in Funäsdalen with the dog handler and three other officers. They drove in silence through the forest. This time Larsson did the driving. Lindman could see that he was very tired. A few kilometres short of Sveg he pulled onto the verge and stopped.

"I can't work it out," Larsson said "Who killed Andersson? It's as if we're only scratching the surface. We have no idea what this is about.

A man from Argentina disappears up a mountain when he ought to be getting away from here as fast as possible. He doesn't *flee* up the mountain, he withdraws there, and then comes back again."

"There's another possibility that we haven't considered," Lindman said. "The man we are calling Fernando Hereira might know something we don't."

Larsson shook his head. "In that case he wouldn't have put on a hood and asked Berggren those questions."

Then they looked at each other.

"Are you thinking what I'm thinking?" Larsson said.

"Possibly," Lindman said. "That Hereira knows, or thinks he knows, that it was Berggren who killed Andersson. And he wants to make her confess."

Larsson drummed his fingers on the wheel.

"Perhaps Berggren isn't telling the truth. She says the man who forced his way into her house asked her who had killed Andersson. He might well have said, 'I know it was you who killed Andersson.'" Larsson restarted the engine. "We'll go on keeping watch on the mountain," he said. "And we'll get tough with Berggren."

They continued to Sveg. The countryside vanished beyond the headlight beams. As they were driving into the hotel courtyard, Larsson's mobile rang.

"It was Rundström," he said when the call was over. "The car was rented in Östersund on November 5. By Fernando Hereira, an Argentinian citizen."

They got out of the car.

"Now we're getting somewhere," Larsson said. "Hereira used his driving licence for an identity document. It could be a forgery, of course, but, for simplicity's sake, let's assume it's genuine. We could be closer to him now than ever we were on the mountain."

Lindman was exhausted. Larsson left his case with reception.

"I'll be in touch," he said. "Are you staying?"

"I'll stay one more day."

Larsson put his hand on Lindman's shoulder. "I must admit it's a long time since I've had somebody to talk to like you. But tell me, honestly: if you'd been in my shoes, what would you have done differently?"

"Not a thing."

Larsson burst out laughing. "You're too kind," he said. "I can stand the odd punch. Can you?"

He didn't wait for an answer, but dashed out to his car. Lindman wondered about the question as he collected his key. It was a new girl in reception. He went up to his room and lay down on the bed. He thought he ought to phone Elena, but first he needed to get some rest.

When he woke he knew he'd been dreaming. A chaotic dream, but all he could remember was the fear. He looked at his watch: 9.15. He'd better hurry if he were going to get some dinner. Besides, he had an appointment with Veronica Molin.

She was waiting for him in the dining room.

"I knocked on your door," she said. "When you didn't answer, I assumed you were asleep."

"It was a strenuous night and a long day. Have you eaten?"

"I have to eat at regular times. Especially when the food is like it is here."

The waitress was also new. She seemed hesitant. Lindman had the impression that Veronica Molin must have complained about something. He ordered a beef steak. Veronica Molin was drinking water. He wanted wine. She watched him with a smile.

"I've never met a policeman before. Not as close up as this, at least."

"What's it like?"

"I think everybody's a bit frightened of policemen, deep down."

She paused and lit a cigarette.

"My brother's on his way here from the Caribbean," she said. "He works on a cruise ship. Maybe I said that already? He's a steward. When he's not at sea he lives in Florida. I've only visited him once, when I was in Miami to clinch a business deal. It took us less than an hour to start quarrelling. I can't remember what about."

"When's the funeral?"

"On Tuesday, eleven o'clock. Are you thinking of coming?"

"I don't know."

Lindman's meal arrived.

"How can you stay as long as this?" he said. "I had the impression that it was difficult for you to get here at all. Now you're staying for ever."

"Until Wednesday. No longer. Then I'm leaving."

"Where to?"

"First London, then Madrid."

"I'm only a simple policeman, but I'm curious about what you do."

"I'm what the English call a 'deal-maker'. Or 'broker'. I bring interested parties together and help them to produce a contract. So that a business deal can take place."

"Dare I ask how much you earn from that kind of work?"

"Presumably a lot more than you."

"Everybody does."

She turned up a wine glass and slid it towards him.

"I've changed my mind."

Lindman filled her glass. He drank her health. She seemed to be looking at him in a different way now, not as warily as before.

"I went to see Elsa Berggren today," she said. "I realised too late that it was not a good time. She told me what had happened last night. And about you. Have you caught him?"

"Not yet, no. Besides, it's not me who's hunting him. I'm not part of the investigation team."

"But the police think that the man who attacked you is the person who murdered my father."

"Yes."

"I tried to get Giuseppe Larsson on the telephone. I do have a right to know what's happening, after all. Who is this man?"

"We think he's called Fernando Hereira. And that he's from Argentina."

"I hardly think my father knew anybody from Argentina. What is the motive supposed to be?"

"Something that happened during the war."

She lit another cigarette. Lindman looked at her hands and wished he could hold them.

"So the police don't believe my theory? About the woman from Scotland?"

"Nothing is excluded. We follow up every lead. That's one of the basic rules."

"I shouldn't smoke while you're eating."

"It doesn't matter. I've already got cancer."

She looked at him in surprise. "Did I hear you right?"

"It was a joke. I'm fully fit."

What he really wanted to do was to leave the table. Go up to his room and phone Elena. But there was something else driving him now.

"A strange sort of joke."

"I suppose I wanted to see how you reacted."

She put her head on one side and looked hard at him.

"Are you making a pass at me?"

He emptied his glass.

"Don't all men do that? You must be aware that you are very attractive."

She shook her head but she didn't say anything and moved her glass away when Lindman tried to give her more. He filled his own glass.

"What did you and Elsa Berggren talk about?"

"She was tired. What I was most interested in was to meet the woman who knew my father and had helped him to buy the house where he died. She had known my mother, but we didn't have much to say to each other."

"I've wondered about their relationship. Apart from the Nazi link."

"She said she was sorry my father was dead. I didn't stay long. I didn't like her."

Lindman ordered coffee and a brandy, and asked for the bill.

"Where do you think this Hereira is now?"

"Perhaps he's up in the mountains. He's still in the district, I am sure of it."

"Why?"

"I think he wants to know who killed Andersson."

"I can't work out what connection that man had with my father."

"Nor can we. It will become clear sooner or later, though. We'll catch up with both the murderers, and we'll find out what their motives were."

"I hope so."

Lindman swallowed the brandy in one gulp, and sipped at his coffee. When he'd signed his bill, they went out to reception.

"Will you let me offer you another brandy?" she said. "In my room. But don't expect anything else."

"I long since stopped expecting anything."

"That doesn't sound quite true."

They walked down the corridor. She unlocked her door. Lindman was standing as close to her as possible without actually touching her. On her desk was a laptop computer with a glittering screen.

"I have the whole of my life in this," she said. "I can still keep working while I'm waiting for the funeral."

She poured some brandy for him from a bottle on the table. She didn't take any herself, but kicked off her shoes and sat on the bed. Lindman could feel that he was getting tight. He wanted to touch her now, undress her. His train of thought was interrupted when his mobile rang in his jacket pocket. It was bound to be Elena. He didn't answer.

"Nothing that can't wait," he said.

"Don't you have a family?"

He shook his head.

"Not even a girlfriend?"

"It didn't work."

He put his glass down and reached out his hand. She stared at it for a long time before taking it.

"You can sleep here," she said. "But please expect no more than me lying beside you."

"I've already said I don't expect anything."

She shuffled along the edge of the bed until she was sitting close to him.

"It's a long time since I met anybody who expects as much as you do."

She stood up. "Don't underestimate my ability to see through people. Do whatever you like," she said. "Go back to your room and come back later. To sleep, nothing more."

When Lindman had finished showering and wrapped himself in the biggest towel, the telephone rang again. It was Elena.

"Why haven't you phoned?"

"I have been asleep. I don't feel well."

"Come back home. I'm waiting for you."

"Just a few more days. I really must sleep now. If we go on talking I'll be awake all night."

"I miss you."

"And I miss you."

I lied, he thought. And a little while ago I denied Elena's existence. The worst of it is that just at the moment, I couldn't care less.

CHAPTER 27

When Lindman woke up the next morning Veronica Molin had already left. There was a message on the computer screen: "I've gone out. Make sure you've left by the time I get back. I like men who don't snore. You are one."

Lindman left the room wrapped in a bath towel. On the stairs to the upper floor he passed a chambermaid. She smiled and bade him good morning. When he came to his room he crept into bed. I was drunk, he thought. I spoke to Elena, but I can't remember what I said, only that it wasn't true. He sat up and reached for his mobile. There was a message. Elena had called. He felt a shooting pain in his stomach. He lay down again and pulled the bedclothes over his head. Just as he used to do as a child, to make himself invisible. He wondered if Larsson did the same? And Veronica Molin? She'd been in bed when he returned to her room last night, but firmly rejected all advances – she just tapped him on the arm and told him it was time to go to sleep. He was feeling extremely passionate, but had enough sense to leave her in peace.

He had never lied to Elena before. Now he had, and he still wasn't sure how much he cared. He decided to stay in bed until 9 a.m. Then he would phone her. Meanwhile he would lie with the bedclothes over his head and pretend he didn't exist.

Nine o'clock arrived. She answered at once.

"I was asleep," he said. "I can't have heard the phone. I slept really soundly last night. For the first time for ages."

"Something scared me. It was something I'd dreamt. I don't know what."

"Everything's OK here, but I'm worried. The days are racing past. It'll soon be the 19th."

"It'll all be fine."

"I've got cancer, Elena. If you've got cancer, there's always a chance that you might die."

"That's not what the doctor said."

"She can't know for sure. Nobody can."

"When are you coming home?"

"Very soon. I'm going to Molin's funeral on Tuesday. I expect to be leaving for home on Wednesday. I'll let you know when I'll arrive."

"Are you going to phone me tonight?"

"You'll hear from me."

The conversation had made him sweaty. He didn't like discovering how easy it was to tell lies. He got out of bed. Staying between the sheets would do nothing to dispel his remorse. He dressed and went downstairs to the dining room. The usual girl was back in reception. He felt calmer.

"We're going to change the television set in your room today," she said. "When would be a suitable time?"

"Any time, no problem. Is Inspector Larsson around?"

"I don't think he was in his room at all last night. His key's still here. Have you arrested anybody yet?"

"No."

He set off for the dining room, but turned back.

"Fröken Molin? Is she in?"

"I arrived at 6 a.m. and passed her on her way out."

There was something else he ought to ask her, but Lindman couldn't remember what it was. His hangover was making him feel sick. He drank a glass of milk then sat down with a cup of coffee. His mobile rang. It was Larsson.

"Awake?"

"Just about. I'm having coffee. What about you?"

"I slept for a couple of hours in Erik's office."

"Has something happened?"

"There's always something happening. But it's still misty in Funäsdalen. Everything's at a standstill, according to Rundström. As soon as the mist lifts today they'll set out with the dog again. What are you doing at the moment? Apart from drinking coffee?"

"Nothing."

"Then I'll call on you. I think you ought to come with me on a house visit."

Ten minutes later Larsson came bounding into the dining room, unshaven, hollow-eyed, but full of energy. He poured himself a cup of coffee and sat down. He had a plastic bag in his hand, and put it on the table.

"Do you remember the name Hanna Tunberg?" he said.

Lindman thought, then shook his head.

"She was the one who found Molin. His cleaning lady, who turned up once a fortnight."

"I remember now. From the file I read in your office."

Larsson frowned. "It seems ages since it was my office," he said. "Though it's not so long really."

He shook his head as if he'd just made a great discovery about life and the passage of time.

"I remember there was something to do with her husband," Lindman said.

"He had a nasty shock when he found Molin's body at the edge of the trees. We had several detailed talks with her, though. It turned out that she hardly knew Molin at all, even though she was his cleaner. He never left her on her own, she claimed. He kept a constant watch over her. And he would never allow her to clean the guest room. Where the doll was. She thought he was unpleasant, arrogant. But he paid well."

Larsson put his cup down.

"She phoned this morning and said that she'd calmed down now and been thinking. She thought she had something else she could tell us. I'm on my way there now. I thought you might like to come with me."

"By all means."

Larsson opened the plastic bag and produced a photograph behind glass in a frame. It was of a woman in her sixties.

"Do you know who this is?"

"No."

"Katrin Andersson. Andersson's wife."

"Why have you brought that with you?"

"Because Hanna Tunberg asked me to. She wanted to see what Abraham's wife looked like. I don't know why. But I sent one of the boys out to Dunkärret this morning to fetch the photograph."

Larsson finished his coffee and stood up.

"Hanna lives in Ytterberg," he said. "It's not far."

*   *   *

The house was old and well looked after. It was beautifully situated with views of the wooded hills. A dog started barking when they parked. A woman was standing next to a rusty old tractor, waiting for them.

"Hanna Tunberg," Larsson said. "She was wearing the same clothes the last time I saw her. She's one of the old school."

"Who are they?"

"People who put their best clothes on when they have an appointment with the police. What's the betting that she's been doing some baking?"

He smiled and got out of the car.

Larsson introduced Hanna Tunberg to Lindman. He found it hard to say how old she was. Sixty, perhaps, or maybe only just over 50.

"I've made some coffee. My husband's gone out."

"Not because we were coming, I hope," Larsson said.

"He's a bit odd. He's not over-fond of the police. Even though he's an honest man."

"I'm sure he is," Larsson said. "Shall we go in?"

The house smelt of tobacco, dog and lingon berries. The living room walls were decorated with elk antlers, tapestries and some paintings with woodland motifs. Hanna Tunberg moved some knitting out of the way, lit a cigarette, inhaled deeply and started coughing. There was a rattling noise in her lungs. Lindman noticed that the tips of her fingers were yellow. She had fetched the coffee and filled the cups. There was a plate of buns on the table.

"Now we can talk at our leisure," Larsson said. "You said you'd been thinking. And that there was something you wanted to tell me."

"I don't know if it's important or not, of course."

"Nobody ever knows that beforehand. But we're all ears."

"It's to do with that woman who used to visit herr Molin."

"You mean fröken Berggren?"

"She was sometimes there when I went to do the cleaning. She always left as soon as she clapped eyes on me. I thought she was odd."

"How exactly?"

"Impolite. I have no time for people who give themselves airs. Herr Molin was the same."

"Was there something particular she did to make you think she was impolite?"

"It was just a feeling I had. That she was looking down on me."

"Because you were a cleaner?"

"Yes."

Larsson smiled. "Very nice buns," he said. "We're listening."

Hanna Tunberg was still smoking and didn't seem to notice that she was spilling ash on her skirt.

"It was last spring," she said. "Towards the end of April. I went to the house to do the cleaning, but he wasn't there. I thought it was odd, because we'd agreed on the time."

Larsson raised his hand to interrupt her.

"Did you always do that? Did you always fix a time in advance when you were going to arrive?"

"Always. He wanted to know. Anyway, he wasn't there. I didn't know what to do. I was quite certain that I hadn't got the wrong day or the wrong time, though. I always wrote it down."

"What happened next, then?"

"I waited. But he didn't come. I stood on a sledge so that I could see in through the window. I thought he might be ill, you see. The house was empty. Then I thought about Abraham Andersson. I knew they were in touch with each other."

Larsson raised his hand again.

"How did you know that?"

"Herr Molin told me once. I don't know anybody around here apart from Elsa," he said. "And Abraham."

"What happened?"

"I thought maybe I should drive to Abraham's place. I knew where he lived. My husband mended a bow for him once. He's a jack of all trades, my husband. Anyway, I went there and knocked on the door. There was a long pause before Abraham answered."

She stubbed out her cigarette and immediately lit another. All the smoke was making Lindman feel ill.

"It was in the afternoon," she said. "It must have been about three. And he wasn't dressed yet."

"Was he naked?" Larsson said.

"I said he wasn't dressed. Not that he was naked. I'd have said if he had been. Do you want me to tell you what happened, or are you going to interrupt all the time?"

"I'll take another bun and keep quiet," Larsson said. "Carry on."

"He was wearing trousers, but no shirt. And barefoot. I asked him if he knew where herr Molin was. He said he didn't. Then he shut the door. He didn't want to let me in. And I knew why, of course."

"He wasn't alone?"

"Exactly."

"How did you know? Did you see anybody?"

"Not then. But I realised even so. I went back to the car. I'd parked some way short of the drive. I was just about to leave when I noticed a car standing behind the garage. It wasn't Abraham's."

"How did you know that?"

"I don't know. I just get the feeling sometimes. Doesn't it happen to you too?"

"What did you do next?"

"I was going to start the engine and drive away when I glanced in the rear-view mirror and saw somebody coming out of the house. It was a woman. When she realised that I was still there she went back inside."

Larsson picked up the plastic bag with the photograph of Katrin Andersson. He handed it over. She spilled ash on it.

"No," she said. "That wasn't her. I was quite a long way away, and it's not easy to remember somebody you've seen in the rear-view mirror. But I'm sure it wasn't her."

"Who do you think it was, then?"

She hesitated. Larsson repeated his question.

"Who do you think it was?"

"Fröken Berggren. But I can't be sure."

"Why not?"

"It all happened so quickly."

"But you had seen her before, hadn't you? And even so you couldn't identify her for sure."

"I'm telling you the truth. It happened so quickly. I only saw her for a few seconds. She came out, saw the car and went back inside."

"So she didn't want anybody to see her?"

Hanna Tunberg looked at him in surprise.

"Is that so strange? If she'd come out of a house where there was a half-naked man who wasn't her husband?"

"The memory works like a camera." Larsson said. "You see something and the image is stored inside your head. You don't need to see a thing for long in order to remember it clearly."

"Some photographs are blurred, though, aren't they?"

"Why are you only telling us this now?"

"I didn't remember until today. My memory's not very good. I thought it might be important. If it was Elsa Berggren. I mean, she had contact with both Herbert and Abraham. Anyway, if it wasn't her, it was certainly not his wife."

"You're not sure that it was Elsa Berggren, but you are sure that it wasn't Katrin Andersson?"

"Yes."

Hanna Tunberg started coughing again, that rattling, scraping cough. She stubbed out her cigarette in irritation. Then she gasped for breath, stood halfway up and slumped forward over the table. The coffee pot fell over. Larsson stood up as she fell. He turned her over, onto her back.

"She's not breathing," he said. "Phone for an ambulance."

Larsson started giving her the kiss of life as Lindman took out his mobile.

Looking back, he would remember the events as if in slow motion. Larsson trying to breathe some life back into the woman lying on the floor, and the thin wisp of smoke rising up to the ceiling from the ashtray.

It took the ambulance half an hour to get there. Larsson had given up by then. Hanna Tunberg was dead. He went to the kitchen and rinsed his mouth. Lindman had seen a lot of dead people – after road accidents, suicides, murders: but only now did he grasp how close death actually is. One moment she'd had a cigarette in her hand and answered "yes" to a question, the next she was dead.

Larsson went out to meet the ambulance.

"It was all over in a second," he said to the man who examined Hanna Tunberg to make sure she was dead.

"We're not really supposed to put dead bodies in an ambulance, but we can't very well leave her here."

"Two police officers are witnesses to the fact that she died a natural death. I'll make sure that goes into the report."

The ambulance left. Larsson looked at Lindman and shook his head.

"It's hard to believe that it can be all over so quickly. Mind you, it's the best kind of death you can possibly wish for."

"As long as it doesn't come too soon."

They went outside. The dog barked. It had started raining.

"What did she say? That her husband had gone out?"

Lindman looked round. There was no sign of a car. The garage doors were open. Nothing inside.

"He seems to have gone for a drive."

"We'd better wait. Let's go in."

They sat without speaking. The dog barked again. Then it, too, fell silent.

"What do you do when you have to inform a relative that some-body's died?" Larsson said.

"I've never had to do that. I've been present, but it was always some-body else who had to do the talking."

"There was only one occasion when I thought seriously about resigning from the force," Larsson said. "Two sisters, aged four and five, had been playing by a pond. Seven years ago. Their father had left them on their own for a few minutes. We never managed to find out what actually happened, but they both drowned. I was the one who had to go and tell their mother about it, taking a priest with me. Their father had broken down. He'd gone out with the children so their mother was left in peace to prepare for the five-year-old's party. That drove me close to giving up. It hadn't happened before, and it hasn't happened since."

The silence wafted to and fro between them. Lindman looked at the carpet where Hanna Tunberg had died. Her knitting was on a table next to the chair, the needles sticking out at an angle. Larsson's mobile rang. Both of them gave a start. Larsson answered. The rain started pelting against the window panes. He finished the call without having said much.

"That was the ambulance. They'd met Hanna's husband. He went with them in the ambulance. We don't need to stay here any longer."

Neither of them moved.

"We'll never know," Larsson said. "A witness steps forward, crossing the threshold that usually holds people back from saying anything. The question remaining is: was she telling the truth?"

"Why shouldn't she have been?"

Larsson was by the window, looking out at the rain. "I know nothing about Borås," he said, "other than that it's a decent-sized town. Sveg is not much more than a village with only a few thousand inhabitants. Fewer people live in the whole of Härjedalen than in a Stockholm suburb. That means that it's harder to keep secrets here."

Larsson left the window and sat down in the chair where Hanna Tunberg had died. Then he sprang to his feet and remained standing.

"I ought to have mentioned this before we got here. I suppose I simply forgot that you are not from these parts. It's a bit like the angels with their halos. Everybody up here is surrounded by little rings of rumour, and Hanna Tunberg was no exception."

"I don't see what you're getting at."

Larsson stared gloomily down at the carpet where Hanna had been lying.

"One shouldn't speak ill of the dead. What's so wrong about being nosy? Most people are. Police work is based on facts and curiosity."

"You mean she was a gossip monger?"

"Erik told me she was. And he always knows what he's talking about. I had that in mind all the time she was speaking. If she'd lived for another five minutes I'd have been able to ask her. Now that's not possible." Larsson went back to the window. "We should be able to conduct an experiment," he said. "We'll put a car where she said she'd parked. Then we'll ask somebody to look in the rear-view mirror while somebody else comes out of Andersson's front door, counts to three and then goes in again. I can guarantee that either the person in the car will see whoever it is at the door perfectly clearly, or not at all."

"So she was lying?"

"Yes and no. She wasn't actually telling a lie, but I suspect that she had either spotted something behind Andersson when he answered the door, or that she peeped in through a window. We'll never know which."

"But you think the gist of what she said was right?"

"That's what I think. She wanted to tell us something that might be important, but she didn't want to tell us how she'd found out about it." Larsson sighed. "I can feel a cold coming on," he said. "I've got a sore throat. No. Not yet. But it's starting to get sore. I'll have a headache a couple of hours from now. Shall we go?"

"Just one question," Lindman said. "Or two, rather. What are the implications if it really was Berggren, as Hanna suggested? And if it wasn't her, who was it? And what does it all mean?"

"I make that three questions," Larsson said. "And they're all important. We can't answer any of them, though. Not yet, at least."

They hurried through the rain to the car. The dog had retired to its kennel and watched their departure in silence. That was the second melancholy dog Lindman had come across in the space of a few days. He wondered how much of what had happened they'd understood.

They were on the point of joining the main road when Larsson pulled into the side and stopped.

"I must phone Rundström. I guess that the mist is as bad as ever. And to make things worse, I heard on the radio this morning that a storm's brewing."

He dialled the number. Lindman tried to think about Elena, but all he could picture was Hanna Tunberg. Gasping for breath, then dying with a rattling sound.

Larsson told Rundström about Hanna Tunberg's death. Then he asked questions – about the mist, the dog, the man on the mountain. It was a short call. Larsson put the phone down and felt his throat.

"Every time I catch a cold I think I'm going to die. It's not an hour since Hanna Tunberg died before our very eyes, and here I am complaining because I think I can feel a cold coming on."

"Why worry about somebody who's dead?"

Larsson looked at him. "I'm not thinking about her," he said. "I'm thinking about my own death. That's all I care about."

Lindman punched the roof of the car. He couldn't control his violent outburst. "You sit here complaining about the beginnings of a cold. At the same time, I could *really* be dying."

He flung the car door open and stormed out into the rain.

Larsson opened his door. "That was thoughtless of me."

Lindman pulled a face. "What difference does it make? Cancer or a sore throat."

He got back into the car. Larsson stayed out in the rain.

Lindman stared through the windscreen, past the raindrops. The trees were swaying gently. He had tears in his eyes. The mist was in his eyes, not on the windscreen.

*   *   *

They drove back to Sveg. Lindman leaned his head against the side window, thinking about where his life was going. He gave up and started again. Elena was there. And Veronica. He wasn't sure where he fitted in.

It was 12.30 when they arrived at the hotel. Larsson said he was hungry. The rain was still pattering on the car roof. They hurried into reception with their jackets pulled up over their heads.

The girl in reception stood up.

"Can you phone Erik Johansson," she said. "He's been trying to get in touch with you. It's urgent."

Larsson took his mobile out of his jacket pocket and cursed. It was switched off. He switched it on and sat on the sofa. Lindman thumbed through a brochure lying on the reception desk. *Old Mountain Pastures in Härjedalen*. Hanna Tunberg was still dying before his eyes. The girl in reception was searching through a file. Larsson was speaking to Johansson.

What Lindman would have liked to do most of all just now was to go to his room and masturbate. That would be the only way of fulfilling last night. And his betrayal of Elena.

Larsson stood up. Lindman could see that the phone call had worried him.

"Is something wrong?"

The girl in reception eyed them inquisitively. Lindman noticed that she'd been working at a computer identical to the one Veronica Molin had in her room. Larsson beckoned Lindman to follow him into the empty dining room.

"It looks as if the man on the mountain may have found a road through the fog that wasn't being watched, and then stolen another car. Erik had just gone home for a meal," Larsson said, "and he saw that he'd been burgled. A pistol and a rifle had been taken. Plus some ammo and a detachable telescopic sight. It must have happened today, early in the morning." He felt his throat again. "It could have been somebody else, of course. But our man is still in the area, he threatens Berggren, he *wants* something although we don't know what. A man like that may have realised that he needed another gun – no doubt he's got rid of the others, if he's got any sense. And who would have a gun in his house? A policeman, of course."

"He would have to have known Johansson's name, and that he was a police officer. And where he lives. How could he have found that out? And when?"

"I don't know. But I think it's time to work backwards. We must have seen something at some point without realising its significance." Larsson bit his lip. "We started looking for a murderer who tried to make us think there were actually two of them. Now I'm starting to wonder if there isn't only one after all, but he's let loose his shadow to put us off the scent."

CHAPTER 28

They had gathered in Johansson's office at 2.15. Lindman had been hesitant about joining them, but Larsson insisted. Johansson was tired and irritable, but most of all he was worried. Lindman sat next to the wall, behind the others. The rain had passed over and the sun, already quite low in the sky, shone in through the open window. Johansson switched his mobile telephone to loudspeaker mode, and Rundström's voice could be heard despite a poor connection. The mist in the mountains of north-west Härjedalen was still there.

"We're marking time here," he said.

"And the road blocks?" Johansson said.

"They're still in place. A Norwegian drunk drove straight into the ditch from shock when he saw police standing in the road. He had a zebra skin in his car, incidentally."

"Why?"

"How should I know? If it had been a bear skin you could have understood it, but I didn't know there were any zebras in Härjedalen."

The connection was lost, then it came back.

"I have a question about the weapons that were stolen," Rundström said. "I know what make of guns and how many, but what about ammunition?"

"Two magazines for the pistol and twelve cartridges for the Mauser."

"I don't like this at all," Rundström said. "Did he leave any clues?"

His voice was coming and going in waves.

"The house was empty," Johansson said. "My wife is in Järvsö visiting our daughter. I don't have any neighbours. The gun cupboard had been broken into."

"No footprints? Did anybody see a car?"

"No."

"The mist will start clearing soon, according to the weather people. But the sun will have set before long. We're wondering what to do. If

299

he's the one who stole the guns there's not much point in our staying here. It would mean he'd already passed through our cordon."

Larsson leaned towards the telephone. "Larsson here. I think it's too soon to withdraw from up there. It might not have been him who broke into Erik's house. But I have a question. Do we know anything about what this Hereira might have in the way of food?"

"Frostman claimed he didn't have anything in his pantry. Maybe some jam. He wasn't sure. On the other hand, the freezer was full. It was worth leaving it on to store all the berries and elk meat he'd been given by friends."

"It's hardly possible to prepare an elk steak on a camping gas stove. Sooner or later he'll have to find a shop and buy some food. Assuming he's not the one who broke into Erik's place."

"We've been checking the houses up here. There's just one solitary old fellow who lives here all the year round. Hudin, he's called, in a place called Högvreten. We've got a couple of officers there. Apparently he's 95 and not exactly a shrinking violet. Apart from him, there are only holiday cottages in the area. You can't say it's over-populated round here."

"Anything else?"

"Not at the moment."

"OK, thanks. We'll talk again later."

Rundström's voice faded away in a buzz of interference. Johansson switched the telephone off.

"Frostengren," said one of the officers. "Wasn't that his name? Not Frostman?"

"Rundström's not very good at names," Larsson said. "Let's have a run-through now. Is there anybody here who hasn't met Stefan Lindman? A colleague from Borås who used to work with Herbert Molin."

Lindman recognised all the faces. He wondered what they would say if he stood up and told them that in a few days' time he would be starting a course of radiation treatment for cancer.

There was a mass of detail and reports to sort out. Larsson urged them to be brief. They couldn't waste time dwelling unnecessarily on minor details. At the same time, he had to make decisions about what was important and what could wait. Lindman tried to listen, but found that his head was full of images of women. Hanna Tunberg getting up from her chair and falling dead on the floor. Veronica Molin, her hand and her back as she lay asleep. And Elena was there as well. Especially Elena. He was ashamed of having told Veronica Molin that there was no-one in his life.

He forced such thoughts out of his mind and tried to concentrate on what was being said round the table. They talked about the weapons used when Molin was murdered. They must have come from somewhere. It could be assumed that Hereira had entered Sweden from abroad, and so it followed that he had acquired them in Sweden. Larsson had a list of guns reported stolen in Sweden in recent months. He glanced through them, then put it on one side. No Swedish border control post had any information about a man called Fernando Hereira from Argentina passing through.

"Interpol are looking into that right now," Larsson said. "I know that South American countries can be hard to deal with. A girl from Järpen disappeared in Rio de Janeiro a few years ago. It was sheer hell trying to get anything out of the police there. She turned up eventually, thank God. She'd fallen in love with an Indian and lived with him for a while in Amazonas. But it didn't last. Now she's a primary school teacher and married to a man who works for a travel agent in Östersund. Rumour has it that her house is full of parrots."

Laughter ran through the room.

"Let's just hope that a suitable Fernando Hereira turns up," Larsson said.

Some more papers were put to one side. There was a preliminary summary of Abraham Andersson's life, but it was far from complete. So far, they'd found nothing at all to link him with Molin. Everybody agreed that in view of what Hanna Tunberg had said, they ought immediately to put more resources into digging up Andersson's past. Lindman could see that Larsson was trying to keep his impatience under control. He knows he'll become a bad police officer if he loses his cool, Lindman thought.

They turned their attention to Hanna Tunberg for a while. Johansson said that she'd been one of the leading lights when the Sveg curling club was formed, and that now it had an international reputation.

"They used to play in the park near the railway station," he said. "I can remember her sweeping the ice clear as soon as it was cold enough in the autumn."

"And now she's dead," Larsson said. "That was a horrific experience, believe you me."

"What caused it?" It was one of the officers who hadn't said anything so far. Lindman seemed to recall that he was from Hede.

Larsson shrugged. "A stroke, maybe a blood clot on the brain. Or a heart attack. She was a chain-smoker. Anyway, the last thing she did before she died was to tell us about Berggren. She thought she'd seen her in Andersson's house some time last spring. Hanna was honest enough to admit that she wasn't sure. If she was right, it could mean at least two things. Firstly, that we've established a link between Andersson and Molin. A woman. And we must also bear in mind that so far, Berggren has denied anything more than a fleeting acquaintance with Andersson."

Larsson reached for a file and picked out a piece of paper.

"Katrin Andersson, Abraham's widow, told the Helsingborg police that she'd never heard the name Elsa Berggren. She claims to have a good memory for names, and that her husband never – I'm quoting here – 'kept any secrets from me'." Larsson snapped the file shut. "That could be a claim that proves to be untrue, of course. We've all heard that phrase before."

"I think we ought to be a bit cautious," Johansson said. "Hanna had a lot of good points, but she also had a reputation for being a nosy parker. People like that sometimes have trouble distinguishing between what's fact and what they've made up."

"What do you mean?" Larsson said, irritated. "Should we take what she said seriously, or should we not?"

"Perhaps we shouldn't be 100 per cent certain that the woman outside Andersson's house really was Berggren."

"If the woman actually was outside the door," Larsson said. "I suspect that Hanna peered in through a window."

"Surely the dog would have barked in that case?"

Larsson reached impatiently for another file. He leafed through it without finding what he was looking for. "I know I've read somewhere that after the murder of Molin, Andersson said that he sometimes had the dog inside the house. This could have been one of those occasions.

Mind you, some guard dogs bark even when they're in the house if they hear a noise outside, I'll grant you that."

"It didn't seem all that alert for a guard dog when I was there," Lindman said. "It appeared to be more of a hunting dog."

Johansson was still sceptical. "Is there anything else that links them? We know that Elsa and Molin were Nazis. If we can believe everything that has emerged so far, that's what they had in common. Two lunatics, in other words, but harmless. Was Andersson a Nazi?"

"He was a paid-up member of the Centre Party," Larsson said grimly. "For a while he was even an elected member of the Helsingborg Town Council. He resigned over a split to do with funding for the local symphony orchestra, but he didn't leave the Party. We can assume that not only was Andersson a man with no links to the unpleasant political movement known as neo-Nazism, but also that he took great exception to it. It would be interesting to know how he'd have reacted if he'd realised that he had a former Waffen-SS officer for a neighbour."

"Maybe he did know," Lindman heard himself saying.

Larsson looked at him. It was quiet in the room. "Say that again."

"I'm just suggesting that we could turn the way we've been thinking on its head. If Andersson had discovered that his neighbour, Molin, was a Nazi, and perhaps Berggren as well, that could indicate that there was in fact a link."

"And what would that be?"

"I don't know. But Molin had hidden himself away in the forest. He wanted to keep his past a secret, no matter what the cost."

"You mean that Andersson might have threatened to expose him?"

"It could even have been blackmail. Molin had done everything he could to disappear from view, to hide his past. He was scared of something. Presumably of a person, but possibly several. If Andersson discovered his secret, the whole of Molin's existence would be under threat. Berggren had bought the house on Molin's behalf. Suddenly some new circumstances arise in which he needs her help again."

Larsson shook his head doubtfully. "Does that really add up? If Andersson had been killed before Molin, I could have understood it. But not afterwards. When Molin was already dead?"

"Maybe it was Andersson who helped the murderer to find Molin?

303

But something went wrong. There's another possibility, of course. Berggren could have realised, or assumed, that Andersson was somehow responsible for what happened to Molin, and took revenge."

Johansson protested. "That can't be right. Are you suggesting that Elsa, a woman in her seventies, dragged Andersson into the forest, tied him to a tree and shot him? That can't be right. Besides, she didn't have a gun."

"Guns can be stolen, as we know," Larsson said, icily.

"I can't see Elsa as a murderer."

"None of us can, but we both know that people who on the surface are as gentle as lambs can commit violent crimes."

Johansson made no comment.

"What Stefan says is worth bearing in mind, of course," Larsson said. "But let's not sit around here speculating. We should be gathering more facts. For instance, we have to find out how much you can see in the rear-view mirror of a car parked in the place described by Hanna Tunberg. Obviously, we should then concentrate on Berggren. Without dropping everything else, of course. Everybody in this room knows that it could take a long time to work out what happened in the forest, but that doesn't mean we should let it take any longer than necessary. We might have a bit of luck and catch that man on the mountain, and find out that he killed Andersson as well as Molin."

Before the meeting closed they phoned Rundström again. The mist was as thick as ever.

4 p.m. Those present at the meeting went their various ways, leaving only Larsson and Lindman in the office. The sun had gone. Larsson yawned. Then he smiled broadly.

"I don't suppose you've discovered a bowling alley on your rambles through Sveg? That's what you and I need right now."

"I haven't even found a cinema."

Larsson pointed at the window. "They show films at the Community Centre. *Fucking Åmål* is on now. It's good. My daughter forced me to see it."

Larsson sat at the desk. "Erik's upset," he said. "I'm not surprised. It doesn't look good for a police officer to have his guns stolen. I suspect that he forgot to lock his front door. It's easily done when you live out in the country. Maybe he left a window open. He's keeping very quiet about how the thief got in."

"Didn't he say something about a broken window?"

"He could have broken it himself. Nor is it absolutely certain that he followed the regulations when he bought the rifle. There are lots of guns in this country that are not kept locked away as the law requires, especially hunting rifles."

Lindman opened a bottle of mineral water. He could see that Larsson was eyeing him keenly.

"How are you feeling?"

"I don't know. I suppose I'm a lot more frightened than I care to admit." He put the bottle back on the table. "I'd rather not talk about it," he said. "I'm more interested in what's happening in the case."

"I'm thinking of spending this evening here in the office. Going through some papers again. I think our discussion today has given us a few new leads. Berggren worries me. I can't fathom her out. If Hanna Tunberg really did see what she said she saw, what does it mean? Erik is right to soft-pedal a bit. It's hard to imagine a woman in her seventies dragging a man into the forest, tying him to a tree and then executing him."

"There was an old detective in the Borås force called Fredlund," Lindman said. "He was abrupt, sullen and slow, but a brilliant investigator. Once when he was in an unusually good mood he said something I've never forgotten. 'You work with a torch in your hand. You point it straight in front of you so that you can see where you're putting your feet, but you should occasionally point it to each side as well, so that you can see where you're *not* putting your feet.' If I understand him rightly he was maintaining that you should always keep checking on what's central. Which of the people involved is the most important?"

"What happens if you apply that to our situation? I've been talking too much today. I need to do some listening."

"Could there be a link between the man on the mountain and Berggren? What she said about being attacked doesn't have to be true. It strikes me now that it could have been my turning up there that triggered that situation. That's the first question: is there a link between her and Hereira? The second question, leading me in a different

305

direction, is: is there somebody else involved in all of this, somebody lurking in the shadows whom we haven't yet identified?"

"Someone who may share the political views of Berggren and Molin? Are you thinking of some kind of neo-Nazi network?"

"We know they exist."

"So, Hereira turns up to dance the tango with Molin. That sparks off a series of incidents. One important consequence is that Berggren decides that Andersson has to be killed. So she sends for somebody suitable from her brown-shirted brotherhood to take care of it. Is that what you're saying?"

"I can hear how crazy it sounds."

"Not *that* crazy," Larsson said. "I'll keep it in mind as I chew my way through the files tonight."

Lindman walked back to the hotel. There was no light in Veronica Molin's room. The girl in reception was peering at her new computer. "How long are you staying?" she said.

"Until Wednesday, if that's all right."

"We shan't be full until the weekend."

"Test drivers?"

"A group of orienteerers from Lithuania are coming to set up a training camp."

Lindman collected his key.

"Is there a bowling alley in Sveg?"

"No," she said, surprised.

"Just wondering!"

When he got to his room he lay on the bed. It was something to do with Hanna Tunberg, he thought. Something to do with her death. He started remembering. The images in his head were elusive. It took time for him to sort them out, to make them hang together.

He was five or six years old. He didn't know where his sisters and mother were. He was at home, with his father. He remembered that it was evening. He was on the floor playing with a car, behind the red sofa in the living room. The car was made of wood, yellow and blue with a red stripe. His eyes were concentrated on the invisible road he'd mapped out on the carpet. He could hear the rustling of newspaper pages. A friendly noise, but not completely without menace. His father sometimes used to read things that annoyed him. That could result in the newspaper being ripped to shreds. "These damned socialists," he would say. It was like leaves on a tree. They could rustle like newspaper pages. Suddenly a gale would start blowing and the tree would disintegrate. He drove the car along a road, winding along the brink of a precipice. Things could go wrong. He knew his father was in the dark green armchair next to the open fire. Before long he would lower his newspaper and ask Stefan what he was doing. Not in a friendly way, not even because he was interested. Just a question to check that everything was in order.

Then the rustling stopped, there was a groan followed by a thud. The car stopped. A rear tyre had burst. He was forced to edge his way carefully out of the driving seat, trying not to send the car tumbling into the ravine.

Stefan slowly stood up and peered over the back of the sofa. His father had fallen to the floor. He still had the newspaper in his hand, and he was groaning. Lindman approached him cautiously. So as not to be completely defenceless, he took the car with him. He would not let go of it. He could use it to escape if necessary. His father looked at him with fear in his eyes. His lips were blue. They were moving, forming words. "I don't want to die like this. I want to die upright, like a man."

The images faded. Stefan wasn't even in them any more, he was looking in from the outside. What had happened next? He remembered his fear, standing there with the car in his hand, his father's blue lips. Then his mother had come in. His sisters were no doubt with her, but he couldn't remember them. It was just him, his father and his mother. And a car with a red stripe. He remembered the make now. Brio. A toy car from Brio. They made better trains than cars. But he liked it because his father had given it to him. He'd have preferred a train. But the car had a red stripe. And now it was hanging over the edge of a precipice.

His mother had pushed him out of the way, screamed, and what followed was like a kaleidoscope: an ambulance; his father in a sickbed, his lips less blue. A few words that somebody must have repeated over and over again. A heart attack. Very slight.

What he remembered now with crystal clarity were the words his father had said to him. "I want to die upright, like a man."

307

Like a soldier in Hitler's army, Lindman thought. Marching for a Fourth Reich that wouldn't be crushed like the Third.

He took his jacket and left the room. Somewhere among all those memories he'd dozed off for a while. It was 9 p.m. already. He didn't want to eat in the hotel and made his way to a hot dog stall he'd noticed by the bridge, next to one of the petrol stations. He ate some mashed potato and two half-grilled sausages while listening to some teenage boys discussing a car parked a few metres away. Then he carried on walking, wondering what Larsson was doing. Was he still poring over his files? And what about Elena? He'd left his mobile in his room.

He walked through the dark streets. The church, the scattered shops, empty premises waiting for someone to make something of them.

When he returned to the hotel, he stopped outside the entrance. He could see the girl in reception preparing to go home. He walked down the street, to the front side of the hotel. There was a light in Veronica Molin's room. The curtains were drawn, but there was a narrow gap in the middle. He slunk into the shadows as the girl from reception walked down the street. He wondered again why she'd been crying that time. A car went past. Then he stood on tiptoe to look through the window. She was wearing dark blue. Silk pyjamas, perhaps? She was sitting at her computer, with her back to him. He couldn't see what she was doing. He was about to move on when she got up and moved out of view. He ducked down then slowly stood up again to look through the window. The computer screen was shimmering. There was some kind of pattern on it, a logo probably. At first he couldn't make out what it was. Then he recognised it. The screen was filled by a swastika.

CHAPTER 29

It was like receiving a powerful electric shock. He was almost knocked backwards. A car came round the corner, and Lindman turned to walk away, ducking into the courtyard of the building next door, which housed the newspaper offices. Only a week ago he'd opened a wardrobe and found an SS uniform. Then he'd discovered that behind a respectable façade, his own father had been a Nazi and even now, after his death, was paying blood money to keep afloat an organisation that might look harmless but nevertheless had murderous intentions. And now came Veronica Molin's computer screen with its shimmering swastika. His first impulse was to go to her room and take her to task. But for what? Because she had lied to him. Not only had she known that her father was a Nazi, but she was one herself.

He forced himself to remain calm, to act like a police officer, to see clearly, analytically, to distinguish between what was fact and what wasn't. In the darkness behind the blacked-out editorial offices of the *Härjedalen*, it was as if everything that had happened since the time he'd been sitting in the hospital cafeteria in Borås and stumbled upon a newspaper report saying that Molin had been murdered finally fell into its logical place. Molin had spent his old age solving jigsaw puzzles, when he wasn't dancing with a doll or dreaming about some absurd Fourth Reich. Now it seemed that the puzzle in which Molin had been one of the crucial pieces was finally finished. The last piece in place, the picture clear at last. Thoughts were racing through his head. It was as if a series of floodgates had been opened and he was now hastily directing all the masses of water into the correct channels. He was forced to hold on tight so as not to be swept off his feet and away with the current.

He stood quite still. Something moved at his feet. He jumped. A cat. It scuttled away through the light from a street lamp.

What is this that I can see? A pattern, absolutely clear. Possibly

309

more than a pattern, possibly a conspiracy. He started walking, as he thought more clearly when on the move. He headed for the railway bridge. The district court-house on the left, all the windows in darkness. He came upon three ladies, all humming a tune. They laughed, said "Good night" as he passed, and he recognised the tune as something by ABBA, "Some of us are crying". He turned off, following the railway line to the bridge. The rails, nowadays only used by occasional peat trains and the so-called Inland Railway during the summer, looked like neglected cracks in a bronze-coloured wooden floor. On the other side of the river, Berggren's side, he could hear a dog barking. He stopped in the middle of the bridge. The sky was full of stars now, it was colder. He picked up a stone and dropped it into the water.

What he ought to do was to speak to Larsson without delay. There again, perhaps not just yet. He needed to think. He had a start, and wanted to make the most of it. Veronica Molin didn't know what he had seen through her curtains. Would he be able to use the start he had to his advantage?

He left the bridge and walked back to the hotel. There was only one thing to do. Talk to her. Two men were playing cards in reception. They nodded to him but concentrated on their game. Lindman stopped at her door and knocked. Once again he had the urge to kick it in, but he knocked instead. She opened immediately. He could see over her shoulder that the computer screen was blank.

"I was about to go to bed," she said.

"Not just yet. We need to talk."

She let him in.

"I want to sleep alone tonight. Just so that you know."

"That's not why I've come. Although I do wonder about that, of course. Why you wanted me to sleep here. Without my being allowed to touch you."

"It was you who wanted to. I do admit that I can feel lonely at times."

She sat down on the bed, and just like last night pulled up her legs beneath her. He was attracted by her, and his wounded anger only made the feeling stronger.

He sat on the creaking chair.

"What do you want? Has something happened? The man on the mountain? Have you caught him?"

"I don't know. But that's not why I've come. I've come about a lie."

"Whose?"

"Yours."

She raised her eyebrows.

"I don't know what you're talking about. And I have no patience with people who don't come straight to the point."

"Then I'll come straight to the point. A few minutes ago you were working at your computer. Your screen was filled with a swastika."

It was a few seconds before the penny dropped. Then she glanced at the window and the curtains.

"Precisely," he said. "I looked in. You'd be right to complain about that. I looked in when I shouldn't have. But it wasn't that I hoped to see you naked. It was just an impulse. And I saw the swastika."

He could see that she was perfectly calm.

"That's absolutely right. There was a swastika on my screen not long ago. Black against a red background. But what's the lie?"

"You take after your father. You claimed the opposite. You said you were trying to protect his past, but in fact it was yourself you were trying to protect."

"What from?"

"The fact that you are a Nazi."

"Is that what you think?"

She stood up, lit a cigarette and remained standing. "You are not only stupid," she said, "you're full of yourself with it. I thought you were better than the run-of-the-mill policeman, but you're not. You're just an insignificant little shit."

"You won't get anywhere by insulting me. You could spit in my face and I wouldn't lose my temper."

She sat down on the bed again.

"I suppose in a way it's just as well you went out snooping," she said. "At least we can get this business out of the way very quickly."

"I'm listening."

She stubbed out her cigarette.

"What do you know about computers? About the Internet?"

"Not a lot. I know there's a lot of Internet traffic that ought to be stopped. Child pornography, for instance. You said you could keep in touch with the whole world, no matter where you were. 'I have the whole of my life in this computer,' you said."

She sat down at her computer and beckoned him to pull his chair closer.

"I'll take you on a journey," she said. "Through cyberspace. I suppose that's a term you must have heard?"

She pressed a button on her keyboard. A faint whirring came from inside the computer. The screen came to life. She pressed various keys. Images and patterns flickered across the screen until it turned red all over. The black swastika appeared gradually.

"This network embracing the whole globe has its underworld, just as the real world does. You can find anything at all there."

She tapped away at the keys. The swastika disappeared. Lindman found himself staring at half-naked Asian girls. She tapped more keys, the girls were replaced by pictures of St Peter's in Rome.

"You can find everything in here," she said. "It's a marvellous tool. You can retrieve information no matter where you are. Just now, at this moment, Sveg is the centre of the world. But there's also an underworld. Endless amounts of information about where you can buy guns, drugs, pornographic pictures of little children. Everything."

She tapped away again. The swastika returned.

"This as well. Lots of Nazi organisations, including several Swedish ones, publicise their opinions on my computer screen. I was sitting here trying to understand. I was looking for the people who are members of Nazi organisations today. How many of them there are, what their organisations are called, how they think."

She tapped the keys again. A picture of Hitler. More tapping, and suddenly she appeared on the screen herself. "Veronica Molin. Broker."

She switched off. The screen went black.

"Now I'd like you to leave," she said. "You chose to jump to a conclusion on the basis of a picture you saw on my screen when you were snooping around and looking in at my window. Perhaps you still think I'm stupid enough to sit here worshipping a swastika. It's up to you to decide if you're an idiot or not, but please go anyway. We've nothing more to say to each other."

Lindman didn't know what to do. She was upset, convincingly so.

"If the situation had been reversed," he said, "how would you have reacted?"

"I'd have asked. Not immediately accused you of lying."

She stood up and flung open the door.

"I can't stop you from going to my father's funeral," she said. "But I shall feel no compulsion to speak to you there, or to shake your hand."

She ushered Lindman out into the corridor and closed the door behind him. He went back to reception. The card players had left. He went up to his room, wondering why he had reacted as he did. He was rescued by a telephone call. It was Larsson.

"I hope you weren't asleep."

"On the contrary."

"Wide awake?"

"Very much so."

He thought he might as well tell Larsson what had happened.

"It's a dangerous habit, peeping into little girls' bedrooms. You never know what you might see," he said, laughing.

"I acted like an idiot."

"We all do sometimes. Not all at the same time, with luck."

"Did you know that you can look up all the Nazi organisations in the world on the Internet?"

"Probably not all of them. What was the word she used? 'Underworld'? There are no doubt lots of different rooms down there. I suspect the really dangerous organisations don't advertise their name and address on the Internet."

"You mean it's only possible to scrape the surface?"

"Something like that."

Lindman sneezed. And again.

"I hope that's not something you've caught from me."

"How's your throat?"

"I have a slight temperature, it's swollen on the left side. People who get to see as much misery as we do often succumb to hypochondria."

"I've enough to cope with in the real world."

"I know. I'm sorry. I put my foot in it again."

"What did you want?"

"Somebody to talk to, I suppose."

"Are you still in Johansson's office?"

"Yes, and I've got coffee."

"I'll be there."

As he passed the front of the hotel he glanced at Veronica Molin's window. He could just see that the light was still on, but the gap in the curtains was gone.

Larsson was waiting for him outside the Community Centre. He had a cigarillo in his hand.

"I didn't know you smoked."

"Only when I'm very tired and need to keep awake."

He broke the end off the cigarillo and trampled the glowing tobacco. They went inside. The bear observed their entry. The building was deserted.

"Erik phoned," Larsson said. "He's a very honest man. He said that he was so depressed at having his guns stolen that he didn't feel up to working tonight. He was going to have a couple of drinks and a sleeping tablet. Maybe not a very good combination, but I don't blame him."

"Any news from the mountain?"

They were in the office by now. There were two thermos flasks on the desk, marked "Härjedalen County Council". Lindman shook his head when Larsson offered him a cup. There were a few half-eaten Danish pastries on a torn paper bag.

"Rundström has been phoning on and off. We've also heard from back-up HQ in Östersund. One of the helicopters we usually hire has broken down. A substitute will be arriving from Sundsvall tomorrow."

"What about the weather?"

"There is no mist on the mountain at the moment. They've moved their base down to Funäsdalen. No joy from the road blocks as yet, apart from that Norwegian drunk. Apparently his grandmother had been a missionary in Africa and brought a zebra skin home with her. There's an explanation for practically everything. Rundström's worried, though. If they're able to carry out a search on the mountain tomorrow and don't find him, it can only mean that he's broken through the cordon. In which case it probably was him who burgled Erik's place."

"Maybe he never did go up the mountain?"

"You're forgetting that the dog picked up a scent."

"He could have doubled back. Besides, don't forget this man is from

South America. It's too cold for him on a Swedish mountainside in the late autumn."

Larsson was looking at a map on the wall. He drew a circle with his finger round Funäsdalen.

"What bugs me is why he hasn't left the area ages ago," he said. "I keep coming back to that. Of all the questions buzzing around in connection with this investigation, that's one of the most important. I'm convinced of it. The only explanation I can think of is that he hasn't finished yet. There's something more for him to do. That thought makes me more and more apprehensive. He runs the risk of getting caught, but still he stays on. He might well have got himself a new set of weapons. Earlier this evening it made me think of a question we haven't yet addressed."

"What did he do with the weapons he used to torture and kill Molin?"

Larsson turned away from the map. "Right. We asked ourselves where he got them from, but not what he did with them. And the fact that he probably disposed of them has set my brain working overtime. What about yours?"

Lindman thought for a moment before replying.

"He goes away. Something has been finished. He throws the weapons away, maybe in the lake, or perhaps he buries them. Then something happens and he comes back. He needs new weapons. Is that what you're thinking?"

"Precisely. But I can't make sense of it. We are wondering if he came back to dispose of Andersson. He obviously had access to a gun if that was the case. It seems very odd if he then went away a second time. If he was the one who broke into Erik's place, does that mean that he's disposed of his weapons twice? That can't be right. We know the man planned everything meticulously. All these guns thrown away suggests the opposite. Is he after Berggren? He asks her who killed Andersson, but he doesn't get an answer, so far as we know. He is insistent. Then he bashes you over the head and disappears."

"How about if we ask the same question as he did?"

"That's what I've been doing all evening."

Larsson gestured towards all the files scattered on every surface in the room.

"I've had that question in mind while I've been going through the most important bits of the material we've got. I've even asked myself if he went to see Berggren to create a false trail because in fact he did murder Andersson. But if that were the case, why is he still here? What's he waiting for now? Is he expecting something specific to happen? Or is he after somebody else? In which case, who?"

"There's a missing link," Lindman said, slowly. "A person. The question is, though, is it a murderer or another victim?"

They sat in silence. Lindman found it difficult to concentrate. He wanted to help Larsson, but he was thinking about Veronica Molin all the time. And he ought to have phoned Elena by now. He looked at his watch. It was 11 p.m. already. She'd be asleep. Too bad. He took his mobile out of his pocket.

"I have to ring home," he said, and went out. He stood beside the stuffed bear, hoping it might protect him.

She wasn't asleep.

"I know you're ill, but do you really have the right to treat me like you are doing?" she said.

"I've been working."

"You're not at work. You're on sick leave."

"I've been pretty busy talking to Larsson."

"And so you don't have time to phone me, is that it?"

"I didn't realise it was as late as this."

No response. Then:

"We have to have a serious talk. Not now, though. Later."

"I miss you. I don't really know why I'm here. I suppose I'm so scared of the day dawning when I have to go to the hospital that I daren't even be at home. I don't know whether I'm coming or going at the moment. But I do miss you."

"Are you sure you haven't met another woman up there?"

That shook him. Hard, in a flash.

"And who would that be?"

"I don't know. Somebody younger."

"Don't be silly."

He could hear that she was depressed, unhappy, and that made him feel even more guilty.

"I'm standing next to a stuffed bear," he said. "He sends his greet-ings."

She didn't answer.

"Are you still there?"

"I'm still here. But I'm going to sleep now. Phone me tomorrow. I hope you'll be able to sleep tonight."

Lindman went back to the office. Larsson was poring over an open file. Lindman poured himself a cup of lukewarm coffee. Larsson pushed the file to one side. His hair was in a mess, his eyes bloodshot.

"Berggren," he said. "I'll have another chat with her tomorrow. I intend to take Erik along with me, but I'll be putting the questions. Erik is too nice with her. I even think he's a bit frightened of her."

"What are you hoping to achieve?"

"Clarity. There's something she's not telling us."

Larsson stood up and stretched.

"Bowling," he said. "I'll ask Erik to have a word with the local authority and see if they can't establish a little bowling alley. Strictly for visiting policemen." Then he was serious again. "What would you ask Berggren? You'll soon be as familiar with this investigation as I am."

Lindman said nothing for almost a minute before replying.

"I'd try to find out if she knew that Erik kept guns in the house."

"That's a good idea, of course," Larsson said. "We'll keep on trying to fit the old girl into the picture. With a bit of luck, we'll find a place for her in the end."

The telephone on his desk rang. Larsson answered. He listened, sat down and pulled a notepad towards him. Lindman handed him a pencil that had fallen to the floor. Larsson checked his watch.

"We're on our way," he said, and hung up.

Lindman could see from his face that something serious had happened.

"That was Rundström. Twenty minutes ago a car drove straight through one of the road blocks. The officers there were very lucky to escape uninjured.

He marked the spot on the map with his finger. It was a crossroads south-east of Funäsdalen. Lindman estimated the distance between there and Frostengren's chalet at about 20 kilometres.

"A dark blue saloon car, possibly a Golf," Larsson said. "The driver was a man. His appearance could be in line with the descriptions we've had previously. The officers didn't have time to see much. But this could mean that our man has broken through the cordon, and that he's on his way here."

Larsson looked at his watch again. "If he really puts his foot down he could be here in two hours."

Lindman looked at the map and pointed to a side road. "He could turn off there."

"All the blocks in Funäsdalen are being moved right now. They'll build a wall behind him. It's here that there is no check at the moment."

He picked up the telephone. "Let's hope that Erik's sleeping pill hasn't knocked him out yet."

Lindman waited while Larsson spoke to Johansson about the road block they needed to set up. He put the phone down and shook his head.

"Erik's a good man," he said. "He'd just taken his sleeping pill, but he's going to stick his finger down his throat and sick it up. He's really set his mind on catching that bastard. Not just because Hereira's most probably the one who stole his guns."

"It doesn't add up," Lindman said. "The more I think about it, the more impossible it gets. Why on earth would he break into Johansson's place and then go back to the mountain?"

"Nothing adds up. But we can hardly start thinking about a third person being mixed up in all this." Larsson interrupted himself. "Maybe that is what happened," he said, "but if so, what does that mean?"

"I've no idea."

"Whoever is in that car could be the one with the guns. And he might start using them. We'll put a stinger out to puncture his tyres. If he starts shooting, we'll keep well out of the way." Then he turned serious. "You're a police officer," he said. "We're very short-staffed just now. Will you come with us?"

"Yes."

"Erik's bringing a gun for you."

"I thought they'd been stolen?"

Larsson pulled a face.

"He had an extra pistol that he presumably hasn't registered either. Hidden away in the cellar. Plus his police issue weapon."

The telephone rang again. Rundström. Larsson listened without saying anything.

"The car is stolen," he said when the call was over. "It was in fact a Golf. Stolen from a petrol station in Funäsdalen. A lorry driver saw it happen. According to Rundström, it was one of the blokes Erik plays cards with."

He was in a hurry now. He shoved several files lying on his jacket into a heap.

"Erik will call out the two police officers in Sveg. Not exactly an impressive squad, but I expect that will be enough to stop a Golf."

Three quarters of an hour later they had set up a road block three kilometres north-west of Sveg. The wind was rushing through the trees. Larsson talked in a low voice to Johansson. The other police officers skulked like shadows back from the side of the road. The headlights from the police cars cut into the darkness.

CHAPTER 30

The car they were waiting for never arrived. Five other cars passed through. Johansson knew two of the drivers. The other three were strangers: two were women, home helps, who lived to the west of Sveg, and a young man in a fur hat who had been staying with relatives in Hede and was now on his way south. All were made to submit their boots for inspection before they were allowed to continue.

The temperature had risen again, and some wet snow was falling, melting the moment it touched the ground. There was no breeze anymore, and every sound was clearly audible. Somebody broke wind, a hand brushed against a car door.

They spread out a map on the bonnet of one of the police cars, and examined it by torchlight. It quickly became wet. Had they made an error? Was there some other route that they'd overlooked? They couldn't see the alternative. All the roadblocks were where they should be. Larsson was acting as a sort of one-man call centre, keeping in touch with the other groups of officers stationed at various points in the forest.

Lindman stayed on the sidelines. He'd been given a pistol of a type familiar to him by Johansson. Snow was falling on his head. He thought about Veronica Molin, Elena, and most of all about November 19. He couldn't make up his mind if the darkness and the trees increased or alleviated his anxiety. There was also a brief moment when it crossed his mind that he could put an end to it all in just a few seconds. He had a loaded gun in his pocket; he could put it to his head and pull the trigger and there would be no need for radiotherapy.

Nobody could see where the Golf could have disappeared to. Lindman heard Larsson getting more annoyed every time he spoke to one of his colleagues. Then Johansson's telephone rang.

"You what?" he shouted.

He signalled for the wet map to be unfolded again as he listened to what was being said. He jabbed his finger onto the map so hard that it made a hole, repeated a name, Löten, then finished the call.

"Shooting," he said. "Some time ago, here, by the lake, Löten, three kilometres from the road to Hårdabyn. The call was from somebody called Rune Wallén. He lives near there, owns a lorry and a bulldozer. He said he was woken by something that sounded like a bang. His wife heard it as well. He went outside, and there was another bang. He counted ten shots altogether. He's a hunter, so he knows what a shotgun sounds like."

Johansson looked at his watch and did some calculations. "He said it took him a quarter of an hour to find my mobile phone number. We're in the same hunting club so he knew he had the number somewhere. He said he'd also spent five minutes discussing with his wife what they should do. He thought at first he'd be waking me up if he called. All of which adds up to the fact that the shooting took place 25 minutes ago at the most."

"Right, let's re-group," Larsson said. "This road block must stay, but a couple of us and some of the men further north will head for the scene. Now we know that guns are being used. Caution is the watchword, no reckless intervention."

"Shouldn't we call a national alert on this?" Johansson said.

"You bet we will," Larsson said. "You can arrange that. Phone Östersund. And take charge of the road block here."

Larsson looked at Lindman, who nodded.

"Stefan and I will go to Löten. I'll phone Rundström from the car."

"Be careful," Johansson said.

Larsson didn't seem to hear. Lindman drove. Larsson spoke to Rundström. Described what had happened, what decisions had been taken. Then he put the telephone down.

"What's going on?" he said. "What the bloody hell is going on?"

After a while, he said, "We could meet a car. We shan't stop, we'll just try and get its make and registration number."

It took them 35 minutes to reach the place described by Rune Wallén. They could see no cars. Lindman slowed down and pulled up when Larsson shouted, pointing at a dark blue Golf at the side of the road, halfway into the ditch.

"Let's back up a bit," Larsson said. "Switch the lights off."

It had stopped snowing. There wasn't a sound. Larsson and Lindman crouched as they ran from the car. They had each taken one side of the road. Both had drawn their guns. They were peering into the darkness, listening intently. Lindman wasn't sure how long they waited, but eventually they heard the sound of a car approaching. The headlights drew nearer in the darkness and the police car came to a halt. Larsson had switched on his torch. It was Rundström on the other side of the blue Golf, and another officer Lindman thought was called Lennart Backman. It occurred to him that there had once been a footballer he admired whose name was Lennart Backman. Who did he used to play for? Was it Hammarby or AIK?

"Have you seen anything?" Rundström shouted.

His voice echoed through the forest.

"The car seems to be empty," Larsson said. "We waited for you to get here before moving in to examine it."

"Who's with you?"

"Lindman."

"You and I will approach the car," Rundström said. "You others stay where you are."

Lindman held his pistol at the ready, simultaneously shining his torch for Larsson. He and Rundström closed in on the Golf from each side.

"There's nothing here," Larsson cried. "Move the cars to give us more light."

Lindman moved the car up and directed the headlights at the Golf.

Wallén had not been mistaken. The Golf was riddled with bullet holes. There were three in the windscreen, the front left-hand tyre had been punctured and there were holes in the bonnet as well.

"The shots seem to have come from straight in front," Rundström said, "possibly slightly to one side."

They shone their torches into the car.

Larsson pointed. "That could be blood."

The driver's door was open wide. They shone their torches on the ground, but could see no trace of blood on the road or on the wet ground on the verge. Larsson pointed his torch into the trees.

"I've no idea what's going on," he said. "No idea at all."

They formed a chain, shining their torches into trees and bushes. There was no sign of anybody, nor of any tracks. They continued into the trees for about a hundred metres before Larsson gave the order to turn back. There was a distant sound of sirens approaching from the east.

"The dogs are on their way," Rundström said, when they were on the asphalt again.

The keys were still in the ignition. Larsson opened the boot. There were some tins of food and a sleeping bag. They exchanged looks.

"A dark blue sleeping bag," Rundström said. "Labelled 'Alpin'."

He searched the bank of numbers in his mobile telephone, then called one of them.

"Inspector Rundström," he said. "I'm sorry to wake you. Didn't you say there was a sleeping bag in your chalet? What colour was it?"

He nodded. Dark blue. It fitted.

"What brand was it?" He listened. "Can you remember if you had any tins of 'Bullen's Party Sausages' in your pantry?"

Frostengren's reply seemed to be comprehensive.

"That's all I wanted to know," Rundström said. "Many thanks for your help."

"So, now we know," he said. "Even though he was half asleep Frostengren could remember that his sleeping bag wasn't labelled 'Alpin'. That needn't be significant, of course. Hereira presumably had some stuff of his own. But the sausages were his."

Everybody realised what that meant. Hereira had broken through the cordon round the mountain.

The police car came racing up, switched off its siren and pulled up. One of the forensic team Lindman had met before got out. Rundström explained briefly what had happened.

"It'll be light in an hour or two," Larsson said. "We must get the traffic boys here. Even if we are in the back of beyond there'll presumably be some traffic on this road."

The forensic officer had some police tape with him and Lindman helped to cordon off the Golf. They positioned the cars so that their headlights lit up not only the Golf in the ditch, but also the road and the edge of the trees. Larsson and Rundström stood back to let the forensic specialist get on with his work. They beckoned Lindman to join them.

"What do we do now?" Larsson said. "None of us understands what's happened, if we're honest."

"Facts are facts," Rundström said, impatiently. "The man we've been hunting in the mountains has broken through our cordon. He steals a car. Then somebody has a surprise in store for him, steps into the road and takes a few pot shots at him. Shoots to kill, because he's aiming at the windscreen. I think we can take it for granted that Hereira didn't get out of the car and shoot at it himself. The man must have been incredibly lucky, unless he's lying wounded or dead somewhere out there in the forest, of course. There could have been blood even if we didn't see any. Has it been snowing, by the way? We had a few millimetres up in Funäsdalen."

"We had some wet snow for about an hour. That's all."

"The dog handler will be here any minute," Rundström said. "He's in his own car and, needless to say, he's had a puncture. But my sense is that Hereira has survived. The stain on the car seat doesn't suggest a serious wound. Assuming it is blood, of course." He went over to the forensic officer and asked him. "It could be blood," he said, when he came back, "but it could also be chocolate."

"Have we got a time scale?" Larsson said. A question apparently directed mainly at himself.

"It was precisely 4.03 when you phoned me," Rundström said.

"So this drama must have taken place between 3.30 and 3.45."

The penny dropped for all of them at the same time.

"The cars," Larsson said, slowly. "Two passed through our road block shortly before Wallén phoned to tell us about the shooting."

All three realised what that meant. The man who did the shooting could have passed through the cordon already. Larsson looked at Lindman.

"Can you remember? The last two cars to pass through?"

"The first was a woman in a green Saab. Erik knew her."

Larsson agreed.

"Then there was another car after that woman had gone. Driving rather fast. What was it? A Ford?"

"A red Ford Escort," Lindman said.

"A young man in a fur hat. Driving back south after visiting some relatives in Hede. The time would fit. First he shoots up this car, and then he passes through our checkpoint."

"Did you check his driving licence?"

Larsson shook his head grimly.

"Registration number?"

Larsson phoned Johansson and explained what had happened. He waited, then put his mobile back in his pocket.

"ABB 303," he said. "Erik's not absolutely certain about the numbers. His notebook got wet and the pages are stuck together. This business is being handled very badly."

"Let's put a marker on that car straightaway," Rundström said. "Red Ford Escort. ABB 303, or something similar. We want the owner now, no delays. We can give Erik a telling-off later."

"Let's try to get it clear what's happened," Larsson said. "There are loads of questions that need answering. Just so we don't overlook something crucial. How could anybody know that Hereira would be coming past in a dark blue Golf at this very spot and at this time? Who stands in the middle of the road and tries to kill him?"

Rundström and Larsson got out their mobiles again. Lindman did the same, but had no idea who to phone. A car drew up with the dog handler, two other officers and Dolly the Alsatian. The dog found a scent immediately. The officers headed into the forest.

Rundström exploded in anger when he'd finished his call. "The bloody computer's down. We can't trace the car," he said. "Why does everything always have to get buggered up?"

"Did it crash or is it a software glitch?"

Larsson was talking to somebody in Östersund and to Rundström at the same time.

"They're putting new data in. They claim it'll be up and running within an hour."

The forensic officer went past. He'd been to his car to exchange his shoes for rubber boots.

"Have you found anything?" Larsson said.

"All sorts of things, but I'll give you a shout if I think it's important."

It was still dark at 6 a.m. The police officers and the dog returned from the forest.

"She lost the scent," the dog handler said. "She's tired as well. You can't push her beyond her limits. We'll have to get some more dogs here."

Rundström was talking non-stop on the telephone. Larsson had unfolded the map again.

"He hasn't got much to choose from. He'll come to two gravel roads. The rest is nothing but trees. He'll have to choose one of these two roads."

Larsson folded the map carelessly and tossed it into the car. Rundström was berating somebody for not "understanding how serious this is". Larsson took Lindman with him to the other side of the road.

"You think clearly," Larsson said. "And you are lucky enough not to be responsible for all this. Even so, you can help us by telling us what conclusions you think we ought to reach."

"You've already asked the most important question," Lindman said. "How could anybody know that Hereira was going to come down this very road tonight?"

Larsson stared at him for a long while before replying. They were standing in the light from one of the police cars' headlights.

"Can there be more than one answer?" Larsson asked.

"Hardly."

"So whoever did the shooting must have been in contact with Hereira?"

"It's the only possibility I can see. Either directly with Hereira, or with a third party who was a link between the two of them."

"And then he stakes out this road, intending to kill him."

"I can't think of any other explanation. Unless there's a leak from the police. Somebody passing on information about where we were setting up roadblocks, and why."

"That doesn't sound plausible."

It occurred to Lindman that the previous evening he'd had the feeling that he was being followed. That somebody was keeping him under observation. But he didn't say anything.

"One thing's certain in any case," Larsson said. "We've got to find Hereira. And we've got to identify the man driving that red Ford. Did you see his face?"

"It was pretty much hidden by his fur hat."

"Erik can't remember what he looked like either. Nor how he spoke. If it was a dialect. But it's far from clear that Erik would have noticed anyway. Remember, he sicked up that sleeping tablet. I don't think he's 100 per cent clear in the head tonight."

Lindman suddenly felt dizzy. It came out of nowhere. He was forced to grab hold of Larsson so as not to fall.

"Are you ill?"

"I don't know. Everything started spinning round."

"You'd better go back to Sveg. I'll get somebody to drive you. Erik is obviously not the only one who's not on form tonight."

Lindman could see that Larsson was genuinely concerned.

"Are you going to faint?"

Lindman shook his head. He didn't want to tell him the truth, which was that he felt as if he could keel over at any moment.

Larsson drove him back to Sveg himself. They didn't speak during the journey. Dawn was breaking. The snow had gone away, but the clouds were still thick overhead. Lindman had noted absent-mindedly that sunrise was about 7.45. Larsson pulled up outside the hotel.

"How do you feel?"

"Same as you. A sleepless night. I'll feel better when I've had a bit of sleep."

"Don't you think it would be best if you went back to Borås?"

"Not yet. I'll stay as arranged. Until Wednesday. Besides, I'm interested to know if that registration number has been linked to an owner yet."

Larsson phoned Rundström.

"The computers are still down. Don't they have any paperwork? Don't they have any back-up?"

Lindman opened the car door and eased himself out. Fear was churning around in his insides. Why don't I say anything? he thought. Why don't I tell Larsson that I'm so frightened that I can't stop shaking?

"Go and get some rest. I'll be in touch."

Larsson drove away. The girl in reception was sitting at her computer.

"You're up early," she said with a smile.

"Or late," he said.

He took his key, went up to his room, sat on the edge of the bed and phoned Elena. She was already at school. He told her what had happened, that he'd been up all night, and that he felt dizzy. She asked when he was coming home, but he raised his voice, couldn't conceal his irritation, and simply said that he needed to sleep. Then he'd make up his mind.

*   *   *

327

It was 1.30 when he woke up. He lay in bed, looking up at the ceiling. He'd dreamt about his father again.

They were paddling in a two-man canoe. There was a waterfall some-where ahead. He'd tried to tell his father that they must turn back before the current became so strong that they'd be forced over the edge, but his father didn't answer. When Stefan turned round, he found that it wasn't his father sitting behind him, but the solicitor Jacobi. He was stark naked, his chest covered in reeds. Then the dream had dissolved.

He got out of bed. He didn't feel dizzy any more. He felt hungry. Even so, his curiosity got the better of him. He tried Larsson's number. Engaged. He showered and tried again. Still engaged. He dressed and discovered that he had no clean underwear left. Phoned again. Now Larsson answered, with a bellowing "Yes?"

"It's Lindman."

"Oh. I thought it was a reporter from Östersund. He's been chasing me all morning. Erik thinks Wallén must have tipped him off about the shooting. If so, he's in for a good rollicking. The Chief of Police is kicking up a stink as well. He's wondering what on earth is going on. Aren't we all?"

"How's it going?"

"We've established the registration number. ABB 003. Erik was out by one digit."

"Who's the owner?"

"A man called Anders Harner. His address is a P.O. box in Albufeira in southern Portugal. One of the officers in Hede knew exactly where that is. He's been there on holiday. But we've got more problems: Anders Harner is 77, and the man in that car was certainly not an old man. None of us has eyesight that bad."

"Perhaps it was his son? Or some other relative?"

"Or the car had been stolen. We're chasing that one up. It's perfectly obvious that nothing to do with this investigation is straightforward."

"Why not say that the crimes are well planned? Any trace of Hereira?"

"We've had three dogs out, and the helicopter from Sundsvall finally turned up. But we've drawn a blank. No sign at all. Which is quite remarkable. How are you, by the way? Have you had some sleep?"

"I don't feel dizzy any more."

"I had a bad conscience. I don't know how many regulations I've broken by roping you into this business, but more important than that is that I shouldn't have forgotten that you're ill."

"I wanted to join in."

"The forensic lad reckons it could well have been Erik's gun that was used last night. It's a possibility, at least."

Lindman went to the dining room. He felt better after a meal, but he was still tired when he went back to his room. There was a stain on the ceiling that looked like a face. Jacobi's face, he thought. I wonder if he's still alive.

There was a knock on the door. He opened it. It was Veronica Molin.

"Am I disturbing you?"

"Not at all."

"I've come to apologise. I reacted too strongly last night."

"It was my fault. I was stupid."

He wanted to ask her in, but there was dirty laundry lying around. Besides, it smelt stuffy.

"The room hasn't been cleaned," he said.

She smiled. "Mine has." She looked at her watch. "I'm due to meet my brother at Östersund airport exactly four hours from now. There's time for us to talk."

He took his jacket and followed her down the stairs. He was just behind her and had to force himself not to reach out and touch her.

Her computer was switched off.

"I've spoken to Giuseppe Larsson," she said. "I had to winkle out of him what happened last night. I gathered from what he said that you might be in the hotel."

"What did he tell you?"

"About the shooting. And that you haven't yet caught the man you're after."

"The question is, how many men are the police after? Is it one or two? Maybe even three."

"Why aren't I being kept informed about what's happening?"

"The police like to work in peace, without being harassed by reporters. And relatives. Especially when they don't know what's actually happened. And especially when they don't know *why* something has happened."

"I still don't believe that my father died because he used to be a

Nazi. Because of something he might have done when he was a German soldier. The war ended more than 50 years ago. I think his death is somehow connected with that woman in Scotland, whose name I remember as Monica."

Lindman decided on the spur of the moment to tell her about the discovery he'd made in Wetterstedt's flat in Kalmar. He didn't know why. Perhaps to establish the fact that they had a secret to share and that both their fathers had been Nazis. He told her without saying how he'd made the discovery, without saying that he'd broken into the flat and found out by accident. He told her about the network, and the foundation called Strong Sweden. About all the dead as well as the living who made contributions to the organisation.

"I still don't know enough," he said in conclusion. "Perhaps that organisation is just a small part of something much bigger? I'm not so naïve that I think there might be a world-wide Nazi conspiracy, but it's clear that Nazi ideas are alive and well. When all this is over I'll talk to my boss in Borås. There must be grounds for the security services to look into this in earnest."

She listened intently to what he had to say.

"You're doing the right thing," she said eventually. "I'd have done the same."

"We've got to fight against this lunacy," he said. "Even if these people are harbouring a hopeless dream, they are spreading the madness further into the world."

She looked at her watch.

"I know you have to collect your brother," Lindman said. "Just answer me one question. Why did you let me sleep here?"

She put her hand on her computer.

"I said that this thing contains the whole of my life. That's not really true, of course."

Lindman stared at her hand and the computer. He was listening to what she was saying, but it was an image that imprinted itself on his mind. She removed her hand and the image disappeared.

"I'll go now. What time's the funeral tomorrow?"

"Eleven o'clock."

He turned and walked to the door. He was about to open it when he felt her hand on his arm.

"You've got to fetch your brother," he said.

His mobile rang in his jacket pocket.

"You'd better answer."

It was Larsson. "Where are you?"

"At the hotel."

"Something very odd has happened."

"What?"

"Berggren has phoned Erik. She wants him to pick her up."

"Why?"

"She says she wants to confess to the murder of Abraham Andersson."

It was 2.25. Monday, November 15.

CHAPTER 31

Larsson phoned at 6 p.m. and asked Lindman to come to Johansson's office. It was cold and windy when he left the hotel. When he reached the church he stopped and turned quickly round. A car went by along Fjällvägen, followed by another. He thought he could make out a shadowy figure next to the wall of the building opposite the school, but he wasn't sure. He continued to the Community Centre. Larsson was waiting for him outside the entrance. They went to the office. Lindman noticed that there were two extra chairs – one for Berggren, he assumed, and the other for her lawyer.

"They're on the way to Östersund now," Larsson said. "She's under arrest, and will be remanded in custody tomorrow. Erik is with her."

"What did she say?"

Larsson pointed at a tape recorder on the desk.

"A tape of the interrogation is on its way to Östersund," he said, but I had two tape recorders. I thought you might like to hear the copy. You'll be on your own here. I have to get something to eat, and rest for a bit."

"You can borrow my hotel room if you like."

"There's a sofa in the other room. That'll do."

"I don't need to listen to the tape. You can tell me what happened."

Larsson sat in Johansson's chair. He scratched at his forehead, as if he'd got a sudden itch.

"I'd rather you listened to it."

"Did she confess?"

"Yes."

"The motive?"

"I think you should listen to the tape. And then tell me what you think."

"You are not convinced?"

"I don't know what I am. That's why I want to hear your reaction."

Larsson stood up. "Still no sign of Hereira," he said. "We haven't

332

found the red Ford either. Nor the man who did the shooting. But we will in the end. I'll be back here in two hours."

Larsson put on his jacket.

"She sat on that chair," he said, pointing. "Her solicitor, Hermansson, was on that one. She'd phoned him this morning. He was already here when we went to pick her up."

Larsson closed the door behind him. Lindman switched on the tape recorder. There was a scraping noise from a microphone being moved. Then he heard Larsson's voice.

GL: So, we are commencing this interrogation and note that today is November 15, 1999. The time is 15.07. The interrogation is being conducted at the police station in Sveg by Detective Inspector Giuseppe Larsson. The witness is Inspector Erik Johansson. The interrogation of Elsa Berggren is being held at her own request. She is being represented by her solicitor, Sven Hermansson. Would you please give us your name and personal details?

EB: My name is Elsa Maria Berggren, born May 10, 1925 in Tranås.

GL: Could you speak a bit louder, please?

EB: My name is Elsa Maria Berggren, born May 10, 1925 in Tranås.

GL: Thank you. Could we have your full Identity Number, please?

EB: 250510-0221.

GL: Thank you. *(More scraping from the microphone, somebody coughed, a door closed.)* So, if you could just move a bit closer to the microphone . . . Now, please tell us what happened.

EB: I want to confess to the murder of Abraham Andersson.

GL: You are confessing to have killed Abraham Andersson with intent?

EB: Yes.

GL: So it was murder, is that right?

EB: Yes.

GL: Have you consulted your solicitor before saying this?

EB: There's nothing to consult about. I admit to having killed him with malice aforethought. Isn't that what it's called?

GL: That's what they usually say, yes.

EB: Then I admit to having murdered Abraham Andersson with malice aforethought.

GL: So you are confessing to having committed murder?

EB: How many times do I have to repeat it?

GL: Why did you kill him?

EB: He threatened to expose the man living nearby who was killed shortly beforehand, Herbert Molin, as a former National Socialist. I didn't want that. He also threatened to expose me as a convinced National Socialist. And he also committed blackmail.

GL: Against you?

EB: No, Herbert Molin. He demanded money from him every month.

GL: How long had that been going on?

EB: Since a year or so after Herbert moved here. Eight or nine years, I suppose.

GL: Are we talking about a lot of money?

EB: I don't know. No doubt it was a lot of money for Herbert.

GL: When did you decide to kill Andersson?

EB: I can't remember the exact date, but after Herbert was killed he contacted me and said he expected me to carry on with the payments. Otherwise he would expose me as well.

GL: What happened then?

EB: He came to my house without phoning first and was very rude. He demanded money. That was no doubt when I made up my mind.

GL: Made up your mind to do what?

EB: Why do I have to keep repeating everything?

GL: You mean you made up your mind to kill him?

EB: Yes.

GL: Then what happened?

EB: I killed him a few days later. Can I have a glass of water?

GL: Of course. *(More scraping noises from the microphone, somebody stood up, then the voices started again. Lindman could see it all enfolding in front of him. Johansson was no doubt sitting closest to the table where there were several glasses and an open bottle of mineral water, and he filled a glass and passed it to her.)* So, you killed him.

EB: That's what I'm sitting here telling you.

GL: Can you tell us how it happened?

EB: I drove to his place in the evening. I took my shotgun with me. I threatened to kill him if he didn't stop trying to blackmail me. He didn't think I was serious, so I forced him to walk out into the trees not far from the house and shot him.

GL: You shot him?

EB: I shot him through the heart.

GL: So you have a shotgun?

EB: For God's sake . . . What do you expect me to have had? A machine gun? I've already said that I had a shotgun with me.

GL: Is it a weapon you keep at home? Is it licensed?

EB: I don't have a licence. I bought it in Norway a few years ago, and brought it to Sweden illegally.

GL: Where is it now?

EB: At the bottom of the River Ljusnan.

GL: So you threw the gun into the river immediately after shooting Abraham Andersson?

EB: I could hardly have done it beforehand, could I?

GL: No, I suppose not. But I have to ask you to answer clearly and directly to my questions, without making unnecessary comments.

(A man's voice interrupted at this point. Lindman presumed it was the solicitor. To his surprise the solicitor spoke with a very broad Småland accent and was difficult to understand. As far as he could work out, Hermansson had said that in his view his client had answered the questions in a perfectly proper manner. He couldn't hear what Larsson said in reply as the microphone was moved again.)

GL: Can you say where you threw the gun into the river?

EB: From the bridge here in Sveg.

GL: Which one?

EB: The old one.

GL: From which side?

EB: The side facing the town. I was standing in the middle of the bridge.

GL: Did you throw the gun or drop it into the water?

EB: I'm not sure. I suppose I dropped it.

GL: Let me take a different line for a moment. A few days ago you were attacked in your home by a masked man wanting to know who had killed Abraham Andersson. Is there anything you said at that time that you wish to change now?

EB: No.

GL: So you didn't make that up to throw us off the scent?

EB: It happened exactly as I said it did at the time. Besides, that pale-looking policeman from Borås . . . what's his name? Lindgren . . . He was also attacked outside my house.

GL: Lindman. Have you a plausible explanation for what happened? For why the man who attacked you wanted to know who killed Abraham Andersson?

EB: Perhaps he was feeling some kind of guilt.

GB: For what?

EB: Because the murder of Herbert might have led to the murder of Abraham Andersson.

GL: So he was right, wasn't he?

EB: Yes. But what did he know? Who is he?

GL: Could it have been then that you decided you should confess?

EB: That obviously played a part in it.

GL: OK, we'll leave that for the moment. Let's go back to what happened at Andersson's place. You said that you – and I'm quoting you word for word, I wrote it down – "forced him to walk out into the trees not far from the house and shot him". Is that correct?

EB: Yes.

GL: Can you describe in detail exactly what happened?

EB: I stuck the gun in his back and told him to start walking. We stopped when we came in among the trees. I stood in front of him and asked him one last time if he realised that I was deadly serious. He just laughed. So I shot him.

(*Silence. The tape was still running. Somebody coughed, the solicitor perhaps. Lindman understood why. There was something wrong here. It was pitch dark in the forest. How had she been able to see anything? Moreover Andersson was tied to a tree when he died. Or at least the police had assumed that he was still alive when he'd been tied to the tree. Lindman suspected that Larsson was beginning to wonder about Berggren's confession, and was asking himself how to proceed. He was probably trying to recall what had been published in the media, and what was known only to the police.*)

GL: So you shot him from in front?

EB: Yes.

GL: Can you say roughly how far away from him you were?

336

EB: Three metres or so.

GL: And he didn't move? Didn't try to run away?

EB: I suppose he didn't believe I was going to shoot.

GL: Can you remember what time it was when this happened?

EB: Round about midnight.

GL: That means it was dark.

EB: I had a strong torch with me. I made him carry it when we walked into the forest.

(Another short pause. Berggren had answered the first question that had worried Larsson.)

GL: What happened after you'd shot him?

EB: I looked to make sure he was dead. He was.

GL: Then what did you do?

EB: I tied him to a tree trunk. I had a washing line with me.

GL: So you tied him up after you'd shot him?

EB: Yes.

GL: Why did you do that?

EB: At that time I had no intention of making a confession. I wanted to make it look as if it was something different.

GL: Something different from what?

EB: A murder a woman could have done. I made it look more like an execution.

(The second question answered, Lindman thought. But Larsson still doesn't really believe her.)

EB: I need to go to the lavatory.

GL: Then we'll take a break here, at 15.32. Erik can show you where it is.

The tape started running again. The interrogation continued. Larsson went back to the beginning, repeated all the questions, but stopped in connection with more and more details. A classic interrogation, Lindman thought. Larsson is tired, he's been working day and night for several days, but he's still in complete control of what he's saying, step by step.

The tape stopped. Larsson had brought the interrogation to a close at 17.02. The last thing he said on the tape was the only conclusion he could draw.

*   *   *

GL: OK, I think we can stop there. What has happened is that you, Elsa Berggren, have confessed to shooting Abraham Andersson, intentionally and after having planned it, at his house at Dunkärret on November 3, shortly after midnight. You have described in detail what happened, and stated that the motive was that you and Herbert Molin had been blackmailed, or threatened with blackmail. You also said that you threw the murder weapon into the River Ljusnan from the old bridge. Is that all correct?

EB: Yes.

GL: Is there anything you've said that you'd like to change?

EB: No.

GL: Is there anything herr Hermansson would like to say?

SH: No.

GL: I must now inform you that you are under arrest and will be taken to the police station in Östersund. Then a public prosecutor will make a decision about remanding you in custody. Your solicitor will explain all this to you. Is there anything you wish to add?

EB: No.

GL: What you have told us is exactly what happened, is that correct?

EB: Yes.

GL: Then I shall conclude the interrogation at this point.

Lindman stood up and stretched his back. It was stuffy in the room. He opened a window and emptied the half-bottle of mineral water. Thought about what he'd heard. He felt the need to stretch his legs. Larsson was asleep somewhere. He wrote a note and put it on the desk. *Short walk, to both bridges and back. Stefan.*

He walked quickly as he was cold. The path by the river was well lit. Again he had the feeling that somebody was following him. He stopped and turned. Nobody in sight. Although, had there been a shadowy figure dodging out of the light? I'm imagining things, he told himself. There's nobody there. He continued towards the bridge from which Berggren claimed to have dropped her shotgun into the river. Not thrown, dropped. Was she telling the truth? He had to assume so. Nobody confesses to a murder they haven't committed unless there is a very special reason to protect the real culprit. In such cases, the culprit is usually a child. Parents sometimes accept the blame to save their children. But otherwise? He came to the bridge, tried imagining the shotgun lying there in the water, then turned back. There was one question that Larsson had overlooked. Why had she chosen just this day to confess? Why not yesterday? Why not tomorrow? Had she only made up her mind finally today? Or was there some other reason?

He came back to the Community Centre and passed behind it. The window was still ajar. Larsson was on the phone. Talking to Rundström, Lindman could hear. The library was still open. He went into the reading room and looked for the Borås local paper. It wasn't there. He went back to the police offices. Larsson was still talking to Rundström. Lindman stayed in the doorway. Looked at the window. Held his breath. He'd been standing out there in the dark and had heard everything Larsson said. He went over to the window, closed it and went back outside. Now he couldn't hear a word of what was being said inside. He went back in. Larsson was finishing his conversation with Rundström. Lindman opened the window again. Larsson looked at him and raised his eyebrows.

"What are you up to?"

"I've just realised that from outside you can hear every word that's said in here, loud and clear, when the window's open. If it's dark you can be right next to the window and not be seen."

"So?"

"Just a thought. A possibility."

"You mean that somebody's been listening to our phone calls?"

"I expect I'm just imagining it."

Larsson closed the window.

"For safety's sake," he said with a smile. "What do you think about her confession?"

"Did it say in the papers that he was tied to a tree trunk?"

"Yes, but not that a washing line was used. I also spoke to one of the forensic boys who examined the scene. He could see no flaw in what she described."

"So she did it?"

"Facts are facts. You no doubt noticed that I was sceptical, though."

"If she didn't do it, if she's protecting the real culprit, we have to ask why."

Larsson shook his head. "We have to start from the assumption that we've got this murder solved. A woman has admitted doing it. If we find the shotgun in the river tomorrow, we can soon establish if the fatal shot came from that gun."

He sat down and started rolling one of his broken-off cigarillos between his fingers.

"We've been fighting on several fronts these last few days. I hope that one of them can now be regarded as closed."

"Why do you think she decided to confess today rather than on any other day?"

"I don't know. Maybe I ought to have asked her that. I suppose she'd only just made up her mind. She may even have had enough respect for us to have decided that we'd get her in the end anyway."

"Would we have done?"

Larsson pulled a face. "You never know. Sometimes even the Swedish police catch a criminal."

There was a knock on the half-open door. A boy came in with a pizza box. Larsson paid the bill and put it in his pocket. The boy left.

"This time I'm not going to crumple it up and drop it in an ashtray. Do you still think it was Hereira who picked up the bill in the dining room that night?"

"Could well have been."

"This is the most continental thing about Sveg," he said. "They have a pizzeria. Not that they normally deliver, but they will if you have the right contacts. Would you like some? I didn't get round to eating. I fell asleep."

Larsson cut the pizza in half with a ruler.

"Police officers soon put on weight," Larsson said. "Stress and careless eating habits. On the other hand, we don't commit suicide all that often. Doctors are worse in that respect. There again, a lot of us die from heart problems. Which is probably not all that surprising."

"I've got cancer," Lindman said. "Perhaps I'm an exception."

Larsson sat with a piece of pizza in his hand.

"Bowling," he said. "That would make you healthy again, no question."

Lindman couldn't help laughing.

"I only have to mention the word bowling and you start laughing. I don't think being serious suits your face."

"What was it she called me? 'That pale-looking policeman from Borås'?"

"That was the only funny thing she said from start to finish. To be honest, I think Berggren is an awful woman. I'm glad she isn't my mother."

They ate in silence. Larsson put the carton and the remains of his pizza on top of the waste-paper basket.

"We're getting the odd bit of information in," he said, wiping his mouth. "The only problem is that it's the wrong stuff. For instance, Interpol in Buenos Aires have sent a mysterious message telling us that there's somebody called Fernando Hereira in jail for life, for something as old-fashioned as counterfeiting. They ask if he's our man. What on earth do you say to that? Do we tell them that if they can prove the bloke has cloned himself, we'll take them seriously?"

"Is that really true?"

"I'm afraid so. Maybe if we have a bit of patience we'll get something more sensible from them. You never know."

"The red Ford?"

"Disappeared into thin air. Like the driver. We still haven't tracked down the owner, Harner. He seems to have emigrated to Portugal. Some might take that with a pinch of salt as he still has a car in Sweden. The national crime squad are looking into it. There's a nation-wide alert for the car. Something will happen, given time. Rundström's a persistent bastard."

Lindman tried to make a summary in his head. His role in this investigation, in so far as he had one at all, had been to ask questions that could be of use to Larsson.

"I take it that you'll be telling the mass media as soon as possible that you have the person responsible for the murder of Abraham Andersson?"

Larsson looked up in surprise. "Why on earth should I do that? If what we think is right, it could mean that Hereira will clear off. If it's true that he came back up to the northern forests to find out about the murder of Andersson, that is. Don't forget that he put Berggren under pressure on that score. I think she was telling the truth about that, at least. Obviously, we'll have to dig into all this. Our first task tomorrow morning will be to look for the shotgun in the river."

"Somebody else could have killed Andersson, using a gun that either the murderer or Berggren threw into the river. Or dropped, as she said."

"Are you suggesting that she confessed to get our protection?"

"I'm just asking questions."

Then he thought of something else that had been troubling him on and off.

"Why isn't there a prosecutor?" he said. "I haven't heard a name, at any rate."

"Lövander," Larsson said. "Albert Lövander. They say that in his younger days he was a pretty good high-jumper, only just below the elite standard. Now he devotes most of his time to his grandchildren. Of course there's a prosecutor involved. We don't work outside the legal system. Besides, Lövander and Rundström are old hands. They talk to each other every morning and every evening. And Lövander never interferes in what we're doing."

"But surely he must have given some general instructions?"

"Only to carry on as we are going."

It was now 9.15. Larsson phoned home. Lindman went out and stood next to the stuffed bear. Then he phoned Elena.

"Where are you?"

"Next to the bear."

"I consulted a map of Sweden today, large-scale. I'm trying to find out where you are exactly."

"We've had a confession. One of the murders might have been solved. It was a woman."

"Who'd done what?"

"Killed a man who'd been blackmailing her. She shot him."

"Was that the man who was tied to a tree?"

"Yes."

"No woman would ever do that."

"Why not?"

"Women defend themselves. They never attack."

"I don't think it's quite as straightforward as that."

"How straightforward is it, then?"

He hadn't the energy to try to explain.

"When are you coming home?"

"I've already said."

342

"Have you thought any more about our trip to London?"

Lindman had forgotten all about it.

"No," he said. "But I shall. I think it sounds like an excellent idea."

"What are you doing just now?"

"Talking to Larsson."

"Doesn't he have a family to go home to?"

"What makes you ask that? Right now he's talking to his wife on the telephone."

"Can you give me an honest answer to a question?"

"Why ever not?"

"Does he know that I exist?"

"I think so."

"Think?"

"I've probably mentioned your name. Or he'll have heard me talking to you on the telephone."

"Anyway, I'm glad you phoned. But don't ring again until tomorrow. I'm going to bed early tonight."

Lindman went back to the office. Larsson had finished his call. He was picking at his fingernails with a straightened paper-clip.

"That window standing ajar," he said. "I've been thinking about what you said. It seems plausible that there was somebody there, listening to what we said. I've been trying to remember when it was open, and when it was closed. Impossible, of course."

"Maybe you should be thinking about what information came from this room, and nowhere else."

Larsson contemplated his hands. "We decided on the road blocks here," he said eventually. "We talked about a man on his way from Funäsdalen towards the south-west."

"I take it you're thinking about the red Ford? The man who did the shooting?"

"I'm thinking more about the suggestion that there might have been a leak from the police. It seems more likely that it was an open window."

Lindman hesitated.

"This last day or so I've had the feeling that somebody has been following me," he said. "I've felt it over and over again. A shadow somewhere behind me. Noises too. But I can't be sure."

Larsson said nothing. Instead he stood up and went to the door.

"Walk over to the wall," he said. "Keep on talking. When I turn the light out, look out of the window."

Lindman did as he was told. Larsson started prattling on about grapes. Why red ones were much better than green ones. Lindman had got as far as the window. Larsson switched off the light. Lindman tried to see what was happening in the darkness outside, but everything was black. Larsson put the light back on, and went back to his desk.

"Did you see anything?"

"No."

"That doesn't necessarily mean that there wasn't somebody there. Or that there wasn't somebody there not long ago. But I don't see what we can do about it."

He pushed aside two small plastic bags lying on top of a file. One of them fell on the floor.

"The forensic boys forgot a couple of plastic bags," Larsson said. "Odds and ends they'd found on the road not far from the blue Golf."

Lindman bent down to look. One of them contained a receipt from a petrol station. Shell. It was dirty, hardly legible. Larsson watched him intently. Lindman studied the text. It seemed a bit clearer now. The petrol receipt was from a filling station near Söderköping. Slowly, he replaced the plastic bag on the desk and looked at Larsson. Thoughts were whirring around in his brain.

"Berggren didn't kill Andersson," he said slowly. "We're into something much bigger than that, Larsson. Berggren didn't kill him."

CHAPTER 32

Snow was falling again. Larsson went to the window to check the thermometer. Minus one. He sat down and looked at Lindman. Lindman would remember that moment, a clear and unmistakable image of a turning point. It was made up of the newly falling snow, Larsson with his bloodshot eyes and the story itself, what had happened in Kalmar, the discovery he had made when he broke into Wetterstedt's flat. He remembered that only a few hours beforehand he had told the same story to Veronica Molin. Now it was Larsson listening with great interest. Was he surprised? Lindman couldn't tell from the expression on his face.

He was trying to create an overall picture. That dirty filling station receipt from a Shell garage in Söderköping was a key that fitted all doors, but in order to draw conclusions he must first tell the whole story, not just parts of it.

What had he realised when he picked up the plastic bag that had fallen from the overladen desk? A sort of silent explosion, a wall being broken through, and something that had been limited all at once became very large. Although they were groping in the dark, looking for a murderer who might be called Fernando Hereira and might come from Argentina, the investigation had been local. They had been looking for the solution in Härjedalen. Now the artificial walls had collapsed. The petrol receipt shot like a rocket through everything they had built, and at last it was possible to see things clearly.

Somebody had filled up with petrol in Söderköping, in a red Ford Escort belonging to a man by the name of Herner who had a P.O. box in Portugal. Then somebody had driven the car across much of Sweden and stopped on a country road west of Sveg, and started shooting at a car that was coming from the mountains. They scraped at the dirty receipt but were unable to read the date, although the time was clearly 20.12. Larsson thought the forensic people would be able to decipher the date, and they must do that as soon as possible.

Somebody sets off from Kalmar for Härjedalen. On the way, in Söderköping, he stops to fill up with petrol. He continues his journey. He tries to kill the man who most probably was responsible for the murder of Molin. Neither Lindman nor Larsson were the type of police officer who believed in coincidences. Somewhere in the Nazi underworld, inhabited by the likes of Wetterstedt and the Strong Sweden foundation, Lindman's visit had stirred up unrest. They couldn't be certain that he was the one who'd broken into the flat. Or could they? Lindman remembered the front door shutting as he left the flat, the feeling that somebody was watching him, the same feeling he'd had these last few days. "Perhaps two invisible shadows make one visible shadow," he said to Larsson. It could be that the shadow following him in Kalmar was the same as the one in Sveg. The conclusion that Lindman was trying to reach was that their thinking had been closer to the truth than they had dared to believe. It was all to do with the underworld where old Nazis had come across something new that enabled the old madness to join up with the new version. Somebody had broken into this shadow world and killed Molin. A shudder had run through the old Nazis. "The woodlice are starting to crawl out from under stones," as Larsson put it afterwards. Who was the enemy of these Nazis? Was it the man who had killed Molin? Could it mean that Andersson had known about more than just the past of Molin and Berggren, that he'd known about the whole organisation, and had threatened to expose it and perhaps even something still bigger? They couldn't know that. But a Ford Escort had been filled up with petrol and driven to Härjedalen by a man intent on killing somebody. And Berggren had decided to take responsibility for a murder she almost certainly hadn't committed. The pattern was becoming clear, and conclusions possible to draw. There was an organisation, to which Lindman's own father was continuing to give support long after his death. Molin had been a member, as was Berggren. But not Andersson. Nevertheless, somehow or other he had discovered its existence. On the surface he was a friendly man who played the violin in the Helsingborg Symphony Orchestra, was a paid-up member of the Centre Party and also wrote trivial pop songs under the pseudonym of Siv Nilsson. Beneath the surface he was a man with more than one string to his bow. A blackmailer who made threats and demands. And maybe, deep down, was upset at the very thought of living close to an unreformed Nazi.

It took Lindman half an hour to work it all out.

"The bolt hole," he said. "Andersson's bolt hole. What did he have hidden in there? How much did he know? We can't tell. But whatever it was, it was too much."

Snow was falling more densely now. Larsson had angled his desk lamp so that it shone out into the darkness.

"This has been threatening for the last week," he said. "Snow. And now we're getting plenty of it. It might melt away, but it could lie. Winters up here are not easy to predict, but they're always long."

They drank coffee. The Community Centre was empty. The library had closed.

"I think it's time for me to go back to Östersund," Larsson said. "All you've told me makes me more than ever convinced that the Special Branch must be brought in."

"What about the information you've had from me?" Lindman said.

"We may have received an anonymous tip-off," Larsson said. "Don't worry, I'm not going to report you for breaking down the door of that Nazi's flat."

It was 10.15. They examined the situation they were in from various angles. Shuffled the pieces around. A couple of hours ago Berggren had been playing a central role. Now she'd been sidelined, at least for the time being. At the front of stage were Fernando Hereira and the man who'd filled a Ford Escort with petrol in Söderköping.

There was a clattering from the entrance to the Community Centre. Johansson eventually trudged in, snow in his thinning hair.

"I very nearly came off the road," he said, brushing the snow from his jacket. "I got in a skid. I was close to catastrophe."

"You drive too fast."

"Very possibly."

"What happened in Östersund?"

"Lövander will sort out the remand procedures tomorrow morning. He came to the police station and listened to the tape, then phoned me in the car."

"Did she say anything else?"

"She didn't utter a word all the way to Östersund."

Larsson had vacated the desk chair, and Johansson sat down with a yawn. Larsson told him about the petrol receipt and the conclusions they'd drawn. He invented a story about Lindman receiving an anonymous call about the Strong Sweden foundation. Johansson was only half listening at first, but soon pricked up his ears.

"I agree," he said when Larsson had finished. "We have to bring in the Special Branch. If we have an organisation calling itself Nazi and killing people, then Stockholm needs to be in on the case. There's been an awful lot of this kind of stuff in Sweden lately. Meanwhile I suppose we'd better keep on hunting for that red Escort."

"Isn't Stockholm doing that?"

Johansson had opened his briefcase and was taking out some faxes.

"They've traced Anders Harner. He says the Escort is his all right, but it's in a garage in Stockholm. A place run by somebody called Mattias Sundelin. I've got his telephone number here."

He called the number and switched his telephone to loudspeaker mode. A woman answered.

"I'm trying to get in touch with Mattias Sundelin."

"Who are you?"

"My name's Erik Johansson and I'm a police officer in Sveg."

"Where's that?"

"In Härjedalen, but that's by the bye. Is Sundelin there?"

"Just a minute, I'll get him."

They waited.

"Mattias here," said a gravelly voice.

"This is Inspector Johansson from the police in Sveg. It's about a red Ford Escort, registration number ABB 003. The owner is Anders Harner. He tells us it's in your garage. Is that correct?"

"Yes, that's correct."

"So you have the car?"

"Not here at home. It's in the garage in town. I rent out garage space."

"But you are certain that the car is there at this moment?"

"I can't be certain about every single car I've got parked there. I have about 90 of them. What's this all about?"

"We need to trace that car. Where is the garage?"

"In Kungsholmen. I can take a look tomorrow."

"No," Johansson said. "We need to know right now."

"What's the hurry?"

"I can't go into that. Please drive in and check that the car is still there."

"Now?"

"Yes. Now."

"I can't do that. I've been drinking wine. I'd be over the limit if I was stopped."

"Is there somebody else who could check? If not, you'll have to take a taxi."

"You can try Pelle Niklasson. I've got his number here."

Johansson wrote it down, thanked Sundelin and rang off. Then he called the new number. The man who answered said he was Pelle Niklasson. Johansson repeated the questions about the red Escort.

"I can't remember if I saw it today. We've got quite a few cars in the long-stay area."

"We need to have confirmation that it is there, and we need it now."

"I'm in Vällingby. Surely you're not suggesting that I should drive all that way at this time of night."

"If not a police car will come to collect you."

"What's happened?"

Johansson sighed. "I'm the one asking the questions. How long will it take you to get there and check if the car's where it should be?"

"Forty minutes. Can't it wait until tomorrow?"

"No. Write down this number. Phone me as soon as you know."

It was still snowing in Sveg. They waited. Thirty-seven minutes later, the phone rang.

"Erik Johansson here."

"How did you know?"

"How did I know what?"

"That the car wasn't here."

Larsson and Lindman sat up and leaned towards the loudspeaker.

"Has it been stolen?"

"I don't know. It's supposed to be impossible to steal a car from here."

349

"Can you explain that a bit more clearly?"

"This is a garage that charges high fees in return for maximum security. No car can be driven away from here without our checking on the person collecting it."

"So everything is recorded?"

"In the computer, yes. I don't know how to run that thing, though. I do mostly maintenance. It's the other lads who look after the computer side."

"Mattias Sundelin?"

"He's the boss. He doesn't do anything."

"Who are you referring to, then?"

"The other lads. Five of us work here, apart from the cleaner. And the boss, of course. One of them must know when the car left, but I can't contact them now."

Lindman raised his hand. "Ask him to fax their personal details through."

"Have you got access to their personal details?"

"They are here somewhere."

He went to look, then returned to the telephone.

"I've found copies of their driving licences."

"Have you got a fax there?"

"Yes, and I know how to use that. I can't send anything until I get the OK from Sundelin, though."

"He knows about it. He gave us your number, remember?" Johansson said, sounding as authoritative as he could. He gave Niklasson the police fax number.

The black fax machine was in the corridor outside the office. Johansson checked that it was working. Then they waited again.

There was a ring, and paper began to emerge from the machine. Four driving licences. The text was barely legible, their faces like black thumbprints. The machine stopped. They returned to the office. Snow was piling up on the windowledge. They passed the photocopies round, and Johansson wrote down the names: Klas Herrström, Simon Lukac, Magnus Holmström, Werner Mäkinen. He read them out, one after the other.

Lindman didn't even listen to the fourth name. He recognised the third one. He took the photocopy and held his breath. The face was

350

just an outline, with no features distinguishable. Even so, he was certain.

"I think we've got him," he said slowly.

"Who?"

"Magnus Holmström. I met him on Öland. When I visited Wetterstedt."

Larsson had barely touched on the visit to Wetterstedt when he told Johansson about what Lindman had said, but he remembered even so.

"Are you sure?"

Lindman stood up and held the photocopy under the lamp.

"He's our man. I'm sure."

"Are you saying he's the one who tried to shoot the driver of the Golf?"

"All I'm saying is that I met Magnus Holmström on Öland, and that he's a Nazi."

Nobody spoke.

"Let's bring Stockholm in now," Larsson said. "They'll have to go to the garage and produce a decent picture of this lad. But where is he now?"

The telephone rang. It was Pelle Niklasson, wanting to know if the faxes had come through all right.

"Yes, thank you, we've got them," said Johansson. "So one of your staff is called Magnus Holmström."

"Maggan."

"'Maggan'?"

"That's what we call him."

"Have you got his home address?"

"I don't think so. He hasn't been working here long."

"You must know where your staff live, surely?"

"I can have a look. This isn't part of my job."

It was almost five minutes before he returned to the telephone.

"He's given us the address of his mother in Bandhagen. Skeppstavägen 7A, c/o Holmström. But he hasn't given a phone number."

"What's his mother's first name?"

"I've no idea. Can I go home now? My wife was extremely pissed off when I left."

"Call her and tell her you won't be back for some time yet. You'll shortly be telephoned by the police in Stockholm."

351

"What's going on?"

"You said that Holmström was new?"

"He's been working here for a couple of months only. Has he done something?"

"What kind of an impression of him have you got?"

"What do you mean by impression?"

"Is he a good workman? Has he any special habits? Is he extreme in any way? When was he last at work?"

"He's pretty discreet. Doesn't say much. I don't really have much of an impression of him. And he's been off work since last Monday."

"Good, thank you. Wait where you are until the Stockholm police phone you."

By the time Johansson rang off, Larsson had already phoned the Stockholm police. Lindman was trying to track down the telephone number, but directory enquiries didn't have a Holmström at that address. He tried to find out if there was a mobile phone number corresponding to Holmström's name and identity number, but he had no luck there either.

After another 20 minutes, all the telephones were silent. Johansson put on some coffee. It was still snowing, but less heavily. Lindman looked out of the window. The ground was white. Larsson had gone to the lavatory. It was a quarter of an hour before he came back.

"My stomach can't cope with this," he said gloomily. "I'm completely blocked up. I haven't had a bowel movement since the day before yesterday."

They drank their coffee and waited. Shortly after 1 a.m. a duty officer phoned from Stockholm to say that they hadn't found Magnus Holmström when they went to his mother's house in Bandhagen. Her first name was Margot, and she'd told them that she hadn't seen her son for several months. He used to call in occasionally when he was working, and to collect his post, but she didn't know where he was living now. They would continue searching for him through the night.

Larsson phoned Lövander, the prosecutor, in Östersund. Johansson sat at his computer and started typing. Lindman's mind drifted to Veronica Molin and the computer she said contained the whole of her life. He wondered if she and her brother had set off for Sveg through the snow, or if they'd decided to spend the night in Östersund. Larsson finished his call to the prosecutor.

"Things are starting to happen now," he said. "Lövander grasped the situation and a new nation-wide emergency call is going out. Everybody will be looking not only for a red Ford Escort, but also for a young man called Magnus Holmström who is probably armed and must be regarded as dangerous."

"Somebody should ask his poor mother if she knows about his political beliefs," Lindman said. "What kind of mail does he receive? Does he have a computer at her home, possibly with e-mail?"

"He must live somewhere," Larsson said. "It's very odd, of course, that he has his mail sent to his mother's address, but lives somewhere else. I suppose this might be what young people do nowadays, moving around from one flat belonging to a friend to another. If that's it, he probably has a hotmail address."

"It suggests he's purposely hiding his whereabouts," said Johansson. "Does anybody know how to make bigger letters on this screen?"

Larsson showed him what to do.

"Maybe they should go looking for him on Öland," Lindman said. "That's where I came across him, after all. And the car was filled up in Söderköping."

Larsson slapped his forehead in irritation.

"I'm too tired," he bellowed. "We should have thought of that from the first, of course."

He grabbed a telephone and started calling again. It took him ages to find the officer in Stockholm he'd spoken to earlier. While he was waiting, Lindman gave him a description of how to find Wetterstedt's house on Öland.

It was 1.30 by the time Larsson finished. Johansson was still tapping away at his keyboard. The snow had almost stopped. Larsson checked the thermometer.

"Minus three. That means it'll lie. Until tomorrow, at least."

He turned to Lindman. "I don't think much more is going to happen tonight. Routine procedures are clicking into place now. A diver can go looking for the gun under the bridge tomorrow morning, but the best thing we can do until then is get some sleep. I'll stay at Erik's place. I can't face a hotel room at the moment."

Johansson switched off his computer. "At least we've taken a big step forward," he said. "Now we're looking for two people. We've even got the name of one of them. That has to be regarded as an advance."

"Three," Larsson said. "We're probably looking for three people."

Nobody contradicted him.

Lindman put on his jacket and left the Community Centre. The snow felt soft under his feet. It muffled all sounds. Occasional flakes of snow were still drifting down. He kept stopping and turning round, but there was no sign that he was being followed. The whole town was asleep. No light in Veronica Molin's window. The funeral was at 11 a.m. later that day. They would have plenty of time to get to Sveg if they had decided to stay in Östersund. He unlocked the front door of the hotel. The two men from yesterday were playing cards again, despite the late hour. They nodded to him as he went past. It was too late to phone Elena now. She'd be asleep. He undressed, showered and went to bed, thinking about Holmström all the time. Discreet, Niklasson had called him. No doubt he could make that impression if he tried, but Lindman had also seen another side of him. Cold as ice and dangerous. He had no doubt at all that it could have been Holmström who had tried to kill Hereira. The question was, did he also kill Andersson? What was still unclear was why Berggren had confessed to that murder. It was possible that she was guilty, of course, but Lindman could not believe it. One could take it for granted that Holmström would have told her anything that wasn't in the newspapers, such as the washing line.

The pattern, he thought, is clearer now. Not complete, there are still some gaps. Even so, it's acquiring a third dimension. He turned off the light. Thought about the funeral. Then Veronica Molin would return to a world he knew nothing about.

He was brought back to consciousness by the sound of the telephone ringing. He fumbled for his mobile. It was Larsson.

"Did I wake you up?"

"Yes."

"I wondered if I ought to phone, but I thought you'd like to know."

"What's happened?"

"Molin's house is on fire. Erik and I are on our way there. The alarm was raised a quarter of an hour ago. A snow plough had gone past and the driver saw the glow among the trees."

Lindman rubbed his eyes.

"Are you still there?" Larsson said.

"Yes."

"At least we don't need to worry about anybody being injured. The place is deserted."

Reception was poor. Larsson's voice was lost. The link was broken. Then he phoned again.

"I thought you'd like to know."

"Do you think the fire has any significance?"

"The only thing I can think of is that somebody knew about Molin's diary but didn't know that you'd already found it. I'll phone again if anything crops up."

"So it has to be arson?"

"I wouldn't like to say. The house was already largely destroyed. It could be natural causes, of course. Erik says they've got a good chief fire officer here in Sveg. Olof Lundin. They say he's never wrong when it comes to establishing the cause of a fire. I'll be in touch."

Lindman put the phone on the bedside table. The light coming in through the window was reflected by the snow. He thought about what Larsson had said. His mind started wandering. He settled down in order to go back to sleep.

It already felt as if he were walking up the hill to the hospital. He was passing the school now. It was raining. Or maybe it was sleet. He was wearing the wrong shoes. He'd got dressed up in preparation for what was in store. The black shoes he'd bought last year and hardly ever worn. He should have been wearing boots, or at the very least his brown shoes with the thick rubber soles. His feet already felt wet.

He couldn't get to sleep. It was too light in the room. He got up to pull down the blinds and shut out the light from the hotel entrance. Then he saw something that made him start. There was a man in the street outside. A figure in the half-light. Staring up at his window. Lindman was wearing a white vest. Perhaps it was visible even though it was dark in the room? The shadow didn't move. Lindman held his breath. The man slowly raised his arms. It looked like a sign of submission. Then he turned on his heel and walked out of the light.

Lindman wondered if he'd been imagining it. Then he saw the footprints in the snow.

Lindman flung on his clothes, grabbed his keys and hurried out of the room. Reception was deserted. The card players had gone to bed. The cards were still there, strewn over the table. Lindman ran out into the darkness. Somewhere in the distance he heard the sound of a car engine dying away. He stood stock still and looked round. Then he walked over to the place where the man had been standing. The footsteps were clear in the snow. He'd left the same way as he'd come, towards the furniture shop.

Lindman examined the footprints. They formed a pattern, that was obvious. He'd seen the pattern before. The man who'd been standing there, looking up at Lindman's window, had marked out the steps of the tango in the glittering, new-fallen snow. The last time Lindman had seen these same footprints, they had been marked out in blood.

CHAPTER 33

He ought to phone Larsson. It was the only sensible thing to do, but something held him back. It was still too unreal, the pattern in the snow, the man underneath his window, raising his arms as if to surrender.

He checked to make sure he had his mobile in his pocket, then started following the tracks. Just outside the hotel courtyard it was crossed by prints from a dog. The dog had then crossed the road after leaving a yellow patch. Not many people were out in the streets. The only tracks visible were from the man he was following. Straight, confident strides. Heading north, past the furniture shop and towards the railway station. He looked round. Not a soul in sight, no shadowy figures now, just this one set of footprints in the snow. The man had stopped to look round when he came to the café, then he had crossed the road, still heading north, before turning left towards the deserted, unlit station building. Lindman let a car drive past, then continued on his way.

He paused when he came to the station. The tracks continued round the building towards the rails and the platform. If his suspicions were correct, he was now following the man who'd killed Molin. Not only killed, but tortured him, whipped him to death, and then dragged him round in a bloodstained tango. For the first time, it struck him that the man might be mad. What they had assumed all the time was something rational, cold-blooded and well planned might be the opposite of that in fact: pure madness. He turned, walked back until he was under a street light, and phoned Larsson. Busy. They'll be at the scene of the fire by now, he thought. Larsson is calling somebody to tell him about it, probably Rundström. He waited, keeping his eye on the station all the time, then tried the number again. Still busy. After a few minutes he tried for a third time. A woman's voice informed him that it was impossible to get through to the required number and would he please try again later. He put the mobile back in his pocket and tried to decide what to do. Then he started walking south towards Fjällvägen. He turned off when he came to a long warehouse and found himself among the railway lines. He could see the station some distance away. He kept walking across the tracks and into the shadows on the other side, then slowly approached the station again. An old guard's van was standing in a siding. He walked round the back of it. He still wasn't close enough to see where the footprints had gone. He stood in the shadow of the guard's van and peered round it.

The snow muffled all sounds, and so he didn't hear the man creeping up on him from behind and hitting him hard on the back of his head. Lindman was unconscious by the time he landed into the snow.

It was pitch dark when he opened his eyes. There was a pounding in the back of his head. He remembered immediately what had taken place – standing by the guard's van, peering out at the station. Then a flash. He knew nothing about what happened next, but he was no longer outdoors. He was sitting on a chair. He couldn't move his arms. Nor his legs. He was tied to a chair, and there was a blindfold round his eyes.

He was terrified. He'd been captured by the man whose tracks he'd followed through the snow. He had done exactly what he shouldn't have done: gone off on his own, without back-up and without warning his colleagues. His heart was racing. When he tried to turn his head he felt excruciating pain in the back of his neck. He listened to the darkness and wondered how long he'd been unconscious.

He gave a start. He could hear somebody breathing close by him. Where was he? Indoors, but where? There was a smell in the room that he recognised, but couldn't place. He'd been in this room before, but where was it? There was a glimmer of light round the edge of the blindfold. He still couldn't see anything, but the light had been switched on. He held his breath and heard muffled footsteps. A carpet, he thought; and the floor's vibrating. An old house with a wooden floor. I've been here before, I'm certain of it.

Then somebody started talking to him in English. A man's voice, coming from his left. It was gruff, the words came out slowly, and the foreign accent was obvious.

"I'm sorry I had to knock you out, but this meeting was necessary."

Lindman made no reply. Every word he said could be dangerous if the man really was mad. Silence was the only protection he had at the moment.

"I know you're a policeman," the voice said. "Never mind how I know."

The man waited for Lindman to reply, but he didn't.

"I'm tired," the voice said. "This has been far too long a journey. I want to go home, but I need the answers to some questions. And there's somebody I want to talk to. Answer just one question: who am I?"

Lindman tried to work out what it meant. Not the words, but what lay behind them. The man talking to him gave the impression of being perfectly calm, not in the least worried or impatient.

"I'd like a reply," the voice said. "You won't come to any harm, but I can't let you see my face. Who am I?"

Lindman realised he would have to respond. It was a very clear question.

"I saw you in the snow under my hotel window. You raised your arms and you'd left some prints in the snow like those in Herbert Molin's house."

"I killed him. It was necessary. I'd spent all those years thinking that I would draw back when it came to it, but I didn't. Perhaps I shall regret it when I'm on my deathbed. I don't know."

Lindman was soaked in sweat. He wants to talk, he thought. What I need is time, time to work out where I am and what I can do. He also thought about what the voice had said: *all those years*. That was something he could latch onto, put a simple question of his own.

"I realise it must have had something to do with the war," he said. "Events that took place a long time ago."

"Herbert Molin killed my father."

The words were spoken calmly and slowly. *Herbert Molin killed my father*. Lindman had no doubt that Fernando Hereira, or whatever he was really called, was speaking the truth.

"What happened?"

"Millions of people died as a result of Hitler's evil war, but every death is individual, every horror has its own face."

Silence. Lindman tried to pick out the most significant bits of what the man had said. *All those years*, that was the war; and now he knew that Fernando Hereira had avenged his father. He'd also mentioned a journey that had been *far too long*. And most important of all, perhaps: *there's somebody I want to talk to*. Somebody besides me, Lindman thought. Who?

"They hanged Josef Lehmann," the voice said. "Round about the autumn of 1945. He deserved it. He had killed many people in the terror-stricken concentration camps he governed. But they should have hanged his brother as well. Waldemar Lehmann. He was worse. Two brothers, two monsters who served their master by making vast numbers of humans scream. One of them finished up with a rope round his neck, the other one disappeared, and if the gods have been incredibly careless he might be still alive. I've sometimes thought I've seen him in the street, but I don't know what he looks like. There are no photographs of him. He had been more careful than his brother Josef. That saved him. Besides, what he enjoyed most was setting up others to carry out the torture. He trained people to become monsters. He educated the henchmen of death."

There was a sigh, or a sob. The man speaking to him moved again. A creaking noise, Lindman had heard it before. A chair, or maybe a sofa that creaked in that way. He'd never sat on it himself.

He gave a start. He knew. He'd sat in exactly the same chair that he was now tied to.

"I want to go home," the voice said. "Back to what remains of my life. But first I must know who killed Abraham Andersson. I must know if I have to bear some of the responsibility for what happened. I can't undo what's already done, but I can spend the rest of my life lighting candles for the Holy Virgin and asking for forgiveness."

"You came along in a blue Golf," Lindman said. "Somebody stepped into the road and shot at you. You escaped. I don't know if you were wounded, but whoever shot you could well have been the person who killed Abraham Andersson."

"You know a lot," the voice said. "But then, you're a policeman. It's your job to know, you have to do all you can to catch me, even if what has actually happened is the opposite and I've caught you. I'm not wounded. You were right: I was lucky. I got out of the car without being hit, and spent the rest of the night hiding in the forest, until I dared to move on."

"You must have had a car."

"I shall pay for the car that was shot up. Once I get home I shall send some money."

"I mean afterwards. You must have taken another car?"

"I found it in a garage by a house at the edge of the forest. I don't know if anybody's noticed that it's missing. The house looked to be deserted."

Lindman thought he could detect the beginnings of impatience in the man's voice. He would have to be more careful about what he said. There was a clinking of a bottle, a top being unscrewed. Some swigs, but no glass, Lindman thought. He's drinking straight out of the bottle. There was a faint smell of alcohol.

Then the man described what had happened 54 years ago. A brief tale, clear, unambiguous, and totally horrific.

"Waldemar Lehmann was a master. A genius at torturing people. One day Herbert Molin entered his life. I'm not sure about all the details. It wasn't until I met Höllner that I realised who had killed my father. After that I was able to find out enough to know that it would be necessary and just to kill Herbert Molin."

The bottle clinked again. The smell of spirits, more swigs. This man is drinking himself silly, Lindman thought. Does that mean he will lose control of what he's doing? He could feel his fear growing, and his temperature rising.

"My father was a dancing master. A peaceful man who loved to teach people how to dance. Especially young, shy people. One day, the man who would hide behind the name of Herbert Molin came to him as a pupil. He'd been granted a week's leave that he was spending in Berlin. I don't know how many lessons he had, but I remember seeing that young soldier several times. I can see his face now, and I recognised him when I eventually caught up with him."

The man stood up. More creaking. Lindman recognised the sound, but it was from the house on Öland, Wetterstedt's holiday home. I'm going mad, Lindman thought in desperation. I recognise a sound from

361

Öland, but I'm in Härjedalen. The noise started again. From the right now. The man had moved to another chair. One that didn't creak. Another memory was stirred in Lindman's mind. He recalled the chair that didn't creak. Where was this room?

"I was twelve at the time. My father gave his lessons at home. When the war started in 1939 he'd had his dance studio taken away from him. One day a star of David had appeared on the door. He never referred to it. Nobody referred to it. We saw our friends disappear, but my father survived. Lurking somewhere in the background was my uncle. He used to give Hermann Goering massages. That was the invisible protection our family enjoyed. Nobody was allowed to touch us. Until August Mattson-Herzén turned up and became my father's pupil."

The voice ground to a halt. Lindman was trying desperately to think where he could be. That was the first thing he needed to know if he were to find a way of escaping. This man he was sharing the room with could be unpredictable, he'd killed Mattson-Herzén, tortured him, he'd behaved exactly like the people on whom he had exacted his vengeance.

The man was talking again. "I used to sit in on the lessons sometimes. Once, our eyes met. The young soldier smiled. I can still remember it. I liked him. A young man in a uniform who smiled. As he never spoke I thought he was German, of course. How could I have known he was from Sweden? I don't know what happened next, but he became one of Waldemar Lehmann's henchmen. Lehmann must have found out somehow or other that Mattson-Herzén was having dancing lessons from one of those disgusting Jews that were still in Berlin, and was being impertinent enough to behave like a normal, free, respectable citizen. I don't know what he did to convince the young soldier, but I do know that Waldemar Lehmann was one of the devil's most assiduous servants. He succeeded in changing Mattson-Herzén into a monster. He came for his dancing lesson one afternoon. I used to sit out in the hall, listening to what went on in the big room after my father had pushed the furniture against the walls to make space for his lessons. The room had red curtains and a shiny parquet floor. I could hear my father's friendly voice, counting the bars and saying things like 'left foot', 'right foot', and imagined his unfailingly straight back. Then the gramophone stopped. There wasn't a sound. I

362

thought at first they were having a rest. The door opened. The soldier hurried out of the flat. I noticed his feet, his dancing shoes, as he left. He generally came out, wiping the sweat from his brow, and gave me a smile, but nothing of that today. I went to the living room. My father was dead. Mattson-Herzén had strangled him with his own belt."

Lindman experienced the rest of what the man had to say as a long, drawn-out scream.

"He'd strangled him with his own belt! Then shoved a shattered gramophone record into his mouth. The label was covered in blood, but I could see that it was a tango. I've spent the rest of my life looking for the man who did that to my father. It wasn't until I happened to bump into Höllner that I discovered who the murderer really was. Learnt that my father's murderer was a Swede, somebody who hadn't even been forced into serving Hitler, never mind giving vent to an utterly pointless and incomprehensible hatred of Jews. He killed the man who had tried to help him overcome his shyness and teach him to dance. I don't know what Waldemar Lehmann did to Mattson-Herzén, I've no idea what he thrashed into him, what he threatened him with. What made him swallow the ultimate Nazi lunacy. It doesn't matter. He'd come to our house that day, not to learn how to dance, but to kill my father. That murder was so brutal, so horrific, that it is beyond description. My father lay dead with his own belt round his neck. He wasn't the only one to die. His wife, my mother, and me and my brothers and sisters – all of us died. We all died with that belt round our necks. We kept our lives going, it's true – my mother only for a few months, until she'd arranged for her children to go abroad. That was the last favour my uncle managed to extract from Goering. Once we were in Switzerland he committed suicide; now I'm the only one of us left. None of my brothers and sisters got beyond their thirties. One brother drank himself to death, a sister took her own life, and I ended up in South America. How I searched for that young man, for that young soldier who killed my father! I suppose that's why I went to South America, where such a lot of Nazis had fled. I couldn't understand how he had the right to go on living after my father had died. I found him in the end, an old man who'd hidden himself with a new name, away up here in the forest. I killed him. I gave him his final dancing lesson, and I was about to go home when somebody killed his neighbour. What makes me anxious is to what extent I am responsible for that."

Lindman waited for him to go on, but nothing was said for a while. He thought about the name Hereira had mentioned, Höllner. Something critical must have happened when they met.

"Who was Höllner?"

"The messenger I'd been waiting for all my life. A man who happened to be in the same restaurant as me one night in Buenos Aires. At first, when I discovered that he was a German emigrant, I was afraid he was one of the many Nazis who hid themselves in Argentina. Then I discovered that he was like me. A man who hated Hitler."

Hereira fell silent again. Lindman waited.

"When I think back, it all seems so simple," he said eventually. "Höllner came from Berlin, like me. And Höllner's father had been given massage treatment by my uncle from the middle of the 1930s. My uncle was indispensable to Goering, who was constantly in pain as a result of his morphine addiction and couldn't tolerate any masseur but my uncle. That was one starting point. The other was Waldemar Lehmann. A man who'd tortured and murdered prisoners in various concentration camps. His brother had been almost as bad. He was hanged in the autumn of 1945, but Waldemar they did not catch. He disappeared in the chaos at the end of the war and couldn't be traced. He was high on the list of war criminals headed by Bormann. They found Eichmann, but not Waldemar Lehmann. One of those looking for him was an English major, called Stuckford. I don't know why, but he was in Germany in 1945 and must have seen the horrors when they entered the concentration camps. He'd also been present when Josef Lehmann was hanged. Stuckford's researches revealed that a Swedish soldier had been one of Waldemar Lehmann's henchmen towards the end of the war, and that, egged on by Lehmann, the Swede had murdered his dancing master."

Hereira paused again. It was as if he needed to gather strength to tell his story to the end.

"Some time long after the war Höllner and Stuckford met at a conference for people trying to trace war criminals. They talked of the missing Waldemar Lehmann. During the conversation Höllner heard about the murder of a dancing master in Berlin, and he also heard that the man responsible was a Swede called Mattson-Herzén. Another Nazi had passed the information to Stuckford while being interrogated, hoping for clemency in return. Höllner told me all this. He also said that Stuckford occasionally visited Buenos Aires."

Lindman heard Hereira reach for the bottle and put it down again without drinking.

"The next time Stuckford was in Buenos Aires I met him, at his hotel. I introduced myself and explained that I was the son of the dancing master. About a year after that meeting I had a letter from England. In it Stuckford wrote that the soldier who'd killed my father, Mattson-Herzén, had changed his name to Molin after the war and was still alive. I'll never forget that letter. Now I knew who had murdered my father. A man who used to give us a friendly smile when he arrived for his lessons. Stuckford's contacts were eventually able to trace Mattson-Herzén to these forests."

He paused again. There is no more, Lindman thought. No more is needed. I've heard the story. Sitting in front of me is a man who has avenged the murder of his father. We were right in thinking that Molin's murder had its origin in something that happened in a war that ended many years ago. It seemed to Lindman that Hereira had finished off for him a puzzle that he'd been working on. There was an irony in that Molin had also spent his old age solving puzzles, in the day-long company of his fear.

"Have you understood what I've told you?"

"Yes."

"Have you any questions?"

"Not about that, but I would like to know why you moved the dog."

Hereira didn't understand the question. Lindman rephrased it. "You killed Molin's dog. When Andersson was dead, you took his dog."

"I wanted to tell you that you were wrong about what happened. You thought I had killed the other man as well."

"Why should we know that we were wrong because of the dog?"

His reply was simple and convincing. "I was drunk when I made up my mind what to do. I still don't understand why nobody saw me. I moved the dog to create confusion. Confusion in the way you were thinking. I still don't know if I was successful."

"We did start asking different questions."

"Then I achieved my aim."

"When you first came, did you live in a tent by the lake?"

"Yes."

Lindman could hear that Hereira's impatience had melted away. He was calm now. There were no more clinking noises from the bottle. Hereira stood up, the floor vibrated. He was behind Lindman's chair now. The fear that had subsided now revived. Lindman remembered the fingers round his neck. This time he was tied up. If the man tried to strangle him, he wouldn't be able to resist.

When Hereira next spoke his voice came from the left. The chair creaked.

"I thought it would die away," the voice said. "All those terrible things that happened so many years ago. But the thoughts that were born in Hitler's twisted mind are still alive. They have other names now, but they are the same thoughts, the same disgusting conviction that a whole people can be killed off if another people or race ordains it. The new technology, computers, the international networks, they all help these groups to co-operate. Everything's in computers nowadays."

Lindman remembered that he'd heard more or less the same phrase from Veronica Molin. Everything's in computers nowadays.

"They are still ruining lives," the voice said. "They'll go on cultivating their hatred. Hatred of people whose skin is a different colour, who have different customs, different gods."

Lindman realised that Hereira's calm was skin-deep. He was close to breaking point, a collapse that could result in his resorting to violence again. He killed Molin, Lindman thought, and he tried to strangle me. He knocked me out, and now I'm sitting here tied to a chair. Unless I'm attacked from behind I'm stronger than he is. I'm 37 and he's nearly 70. He can't let me go because in that case I'd arrest him. He knows that he's captured a police officer. That's the worst thing you can do, whether you're in Sweden or Argentina. Lindman had no doubt that the man in this room with him could kill him if he wanted to. He'd just finished telling his story of what happened, he'd made a confession, so what options were open to him? Running away, nothing else. And in that case, what would he do with the police officer he'd captured?

I haven't seen his face, Lindman thought. As long as I haven't seen his face he can go away and leave me here. I must make sure he doesn't take off this blindfold.

"Who was the man in the road who tried to shoot me?"

The man seemed impatient again.

"A young neo-Nazi. His name's Magnus Holmström."

"Is he Swedish?"

"Yes."

"I thought this was a decent country. Without Nazis. Apart from the old ones from Hitler's generation who aren't dead yet. Who are still hiding away in their bolt holes."

"There's a new generation. Not many of them, but they do exist."

"I'm not talking about the young men with shaven heads. I'm talking about the ones who dream in blood, plan genocide, see the world as a feudal empire ruled by white men."

"Magnus Holmström's like that."

"Has he been arrested?"

"Not yet."

Silence. The bottle clinked.

"Was it her who asked him to come?"

Who did he mean, Lindman wondered. Then he realised that there was only one possibility. Elsa Berggren.

"We don't know."

"Who else could it have been?"

"We don't know."

"But there must have been a motive, surely?"

Be careful now, Lindman thought. Don't say too much. Not too little either, make sure you get it right. But what is right? He wants to know if he's to blame. Which he is, of course. When he killed Molin, it was like turning over a stone: the woodlice scattered in all directions. Now they want to get back under the stone, they want somebody to put it back where it was before all this trouble started in the forest.

There were still a lot of things he didn't understand. He had the feeling that a link was missing, some thread holding everything together that he hadn't found yet. Nor had Larsson, nobody had.

He thought about Molin's house, burning down in the forest. That seemed a question it wasn't too dangerous to ask.

"Was it you who set fire to Molin's house?"

"I assumed the police would go there, but perhaps not you. I didn't know for sure, but it seemed to be a possibility. I was right. You stayed in the hotel."

"Why me? Why not one of the other officers?"

The man didn't answer. Lindman wondered if he'd overstepped the mark. He waited. All the time he was searching for a chance to get away, to get out of this room where he was tied to a chair. To do that he must first establish were he was.

The bottle clinked again. Then the man stood up. Lindman listened. He couldn't feel any vibrations in the floor. Everything was still. Had the man left the room? Lindman strained all his senses. The man didn't seem to be there. Then a clock started striking. Lindman knew where he was. In Berggren's house, it was her clock.

The blindfold was suddenly ripped off. It happened so quickly that he didn't have time to react. He was in Berggren's living room, on the very chair he'd sat on when he first went there. The man was behind him. Lindman slowly turned his head.

Fernando Hereira was very pale. Unshaven and with dark shadows under his eyes. His hair was grey and unkempt. He was thin. His clothes, dark trousers and a blue jacket, were dirty. The jacket was torn near the collar. He was wearing trainers. So this was the man who'd lived in a tent by the lake, killed Molin so brutally, then dragged him round in a bloodstained tango. It was also the man who had attacked him twice, the first time almost strangling him, the second time only an hour or so ago, by hitting him hard on the back of the head.

The clock had struck the half-hour, 5.30 a.m. Lindman had been unconscious for longer than he'd thought. On the table in front of the man was a bottle of brandy. No glass. The man took a swig, then turned to face Lindman.

"What punishment will I get?"

"I can't tell you that. It's up to the court."

Hereira shook his head sadly. "Nobody will understand. Is there a death penalty in your country?"

"No."

Hereira took another swig from the bottle. He fumbled as he put it down on the table. He's drunk, Lindman thought. He's losing control of his movements.

"There's somebody I want to talk to," Hereira said. "I want to explain to Molin's daughter why I killed her father. Stuckford told me in a letter that Molin had a daughter. Perhaps he had other children as well? Anyway, I want to talk to the daughter. Veronica. She must be here."

"Molin will be buried today."

Hereira gave a start. "Today?"

"His son, too, has arrived. The funeral's at 11.00."

Hereira stared at his hands. "I can only cope with talking to her," he said after a while. "Then she can explain it to whoever she likes. I want to tell her why I did it."

Lindman had been given the opportunity he'd been hoping for.

"Veronica didn't know her father was a Nazi. She's very upset now that she does know. I think she'll understand, if you tell her what you've told me."

"Everything I've said is true." Hereira took another drink from the bottle. "The question is, will you allow me the time I need? If I let you go and ask you to contact the girl on my behalf, will I have the time I need before you arrest me?"

"How do I know that you won't treat Veronica as you treated her father?"

"You can't know that. But why should I? She didn't kill my father."

"You attacked me."

"It was necessary. I regret it, of course. I'll let you go. I'll stay here. It's nearly 6 a.m. You talk to the girl, tell her where I am. Once she's left me, you and the rest of the police can come and collect me. I know I'll never return home. I'll die here, in prison."

Hereira was lost in thought. Was he telling the truth? Lindman knew that it wasn't something he could take for granted.

"Needless to say, I won't let Veronica come to you on her own," he said.

"Why not?"

"You've already shown that you do not hesitate to use violence."

"I want to see her on her own. I will not lay a finger on her."

Hereira slammed his fist down on the table. Lindman could feel his misgivings rising.

"What if I don't go along with what you are asking?"

Hereira looked hard at him before answering. "I'm a peaceful man,

369

though it's true that I've used violence on others. I don't know what I'd do. I might kill you, I might not."

"I can give you the time you need," Lindman said, "and you can talk to her on the telephone."

He could see the positive glint in Hereira's eye. He was tired, but far from resigned.

"I'm already committing myself to more than I should," Lindman said. "I'll guarantee you the time you need, and you can talk to her on the telephone. I'm sure you realise that as a police officer, I shouldn't be doing this."

"Can I trust you?"

"You don't really have a choice."

Hereira hesitated. Then he stood up and cut the tape tying Lindman to the chair.

"We have to trust each other. There's no other possibility."

Lindman felt dizzy as he walked to the door. His legs were stiff, and the back of his neck was extremely sore.

"I'll wait for her to phone," Hereira said. "I'll probably talk to her for about an hour. Then you can tell your colleagues where I am."

Lindman crossed the bridge. Before leaving the house he'd made a note of Berggren's telephone number. He paused at the place where a police diver would start looking for a shotgun on the riverbed an hour or two from now. He was exhausted, but he tried to think clearly. Hereira had committed murder, but there was something appealing about him, something genuine, when he'd tried to convince Lindman that he wanted to talk to Molin's daughter, try to make her understand, hope that she would forgive him. He wondered again if Veronica and her brother had spent the night in Östersund. If so, he'd have to ring round all the hotels to find her.

It was 6.30 when he got back to the hotel. He knocked on her door. She opened it so quickly that he almost recoiled. She was already dressed. Her computer was shimmering in the background.

"I have to talk to you. I know it's early. I thought you might have stayed in Östersund for the night, because of the snow."

"My brother never showed up."

"Why not?"

"He'd changed his mind. He phoned. He didn't want to go to the funeral. I got back here late last night. What is so urgent?"

Lindman started back to reception. She followed him. They sat down and without more ado he told her what had happened during the night and about her father's murderer, Fernando Hereira, who was waiting in Berggren's house for her to phone him, and possibly even forgive him.

"He wanted to meet you," Lindman said. "I didn't agree to that, of course."

"I'm not afraid," she said after a while. "I wouldn't have agreed to go there, though. Of course not. Does anybody else know about this?"

"Nobody."

"Not even your colleagues?"

"Nobody. He speaks English."

She looked hard at him. "I'll talk to him, but I want to be alone when I phone him. When the call is over, I'll knock on your door."

Lindman gave her the paper with the telephone number. Then he went to his room. As he opened his door it struck him that she might already have phoned Hereira. He looked at his watch. In 20 minutes he would contact Larsson and tell him where he could find Hereira.

He went to the bathroom, but found that there was no toilet paper left. He went back to reception. He saw her through the window. Veronica Molin, out in the street. In a hurry.

He stopped short. Tried to work it out. Thoughts were racing around his head. There was no doubt that Veronica Molin was on her way to Hereira. He ought to have foreseen that. Something in direct contrast to what he'd previously thought. It's something to do with her computer, he thought. Something she'd said. Maybe something I'd thought without really understanding the implications. His alarm was growing apace. He turned to the girl who was on her way to the dining room.

"Fröken Molin's key," he said. "I must have it."

She stared at him in bewilderment. "She's just gone out."

"That's why I need her key."

"I can't give it to you."

Lindman slammed his fist on the desk. "I'm a police officer," he roared. "Give me the key."

She took the key from beneath the desk. He grabbed it, raced along

371

the corridor and opened her door. The computer was on. The screen was glowing. He stared at it in horror.

Everything fell into place. Now he could see how it all hung together. Most of all he could see how catastrophically wrong he'd been.

CHAPTER 34

It was 7.05 a.m. and still dark. Lindman ran. Several times he slipped and almost fell in the snow. He ought to have recognised long ago what was now obvious, absolutely clear and simple. He'd been too lazy. Or his worries over what lay in store for him at the hospital had been too great. I ought to have caught on when Veronica Molin phoned and asked me to come back, he thought. Why wasn't I suspicious? I'm only now asking all the questions that cried out to be asked even then.

He came to the bridge. Still not light. No sign of Larsson or a diver. How long was it taking for Molin's house to burn down? He took out his mobile and tried Larsson's number. The same female voice asking him to try again later. He very nearly threw the telephone after the shotgun, to the bottom of the river.

Then he saw somebody coming towards him over the bridge. He could see from the light of the street lamps who it was. During his early days in Sveg he'd had coffee with the man in his kitchen. He tried to remember his name. The man who'd never travelled further afield than Hede. Then he got it: Björn Wigren. The man recognised Lindman.

"Are you still here?" he said, in surprise. "I thought you'd gone home. I do know one thing, though: Elsa hasn't committed murder."

Lindman wondered how Wigren knew she'd been arrested and taken to Östersund. But that didn't matter for the moment. Perhaps Wigren could be of some use.

"Let's talk about Elsa Berggren later," he said. "Just now I need your help."

Lindman searched through his pockets for paper and pencil, but found nothing.

"Have you anything to write with?"

"No. I can go home and fetch something if it's important. What's happening?"

His curiosity is something awful, Lindman thought, looking round. They were only just onto the bridge.

"Come over here," he said.

They went to where the bridge joined the road. There was a drift of virgin snow there. Lindman squatted down and wrote in the snow with his finger.

ELSA'S HOUSE. VERONICA. DANGEROUS. STEFAN.

He stood up. "Can you see what I've written?"

Wigren read it aloud. "What does it mean?"

"It means you should stand here and wait until some police officers and a diver turn up. One of the officers will probably be Larsson. Or it might be a man called Rundström. Erik Johansson could well be there as well, and you know him. In any case, show them this message. Is that clear?"

"What does it mean?"

"Nothing that affects you for the moment, but it's very important for the police. Wait until they get here."

Lindman was trying hard to sound authoritative. "Stay here," he repeated. "Is that understood?"

"Yes. But I'm curious, of course. Is it to do with Elsa?"

"You'll find out soon enough. The important thing right now is that this message is crucial. You'll be doing the police a great service if you make sure they see it."

"I'll stay here. I was only going out for a morning stroll."

Lindman left Wigren and ran over the bridge, trying to call the police emergency number at the same time. Same voice. He swore, and put the telephone back in his pocket. He couldn't wait any longer. He turned left and stopped when he came to Elsa Berggren's house. Tried to keep calm. There's only one thing to do, he told himself. I have to be as convincing as possible. I must give the impression that I don't know anything. Veronica Molin must carry on believing that I'm still the idiot she's had every reason to think I am so far.

He thought about the night when she'd let him sleep by her side. No doubt she'd got up while he was asleep and searched his room. That was why she'd let him sleep in her bed. Not even then had the penny dropped. He'd been vain and conceited, and he'd also betrayed Elena. Veronica had made the most of his weakness. Not that he could blame her.

He went through the gate. Everything was very still. A faint band of light had appeared in the sky over the hills to the east. He rang the bell. Fernando Hereira peeped out from behind the curtain covering the glass part of the front door. Lindman was relieved to see that nothing had happened to him yet. When he'd gone to Veronica's room he was still worried in case anything would happen to *her*, but as soon as he saw what was on her computer screen, everything changed. From that moment it was Hereira he was worried for. It made no difference that what was taking place now was a meeting between a woman and the man who had murdered her father. Hereira had the right, as everybody else did, to have their actions tried in a court of law.

Hereira opened the door. His eyes were unusually bright. "You've come too soon," he said, brusquely.

"I can wait."

The door to the living room was ajar. Lindman couldn't see her. He wondered if he ought to tell Hereira the truth straightaway, but decided to wait. She might be standing behind the door, listening. He knew now that Veronica was capable of anything at all. He must draw out this meeting for as long as possible, so that Larsson and the rest had time to get here.

He nodded towards the lavatory. "I'll join you in a moment," he said. "How's it going?"

"As I hoped it would," Hereira said. His voice sounded tired. "She's listening. And it seems as if she understands. I don't know if she'll forgive me, though."

He went back into the living room, somewhat unsteadily. Lindman locked himself in the lavatory. The worst was still to come – looking Veronica in the eye and convincing her that he knew no more now than he had known half an hour ago. On the other hand, why should she suspect that he'd suddenly understood what he'd failed to understand before? He tried Larsson's number. When he heard the voice yet again he nearly panicked. He flushed the lavatory and emerged into the hall. He went to the front door and coughed loudly as he turned the key to unlock it. Then he went to the living room.

Veronica was in the chair he'd been tied to. She looked at him. He gave her a smile.

'I can wait outside," he said in English. "If you haven't finished, that is."

'I'd like you to stay," she said.

Hereira had nothing against that either.

As if by chance Lindman sat on the chair nearest to the front door. It also gave him a clear view of the windows behind the other two. Veronica was still looking hard at him. It was obvious to Lindman now that she had always tried to see right through him whenever they were together. He returned her gaze, repeating over and over to himself: I know nothing, I know nothing.

The bottle was still on the table. Lindman could see that Hereira had drunk half of it, but he'd pushed it to one side and screwed on the cap. He started speaking. About the man called Höllner in a Buenos Aires restaurant, who, purely by chance, had been able to tell him who had killed his father. Hereira gave a detailed account of the meeting, explaining when and where he'd met Höllner, and how they had eventually realised that Höllner was almost a messenger sent by some divine power to provide the information he'd been looking for. Lindman approved: the more Hereira spun out his story, the better. Lindman needed Larsson to be here, he wouldn't be able to cope with the situation on his own.

Then he gave a start.

Neither Hereira nor Veronica seemed to have noticed anything. A face had fleetingly appeared in the window behind Veronica. Wigren. Lindman could see him from the corner of his eye. There was no limit to the man's curiosity. So he'd left the bridge, he hadn't been able to control his inquisitiveness.

The face appeared again. It was obvious to Lindman that Wigren hadn't realised he'd been spotted. What can the man see? Lindman wondered. Three people in a room, engrossed in a serious, not heated conversation. He might be able to see the bottle of brandy from the window, but what is there about this situation that could possibly be "dangerous"? Nothing. No doubt he wonders who the man is, and it's possible that he didn't see Veronica when she came to visit Elsa Berggren. He must think the policeman from the south of Sweden that he bumped into on his morning stroll is mad. He must also wonder why they are in Elsa Berggren's house when she's somewhere else. And how did they get in?

Lindman could hardly keep his anger in check. He couldn't imagine that Larsson or anybody else would see the message in the snow by the bridge. And now there was no-one waiting for them.

The face disappeared again. Lindman said a silent prayer, hoping that Wigren would go back to the bridge. It might not be too late. But then the face appeared once more, this time in the window behind Hereira. Lindman thought there was a risk that Veronica might see him if she turned her head.

A mobile phone rang. Lindman thought at first it was his, but the tone was different. Veronica picked up her handbag, which was on the floor beside her chair, took out the telephone and answered the call. Whoever it is phoning, it's giving me more time, Lindman thought. And time is what I need most of all. Wigren hadn't reappeared. Lindman dared to hope that he had gone back to the bridge after all.

Veronica listened to what the caller was saying without speaking herself. Then she switched off and returned the phone to her handbag. When she took her hand out, it was holding a pistol.

She stood up slowly and took two steps to one side. From there she could cover both Lindman and Hereira. Lindman held his breath. Hereira didn't seem to grasp at first what she had in her hand. When it dawned on him that it was a gun, he also started to stand up, but he sat down again when she raised the pistol. Then she turned to Lindman.

"That was stupid," she said. "Of both of us."

She was pointing the gun at Lindman now. Holding it in both hands, steady as a rock.

"That was the receptionist at the hotel. She phoned to tell me that you had taken my key and gone into my room. And of course, I know I didn't switch off the computer."

"I don't know what you're talking about." It was pointless trying to talk himself out of the situation, but he had to try. He glanced at the window. No sign of Wigren. He could only hope. This time she had noticed his glance. Without lowering the gun she edged closer to the nearest window, but evidently saw no-one outside.

"So you didn't come on your own?" she said.

"Who did I have to bring with me?"

She stayed by the window. It struck Lindman that the face he'd found so attractive before now seemed sunken and ugly.

"There's no point in telling lies," she said. "Especially when you're no good at it."

Hereira stared at the gun in her hand. "I don't understand," he said. "What's going on?"

'It's just that Veronica is not what she pretends to be. She might devote part of her time to business deals, but she spends the rest of her life spreading the cause of Nazism throughout the world."

Hereira stared at him in astonishment. "Nazism?" he said. "She is a Nazi?"

"She's her father's daughter."

"Perhaps it's better if I explain it myself to the man who killed my father," said Veronica.

She spoke slowly and in perfect English, a person with no doubt as to the justice of her cause. To Lindman, what she said was just as frightening as it was clear. Molin had been his daughter's hero, a man she'd always looked up to and in whose footsteps she had never hesitated to follow. But she wasn't uncritical of her father: he had stood for political ideals that were now out of date. She belonged to a new era that adopted the ideals championing the absolute right of the stronger, and the concepts of supermen and sub-human creatures and adapted them to contemporary reality. She described raw and unlimited power, the right of the strong few to rule over the weak and the poor. She used words like "unfit", "sub-humans", "the poverty-stricken masses", "the dregs", "the rabble". She described a world in which people in poor countries were doomed to extinction. She condemned the whole of Africa, with just a few exceptions where despotic dictators were still in charge. Africa was a continent that should be left to bleed to death, that should not be given aid, but isolated and allowed to die. The new age and new technology, the electronic networks, gave people like her the upper hand and the instruments they needed to consolidate their sovereignty over the world.

Lindman listened to what she had to say, persuaded that she was mad. She really did believe what she was saying. Her conviction was ineradicable and she really did have no inkling of how lunatic she sounded, and that her dream could never come true.

"You killed my father," she said. "You killed him, and therefore I'm going to kill you. I know that you didn't leave here because you wanted to know what had happened to Abraham Andersson. He was an insignificant person who had somehow found out about my father's past. So he had to die."

"Was it you who killed him?"

Hereira had understood now. The man standing alongside Lindman had just emerged from one lifelong nightmare only to land in a new one.

"There's an international network," Veronica said. "The Strong Sweden foundation is a part of it. I'm one of the leaders, invisible in the background, but I'm also a member of the small group of people who run the National Socialist network on a global level. Executing Andersson to be certain that he could never reveal what he knew was not a problem. There are plenty of people who are always ready to carry out an order, without question, without hesitation."

"How did Andersson come to discover that your father was a Nazi?"

"In fact it started with Elsa. An unfortunate coincidence. Elsa has a sister who was for many years a member of the Helsingborg Symphony Orchestra. She mentioned to Andersson, when he decided to move up here, that Elsa lived in Sveg and was a National Socialist. He started spying on her, and eventually on my father as well. When he began blackmailing my father, he signed his own death warrant."

"Magnus Holmström," Lindman said. "Is that his name, the man you ordered to kill Abraham Andersson? Was it you or him who threw the shotgun into the river after Andersson's death? And forced Elsa Berggren to confess to the murder? Did you threaten to kill her as well?"

"You know quite a lot," she said. "But it won't help you."

"What do you mean to do?"

"Kill you," she said calmly. "But first I shall put down the man who murdered my father."

"Put down." She's barking mad, Lindman thought. Stark raving lunatic. If Larsson didn't turn up soon he'd have to try to disarm her. He couldn't reckon with any help from Hereira, he'd had too much to drink. There was no hoping he might be able to persuade her to change her mind. He was certain he was dealing with a madwoman. She wouldn't hesitate to use her weapon.

Time, he thought. That's all I need, time. "You'll never get away," he said.

"Of course I shall," she said. "Nobody knows where we are. I can shoot the man who killed my father, and then you. I'll arrange it to look as if you shot him and then killed yourself. Nobody will think it strange that a policeman with cancer should commit suicide, especially after he's just killed another human being. The weapon can't be traced to me. I shall go from here to the church where my father will be buried a few hours from now. It will never occur to anybody that a daughter about to bury her father would that same morning be killing two other people. I will be standing by the coffin. The daughter in mourning. And I will be delighted about my father being avenged before he is buried."

Lindman heard the faintest of noises in the hall. He knew at once it was the front door being opened. He shifted in his chair, as if to stretch his back, and caught sight of Larsson. Their eyes met. Larsson was moving silently. He had a gun in his hand. I must tell him what's happening, he thought.

"So you shoot us both, one then the other," he said. "With that notoriously inaccurate pistol. Forensic will smell you a mile off."

She stiffened. She was on her guard. "Why do you raise your voice?"

She moved rapidly so that she could see into the hall. Larsson wasn't there, but he can't have missed what Lindman had said.

Veronica stood motionless, listening. She seemed to Lindman like an animal in the night, alert for the slightest sound.

Then everything happened very quickly. She started again, this time towards the doorway. Lindman knew she wouldn't hesitate to shoot. She was too far from him that he could throw himself at her before she had time to turn and shoot at him. From that range she couldn't miss. As she reached the door he grabbed the lamp on the table beside the chair and flung it at one of the windows with all the strength he could muster. The pane shattered. At the same time he threw himself at Hereira in such a way that both he and the sofa tumbled over backwards. As he fell down at the side of Hereira, he saw her turn. She had her gun raised. She fired. Lindman closed his eyes and had time to think that he was about to die before the bang came. Hereira's body jerked. There was blood on his forehead. Then another bang. When Lindman realised he hadn't been hit this time either, he looked up and saw Larsson lying on the floor. Veronica had disappeared. The front door was wide open.

Hereira was moaning, but the bullet had only grazed his temple. Lindman jumped up, scrambled over the overturned sofa and rushed to Larsson who was lying on his back, clutching at a point between his neck and his right shoulder. Lindman knelt beside him.

"I don't think it's too bad," Larsson said.

He was white in the face, from pain and shock. Lindman fetched a towel from the cloakroom and pressed it against Larsson's blood-covered shoulder.

"Phone for help," Larsson said. "Then go and look for her."

Lindman called the emergency number from the hall. He knew he was shouting down the line. As he spoke he could see Hereira get up from behind the sofa and slump down on a chair. The operator in Östersund said that reinforcements and an ambulance would be despatched without delay.

"I'll be all right," Larsson said. "Don't hang about. Go and find her. Is she mad?"

"Completely off her head. She's a Nazi, just as much as her father was, maybe even more fanatical."

"No doubt, that explains everything," Larsson said. "At the moment I'm not really sure what, though."

"Don't talk. Lie still."

"I wasn't thinking straight," Larsson said. "You'd better stay here until the reinforcements arrive. She's too dangerous. You can't go after her by yourself."

But Lindman had already picked up Larsson's gun. He had no intention of waiting. She'd shot at him, tried to kill him. That made him furious. She had not only fooled him, she had tried to kill him, Hereira and Larsson. There could easily have been three dead bodies on Elsa Berggren's floor instead of two people with slight wounds and one unscathed. As Lindman picked Larsson's gun up, he made up his mind that he was a man with cancer who was determined not to miss the chance of undergoing treatment and being cured. As he left the house, Wigren was standing by the gate. When he saw Lindman he started running away. Lindman yelled at him to stop.

Wigren's jaw wouldn't keep still and his eyes were staring. I ought to thump the bastard, Lindman thought. His insatiable nosiness very nearly killed the lot of us.

"Where did she go?" he roared. "Which direction?"

Wigren pointed to the road along the river to the new bridge.

"Stay here," Lindman said. "This time don't move an inch. There are police and an ambulance on the way."

Wigren nodded. He asked no questions.

Lindman started running. A face stared from one of the houses. He tried to make out Veronica's footprints in the snow, but there had been too much traffic, too many walkers. He stopped to cock his gun, then ran on. It was still only half light. Heavy clouds were motionless in the sky. He stopped when he came to the bridge. There was no sign of Veronica. He tried to think. She didn't have a car. Something unplanned had happened. She was on the run and forced to make impromptu decisions. What would she have done? A car, he decided. She would find herself a car. She would hardly dare go back to the hotel. She knows that I've seen what was on her computer screen, a swastika and underneath it a letter in which she discussed old Nazi ideals that would last for ever. She realises that what's in the computer doesn't matter any more. She's shot three people, and she doesn't know if any of them have survived. She has two possibilities: try to run away, or give herself up. And she won't give up.

He crossed the bridge. There were two petrol stations on the other side. Everything seemed calm. Some drivers were filling their tanks. Lindman paused and looked around. If somebody had produced a gun and tried to steal a car there would have been turmoil. He tried to put himself in her position. He still thought she would look for a car.

Then he heard an alarm bell in his mind. Was he thinking along the wrong lines? Behind her cool, calm exterior he'd seen a confused, fanatical person. Maybe she would react differently? He looked at the church to his left. What had she said? *My father will be avenged before he is buried.* He continued staring at the church. Was it possible? He didn't know, but he had nothing to lose. He could hear sirens in the distance. He ran to the church. When he saw that the main door was ajar he was immediately on his guard. He only opened it wide enough for him to slip inside. It creaked slightly. He stood close to the wall of the porch. The sirens were no longer audible. The walls were thick. Slowly he opened one of the doors into the church. There was a coffin at the far end, in front of the altar. Molin's coffin. He squatted down, aiming Larsson's gun with both hands. There was nobody there. He crept inside, ducking down behind the back pew. Everything was quiet. He peered cautiously over the back of the pew. There was no sign of her. He must have been wrong, and thought he might as well leave the church when he heard a sound coming from the choir. He wasn't sure what it was, but there was somebody in the vestry, behind the altar. He listened. He heard nothing. Perhaps he was mistaken. Nevertheless, he didn't want to leave until he was certain that the church was empty. He walked down the centre aisle, still crouching, his gun at the ready. When he reached the coffin he stopped and listened. He looked up at the altar-piece. Jesus was on the cross, with a Roman soldier kneeling in the foreground. There was no sound from the vestry. At the altar rail he stopped again to listen. Still no sound. Then he raised his gun and entered the vestry. It was too late by the time he saw her. She was standing beside a tall cupboard, next to the wall at the side of the door. Motionless, with the gun pointing straight at his chest.

"Drop the gun," she said.

Her voice was low, almost a whisper. He bent down and put Larsson's pistol on the stone floor.

"You won't even leave me in peace inside a church," she said. "Not even on the day my father's going to be buried. You should think about your own father. I never met him, but from what I've heard he was a good man. True to his ideals. It's a pity he wasn't able to pass them on to you."

"Was it Emil Wetterstedt who told you?"

"Perhaps, but that hardly matters now."

"What are you going to do?"

"Kill you."

For the second time that morning he heard her say it, that she was going to kill him. This time, though, he hadn't the strength to feel afraid. He could only convince her that she should give up, or hope that circumstances would arise enabling him to disarm her. Then it occurred to him that there was a third possibility. He was still in the doorway. If she let her attention wander he would be able to throw himself backwards into the main part of the church. Once there he could hide among the pews, and possibly even escape outside.

"How did you know I was here?"

She still spoke in the same low voice. Lindman could see that she was holding the gun just as steadily as before. It was aimed now at his legs, not his chest. She's going to pieces, he thought. He shifted his weight onto his right leg.

"Why don't you give up?" he said.

She didn't answer, simply shook her head.

Then came the moment he was waiting for. The hand holding the gun dropped down as she turned to look out of the window. He flung himself backwards as fast as he could, then started running down the centre aisle. He expected the shot to come from behind at any second, and kill him.

All of a sudden he fell headlong. He hadn't seen a corner of the carpet sticking up. As he fell, he hit his shoulder against one of the pews.

Then came the shot. It smashed into the pew beside him. Another shot. The echo sounded like a thunderclap. Silence. He heard a thud behind him. When he looked round, he could see her, just in front of her father's coffin. His heart was pounding. What had happened? Had she shot herself? Then he heard Johansson's agitated, shrill voice from the organ loft.

"Lie still. Don't move. Veronica Molin, can you hear me? Lie still."

"She's not moving," Lindman shouted.

"Did she hit you?"

"No."

Johansson shouted again. His voice echoed round the church. "Veronica Molin. Lie still. Keep your arms outstretched."

Still she didn't move. There was a clattering on the stairs from the organ loft and Johansson appeared in the centre aisle. Lindman scrambled to his feet. They approached the motionless body with trepidation, Johansson with his pistol held in both hands before him. Lindman raised his hand.

"She's dead." He pointed. "You hit her in the eye."

Johansson gulped and shook his head. "I aimed for her legs. I'm not that bad a shot."

They walked up to her. Lindman was right. The bullet had entered her left eye. Right next to her, on the lower edge of the stone underhang of the pulpit was an obvious bullet mark.

"A ricochet," he said. "You simply missed her, but the bullet bounced off the pulpit and killed her."

Johansson shook his head in bewilderment. Lindman understood. The man had never shot at a human being before. Now he had, and the woman he'd tried to hit in the leg was dead.

"It couldn't be helped," Lindman said. "That's the way it goes sometimes. But it's over now. It's all over."

The church door opened. A verger was staring at them in horror. Lindman patted Johansson on the shoulder, then went to the verger to explain what had happened.

Half an hour later Lindman arrived at the Berggren house and found Rundström there. Larsson was on his way to hospital, but no Hereira. The ambulance man said Larsson had told him that Hereira had melted into thin air.

"We'll get him," Rundström said.

"I wouldn't bet on it," Lindman said. "We don't know his real name, he might have several different passports. He's been very good at hiding so far."

"Wasn't he wounded?"

"Just a scratch on his forehead."

A man in overalls appeared. He was carrying a dripping wet shotgun that he put on the table. "I found it straightaway. Has there been a shoot-out in the church?"

Rundström brushed aside the question. "I'll fill you in later," he said. Rundström eyed the shotgun. "I wonder if the prosecutor will be able to nail Berggren for all the lies she's told us," he said. "Even if it was this Holmström who killed Andersson and threw the shotgun into the river. He's obviously the arsonist as well. Molin's house has been well and truly torched."

"Hereira told me he had started the fire. To confuse the police," Lindman said.

"So much has happened that's beyond me," Rundström said. "Larsson's in hospital, and Erik's in the church, having killed Molin's daughter. It seems to me that you, Stefan Lindman, the police officer from Borås, are the only person who can bring me up to speed on what's been happening on my patch this morning."

Lindman spent the rest of the day in Johansson's office. The conversations he had with Rundström lasted for hours, thanks to the continual interruptions. At 1.45 Rundström received a call informing him that Holmström had been arrested in Arboga, still in the Ford Escort they'd put a marker on. It was 5 p.m. by the time Rundström declared that he felt sufficiently in the picture. He accompanied Lindman to his hotel. They said their goodbyes in reception.

"When are you leaving?"

"Tomorrow. The morning flight to Landvetter."

"I'll arrange for somebody to drive you to the airport."

They shook hands.

"It's all been very peculiar," Rundström said, "but I reckon that somehow or other I've come round to understanding most of what's been going on. Not everything. You never do understand everything. There are always gaps. But most of it. Enough to solve the murders."

"Something tells me you'll have problems in catching Hereira," Lindman said.

"He smoked French cigarettes," Rundström said. "Do you remember the butts you found down by the lake, and gave to Larsson?"

Lindman remembered. "I agree," he said. "There are always gaps. Not least this mysterious person named "'M.', in Scotland."

Rundström left. Lindman took it that Rundström hadn't read Molin's diary. The girl in reception was ashen.

"Did I do the wrong thing?" she asked.

"Yes. But it's all finished now. I'm off tomorrow. I'll leave you to your test drivers and Baltic orienteering specialists."

That evening he had dinner in the hotel, then phoned Elena and said he'd be coming home. He was on his way to bed when Rundström phoned to say that Larsson was doing pretty well in the circumstances. The wound was serious, but not life-threatening. Johansson was in a much worse state. He'd had a nervous collapse. Rundström ended by telling Lindman that Special Branch was now involved.

"This is going to be splashed all over the media," he said. "We've turned over a very large stone. It's already obvious that this Nazi network is far more extensive than anybody ever dreamt of. Think yourself lucky that the reporters won't be gunning for you."

Lindman lay awake for ages after that. He wondered how the funeral had gone. Most of all it was memories of his father flooding through his mind. I'll never understand him, he thought. I won't ever be able to forgive him either, even if he is dead and buried. He never showed his true face to me and my sisters. I had a father who worshipped evil.

The following morning Lindman was taken to the airport in Frösön. Just before 11 a.m. his plane touched down at Landvetter. Elena was there to meet him, and he was extremely pleased to see her.

Two days later, on November 19, sleet was falling in Borås as Lindman walked up the hill to the hospital. He felt calm, and was confident of coping with whatever was in store for him.

He had coffee in the cafeteria. Copies of last night's evening papers were piled up on a chair. The front pages were full of what had been going on in Härjedalen, and about the Swedish branch of a world-wide network of Nazi organisations. The head of Special Branch had made a statement. "This is a shocking exposure of something that goes much deeper and is much more dangerous than the neo-Nazis, all those tiny groups dominated by skinheads that have been associated with Fascist aspirations hitherto."

Lindman put the newspapers down. It was 8.10 a.m. Time for him to go to the people who were waiting for him.

Hereira was still at large. Lindman wondered where he had got to, and hoped the man would get back to Buenos Aires. Smoke a few more French cigarettes in peace and quiet. The crime he'd committed had been atoned for long ago.

EPILOGUE

Inverness / April 2000

On Sunday, April 9, Stefan collected Elena early in the morning. On the way from Allégatan to Norrby he'd started humming. He couldn't remember when he'd last done that. Nor did he know at first what it was he was humming. A tune of somewhere far from Sweden, he seemed to recall, as he drove through the empty streets. Then it dawned on him that it was something his father used to play on the banjo. "Beale Street Blues". Stefan also remembered his father saying that it was a street that really did exist, possibly in several North American cities, but certainly in Memphis.

I remember his music, Stefan thought; but my father, his face, his lunatic political opinions, have all started to fade into oblivion. He emerged from the shadows to tell me who he really was. Now I've kicked him back. The only way I'm going to remember him now and in future is by the bits of tunes that have stuck in my head. Maybe that provides him with a redeeming feature. As far as Nazis were concerned, the Africans, their music, their traditions, their way of life – everything was barbaric. Africans were sub-human creatures. Although the black American athlete Jesse Owens was the star of the 1936 Olympics, Hitler refused to shake his hand. But my father loved the music of black men, the blues. He made no attempt to hide it either. Perhaps that's where I can find a crack in his defences, a reason for thinking that he hadn't given himself entirely to evil and to contempt for his fellow men. I'll never know if I'm right, but I have the right to believe what I want to believe.

Elena was waiting for him at her front door. On the way to the airport they talked about which of them was looking forward more to the trip. Elena who had seldom been even a few kilometres from Borås, or Stefan whose doctor had given him hope that he'd overcome his cancer, thanks to the radiotherapy and the subsequent operation. They didn't agree on the answer, but it was only a game.

They left for London Gatwick on a British Airways flight at 7.35 a.m. Elena was afraid of flying and clutched Stefan's hand as the aircraft took off and flew out to sea north of Kungsbacka. As they carved their way through the clouds, Stefan experienced a feeling of liberation. For six months he'd lived with a fear that hardly left him. Now it had gone. It wasn't absolutely certain that he was or would ever be fully fit: his doctor had told him he would have to have tests for five years, but to lead a normal life again, not be forever on the look-out for symptoms, not to nourish the fear he had harboured for so long. Now that he was in the aeroplane, he felt that at last he'd really taken that vital step away from the fear, and back to something he'd long been waiting for.

Elena looked at him.

"A penny for your thoughts."

"What I haven't dared to think for half a year."

She said nothing, but took hold of his hand. He thought he would burst out crying, but he managed to keep control of himself.

They landed at Gatwick, and after passing through passport control they went their different ways. Elena to spend two days in London visiting a distant relative from Krakow who had a grocer's shop in one of London's suburbs. Stefan would be continuing his journey on a domestic flight.

"I still don't understand why you have to make this extra trip," Elena said.

"Don't forget that I'm a police officer. I want to follow things through to the bitter end."

"But you've arrested the murderer, haven't you? Or one of them, at least. And the woman is dead. You know why it all happened. What more is there to find out?"

"There are always gaps. Perhaps it's only curiosity, something only indirectly linked."

She eyed him severely. "It said in the newspapers that an officer had been wounded and another one had been in extreme danger. I wonder when you're going to admit to me that you were the one in danger? How long do I have to wait?"

Stefan said nothing, merely flung wide his arms.

"You don't know why you have to make this extra journey," Elena said. "Is that it? Or is there something you don't want to tell me? Why can't you just tell me the truth?"

"I'm trying to learn how to do that. But I have told you the truth. It's just that there's one last door I want to open, and find out what's behind it."

He watched her melt into the crowd heading towards the exit, then made for the transit desk. The tune he'd had in his head earlier came back to him.

If he'd managed to understand rightly what they said over the loudspeakers, the flight would take an hour. He fell asleep and didn't wake up until they landed at Inverness airport. He walked towards the ancient terminal and registered that the air was fresh and clear – just as he remembered it from Härjedalen. In Sveg, the wooded hillsides surrounding the little town had been a dark, threatening circle. The countryside was different here. High, sharply outlined mountains in the distance to the north, elsewhere fields and heaths, and the sky seemed to be low, almost touchable. He collected the key to his rented car, and felt a vague worry about having to drive on the left-hand side of the road. The road was narrow. He was annoyed by the sluggishness of the gear box. He wondered if he would do better to go back and upgrade, but soon gave up on that thought. He wasn't going far, only to Inverness and back, with perhaps the occasional excursion.

The travel agent had booked him into a hotel called Old Blend for two nights, in the town centre. It took him a while to find it. He caused chaos at two roundabouts, but could breathe a sigh of relief when he eventually parked outside the hotel, a three-storey, dark red brick building. Yet another hotel, but the last one in his quest to find out why Herbert Molin had been murdered. He now knew the circumstances, and he'd met the man who killed him. He didn't know the whereabouts of the presumed murderer, Fernando Hereira.

Giuseppe had phoned from Östersund a few days ago and told him that the Swedish police and Interpol had drawn a blank. Presumably he was back in South America by now, using a different name – his real one. Giuseppe didn't think they would ever find him. Even if they did, the Swedish authorities would never manage to have him extradited. Giuseppe promised to keep Stefan informed. He'd also asked about Stefan's state of health, and been pleased about the latest diagnosis.

"What did I tell you?" he said with a laugh. "You were succumbing to doom and gloom – I've never met anybody as depressed as you were."

"Perhaps you haven't met many people with a death sentence hanging round their neck. Or *inside* their neck, to be more precise. But you had a bullet in your shoulder."

Giuseppe turned serious. "I keep wondering if she shot to kill me. I remember the look on her face. I'd like to think that she shot to wound me, but I don't really believe it."

"How are you now?"

"A bit stiff in the shoulder, but much better."

"What about Johansson?"

"I've heard that he's thinking of applying for early retirement. This whole business has hit him hard. I saw him the other day. He looked very thin." Giuseppe sighed. "I suppose things could have been much worse."

"One of these days I'll take Elena to a bowling alley. I'll knock over a few skittles and think of you."

"When Molin was killed, we had no idea what we were letting ourselves in for," Giuseppe said. "But what we stumbled upon is something very big. It's more than a network of Nazi organisations. It's grounds for facing up to the fact that Fascism is alive and kicking, albeit in a different guise."

Giuseppe said that Magnus Holmström's case would come to court the following week. He had asserted his right to remain silent, but even so there was enough evidence to convict him and earn him a long jail sentence.

It was over – but there was one connection that Stefan still wanted to look into. He hadn't mentioned it to Giuseppe. It was to be found in Inverness. Even if Veronica Molin's attempt to invent an explanation for her father's death had failed – the only weak move she'd made during those dramatic weeks – there had in fact been a real person hidden behind the letter "M." in Molin's diary. Stefan had been helped by a clerical assistant called Evelyn who'd worked for the police in Borås for many years. Together they'd searched for and eventually found the report on the visit to Borås by a party of British police officers in November 1971, with a list of names. They'd even found a photograph on the wall of an archive room. The picture was taken outside the police station. Olausson was there, posing with four British police officers, two of them women. One of those, the older one, was called Margaret Simmons. Stefan sometimes wondered how much Veronica knew about her father's visit to Scotland. She hadn't used the name Margaret when she'd tried sending them off on a false trail: she'd said the woman's name was Monica.

Molin was not in the picture, but he had been there. It was then, in November 1971, that he'd met this Margaret; and the following year he'd gone to Scotland to see her and written about her in his diary. They had gone for long walks in Dornoch, a coastal town north of Inverness. Stefan thought that maybe he ought to see what it looked like; but Margaret Simmons no longer lived there: she'd moved when she retired in 1980. Without asking his reasons, Evelyn had helped Stefan to trace her. In the end, one day in February, just when he'd started to believe he was going to live and eventually return to work, she phoned him in triumph and supplied him with an address and a telephone number in Inverness.

And that's where he now was, and that was as far as his advance planning had gone. He had to decide what to do: should he phone, or find the street and knock on her door? She was 80. She might be ill or tired and not at all willing to receive him.

He was given a friendly welcome by a man with a loud, powerful voice. His was room number 12 on the top floor. There was no lift, just a creaking staircase and a soft carpet. He could hear a television set somewhere. He climbed to his room, put down his suitcase and went to the window. Traffic was buzzing around down below, but when he lifted his gaze he could see the sea, the mountains and the sky. He took two miniature bottles of whisky from the minibar and emptied them, standing at the window. The feeling of liberation was now even stronger than before. I'm on my way back, he thought. I'm going to survive. When I'm an old man I'll look on this as a time that changed my life, rather than putting an end to it.

Afternoon turned into evening. He'd decided to wait until the next day before contacting Margaret Simmons. It was drizzling outside. He walked to the harbour, and wandered from quay to quay. He felt impatient. He wanted to start work again. All he'd lost was time. But what was time? Anxious breaths, morning turning into evenings and then new days? He didn't know. He thought of those chaotic weeks in Härjedalen when they'd first been looking for a murderer, and then for two, as almost unreal. Then came the moment after November 19, when he entered his doctor's surgery on the dot of 8.15, and set in train his radiotherapy course. How would he describe that time if he were to write himself a letter? Time had seemed to stand still. He'd lived as if his body were a prison. It wasn't until mid-January, when he'd put it all behind him, the radiotherapy and the operation, that he'd recovered his grasp of time as something mobile, something that passed by, without ever returning.

He had dinner at a restaurant close to the hotel. He'd just been handed a menu when Elena phoned.

"How's Scotland?"

"Good. But it's hard driving on the left."

"It's raining here."

"Here too."

"What are you doing right now?"

"I'm just about to have dinner."

"How's it going with your talks?"

"I've done nothing about that today. I'm starting tomorrow."

"Come when you said you'd come."

"Why wouldn't I?"

"When you were ill you drifted away from me. I don't want that to happen again."

"I'll be there."

"I'm going to have a Polish dinner tonight with relations I've never met before."

"I wish I could be there."

She burst out laughing. "You're a liar. Pass on greetings to Scotland."

After his meal he went walking again. Quays, promenades, the town centre. He wondered where he was heading for. His real destination was inside himself.

He slept deeply that night.

*   *   *

The next morning he rose early. It was still drizzling over Inverness. After breakfast he phoned the number he'd been given by Evelyn. A man answered.

"Simmons."

"My name's Stefan Lindman. I'd like to speak to Margaret Simmons."

"What about?"

"I'm from Sweden. She visited Sweden in the 1970s. I never met her, but a colleague of mine who's a police officer talked about her."

"My mother's not at home. Where are you calling from?"

"Inverness."

"She's at Culloden today."

"Where's that?"

"Culloden is a battlefield not far from Inverness. The site of the last battle to take place on British soil. 1745. Don't you learn any history in Sweden?"

"Not much about Scotland."

"It was all over in half an hour. The English slaughtered everybody who got in their way. Mum likes to wander around the battlefield. She goes there three or four times a year. She goes to the museum first. They sometimes show films. She says she likes to listen to the voices of the dead coming from under the ground. She says it prepares her for her own death."

"When's she due home again?"

"This evening. But she'll go straight to bed. How long does a Swedish policeman stay in Inverness?"

"I'm leaving tomorrow afternoon."

"Call tomorrow morning. What did you say your name was? Steven?"

"Stefan."

That concluded the call. Stefan decided not to wait until the next day. He went down to reception and asked for directions to Culloden. The man smiled.

"Today's a good time to go there. The weather's the same as when the battle was fought. Mist, rain, and a breeze."

Stefan drove out of Inverness. It was easier this time, coping with the roundabouts. He followed the signs off the main road. There were two coaches and a few cars in the car park. Stefan gazed over the moor. There were poles with red and yellow flags a few hundred metres apart.

He assumed they marked the lines of the opposing armies. He could see the sea and the mountains in the distance. It seemed to him that the generals had chosen an attractive place for their soldiers to die in.

He bought a ticket for the museum. There were school classes wandering here and there, looking at the dolls dressed up as soldiers and arranged in violent scenes of battle. He looked around for Margaret. The photograph he'd seen was taken almost 30 years ago, but even so, he was sure he would recognise her. He couldn't see her in the museum, though. He went out into the gusting wind to the battlefield. The moor was deserted. Nothing but the red and yellow flags smacking against the poles. He went back inside. The children were on their way into a lecture room. He followed them. Just as he got in the lights went out and a film started. He groped his way to a seat in the front row. The film lasted half an hour, with scary sound effects. He stayed put when the lights came on again. The children jostled their way out, frequently being urged by their teachers to calm down.

Stefan looked round. He recognised her immediately. She was in the back row, wearing a black raincoat. When she stood up, she leaned on her umbrella and was careful where she placed her feet. She walked past him and glanced in his direction. Stefan waited until she'd left the lecture room before following her. There was no sign of the children now. A woman, knitting behind a counter, was selling postcards and souvenirs. There was the sound of the radio and the clatter of china from the nearby café.

Margaret Simmons was making for the wall encircling the battle-field. It was raining, but she hadn't raised her umbrella. The wind was too strong. Stefan waited until she'd passed through the gate and disappeared behind the wall. He wondered where all the children had got to. She was heading for one of the paths that meandered through the battlefield. He kept his distance, thinking that he'd made the right decision. He wanted to know why Molin had written about her in his diary. She'd been the exception. Molin had described how he'd crossed over the border and entered Norway, enjoyed an ice cream and eyed the girls in Oslo; and then the awful years in the Waffen-SS. The years that had warped his nature and turned him into a henchman of Waldemar Lehmann. Then came the journey to Scotland. If he remembered rightly, it was the longest section in the diary, longer even than the letters he'd sent home from the war.

He would soon catch up with her and be able to place the final piece in the jigsaw puzzle that was Herbert Molin. At regular intervals along the path were gravestones. Not for individual lost soldiers, but for the clans whose men had been massacred by the English artillery. Margaret Simmons is walking though a battlefield, he thought. Molin spent some years in a battlefield, but he escaped the machine-gun and rifle fire. He was murdered by somebody who traced him to his cottage in Härjedalen.

The old woman leant on one of the gravestones beside the path. Stefan stopped as well. She looked at him, then continued along the path. He followed her to the middle of the battlefield; a Swedish police officer who still hadn't reached his fortieth birthday, 30 metres behind a Scottish lady who had also been a police officer and now spent her time preparing for death.

They came to a point between the red and yellow flags. She stopped and turned to look at him. He didn't look away. She waited. He saw that she was heavily made up, short and thin. She tapped the ground with her umbrella.

"Are you following me? Who are you?"

"My name is Stefan Lindman, I'm from Sweden. I'm a police officer. As you used to be."

She brushed aside her hair, that had blown into her face. "You must have spoken to my son. He's the only one who knows where I am."

"He was most helpful."

"What do you want?"

"You once visited a town in Sweden called Borås. It's not a very big place – two churches, two squares, a dirty river. You were there 28 years ago, in the autumn of 1971. You met a policeman by the name of Herbert Molin. The following year he came to see you in Dornoch."

She eyed him up and down, saying nothing.

"I'd like to continue my walk if you don't mind," she said eventually. "I'm getting used to the idea of being dead."

She started walking again. Stefan walked beside her.

"The other side," she said. "I don't want anybody on my left."

He changed sides.

"Is Herbert dead?" she said, out of the blue.

"Yes, he's dead."

"That's the way it goes when you're old. People think the only news you want to hear is that old aquaintances are dead. You can really put your foot in it if you don't know."

"Herbert Molin was murdered."

She gave a start and stopped in her tracks. For a moment Stefan thought she was going to fall over.

"What happened?" she asked after a while.

"His past caught up with him. He was killed by a man who wanted to avenge something he'd done during the war."

"Have you caught the murderer?"

"No."

"Why not?"

"He got away. We don't even know his real name. He has an Argentinian passport in the name of Hereira, and we think he lives in Buenos Aires. But we assume that that is not his real name."

"What had Herbert done?"

"He murdered a Jewish dancing master in Berlin."

She'd stopped again. She looked round at the battlefield.

"The battle they fought here was a very strange one. It wasn't really a battle. It was all over in a very short time."

She pointed. "We were over there, the Scots, and the English were on that side. They fired their cannons. The Scots died like flies. When they finally got round to attacking the English it was too late. There were thousands of dead and wounded here in less than half an hour. They're still here." She started walking again.

"Molin kept a diary," Stefan said. "Most of it's about the war. He was a Nazi, and fought as a volunteer for Hitler. But maybe you knew about that?"

She didn't answer, but rapped her umbrella hard onto the ground.

"I found the diary, wrapped in a raincoat in the house where he was murdered. A diary, a few photographs and some letters. The only thing in his diary that he took the trouble to write up properly was the visit he made to Dornoch. It says that he went for long walks there with 'M.'."

She looked at him in surprise. "Didn't he write my name in full?"

"All he put was 'M.'. Nothing else."

"What did he say?"

"That you went for long walks."

"What else?"

"Nothing."

She walked on without speaking. Then she stopped again.

"One of my ancestors died on this very spot," she said. "I'm partly descended from the McLeod clan, even if my married name is Simmons. I can't really be certain that it was just here that Angus McLeod died, of course, but I've decided it was."

"I have wondered," Stefan said. "About what happened."

She looked at him in surprise. "He'd fallen in love with me. Pure stupidity, of course. What else could it have been? Men are hunters, whether they're after an animal or a woman. He wasn't even good-looking. Flabby. And in any case I was married. I nearly died of shock when he phoned out of the blue and announced that he was in Scotland. It was the only time in my life that I lied to my husband. I told him I was working overtime whenever I met Herbert. He tried to talk me into going back to Sweden with him."

They had come to the edge of the battlefield. She started back on a path alongside a stone wall. It wasn't until they'd returned to their starting point, the gate in the wall, that she turned to look at Stefan.

"I usually have a cup of tea at this time. Then I go out again. Would you join me?"

"Yes, thank you."

"Herbert always wanted coffee. That would have been enough in itself. How could I live with a man who didn't like tea?"

In the cafeteria some young men in kilts were sitting at one table, talking in low voices. Margaret chose a window table from where she could see the battlefield, and beyond it Inverness and the sea.

"I didn't like him," she said firmly. "I couldn't shake him off, even though I'd made it clear from the start that his journey was a waste of time. I already had a husband. He might have been a bit of a handful, and he drank too much, but he was the father of my son and that was the most important thing. I told Herbert to come to his senses and go back to Sweden. I thought he'd done that and left. Then he phoned me at the police station. I was afraid he might come to my home, so I agreed to meet him again. That was when he told me."

"That he was a Nazi?"

"That he'd *been* a Nazi. He had enough sense to realise that I'd experienced Hitler's brutality during the air raids here in Britain. He claimed to regret it all."

"Did you believe him?"

"I don't know. I was only interested in getting rid of him."

"But you still went for walks with him?"

"He started using me as a mother confessor. He insisted it had been a youthful mistake. I remember being afraid that he might go down on his knees. It was pretty awful in point of fact. He wanted me to forgive him. As if I were a priest or a messenger from all those who'd suffered in the Hitler period."

"What did you say?"

"That I could listen, but that his conscience had nothing to do with me."

The men in kilts stood up and left. The rain was now beating against the window pane.

She looked at him. "But it wasn't true, is that it?"

"What do you mean?"

"That he regretted it."

"I believe that he was a Nazi until the day he died. He was terrified about what had happened in Germany, but I don't think he gave up his Nazi beliefs. He even handed them down to his daughter. She's dead too."

"How come?"

"She was shot in an exchange of fire with the police. She damn nearly killed me."

"I'm an old woman," she said. "I have time. Or maybe I don't. But I want to hear the whole story from the start. Herbert Molin is starting to interest me, and that's something new."

When Stefan was on the flight back to London, where Elena was waiting for him, he thought that it was only when he told the story to Margaret, in the cafeteria at the museum in Culloden, that he grasped the full seriousness of what had happened during those weeks in autumn, in Härjedalen. Now he was able to see everything in a new light, the bloodstained tango steps, the remains of the tent by the black water.

Most of all he saw himself, the person he'd been at that time, a man like a quivering shadow at the edge of a remarkable murder investigation. As he told the story to Margaret it was as if he'd become a pawn in the game: it was him, but then again not him, a different person he no longer wanted anything to do with.

When he came to the end, they sat there in silence for ages, staring out at the rain, which was easing off now. She asked no questions, merely sat there stroking her nose with the tip of a lean finger. There were not many visitors to Culloden that day. The girls behind the counter in the cafeteria had nothing to do, and were reading magazines or travel brochures.

"It's stopped raining," she said eventually. "Time for my second walk among the dead. I'd like you to come with me."

The wind had veered from the north to the east. This time she took a different path, apparently wanting to cover the whole of the battlefield in her walks.

"I was 20 when war broke out," she said. "I lived in London then. I remember that awful autumn of 1940, when the siren went and we knew somebody would die that night, but didn't know if it would be us. I remember thinking that it was Evil itself that had broken loose. They weren't aeroplanes up there in the darkness, they were devils with tails and clawed feet, carrying bombs and dropping them on us. Later, much later, when I'd become a police officer, I realised that there was no such thing as an evil person, people with evil in their soul, if you see what I mean. Only circumstances that induce that evil."

"I wonder what Molin thought about himself."

"If he was an evil person, you mean?"

"Yes."

She pondered before replying. They'd stopped by a tall cairn at the edge of the battlefield so that she could retie a shoelace. He tried to help her, but she refused.

"Herbert saw himself as a victim," she said. "At least, he did in his confessions to me. I know now it was all lies. I didn't see through him at the time, though. I was mainly worried that he'd become so lovesick that he'd stand outside my window howling."

"But he didn't?"

"Thank God, no."

"What did he say when he left?"

"'Goodbye'. That's all. Maybe he tried to kiss me. I can't remember. I was just glad to see the back of him."

"Then you heard nothing more of him?"

"Never. Not until now. When you came here and told me your remarkable story."

They'd reached the end of the battlefield for the second time and started walking back again.

"I never believed that Nazism had died with Hitler," she said. "There are just as many people today who think the same evil thoughts, who despise other people, who are racists. But they're called different names, and use different methods. There are no fights between hordes of warriors on battlefields nowadays. Hatred of people you despise is expressed in a different way. From underneath, you might say. This country, and indeed the whole of Europe, is being blown apart from the inside by its contempt for weakness, its attacks on refugees, its racism. I see it all around me, and I ask myself if we are able to offer sufficiently firm resistance."

Stefan opened the gate, but she didn't follow him out.

"I'll stay here a bit longer. I haven't really finished with the dead yet. Your story was remarkable, but I still haven't had an answer to the question I've been asking myself, of course."

"Which question is that?"

"Why did you come here?"

"Curiosity. I wanted to know who was the person behind the letter 'M.' in the diary. I wanted to know why he had made that journey to Scotland."

"Is that all?"

"Yes. That's all."

She brushed her hair out of her face and smiled.

"Good luck," she said.

"What with?"

"You might find him one day. Aron Silberstein who murdered Herbert."

"So he told you what had happened in Berlin?"

"He told me about his fear. The man called Lukas Silberstein who had been his dancing master had a son called Aron. Herbert was afraid

404

someone would take revenge, and he thought that is where it would come from. He remembered that little boy, Aron. I think Herbert dreamt about him every night. I have an instinct that he was the one who tracked Herbert down in the end."

"Aron Silberstein?"

"I have a good memory. That was the name he told me. Anyway, it's time for us to say goodbye. I'm going back to my dead souls. And you're going back to the living." She stepped forward and stroked him on the cheek. He watched her marching resolutely back onto the battle-field. He kept watching her until she was out of sight. This marked the end of his thoughts about what had happened last autumn. Somewhere in the Östersund police archives was a diary that had been hidden away, with a raincoat. Also in the package were the letters and photographs. Now he had met Margaret Simmons. She'd not only told him about Molin's journey to Scotland; she'd also given him the name of the man who called himself Fernando Hereira. He went into the museum and bought a picture postcard. Then he sat down on a bench and wrote to Giuseppe.

Giuseppe, It's raining here in Scotland, but it's very beautiful. The man who killed Herbert Molin is called Aron Silberstein. Best wishes, Stefan.

He drove back to Inverness. The man in the hotel reception said he would post the card.

The rest of his time in Inverness was spent waiting. He went for a long walk, he had dinner at the same restaurant as on the previous day, and he talked for an age on the telephone to Elena in the evening. He was missing her and now no longer had a problem telling her so.

He flew to London the next afternoon. He took a taxi from Gatwick to the hotel where Elena was staying. They spent three more days in London before going home to Borås.

Stefan Lindman started work again on April 17, a Monday. The first thing he did was to go to the archive where the picture of the visiting group of British police officers in 1971 was hanging on the wall. He took it down and put it in a box with other photographs from that visit. Then he returned the box to its place, hidden away in a corner cupboard.

He took a deep breath, and resumed the work he'd been missing for so long.

AFTERWORD

This is a novel. In other words, I'm not describing events, people and places exactly as they are, or have been, in real life. I take liberties, move crossroads, repaint houses and most of all I construct fictional events where necessary. And it is sometimes necessary. The same applies to the people in this book. I very much doubt if there is a detective inspector in the Östersund police force called Giuseppe, to take one example. This means that nobody should think that any of my characters have been based on themselves. It is not possible altogether to avoid similarities with living people, however, and if there are any such similarities in this book, they are pure coincidences.

But the sun does rise at about 7.45 a.m. at the beginning of November in Härjedalen. In among all the fiction there may well be quite a number of other convincing truths.

Which was of course the intention.

H.M.
Göteborg, September 2000